HAVENWOOD FALLS VOLUME THREE

A HAVENWOOD FALLS COLLECTION

R.K. RYALS   HEATHER HILDENBRAND   BELINDA BORING

HAVENWOOD FALLS BOOKS

Forget You Not by Kristie Cook

Old Wounds by Susan Burdorf

Fate, Love & Loyalty by E.J. Fechenda

Covetousness by Randi Cooley Wilson

The Winged & the Wicked by T.V. Hahn & Kristie Cook

Alpha's Queen by Lila Felix

Ink & Fire by R.K. Ryals

Lose You Not by Kristie Cook

Tragic Ink by Heather Hildenbrand

Nowhere to Hide by Belinda Boring

Flames Among the Frost by Amy Hale

Rock Me Gently by Susan Burdorf

From the Embers by Amy Miles

Defying Gravity by Kallie Ross

More books releasing on a monthly basis

Also try the YA line, Havenwood Falls High

Stay up to date at www.HavenwoodFalls.com

INK & FIRE

R.K. RYALS

~ A Havenwood Falls New Adult Novella ~

Havenwood Falls

Ink & Fire

R.K. Ryals

ABOUT THIS BOOK

Welcome to Havenwood Falls, home to sexy men, strong women, and neighbors who bite. Discover supernatural mystery, thrills, and romance in a place where everyone has a deep, dark, and often deadly secret.

It takes the fallen to save the damned.

Harper Sinclair doesn't own any books. If she can avoid it, she doesn't read or write at all. Words are dangerous. Beyond the cover of a book, words rearrange themselves for Harper, becoming messages from beyond. Brutal messages. Terrible messages. When she writes, awful things flow from her fingers. She's a spiritual writer haunted by demons.

Lucas Fox is one of the fallen, an angel whose murderous past keeps him from Heaven, and whose protective, chivalrous nature keeps him from Hell. He lives between worlds, content to enjoy his vices while doing just enough to keep him out of the underworld.

But when Harper is forced to sign a contract for a house she buys in Havenwood Falls, the words that appear aren't her name. Instead, she pens a dire message threatening a fallen angel whose old alliance with a ruler of Hell has made him the target of a powerful demon lord. A warning that draws Lucas Fox to Havenwood Falls to settle old scores and puts Harper Sinclair directly in the line of danger.

OTHER BOOKS BY R.K. RYALS

PARANORMAL ROMANCE BOOKS:

The Redemption Series

Redemption

Ransom

Retribution

Revelation

The Acropolis Series

The Acropolis

The Labyrinth

Deliverance

The Thorne Trilogy

Cursed

Possessed

Dancing with the Devil

In the Land of Tea and Ravens (Standalone book)

FANTASY BOOKS:

The Scribes of Medeisia Series

Mark of the Mage

Tempest

Fist of the Furor

City in Ruins

The Standalone Embrace Yourself Series

The Story of Awkward

An Introvert's Tale

CONTEMPORARY ROMANCE READS:

The Singing River

Hawthorne & Heathcliff

The Best I Could

Sex & Such

Capture the World

For those who know the power behind words.

Words are mighty warriors that can shake mountains even when whispered.

By that sin fell the angels.
—William Shakespeare

PROLOGUE

*D*anger rises in the darkness. Shadows weave in and out of nothingness, the Infernum a screaming mess of imagined pain, for the fear of pain is often much worse than the actual hurt.

Distorted, faceless creatures march through an empty space filled with evil intentions. Trapped, they beg for mercy.

In the midst of chaos, a man's face appears, as beguiling as it is dreadful. Hair the color of midnight, dark eyes touched with crimson, and a hard face lined with smoke and madness stares into emptiness.

The Infernum swallows its prisoners whole.

But not for long. Not for one of them.

"The time has come." Lips curl in a sickening smile, a forked tongue darting out to taste the air.

CHAPTER 1

 y aunt once told me that anything I ever needed to know about life I could find in a Van Morrison song. Apparently, she'd experienced all of her firsts to his music: first date, first kiss, and her first time losing her virginity. I say first because my aunt is continually losing her virginity. Something about taking it back and starting over every time she feels let down by an experience. At forty-eight years old and after a recent less-than-satisfying encounter, Eloise Sinclair is now a virgin again.

Hanging turquoise beads *click click* together as Eloise exits the back of her new age shop Into the Mystic, cradling a steaming mug, the contents smelling suspiciously of mugwort and bourbon. The mugwort is for enhancing her psychic abilities. The bourbon is for her nerves.

A long-sleeved purple tunic swings against polka-dotted leggings as she approaches me, wisps of auburn hair falling into perceptive brown eyes. "The Pen Is Mightier Than the Sword."

She raises her mug at me. The Van Morrison song title is all it takes. I've heard way too much of my aunt's music playlist. She's relating my life to the song.

"Do your clients enjoy translating Morrisonese, or is this just for my benefit?" I grimace at the song choice. "Wrong one for me."

"You assume."

"If this is about the meeting I have at the plaza this afternoon—"

"It's about your fate," Eloise cuts me off cryptically.

My family makes deals with destiny, usually other people's. It pays the rent and the utility bills. The mugwort and the bourbon, too. For prices ranging anywhere from one hundred to three hundred dollars an hour—all depending on the type of reading—my aunt Eloise can discern a client's future, past, or present.

She is psychic. I am, too. Only, my abilities come with a curse. A rather inconvenient one.

Eloise studies me over the rim of her mug, her gaze raking over my loose brown hair and makeup-less green eyes before dropping to my solid navy sweatshirt and skinny jeans. "You couldn't have tried a little harder for such a momentous occasion?"

I glance down at myself. "For picking up a set of keys?"

"Hmm."

My gaze roams over the shop, careful not to linger on anything too long. This shop and the basement apartment downstairs are home. For the last twenty-three years, it has been everything. The purple walls, the brightly painted bookshelves stocked with new age books, the scarf-covered tables littered with candles, the glass cases full of jewelry and crystals, the mauve and gold chaise lounge, the stuffed blue-checked chairs, the herbal tea counter, and the beaded curtains leading to the basement stairs and the back of the shop all wail at me. Memories have a way of making inanimate objects speak.

Or maybe I am just super emotional.

"Did you 'hmm' at me?" I ask, following Aunt Eloise to the front door.

She flips over the open sign, arches a brow, and hmms again.

Outside, the morning sun sweeps like spilled pastel paints down Eleventh Street, the rays turning the light dusting of snow on the shop rooftops on the other side of the square into glitter. The sun brings the stores—Backwoods Sport & Ski, Howe's Herbal Shoppe, and Tragic Ink—to life. Like a necromancer raising the dead. Darkness touched by light.

I have a lot of experience with darkness, with beasts, and with life.

That's what happens when your psychic abilities are tied to evil.

Eloise calls what she does spiritually guiding people's lives.

I sentence them to damnation.

Spiritual writing, my aunt calls it. Communication from the dead translated through written words. It all sounds so harmless.

I was barely old enough to write when I scribed my first message. Wide-eyed and excited, I handed the note to a man in town, the words *u will die and deemuns will feest on ur sol* scrawled in crayon. As if this was a completely normal thing for a gap-toothed five-year-old girl to do. As if I was delivering a winning lottery ticket rather than a death sentence.

Turns out, people don't like knowing when they're going to die. They like even less knowing their souls are indulgent treats for demons.

The man cried. I didn't come out of my room for two days.

Worse yet, he was a mortal, and he *died*.

That night, the Court of the Sun and the Moon came for me, everyone solemn-faced and full of regret. A world of secrets was revealed—secrets about the town I lived in and the people I loved. Havenwood Falls, Colorado, is a sanctuary for people and creatures with supernatural abilities. It's also home to mortals. Oh, and ironically, demons, but not the kind of demons that like me. Not the soul-sucking terrible horrible creatures that I seem to channel.

The rules of our town are simple: protect the secret and don't kill the mortals.

At five years old, I was off to a bad start.

My aunt pats me on the cheek, breaking me out of my thoughts, her hand warm from the mug. "Hmm."

Nothing good ever comes from Eloise's hmms.

Snatching her mug, I gulp down the mugwort and bourbon. For the nerves, not the mental enhancement.

"It's a house," I say. Not just any house. *My* house. My first house. A place all my own, completely book- and writing-free. That's a lot more difficult than it sounds.

Words are everywhere. On television, clothes, signs, groceries, phones . . . the list goes on forever. I've trained myself to look at things without actually *looking* at them. If it's possible to avoid my "gift," then I do it.

The bell at the front of the store *dings*.

"You're not going to want the chamomile or candles," Eloise says from behind one of the displays. She doesn't have to see the customer to know why she's come. "It's oolong tea and a charged black tourmaline crystal for you. Trust me. You have all kinds of negative energy attached to you, and it is not good for your health."

At least her gift doesn't kill people.

I'm still stuck on Eloise's hmms.

The hmms chase me through the rest of the morning and through the streets of Havenwood Falls. It's too early for my meeting at the plaza when I leave my aunt's shop, so I am in no hurry when I hit Main Street on foot, my hands tucked deep within my coat pockets. I have a bad habit of facing my weaknesses while also avoiding them. This is why I find myself standing in front of Shelf Indulgence, a bookstore on Main Street, the smell of coffee wafting from Coffee Haven next door.

My eyes drift over the large showcase window so quickly that everything inside is merely a blur, before my gaze falls to my feet, puffs of air the only thing between me and the ground. Shelf Indulgence is my own personal hell. A place full of everything I wish I could touch and see. A place full of everything I wish I could *be*. The owner, a witch named Sedona Mathews, always decorates the showcase window with wildly creative displays. I'm both tempted and afraid to look at it. I am blind without being blind, my mind used to counting steps and knowing exactly where everything is, so that I can avoid anything new and potentially dangerous. My mind hates change, but my heart craves it.

"Harper?" a familiar female voice calls.

A pair of small brown boots settle next to mine on the sidewalk, and I let my gaze slide up them, over Thanksgiving-themed leggings and a long burgundy tunic to a pale face surrounded by silvery blond hair. Her skin positively glows. Concerned turquoise eyes stare at me. Willow Fairchild, the owner of Coffee Haven, and as of a few months ago, a new mother. Motherhood agrees with her.

She smiles. "It's been a few days since I saw you down this way. Do you have any new photographs for me? Your last set was popular with the customers."

I try to talk and can't, my words caught somewhere between the emotions building within me and the desire to walk inside Coffee Haven to see the new artwork Willow has displayed.

Silence stretches between us.

Reaching out, Willow squeezes my shoulder gently. "You let me know when you do, okay?" Profound understanding colors her eyes a deeper shade of turquoise, and I know she senses my unease and troubled thoughts. Willow, like many of the town's residents, is a supernatural, an empathetic fae with the power to sense emotions.

Throwing me a final smile, she enters Coffee Haven. A blast of warm air and the smell of blueberry scones hits me. I inhale, sucking in the scent and the warm feeling that comes with it.

Cars and pedestrians meander slowly around my spot on the sidewalk, and I turn away from the bookstore and coffee shop, my gaze settling on the town square across the street and a sparkling fountain in the distance. A work truck is parked near the curb, and a man leans against it, a cup of coffee cradled in his hands. Like with most of the locals, I've seen him before, but I don't know him. I'm not a social person, even though I think I could be if things were different.

This man is broad, a beard protecting his face from the cold, and he sips the coffee, watching me. When my eyes catch his, he pauses, dips his head, and lifts his cup. There are secrets lurking in his gaze, and even though it's unnerving to find him observing me, I don't feel threatened. I have a strange feeling he's studying me for the same reason I study him back. Secrets. There are secrets everywhere in this town.

Today, however, secrets are the least of my concerns. Today, I'm making Harper history. Giddy excitement fills me, the emotions overwhelming everything else, and I slip down the street. Away from the stranger. Away from Shelf Indulgence and my wishes. Away from Willow Fairchild and her empathetic understanding.

Away from everything I know and toward something new.

CHAPTER 2

The minute I walk into the Turner Real Estate office, I know I'm in trouble.

There isn't much to the small space. Part of Miller's Plaza on the west side of town and right off of the street, it is basically a king-sized cubicle. A large desk rests against the back wall with two burgundy-cushioned chairs positioned before it and bookshelves flanking it. An area rug is thrown over old wooden floors, and a small hallway off to the side leads to whatever is kept in the back.

It's not the office that bothers me. It's the stack of papers fanned out across the desk.

I let my gaze slide quickly over the pages before dropping it to the floor.

Jeanine Turner, a tall, slender, raven-haired woman, greets me at the door, her smile a little too perky, her eyes way too sharp.

"Today is your day, Harper Sinclair!" She high-fives the air. "I just have one place we missed in the paperwork the other day that I need you to sign. Nothing serious. It's mainly for my own personal records."

My mouth turns to sawdust. "My aunt takes care of my paperwork."

Jeanine waves away my words. "It's one signature. We got the legal stuff in closing. This is for my records. I don't know if the pages stuck together or if Eloise overlooked it. You can sign your name, can't you?"

Her condescending tone stiffens my spine. I'm not illiterate, and she knows it. What she doesn't know is what's actually wrong with me. Because Jeanine is mortal, I'm not at liberty to discuss my demon-possessed writing skills.

Jeanine slides behind her desk, steeples her fingers, and says, "We can wait on your aunt, but I leave for vacation in," she checks a clock on the wall, "ten minutes."

I don't check the time. Even though my abilities don't seem to include a problem with numbers, I only look at them when absolutely necessary, and usually only long enough to keep track of the day.

As for Jeanine, she's lying. I can smell it on her, and I'm not even a shifter. Technically, I am just as human as she is. Just with extrasensory abilities.

This is what I get for using a mortal agency. The Court has ways of working around my issues, which is why I'm still in Havenwood Falls. I can't risk leaving.

I start to sit in one of the cushy chairs, and then decide against it. "I need this done now."

I *want* this done now.

"Then I suggest you sign on the dotted line. I'd hate to hold the keys on a technicality."

I make my living as a nature photographer. Vintage cameras. Old film. Hours spent inside a darkroom. Days spent hiking in the mountains. Jeanine reminds me of a buzzard, a scavenger reeking of decay. I'm the roadkill.

For business and financial matters, I gave power of attorney to my aunt, but I'm legally able to sign if necessary.

I don't want to wait a week to move into my home, and because I'm terrible with confrontation, I don't call her bluff on the vacation. Honestly, I *don't want* to call her bluff. I want this home in every sense of the word. I want it to be mine. Something with my actual signature on it. Not my aunt's or someone's from the Court. *Mine.*

Sitting, I lock gazes with Jeanine. "I need a pen."

The ballpoint she hands me feels foreign and heavy in my fingers.

Jeanine slides a sheet of paper in front of me, the signature line clearly marked by a red sticky flag. Words dance, and I try not to look at them, my gaze focused on the tab. It's the color of blood.

I set the pen against the paper.

The world falls apart.

Dark energy rushes me, overwhelmingly tragic, the power turning my fingers into monsters. Words whisper through my head. Dreadful words. *Death. Blood. Mine.* I am a prisoner to the pain and the agony. The demons howl, each of them begging me to channel them.

If I could fall to my knees and beg them to stop, I would. A tear slips down my cheek, and I fight, sweat beading up along my brow as I try to drop the pen. Not fighting feels like giving up.

"Please," I whimper.

"Write it!" One voice is more persistent than the rest. My hand spasms, the world going black. The way it always does.

Jeanine Turner screams.

When I come to, my hand remains poised over the paper, the ballpoint pen having left a line of frantically scrawled words. *You will have a place in Hell, Lucas Fox. Cast and chained in the Infernum of darkness. Death to the messenger. Death to those who give her sanctuary.*

I inhale . . . or try to.

An invisible vise grips me by the neck, cutting off my oxygen supply, and I claw at my skin desperately. It makes no difference. I belong to a world of darkness.

With little effort, the spirit attached to me lifts me off the chair and throws me across the room.

My head slams against the office's glass entrance, my vision blurring. Adrenaline and fear pump through my system, dulling the pain. People move on the sidewalk beyond, and I panic even while gasping for air. I can't let anyone see me like this. First rule of thumb: protect the humans.

Still struggling to breathe, I crawl back across the room, a trail of blood dripping behind me. Jeanine's screams rise, shrill and deafening, the sound a jackhammer in my head.

The Court is going to kill me.

My knees and hands dig into the wooden floor, my heart racing as

I lurch into the back hallway. Two doorways greet me, and I propel myself through the closest one, my body landing on a tiled bathroom floor. Slamming the door, I lock it.

The demon relinquishes me, and I drag in air through my lungs, his words etched into my brain. *Death to the messenger. Death to those who give her sanctuary.*

Death simply because I wanted something to call mine. Death simply because I wanted to be able to write my own name.

Tears mingle with blood on the floor beneath me. Red on black on white. The story of my life.

CHAPTER 3

"*H*arper?"

My aunt's voice is like a balm on an open wound, and even though I want nothing more than to throw open the bathroom door and run into her arms, I don't. I remain in a fetal position, my cheek pressed against a floor I hope has been cleaned in the last week. It's too potpourri-y in here, which is never good. No one uses potpourri this strong unless they're trying to hide something. Mold. Urine. Germs.

"Harper," my aunt tries again.

"It's bad this time," I tell her, my gaze on the crack under the door. She's wearing tennis shoes, which means this is serious. Aunt Eloise owns one pair of tennis shoes—a pair of neon yellow Velcro monstrosities—and she only wears them when there's an emergency and she's in a hurry. Otherwise, she dons outrageously colored boots or ballet flats. The bright tennis shoes look like caution tape and rightly so.

Jeanine Turner yells something unintelligible from her office.

Aunt Eloise answers her with, "It's fine. Everything's okay. She just has a thing for bathrooms." She raps on the door. "Harper, honey, you've got to open up. You're scaring the mortal."

I glare at her feet. "This is why you were 'hmming' at me earlier, isn't it? You knew!"

"She flew across the room!" Jeanine roars, her voice rising. "Explain that!"

"Addie, why don't you take Mrs. Turner out for some fresh air?" another voice breaks in.

I would know that voice anywhere. Saundra Beaumont. A powerful witch of one of the founding families of the Luna Coven. She also serves on the Court of the Sun and the Moon, a court that basically runs Havenwood Falls. All of the members are from old blood and old money.

"I didn't mean to," I immediately defend.

A pair of navy high heels joins Eloise's worn sneakers. Old family blood versus us.

"Calm yourself, Harper," Saundra says firmly. "We can fix what happened here." Papers rustle, and I cringe. "As for what you wrote, that's another story."

"I'm sorry." Apologizing is habit for me. I've been practicing the art of apology ever since I first entered the Court of the Sun and the Moon. Then, I had been an awestruck child standing in a windowless room in the City Hall's basement, candlelight flickering off of sympathetic faces.

Oh, how I have fallen.

The message I wrote at five years old isn't the only message I've scribed. I did learn how to read and write, after all. Not to mention it's hard to completely avoid words, especially as a child, but the Court has steadily protected me and the people I inadvertently threatened while I learned to be what I am now: detached from the world. As far as I know, I've only caused one death with my curse.

"I just want the keys to my house," I say weakly. No potpourri for my bathroom. I will scrub my toilets.

"Come out," Saundra soothes. "Get medical attention. Go home with your aunt. What's happening to you is wrong, Harper. No one should have to see their family . . ." She pauses, and I know she's looking at my aunt. When her voice comes again, it's closer to the floor, surprising me. I'm having a hard time imagining the silver-haired, suit-wearing woman stooping. "Generational curses be damned. We protect the supes and the mortals, Harper. We made a promise to you and to your aunt. You can't help what's happening to you."

"He's coming," I whisper. From the paper she's holding, she knows who I mean.

"We'll have someone stronger here to meet him."

Finally sitting up, I reach over and flip the lock on the door. My aunt opens it, her concerned gaze finding my face. She looks every bit the eccentric with her colorful clothes, tennis shoes, and hoop earrings. Saundra is her opposite in every way.

I stare up at them. "I still want the keys to my house."

Arching a brow, Saundra lifts her hand, a set of keys dangling from her fingers.

Taking them, Eloise leans down next to me and presses them into my hand. "I didn't know this would happen. I saw something big, but not this . . . darkness." She starts to hug me, and then stops. I don't do hugs. "Let's get you cleaned up. The Court will take care of the rest."

Amnesia spells. Wards. Secrets. The Court of the Sun and the Moon runs this town on magic and mystery.

"My soul hurts," I breathe.

"Oh, honey, I know." She smooths a hand over my blood-dampened hair, and murmurs, "Harpists harp harping. Angels airily dancing. On clouds, casting glances. Their eyes glowing brightly. Guarding. Guiding. And that's how I got my name. Or so my mother says."

"No Van Morrison right now."

"It's not Van Morrison," Eloise reveals. "Your mother wrote that."

"Really?" Even if she's lying, it's a good distraction.

"Really. Right before she died, she took your dad's hand and said, 'Name her Harper.' We figured it was an omen. They say people see things right before they die."

I killed her, too, I think.

Eloise helps me to my feet, throws a coat around my shoulders, pulls a hoodie up over my head, and leads me out a back door at the end of the hall. Past witches I don't stop to talk to and a dazed Jeanine

Turner. She won't remember this tomorrow. Quite possibly, she won't even remember her vacation.

I fist my hand around the keys until the metal bites into my flesh.

⁓

THAT NIGHT, after hours of forced wakefulness, I fall into a deep, exhausted sleep, my sore body curled around a pillow, blankets wrapping me, and my aunt's familiar apartment surrounding me.

Then, I dream.

NIGHT SWALLOWS THE DAYLIGHT.

I am standing on a mountain, a brisk wind lifting my hair against my face. There's snow on the air, the smell of it heavy and thick.

A full moon shines down on a silver world, on a sleepy town full of people I've known forever. Streets, shops, parks, and cemeteries I could walk in my sleep spread out like pieces on a board game.

My town. No road map. No signs.

Words are dangerous, so I navigate without them. My mind is an atlas of landmarks. Over two miles of stamped images: avenues named after the Old Families, a town square, a park with a lake, a ski resort, a myriad of residences ranging in income and style, and mountain trails. Housing developments dot the town: Havenwood Heights, Creekwood, Havenstone, and Havenwood Village. Shops I rarely visit out of fear stare up at me: Howe's Herbal Shoppe, Soothing Sips, Coffee Haven, Callie's Consignments, Shelf Indulgence, and Tragic Ink among many.

In the mountains are other things—Cooley Creek, Mathews River, Smalls Falls, Peacock Lake, Bels Creek, Hale Creek—beautiful landmarks I've made a living hiking so that I can capture the animals and flora on film, being careful not to snap pictures of the shifters and other supernatural creatures that prowl the trails with me.

Somewhere in the forest, a wolf howls.

"It's a beautiful town," a gravelly voice says, the words a part of the wind. "What a shame it would be if I destroyed it."

"*Why would you destroy it?*" My words sound far away, as if I'm floating outside of my body instead of inhabiting it.

"*Because I can.*" Evil doesn't always need a reason to do things. "*Can't you see the future, psychic?*"

Above me, the moon turns red. Something wet and sticky drips on my face, and I swipe at it, horrified when my hand comes away covered in a substance that looks suspiciously like blood.

Black shadows so dark even the night can't hide them drop out of the sky, descending on the town. Screams rise from the streets below. Agonizing *screams.*

"*They're dying,*" the voice gloats. "*They're all dying.*"

"*No!*"

From the edge of the woods, animals emerge. They crawl toward me, all of them wounded, blood spilling out of their sides. Shifters. All *of them are shifters. Shifters I know. People I spend every day passing on the streets. People I talk to. Friends.*

"*Help us,*" they beg.

Blood. There's so much blood.

The shifters crawl closer, reaching, their prone figures so close I can see the agony etched into their faces.

"*No!*" I scream.

Closing my eyes, I cover my ears and fall to my knees.

Only, I don't hit the ground. My knees land on air, and I am falling, falling, falling.

WHEN I COME TO, I stare into a dark room touched by a night-light that's been in my aunt's apartment for as long as I can remember. It's shaped like a star, and I used to make wishes on it. *Star light, star bright, first star I see tonight.*

That was before I learned wishes are scary things. That was before I learned it is much easier to wish for something than it is to make it happen.

CHAPTER 4

*L*ight finger-shaped bruises form around my neck, and I spend the next few days pulling the collar of my coat up, my hair swinging loose. Other than the bruising and a mild concussion, the worst thing I suffer is a blow to my pride. Nothing yells adulting quite like being found in a fetal position on the bathroom floor covered in blood and shame.

After three days of sweat-inducing terrifying nightmares—the same one every night—sympathetic stares, Court interrogations, and my aunt's outrageous herbal concoctions, relief washes over me the minute I step into the driveway of my new home. It's perfect. A remote, fully furnished, one-bedroom log cabin in the mountains, the home is everything I had worked to achieve: independence.

Inhaling the cold mountain air, I sling a camera bag over my shoulder before tugging the single rolling suitcase after me. My life in one bag and one suitcase. I don't know if that's sad or impressive.

Mine.

My fingers tremble when I insert the key in the lock, the sound of it clicking open like fireworks on the Fourth of July.

Now would be a good time for intro music, something about freedom and home, but all I get is the heavy arched door creaking open on its iron hinges. The door is part of the reason I love the place.

Sunlight spills in like a spotlight on stage, revealing a stuffed leather sofa, wood-burning fireplace, and stone-accented kitchen, but the best part is what the place is missing.

No television. No books. No cell phones. No signs.

No trouble.

You will have a place in Hell, Lucas Fox. Cast and chained in the Infernum of darkness. Death to the messenger. Death to those who give her sanctuary.

The message haunts me, but I push it away. I'm sick of evil controlling my life.

Setting the suitcase and camera bag inside the entry, I switch on the lights and quietly shut the door behind me, my fingers running over the frame. *Home.* Excitement burrows a den in my heart.

Unable to stop smiling, I move through the house doing mundane things I never thought I'd appreciate: starting a fire, unpacking clothes, and sweeping the floors with a broom I find in the hallway utility closet.

My fireplace. My dust. My broom.

In the middle of my living room, I take it all in, embarrassed by the tears pricking the back of my eyes. I am proud of this.

"They tell me you're the messenger," a low voice says from the direction of the kitchen.

I freeze, goosebumps rising on my skin, my fingers gripping the broom in my hand so hard my knuckles turn a mottled shade of red, the flesh around it pallid.

Death to the messenger.

Chest heaving, I turn slowly.

A man—no, a golden *Adonis*—leans against the island bar separating the kitchen from the living area. He's tall, over six feet, with blond hair cropped close to his head and eyes so blue, it's like looking at the sky. Jeans rest low on his hips, and a white button-up shirt hugs a muscular frame too magnificent to be covered up.

He's too *everything* to be human, *and* he came out of nowhere. This should be what frightens me the most, but sadly, I'm used to strange things happening to me. Or, more accurately, me *doing* strange things. Like me relaying demonic words and images I shouldn't see or me being hurled across an office by an evil entity. This, however, would be the first time an actual man appeared.

Considering my gifts, he can be only one thing.

I wield the broom like a sword. "I don't know what you are or what you want, but know that I won't go down without putting up one hell of a fight."

He studies me, his gaze flicking over the bruises on my neck before falling to the broom. "Congratulations, Ms. Sinclair. I've got to say, this is the first time I've ever been challenged with a broom." Pushing away from the bar, he steps toward me.

I stumble backward. He knows my name.

"I'm not here to harm you," he promises.

Jabbing the air with my makeshift weapon, I circle toward the front door and then stop, because I refuse to leave my house. "Prove it. Keep your distance." He pauses, and I swallow tears. There's nothing worse than feeling the urge to cry when angry. "Why won't all of you leave me alone? You can't let me have even this? Stealing words from me wasn't enough? Taking away a normal life wasn't enough?"

His chin rises, and I can't help but notice how sharp his face is. He's more rugged than beautiful. Terrifying even.

"I'm not a demon," he reveals.

My grip on the broom loosens and then tightens again. "You're lying. You can't be anything else. Only demons and evil spirits come to me."

"They come to you in messages. Do I look like a message to you?" he asks.

"Do the bruises on my neck look like a message?"

"Quite frankly, yes."

The broom wavers. "What are you?"

He smirks. "More like *who* am I? You should know. You channeled the asshole who threatened me."

You will have a place in Hell, Lucas Fox. Cast and chained in the Infernum of darkness. Death to the messenger. Death to those who give her sanctuary.

The broom hits the floor. "Lucas Fox."

"I never did understand the mortal need for last names."

He's moved closer while speaking, and I keep backing away, circling so that I'm not caught against a wall.

"Heritage. Family," I reply, unsure why I care. At one point, I have to climb on the arm of my new couch.

Lucas's eyes twinkle. "They didn't tell me you were so young . . . or so intriguing."

"Who are they?"

"The Court. Your town's Court. You know, the whole Sun and Moon thing?"

Startled, I almost fall off the sofa, my fingers finding purchase on the leather. "The Court sent you?"

Lucas stops in front of the couch, and I drop down behind it, the sofa a shield between us.

"They would have told me." I glance around frantically. "S-supernatural newcomers are supposed to register with the Court. The wards . . . they'll know you're here." I shake a finger at him. "Demons aren't immune."

He smiles. "They summoned me with quite an interesting message. I told you I'm not a demon, and I'm not very good with rules. They'll know I'm here when I'm ready for them to know. Going to them first would have been a lot less interesting than this." Glancing at the floor, he cocks a brow. "I kind of miss the broom. You looked cute with it."

What dignity I have left bristles at his comment. "You've got a lot of . . ." The words trail off, my eyes widening. Only one kind of supernatural being is immune to the Court and the wards, and as far as I know, not many of them make their homes in Havenwood Falls. "You're an angel." Shock colors my words.

He dips his head. "Well done, Harper." Spreading his arms wide, he adds, "Now that we've gotten that out of the way, do you want to tell me why I smell Hell on you?"

I may not watch television or read any books, but I do listen to a lot of audiobooks on CDs from which my aunt removes the labels. Mostly science fiction and romance, because sci-fi is cool and romance is, well, romance.

The last thing a girl ever wants to hear from anyone—it doesn't matter who it is—is that they smell like Hell.

It takes everything I've got not to sniff myself. "Hell has a smell?"

He laughs, the sound masculine and deep. It gives me an odd feeling, as if it's the kind of laugh that gives purpose to life, which seems weird, and yet . . . maybe not. Every time I've accidentally channeled a demon over the years, it felt like something was stolen from me. This laugh—an *angel's* laugh—gives something back.

For a woman drowning in darkness, it's a heady feeling.

"It doesn't smell like mortals would assume," Lucas assures me. "It's not all brimstone and sulfur." His eyes shine. "It smells like sin."

"Which is bad, right?"

"To some." The way he arches his brows suggests he isn't one of the "some."

My mouth gapes. "You're fallen." The words come out on a whisper. It doesn't take much to figure out what he is. Lucas has that *how can something that looks so good be so bad* feel to him, and he definitely doesn't smell like Hell.

He sits on the arm of the couch, and I'm tempted to lunge for my broom. Fallen angels have to be fallen for a reason, right?

"Don't look so horrified," he says. "Considering the evil you channeled, you're going to be glad I am who I am. I feel him. He shouldn't be coming, but he is. You and this town are going to need me."

His warning makes my heart race, and I touch the bruises on my neck. "If he's a demon—"

"He's more than a demon. He's an archdemon. A lord of Hell. A part of the highest order in the underworld. You called royalty, Ms. Sinclair."

I am pretty sure I've forgotten how to breathe.

Lucas stands. "You have a nice home."

A thank you hangs off the tip of my tongue, but it never makes it out of my mouth before Lucas suddenly vanishes.

My legs give out, and I sink to the floor, the fire crackling in the hearth the only sound in the room. The blaze should warm me, but I feel cold. *Way* too cold.

Fallen angels. Archdemons.

I own a house. I don't know why I cling to that thought. Maybe because, with everything happening to me, I need a reminder that a little piece of me remains.

There's only one remedy for the sick feeling in my stomach: grilled cheese sandwiches.

That's the thing with issues like mine. After years of having to face the monsters under my bed, or in my case, out of accidental messages, I've had to find ways to cope. Wine is a pretty good remedy. Hell, there've been times I've just thrown back the hard stuff, but drunkenness means losing control. Losing control means forgetting not to read messages or write. That leaves food. Forget ice cream. There's nothing better for stress eating than carbs and melted cheese. And butter.

Oh, the butter.

*B*arely twenty-four hours into living on my own, and I'm back in town, the sun shining down on my uncovered head, my coat pulled tightly closed. Despite growing up in the mountains, I am always cold, which is the reason I have a tendency to tuck insole foot warmers into the bottom of my boots and hand warmers into the pockets of my coat. If I can keep my feet warm, the rest of me manages.

Pedestrians crowd the sidewalk despite the late November temperatures, most of them taking advantage of the Thanksgiving week sales. Murmurs of conversation ride the wind, puffed breaths mingling with the smells of coffee and food.

I pause outside my aunt's shop, the words Into the Mystic New Age Books and Gifts burned into a wooden sign hanging above my head. I don't look up at it. My breath leaves condensation on the store's glass door, the heat clouding the interior.

My stomach hurts. Anxiety, maybe? Or the ridiculous amount of greasy grilled cheese sandwiches I inhaled the night before.

The bell dings when I enter. "Aunt Eloise," I call, "we need to talk."

Beads clink together. "What do you think about reserving an area of the park for storytellers at the psychic fair this year? Maybe dressed as authentic minstrels?" In white tights and a top covered in swirly colors, my aunt looks like a lollipop. A lollipop that's avoiding eye contact. "Imagine how enthralling and vivid it would be."

Every year on the spring equinox, Eloise runs an Into the Mystic New Age and Psychic Fair in Town Square Park. She starts planning the next year's event as soon as the current one ends, and as much as I love helping her come up with ideas, I know a distraction when I see one.

"The Court sent me an angel. A *fallen* angel." The statement sits in the air between us, heavy and accusing.

Eloise tugs on one of her hoop earrings. She has eight earrings in all, most of them studs and none of them the same color. "I know. Saundra informed me." She tugs harder on the hoop. "Technically, they sent you the angel your message called out by name."

"Hmm." It feels good to throw out a few hmms of my own, instead of receiving them.

"He's a warrior," Eloise tries again. "There aren't many high-ranking supernaturals who don't know who Lucas Fox is."

"Hmm." My arms cross.

"He fell from the highest order an angel can fall from. He's one of the most powerful of his kind. That's all I know, Harper."

"Is he dangerous?" I ask, dropping my arms. "Because he just showed up at my house. Out of nowhere."

Moving past me to the table she keeps stocked with candles, she begins sorting them. First by size and then by color. "The Court wouldn't bring in someone dangerous."

"That's a lie," I snap, surprising us both. "I'm dangerous, and they let me live here."

"Harper—"

"Is he dangerous to *me*?"

I leave what I really want to ask unsaid. She knows. Because of my curse, I should have never taken the pen. I should have never attempted to write my name. I not only put people in danger, I put the entire town at risk. The Court has every right to punish me.

A sudden brilliant light fills the room, followed by a familiar golden visage. "Give me a little credit, sweetheart. I don't punish people unless I have a personal reason to."

Eloise knocks over two of her candles. I nearly fall into a display of essential oils.

"I expected a little fanfare, but nearly fainting . . . I'm humbled." Lucas Fox saunters across the shop, his blue eyes glinting.

Eloise rights the candles. "I had heard you were arrogant."

He smiles. "I had heard you were charming."

"I haven't heard anything." Frustration turns my voice into a growl. "And that light thing," I wave at Lucas, "you couldn't have done that when we first met?"

Lucas roams the shop, an appreciative gleam in his eyes. "I'm not sure what smells better. The scotch you have put away or the holy water you've got for sale." Pausing at a rack, he lifts a vial of clear liquid. "What proof is this, you think?" Popping the top off, he sniffs it. "Fifty percent, at best."

Curiosity gets the better of me. "Holy water?"

Lucas replaces the vial. "Angels can't get drunk on alcohol, but holy water," he laughs, "let's just say it's intoxicating."

I try so hard not to smile and fail.

Pointing at me, he winks. "There you go. I knew you had it in you. You're going to need it." He glances at Eloise. "You've got a witch, a shifter, and a fae coming in three, two . . ."

The bell above the door dings.

Saundra Beaumont is the first to storm in, looking like the avenging angel Lucas is supposed to be. Close on her heels is Elsmed Fairchild, a one-hundred-and-two-year-old male fae with frosty blue eyes and a bone to pick. Bringing up the rear is Ric Kasun, Havenwood Falls' sheriff and a wolf-shifter. At six foot four and built as solidly as the black Chevy truck he drives around town, he looks in no mood to play games. All of them are from old families, all of them are representatives of the Court of the Sun and the Moon, and all of them are pissed.

"Close up shop," Saundra commands Eloise. "Now."

My aunt wastes no time obeying, knocking over more of the candles in her haste to flip the open sign to closed.

Saundra turns to Lucas. "You want to explain to me why you're not standing in court right now? Why you had the audacity to summon us *here!*"

Completely unfazed, the angel circles behind the store's checkout counter, stoops to retrieve something off of the shelves built beneath, and rises with a bottle of scotch and a glass. He pours the liquid.

"Want some?" he asks. The question is met with hard stares. Lucas shrugs, downs the amber-colored liquid, and then tips the empty glass at me. "I figured the familiar setting would make this a lot easier on the girl."

Elsmed's glacial eyes swing my way. He has silver hair, a flat nose, and a long chin, and I find myself thinking he'd be just as intimidating as an iceberg as he is as a fae. "Speaking of court—"

"She didn't get the summons," Lucas interrupts. "I intercepted it."

While they argue, I stumble, catching myself. The stomach pain I'd felt when I arrived at my aunt's shop worsens. My head pounds, my skin itching. The fading bruises around my neck tingle.

Something is wrong with me.

Ric Kasun frowns, his muscles tense when he advances on the fallen angel. Even out of uniform—his broad frame in flannel, jeans, and boots—he looks every bit the sheriff this town needs. He removes a pair of sunglasses perched on his nose, revealing silvery blue eyes framed by black hair and a scruffy jaw. "There are rules in place here, Mr. Fox."

Lucas's gaze hardens, his smirk wiped away. For the first time since I've met him, he scares me. "I'm not breaking the law, Sheriff. I just changed the Court's venue. Should I remind all of you that I'm here to help your town, not hurt it?"

"We have a certain way we do things," Saundra inserts.

"I'm becoming well aware of that," Lucas mumbles. Setting down his glass, he straightens to full height, putting him eye to eye with Sheriff Kasun. "My first priority is the girl and the archdemon using her as a conduit. You don't want a demon like him anywhere near your Court." He comes around the counter, leaving nothing between him and the Court members. "Let me give you a rundown on how archdemons play games. Leviathan—Levi to make things simple and because I seriously don't like the bastard—won't set off your wards. He's not like the demons you have in residence here. He has an eternity of tricks up his sleeve. You won't know he's coming until he shows up."

My heart begins to race, and I tug at my shirt as heat washes over me. I am hot, *so very hot*, and I *never* get hot.

Ric's eyes narrow. "Talk to us, angel. Why won't our wards detect him?"

"Because he has other ways of getting into your town." Lucas's gaze finds me. "It starts with nightmares, terrible visions full of death. Then the marks come."

I can't breathe. My world has narrowed to the heat in my skin and the look Lucas gives me. Blue eyes. There are too many blue eyes in this room.

My vision blurs.

Lucas approaches me, a hazy figure in a shop full of mystical things.

"What are you doing?" I gasp, my words sounding so very far away, as if I'm yelling inside an echoing tunnel.

I want to back away, but I can't.

"Angel," Ric warns, a low growl escaping him. His wolf is on high alert.

When he reaches me, Lucas grabs the hem of my sweatshirt, fisting the material in his hands before jerking it up past my bra, his gaze locking with mine. "Don't look down."

The Court members gasp.

"Oh, my God!" Eloise exclaims. "What's happening to her?" She starts to rush toward me, but Lucas pushes me toward the counter.

"Keep your distance," he says. "You're psychic, and she's a conduit. You touch her now, and you're just as likely to suffer." He leans forward. "Deep breaths, Harper."

I inhale, exhale, and inhale again. Oxygen rushes into my system, clearing my vision and making me horrendously lightheaded.

Putting a little distance between us, his hands still wrapped in my shirt, Lucas finally gives me space enough to look down.

"Prepare for the worst," he advises.

My gaze falls, my breath catching in my throat. Shock and horror turn me mute, trapping any noises or words I'm tempted to make or say. Claw marks run across my stomach, ending just beneath my ribs.

Saundra Beaumont bears down on us, her face stormy. "What does this mean?"

"It's exactly what it looks like," Lucas replies. "Demonic possession. Well, a form of it. He's not directly inhabiting her body, but he's siphoning power and energy. When the time comes, Levi will use Harper to get into Havenwood Falls. She's his portal. By the time the wards detect him, he will have caused a lot of destruction."

My aunt begins to cry, her tears an eerie song in a tense room of silence.

"But the archdemon wants *you*, right?" Saundra asks finally, her deep brown eyes locked on Lucas.

"All because I wanted to write my name," I whisper, mostly to myself.

Lucas lets my shirt drop, but he doesn't release me, his gaze swinging to the witch. "He holds a grudge against me."

Saundra's jaw tenses. "Can you defeat him?"

"Them," Lucas corrects. "There are two demons attracted to Harper. One can trip your wards, but don't underestimate her. Because I'm not sure why I feel her, and I don't know why she's linked with the psychic."

"Two!" Eloise's sobs grow. It sounds like her heart is breaking. Maybe it is.

"Shit!" Ric swears. "This is a security nightmare!" He glances at me, and I know what he's really thinking by the sympathetic look in his eyes. *I'm* the security nightmare. His heart is too big to admit it, too big to blame me out loud.

Ric turns to Saundra. "We need to keep them out of the town. I don't have any desire to tie up with an archdemon or a stranger, but I'll be damned if I let them hurt anyone in Havenwood Falls."

"What can you do to help?" Elsmed steps forward, his disconcerting eyes studying the fallen angel. "On Saundra's request, we summoned you to fix this problem."

Lucas's gaze finds mine again. "I have some favors I plan to call in."

The way he says it—the way he *looks* at me—is oddly reassuring. His hands are warm against the skin of my waist, and I find myself struggling with the need to push him away and the desire to pull him closer. Stranger or no, he looks like salvation.

With a small wink, he releases me, and turns to Saundra. "You and your witches may have to spell a few people, but I'll do my best to keep it contained."

"And you don't know when he'll come?" Saundra asks.

"It depends on how much strength he's gained. Any advantage I have will depend on how weak being in the Infernum has made him." The look he gives her tells a thousand stories. "You know what the Infernum does, witch. You hold a key that opens a portal into part of it. It's a potent feeling finding a weakness that can trap something powerful, isn't it? I have friends in very high places. Low ones, too. I am impressed by what you've done with the Blue Dragon Dagger."

Saundra's eyes fill with understanding and wisdom too deep to fathom. I've known the Court members since I was a child, but I don't think I truly realized how much they knew about this strange world we live in. Until now. They know things I can't even fathom. Things I'm not sure it's safe for me to know. Things I wonder if I *should* know.

Saundra sighs, swipes her hands down her black business suit, and says, "Just get that devil and anyone working with him out of my town, angel."

Lucas bows, and although it comes off as sarcastic, respect flickers in his gaze. "My pleasure, my lady."

"And follow close on his heels while you're at it," Saundra adds.

Lucas grins. "Aw, I see just how much you're going to miss me."

Saundra studies him, her lips twitching. "I don't know whether you're one of the good guys or one of the bad, Lucas Fox, and that unnerves me."

"We're all walking a blurred line, witch. It often takes being bad to save the good."

Something about his words stirs the Court members. They fidget, and I wonder just how many secrets the Court of the Sun and the Moon holds.

I'm not sure I have time to care. If the nightmares I've been having

the last few days and the claw marks on my flesh are any indication,
I'm a ticking time bomb.

CHAPTER 6

Once the door closes behind the court members, Aunt Eloise spins, the alarm on her face turning into grim concern. "Maybe you should consider moving back in."

"No way!" The words pop out much more vehemently than I intend them to. "No." Softening my voice, I approach her, head shaking. "I can't."

"Not for good, Harper." She tugs on her earrings, and I know if she doesn't stop, she's going to make herself bleed. "Just until all of this is over."

With a touch of annoyance, she glances at a spot over my shoulder. At the counter, Lucas pours another glass of scotch.

"Don't mind me." He salutes us with the liquor.

I ignore him. "If I come back now, I'm letting them win."

The monsters are *not* allowed to win. They've taken too much from me. Innocence. Youth. Magic.

They won't take my life.

Eloise's face reddens, and a tear trickles down her cheek. She swipes at it angrily. "I promised your parents I'd do my best by you."

She starts to grab me by the arms, and then stops, her hands dropping to her sides. It's disconcerting to see her so upset. Aunt

Eloise never cries; she sings Van Morrison and makes herbal remedies until everything in her world is right again.

"I don't know how to help," my aunt admits.

There's nothing worse than feeling helpless. Nothing worse than not being able to rescue the people you love the most. Nothing worse than being afraid you're going to hurt not only innocent bystanders, but the people you care about. It's a nightmare I will never wake up from.

"It's better for her in the mountains," Lucas interjects. "Less casualties if something goes wrong."

Eloise stares at him, her gaze intent. Minutes tick by like years. "Don't fail, angel," she says finally, voice wavering. "Please don't fail."

"Levi was bound to find a way to get to me eventually. If not through your niece, then another way. I promise you, I fully intend to give him the fight he deserves." He looks to me. "We should go."

"Together?" A million thoughts flood my head, and none of them are good.

Me. Him. Strangers.

Maybe he senses my unease because he comes to me, a sardonic tilt to his lips. "I like my coffee black, music that beats so hard you can feel it in your pulse, and gambling. But only if I know I'm going to win. I don't do long walks on the beach, but watching sunsets from the clouds," he shrugs, "it does it for me." He offers me his hand. "Now that you know something about me, does that help?" Frustration colors his gaze, and I don't know if I'm the reason behind it or if it's the demon haunting me.

After a moment's hesitation, my hand touches his.

He pulls me into him, startling me. Bright light flashes, and I shut my eyes against the glare.

When I open them again, we're inside my cabin in the mountains, his embrace cloaking me. He's massive, his muscular frame making me feel much, much smaller than I actually am. His heart beats against my cheek, his chest rising and falling with each breath. It's too intimate, and I have to fight the need to struggle.

"You're not used to being held, are you?" Lucas asks, head bent, his breath whispering against my neck.

Shudders race through me. "It hurts." Emotions, old and new, play a complicated game of hide and seek within me. To hide it, I push against him. "My stomach," I lie, even though it *does* pain me.

Immediately, he lets go. "Let me see it."

"What? No." I back away from him. "It's fine."

A smile flits across his face, the expression gone as fast as it appears. "Sit."

"Seriously, I'm good."

"No creams or medicines will fix demonic wounds." He urges me toward the sofa. "I can help."

When he drops to his knees in front of me, I start to shoot up, but he grips my waist, holding me in place. His hand slips under the hem of my shirt.

I look anywhere and everywhere except at him.

Cool air rushes against my skin, aggravating the raw wound and making me increasingly aware that I am not alone. His fingers run gently over my ribs.

I tense, electric tingles shooting all the way down to my toes. Birds flap frantic wings inside my stomach.

"Relax," Lucas soothes.

He touches the claw marks, and I hiss. Beneath his fingers, cool heat flares, and the pain from the injury subsides. The pad of his thumb dips toward my navel.

Hugging my middle, I fly off the sofa.

From his place on the floor, Lucas watches me. "I make you uncomfortable." It's a statement, not a question.

"I don't know. I—"

"Do you want to have sex?"

The question is so abrupt, so unexpected, that I'm pretty sure I squeak. "What?" My eyes widen. "Did you . . ." Pausing, I stare, inhale, and then, "Did you just proposition me?"

I mean, did he?

He stands, completely comfortable with himself and the situation. "I asked if you wanted to have sex."

A crazed laugh escapes me. "I don't even know you."

He shrugs, unconcerned. "I don't always know the women I sleep with."

My mouth falls open. "Are you serious right now?"

"The pleasures of the flesh are an enjoyable way for you to get over this fear you have of being touched."

The hell?

"I don't have a fear . . ." I wag a finger at him. "You know what? I don't like you."

"You'd like me much better if you had sex with me."

The snort that slips out of me is completely unrefined. "You know, that's not even worth a response."

Turning away, I busy myself by trying to start a fire. Lucas joins me, nods at the hearth, and then steps back when the wood within bursts into flames.

I glare, annoyed. "I could have done that."

"All you have to do is say no," Lucas says, and I know he's not talking about the fire.

My chin rises. "No."

He leans against the stone fireplace. "You're going to have to find a way to feel comfortable around me fast, Harper. The things that will happen to you won't be pretty. You need to be okay with me helping you with that."

"By having sex?"

"By opening yourself up in any way you feel comfortable doing so. Sex is just a fun suggestion."

Emotions swell like a tsunami inside of me, the strength of it threatening to knock me into the fire. "Do you have a lot of experience with things like this?"

"Demons or sex?"

I throw him a look.

He grins, and then sobers. "I've done a lap or two around the demonic block. Dealing with demons is complicated. Sometimes the experiences are bad. Other times, they're surprisingly good. I even call a few demons friends."

This, I find interesting. "The good demons? There's a few in town. There's one, she—"

"There are *decent* ones. Never confuse decent with good." Memories spark in his gaze, the resulting smile crinkling the corners of his eyes. "Or maybe it's just the ones I've come into contact with. The demons I know wouldn't appreciate being called good. I doubt they'd even appreciate being called decent."

The demon talk is becoming too much for me.

"They call me a generational curse," I blurt out, stepping back. Lucas keeps his distance, the flames from the hearth shadowing his face. "My father is psychic, but my mother was mortal."

Shut up, Harper, I tell myself.

My heart couldn't give a shit about what my logic thinks. I never get a chance to babble, except with Eloise. Having Lucas here is like having a therapist I don't have to pay for, who's being forced to stay and listen. Bless him. "My parents had trouble getting pregnant, so it was this huge thing when they discovered they were having me."

Pausing, I go into the kitchen and pull out a loaf of bread from a box on the counter. It's homemade sourdough wrapped just for me by the supe who works in the bakery section of our local supermarket. No labels. "Do you eat grilled cheese?"

He told me to be comfortable. Grilled cheese makes me comfortable.

Lucas's brows arch. "What happened to your parents?"

Sighing, I rest my hands on the counter. "Something went wrong with the pregnancy. I wasn't going to make it. The doctors told her it would be best to terminate. For her sake." My heart breaks for a woman I never knew. "My mother had a breakdown over it. She couldn't accept the idea of losing me, so Dad took it before the Court and begged them to do something—a spell, a ritual, or anything—to save me. They refused."

I swallow hard. "You know, I hated the Court for that when I found out. By then, I was ten years old. My aunt sat me down and said," changing my voice, I try to imitate Eloise, "'You've got to understand, Harper. It's not a simple thing trying to cheat death. It often hurts others worse than the person dying.'"

Abandoning the bread, I move back into the living room. "My aunt is right. She has this uncanny knack for being right about things."

I cringe. "My parents heard of a sorceress in Louisiana who did black magic. So they went to her. She saved my mother's pregnancy, but what she neglected to tell them was that, by doing so, my mother would be forfeiting her life and I'd be hounded by evil."

Lucas remains unmoving by the fire. He's too still, as if he's a sculpture rather than an angel. "And your father?"

"When my mother died in childbirth, he blamed himself for her death. It was too much on him, so he left. My aunt raised me." My chin dips, my gaze tracing the wood grain on the floor. "I tried to find my dad a few years ago. He's in California. Married with two kids. He doesn't remember Havenwood Falls, my mother, or me. The Court protects the town by ensuring people who leave here forget it." My gaze finds Lucas. "It's for the best. I think he's happy now."

"He knows something is missing. A spell can't take that away," Lucas says.

Swallowing past a sudden thickness in my throat, I ask, "How do you know?"

"Because I have a lot of practice with magic and a deep history with witches."

He steps away from the fire. The afternoon light from the one window in the living room grazes his face.

I haven't bothered with turning on the lights, and I don't know if it's because I'm more comfortable in the natural light from outside or because I've grown used to dark corners.

Firelight and slanted sunshine transform the room into something wholly unrealistic and yet entirely too real.

Lucas stops before me. "Magic and the supernatural tend to make mortals uncomfortable. Even dangerous. No one likes feeling weak." He glances at the window and at the snow-touched mountains beyond. White brilliance. "Those with differences have to protect themselves. They have to do things in order to protect their families, things that don't sit well with them, but magic has its limitations. It can get rid of memories, but the emptiness the memories leave behind is always there, lurking."

"You sound like you should get along better with Saundra Beaumont—with *all* of the Court—better than you seemed to today."

Lucas's gaze swings back to me. "Let's just say we understand each other, but I'm less willing to confine myself to one place."

He leans forward, putting him so close I can make out every detail of his face. It's unnaturally perfect, rugged and covered in stubble. Just enough to be sexy.

He's a mirage. I don't know how I know it, I just do. Maybe it's the psychic in me, the psychic I could have been if I hadn't been cursed. Looking at Lucas is like staring at a man who never changes. A man who never has to sleep or eat. A man who never has to shave. A man who just *is*.

"What kind of angel were you?" I whisper.

"What kind am I?" he corrects. "Being fallen doesn't make me any less of what I was." His gaze searches mine, and then, "A Seraph. I am a Seraph. The best and worst kind of angel." There's nothing human in the way he looks when he says it.

"What made you fall?"

We are nearly nose to nose when he replies, "I murdered a man."

If hearts could stop beating, mine would quit. Instead, it races, as if beating faster can get it far away from the creature in front of me. Except my body traps my heart, forcing it to face a moment it wants to avoid.

Hearts are cowardly things.

Bodies are shockingly resilient.

I don't run. I don't run because I've murdered a man, too, and although I wasn't wholly responsible—hell, I'd only been a child—the guilt remains. I *feel* like I murdered him.

"I can't judge someone for something I've done," I breathe, surprising him.

He straightens, amusement lightening his eyes. "Bonding over murder. I'd say that's a first."

He doesn't ask me who I killed. Either the Court has supplied him with the information or he doesn't care.

I don't care for the humor. "Did you mean to do it?" We may have something in common, but I never meant to hurt anyone.

For a moment, I think he's not going to answer, but then he touches my face, startling me. "I was trying to save someone not too unlike you. He was hurting her. I shouldn't have interfered. I wasn't supposed to interfere, but I did. He's dead, and I'm fallen."

From the way he drops his gaze, I know he hadn't intended to answer me. Maybe he'd planned to lie.

"Thank you." If I'm stuck with an angel who's supposed to help me fight demons, I can at least appreciate his honesty.

"What's it going to be like when the archdemon comes?" I ask out of nowhere. "If I'm a portal for him, will he," I look down at my stomach, "burst out of me?"

If I'm going to be a conduit for a demon, then I want to go into it as knowledgeable about it as possible. Knowledge is power.

Lucas laughs, the sound deep and thrilling. "You must read a lot of science fiction."

"*Listen*," I correct. "I listen to a lot of science fiction. On audiobook." My hands press against my stomach, and I know by the way it doesn't pain me that the claw marks are gone. "Will it hurt?"

I try to hide the fear I'm feeling, but my voice cracks.

Lucas places his hand over mine on my stomach, squeezing my fingers just enough to be reassuring. "He won't physically burst out of you, but he will torment you. Be prepared for that. He'll use your energy to bring himself into the physical world, so he'll need you near."

Relief is a pleasant feeling that's all too fleeting.

I won't be giving birth to any grotesque beings, but the demon *can* harm me. As a psychic from a long line of psychics, I know enough about spirits to know they have the ability to harm someone they're attached to. The physical stuff is rarer—it takes a lot of energy for a spirit to manifest—but it's possible.

I have another question, but I leave it unasked.

If this demon is strong enough to nearly strangle me in Jeanine Turner's office and claw me at my aunt's shop, what's to stop him from killing me?

"How about that grilled cheese sandwich now?" I ask instead.

Lucas smiles. "Okay."

CHAPTER 7

*T*he last thing I remember before falling asleep is the way the sun moved over the living room as it set, cloaking the house in darkness, the fire in the hearth crackling.

Lucas sat on the end of my couch while I curled against the opposite end, a blanket wrapped around my shoulders. Empty plates rested on the kitchen counter, the silence in the room a lullaby urging my eyes to close.

I fought it, but in the end, weariness won out over wariness.

The angel watching me couldn't be any worse than the archdemon haunting me.

On the heels of another nightmare, debilitating nausea wakes me, and I find myself in my bed, my bare feet tangled in sheets I've apparently been fighting. My room is dark, the window to the side of my queen-sized four poster bed revealing a snowy ground under a star-dotted sky.

My breath comes fast, and I swallow the rising bile in my throat.

The nausea worsens.

Kicking myself free of the sheets, I tumble out of my bed, my knees hitting the floor hard before I drag myself toward the bathroom adjoining the bedroom.

I gag.

Hands lift me, and I struggle.

"Shh," Lucas's voice soothes. "It's me."

The bathroom light clicks on, casting a glow over soft yellow walls and ivory-tiled floors. Sunshine and sunflowers.

My stomach cramps, and I fight the angel holding me. "Please."

He sets me down in front of the toilet just as the vomiting begins. It comes so hard and so fast, I can't breathe through the heaving. Worse yet, blood gushes from my mouth. Straight blood, the metallic taste of it making the nausea sweep me in increasing waves.

My hands grip the porcelain, desperate for the coolness.

Lucas sits behind me, his long legs swallowing me, his thighs embracing me. Pulling my hair back, he fists it in one of his hands.

"I'm dying," I manage to gasp.

"No," he assures me, "but you're going to feel like you are."

The cramps subside, and I sag against his chest, too afraid and spent to be embarrassed. Lucas leans away from me and reaches into a cabinet under the sink. A pile of folded washcloths sits on a shelf. Taking one, he squeezes it in his fist. When he places it against my face, it's wet. The cool moisture feels so good against my heated flesh; I don't even care how he dampened the material.

"Have you been going through my house?" I ask weakly, accepting the cloth.

He drops his arm and slides it around my waist. "Preparation."

Silence.

The embarrassment finally washes over me, thick and uncomfortable. "Oh, God."

Lucas's arm tightens. "It's only going to get worse. The stronger he becomes—the more energy he pulls—the weaker and sicker you're going to be. I can't stop him until he's here. I can't go where he is."

A solitary tear slips down my cheek. It's all I care to give the being tormenting me. One tear packed full of fear and resentment.

"I bet this makes me the first girl you've ever watched vomit blood," I say, trying to lighten the mood. It comes off too soft to be funny.

Lucas combs my hair with his fingers. "You're the first girl who's ever channeled a demon with a vendetta against me. You shouldn't have been drawn into this. If I was able to enter where he is, you wouldn't be his way of getting to me. You also wouldn't be my way of reaching him."

Something in his voice catches me off guard. "Do I hear regret?"

"Don't push it," he mumbles.

I can't help it; I laugh.

Nausea slams into me again, out of nowhere, and the laughter ends on choking sobs.

Lucas rushes to help. I heave over and over until there's nothing left. Until I'm a crumpled mess of weakness. As limp as the washcloth.

Blood and anguish.

A burning pain replaces the nausea in my gut, and I cry out.

Growling, Lucas stands, dragging me up with him. "Damn you, Levi."

Without bothering to ask, he tugs my shirt up and off. Drained, my head hangs, my gaze falling on fresh claw marks on my skin, deeper than the ones that had been there before. Blood drips from the wound, the liquid soaking into the band of my jeans.

Lucas unbuttons my pants.

"What are you doing?" I try struggling, but spots dance before my eyes.

"Remember earlier when I suggested we have sex?" he asks while dragging my jeans down over my thighs. "Maybe you ought to have taken me up on the offer. Into the shower with you." He leaves my bra and underwear on, but everything else goes.

Near the bathroom's entrance is a small stand-up shower. Lucas slides the beveled glass door open and steps inside, bringing me with him. The stall is barely big enough for one person, much less two, but this doesn't deter him.

"Hold on for me, Harper." Resting my hand on the bar inside, he releases me, and with a swiftness that doesn't help my lightheadedness, he sheds his clothes, chucks them outside, and slides the door shut.

"What—?" He turns on the shower, and the initial blast of cold water tears a yelp out of me that drowns out any protests.

Pulling me against him, *all* of him, Lucas slides his hands over my wound. "I can't stop the nausea, but *this* I can fix."

Cool heat flares where he touches me. Blood mingles with water at our feet.

The world spins away from me, making all of this seem surreal: his hands against my skin, the warming water pounding us, the blood, and the sensations pouring through me.

Lucas slips his fingers into the sides of my panties, and when I don't fight him, he slides them down before unsnapping my bra.

His arms circle me, steam rising around us.

I'm ashamed to admit my brain is too foggy and my body too weak to remember much about the shower. He washes me, gently stroking my skin while silently cursing the demon under his breath. He also makes promises to me. Promises to avenge everything Levi has done.

Afterward, he enfolds me in a terry cloth towel, helps me brush my teeth, and carries me to the bed. I'm a limp doll with a sodden heart.

The mattress dips when he sets me on it, and I clutch his bare arms. "Stay . . . please."

His blue eyes darken.

Unlike me, he's not wearing a towel. He's comfortable in his nudity, comfortable with *himself* in a way most people can only hope to be, and I draw strength from that.

He climbs into the bed in front of me, and I curl into his chest. His arm slides over my waist, my towel the only thing separating us.

He's warm, and even though he couldn't stop my vomiting, he feels safe.

Sudden tears leak down my cheeks, the ferocity of them frightening. Shaking me. These tears have nothing to do with the demon and everything to do with me. These tears are deeper. Personal.

For the first time since I was a child, I let someone hold me. And he's not only someone, he's a stranger. A *Stranger*.

Ever since my father left Havenwood Falls and I accidentally caused the death of the man in town, I have pushed people away. Even Aunt Eloise. For years, I stepped out of her hugs because anything longer than a brief touch was too much.

"Let someone help you," she had begged.

I was scared of hurting people and of getting hurt.

Sobs wrack my body. I cry for Eloise. I cry for my mother. I cry for my father. I cry for *myself.* Years of tears.

Tipping my face up gently, Lucas studies my tear-stained eyes, and then kisses me, his lips closing over mine, his warm mouth catching my teardrops.

Tender. Soothing. Fleeting.

Gone as quick as it began.

"Quit thinking," he whispers. "Pain can be so deep that it's hard to bring the people you're too close to into that hurt. Sometimes it takes giving it to a stranger before you can open up to someone else."

"How—"

"Just trust I know."

I stare at him through eyes swollen from tears and madness. "Do you have anyone you're close to?"

"A few."

"Someone you love?"

"Friends."

I let the word sink in, and then, "Have you ever been in love?"

"No." The answer comes too fast.

"You're a high-ranking fallen angel, and you're telling me after all of the years you've existed—"

"An eternity."

I glare, but fatigue takes all of the bite out of it. "You could have kept the eternity part to yourself because now that just makes this," I point from him to me, "weird."

He chuckles. "No, it makes me experienced."

"Not helping. Now I'm self-conscious." My lips curl into a smile. "And you're changing the subject. You can't tell me that in an *eternity* you haven't fallen in love at least once."

With his finger, Lucas traces a line from my forehead to my nose. "Three times," he admits carefully. "Once before my fall. Two after. A mortal in the middle ages, a demon, and a witch."

"What happened?" I ask.

His finger drops to my lips. "The mortal died. The witch and the demon fell in love with each other."

I stare, unable to speak.

"And you, my little psychic?"

My head shakes.

"No one?"

Taking his finger, I remove it from my lips. "It's hard to do relationships when you have to limit yourself so much. No cell phones, no texting each other, no movie theaters, or restaurants with fancy-scripted menus." Reaching out, I caress his face, surprising myself with my boldness. He leans into my touch, the gesture boosting my confidence. "I had crushes. I even tried the whole boyfriend thing, but," my fingers run through the stubble on his face, fascinated with the roughness, "it didn't work out."

"What about when you were in school?"

I shrug, one bare shoulder rising. "I was kept separated. There are two high schools in Havenwood Falls: Havenwood Falls High and the Sun and Moon Academy. The latter is a private school for supernatural students who don't or can't fit into the public school system. Guess where I went?" My lips curl. "They tried teaching me to read and write. I learned, but not without consequences. It took everything the Court's witches had to keep the evil things I kept channeling contained. So, they developed a new way to teach me. I listened to audio textbooks and took verbal tests. Each of the Court members worked with me. Alone. I owe them so much."

Tears prick my eyes again. "This town . . . it's everything to so many people. To me." I inhale. "Saundra Beaumont and her granddaughter, Addie, helped teach me science by doing experiments with me. Addie's a year older than me, and it helped that I wasn't the only child. The shifters would let me join them in the woods, tracking and learning. What I couldn't learn outside the classroom, they found other creative ways to teach me. There's a coffee shop in town, Coffee Haven, owned by a fae, Willow Fairchild. She displays art from local artists in the shop, and she'd bring pieces to show me outside. All kinds. Oil. Water color. Photography. I fell in love with the photography. Then . . ." My words trailing off, I cover my eyes. "You need to tell me to shut up."

His hand cups my hip, and even through the towel, the touch

burns. "Talk, Harper. Talk as much and as long and as big as you need to."

I drop my hands, my incredulous gaze finding his face. "Where did you come from?" He just doesn't seem real.

"From Hell," he answers soberly. "From Hell and Heaven and everything in between. From myth and legend. From gods and goddesses. From the beginning of time until the end."

"Why does that sound sad?" I ask.

"Because eternity is a very long time."

Now I know why this feels so good and hurts so much. We are both lonely strangers. To each other, and maybe even to ourselves.

This time, I kiss him, my hands framing his face, my lips tentative. He opens for me, and our tongues slide together, the sensation sending a pool of heat to my core.

His hand tightens on my hip, his fingers digging into the towel.

My fingers slip into his hair, and suddenly I don't care if I don't know him. I don't care if he isn't human.

He runs his hand up my side, his fingers brushing the edge of my breast, and I arch against him.

"Harper," he whispers.

"Please," I whisper back.

He undoes the towel I'm wearing and replaces it with his skin. His mouth leaves mine, his lips leaving a trail of fire down my jaw, my neck, and my breasts.

I close my eyes because the feel of him is so much better than anything I could have imagined. He doesn't demand anything. He simply gives, and I wonder if it's because I'm not experienced.

What is happening with my life?

This isn't the way I saw any of my firsts.

I certainly don't hear any Van Morrison music.

Instead, I *feel* everything. The hard length of him against my thigh. His hands sliding over parts of me I've never shared with anyone else. His mouth creating heat in places that make my face burn.

Waves of pleasure so intense it's almost painful.

When his mouth returns to mine and he presses into me, I meet his thrust with my hips, my body tense because I expect pain.

There isn't any.

Startled, I meet his gaze.

Holding himself above me, his arms caging me in, he says, "Relax. This much I can do, too. You've endured enough pain."

The tension leaves my body, and he thrusts deeper, my body taking all of him.

My legs wrap around his waist, my fingers digging into his shoulders.

"Oh, God," I breathe.

Chuckling, he kisses the side of my neck, and then whispers, "Now let me show you what heaven feels like."

CHAPTER 8

*L*ucas isn't in the bed when I wake.

I rise with the sun, my body sore, my mind so full of thoughts I don't quite know where to put them all, and I'm glad he's gone.

Too much, too fast, I think.

First house. First time having sex. First time having sex with an *angel*. First one-night stand. Vomiting blood. All within days, even hours and minutes, of each other, because I'm an over-achiever like that.

I grab the pillow next to me, stuff my face into it, and scream. A good scream, not the bad kind. Unlike Aunt Eloise, I have no desire to take back my virginity.

If anything, I want to thank Lucas. It might not have been what I imagined—sex with someone I've had at least three dates with or a guy I am head over heels in love with—but it was everything I needed. Right now. At this moment.

Throwing my legs over the side of the bed, I rush to my closet, quickly donning the usual skinny jeans and sweatshirt. Heavy coat. A knit cap. Solid colors. No words.

My camera bag sits on the living room floor, and I sling it onto my shoulder.

Everything outside looks and feels new. The snow on the ground, the white powder dusting the trees, the way the rising sun paints the sky a rainbow of blues, pinks, and purples. The way the air smells, crisp and tinged with smoke.

Taking my camera out of my bag, I turn back to my cabin, focus the shot, and shoot a picture of the arched front door.

"I've heard of people skipping out on one night stands, but never on me. I think I'm offended."

Smiling, I spin to find Lucas standing in the snow, his hands cradling two cups of coffee, and I know by the way he's gripping one of them, he's hiding a logo.

"You went into town?" I ask.

"More like blinked in and out. Here." He hands me a plain white Styrofoam cup.

The awkwardness of our situation slams into me like a high-speed train. "I don't drink—"

"It's hot chocolate."

Accepting the cup with my free hand, I sniff the contents. "How did you know? I didn't tell you . . ." My gaze swings to Lucas, then back to the cup, my eyebrows practically shooting to my hairline. "How *did* you know?"

His silence is telling.

I groan. "Oh, no . . . don't tell me."

He smirks. "It's an angel thing. Well, a Seraph thing, though a few other castes can do it as well. If it makes you feel better, I can't really read your thoughts. I don't know why. Maybe the demons? You've trained yourself to block out demons for so long, it's like trying to break through an incredibly sophisticated security system. I only get small things from you. Things like the fear of touch. Hot chocolate."

He walks toward me, and he's so brilliant surrounded by the snow and the sky, I rush to set my cup in the snow. From a crouch, I lift my camera.

The *click* is loud in the still morning.

"So, all those things I told you," I ask, still crouching, "you didn't see them in my head?"

He crouches in front of me. "No, and it's refreshing having to guess. Most people make it too easy." Touching my camera, he raises his brows. "You know this won't develop, right?"

"The picture of you?" I'm unable to hide my disappointment. "Why?"

"Seraph means fiery one. The only thing you're going to get on that film is a walking blaze. Since I'm fallen, you'll get a touch of blue fire in there, too."

Standing, I peer down at him. "You like being fallen, don't you?"

"What makes you think that?"

"The way your eyes light up when you say it."

He stands, instantly towering over me. "It bothered me at first, but over the years I've learned to embrace it and what it means. Blurred lines exist for a reason. Some of the best warriors exist in the gray area." Tapping his head as if it's a treasure chest full of knowledge, he smiles. "Half your town's Court among them. Besides," his gaze slides over the snow-covered mountain, "I've been fortunate enough to fight alongside beings and people I would not have fought with if I was still a Risen." His eyes find mine. "And the ones I fought alongside were in the right. Not all demons are bad. Not all angels are good. Not all people are innocent."

Fierce passion makes his eyes glow, lightening them until they are almost colorless, and I suddenly understand why he's a fiery one.

Stooping, he picks up my hot cocoa. "Come on, I've got you a present, and if you're in the mood to take pictures, it's the perfect place for it."

He saunters away.

I rush to catch up with him, camera in hand. "There isn't a place on Mt. Souza, or any mountains around Havenwood Falls for that matter, I don't know."

"Oh, it's not a part of the mountain. It's more of a thing."

We march through the snow, hitting a trail just behind the cabin. My boots leave deep prints in the white powder. His boots leave no marks whatsoever.

"Another Seraph thing?" I ask, indicating the snow. "Just what all *can* you do? Other than healing demonic wounds, vanishing, and reading thoughts."

Lucas glances at the ground. "A lot." When he lifts his head, his eyes are shuttered. "Too much." The tone of his voice tells me everything I need to know. Despite his arrogance, Lucas is not a flashy angel.

Reaching the top of an incline, he turns and offers me his hand. Even though it isn't steep, I accept his help.

A shallow hollow spreads out before us, mountain slopes rising on three sides, majestic and full of power. A cold, pine-scented wind reddens my cheeks before whistling into the valley.

Nature sings.

"One of my favorite places," I breathe, lifting my camera.

"Not yet," Lucas says, stopping me. He gazes out over the space, and then points. "There."

From the edge of the valley, something lopes toward us, a dark blur on snow. "What is that?"

"A favor." He grins. "From a friend."

I edge toward the angel, unease trickling down my spine. "Is that . . . *oh.*"

From the snow, a lion approaches us, his face surrounded by a magnificent fiery mane, his eyes narrowed. Wings protrude from his back, the appendages large enough to envelop him. The closer he draws to us, the more magnificent he becomes.

I blink, and he's in front of me.

Words fail me.

Resting on his haunches in the snow, the lion studies me. Like Lucas, he leaves no tracks in the snow. I am tiny compared to him. Strangely, he doesn't dwarf Lucas at all.

"Meet the Destroyer," Lucas introduces.

"Destroyer?" I whisper, awed. I have met too many supernatural beings in my life to be cowed, but impressed . . . oh, I am most certainly impressed.

Lucas pats the beast on the shoulder. "Or Desi for short."

The lion glares. "You go too far, angel."

"Don't be fooled," Lucas tells me, ignoring the creature. "He likes it."

"What . . . how . . ." Inhaling, I try again. "*Where* did he come from?" My gaze flies to the lion. "*You*, I mean. Where did you come from?"

Lucas answers for him, a secret smile on his lips. "A very powerful gargoyle friend of mine out of France. He has a thing for collecting ancient weapons."

"Weapon? *That* does not look like a weapon!" The lion growls, and I step back. "No offense or anything. I just . . ." I shake my head. "I think I'm going to shut up now."

"Into the mace, Desi," Lucas snaps, startling me.

Grumbling, the lion stretches out in the snow, folds his wings over himself, and then vanishes. *Poof.* Gone. In his place is an intricately carved wooden club, the end of it covered in bronze thorns.

Time out.

"Did," I gesture at the club, "*that* lion just turn into a baseball bat on steroids?"

The mountains echo when Lucas laughs.

Setting our drinks in the snow, Lucas swipes the steroid-bat off the ground and offers it to me. "It's a mace, a much more popular weapon a long time ago. It's yours, for now."

I stare at it. "Not that I don't appreciate this, but I wasn't expecting to wake up this morning to hot cocoa and a new pet, *er*, mace."

"He'll be an invaluable ally for you."

Tucking my camera into the bag on my shoulder, I let Lucas place the weapon in my hands. It's surprisingly light considering it was just a massive, flying male lion.

"I don't like the way you're giving this to me," I say quietly. "This gift comes with too many unsaid things."

Reaching out, he tucks a strand of hair behind my ear before pulling my knit cap down over it. "You are stronger than you know, Harper. You don't get ruffled easily. You take pain better than most mortals I've met. You've been locked away from your abilities out of fear, and when that fear is gone, you're going to discover a whole new woman locked inside of you, too. It takes an awful lot of power to keep a Seraph out of your head. Until then," he winks, "Desi here will be a friend. He's a sentient weapon, which means you can fight with him, use him for information, or even let him fight for you when you can't. I'd teach you how to use a sword or some other form of defense, but we're running out of time."

"What about you?" I ask, my hands gripping the weapon. "Couldn't you use the mace?"

Lucas ducks his head. "Seraphs are nearly invincible. I say nearly because we do have weaknesses. Not many, but we do. If Leviathan is threatening me, he's got something he knows will harm me." At my look of alarm, he tips my chin up. "I'll destroy him no matter what happens to me. This has been a long time coming. This has nothing to do with your town or you. It's not your fault."

I'm not worried about the demon's destruction; I'm worried about Lucas. He may have charged into my life too quickly, like a flame sparking, but now that he's here, I want to know more about him. I want to know more about what and who he is. I want *time*. My abilities have always left me with little time. Scrawl a message to a guy in town. He dies. Scrawl a message threatening an angel, and my life becomes a fast-paced action novel. In audio.

I hug the weapon to myself. "What did you do to the archdemon?"

Lucas glances at the valley beyond. "When the world was ancient, Leviathan was considered a god. He was worshipped as one. His need for power, his greed, and his cruelty grew. His possessed followers were sacrificing humans for him, specifically young virgins. In his bid for supremacy, he nearly wiped out whole cities of mortals. Archdemons are a pain in the ass. For even their own kind." His gaze returns to mine. "This was the time of the gods, of the Greeks, of the Romans, and of great power. Before I fell, I was commanded to take down Leviathan before he caused more destruction. The battle wasn't an easy one. It took me and a legion of warriors to take down Levi and his minions." His eyes go distant. "A dragon of the heavens against a dragon of the seas and the land. In the end, I managed to lock him away in the Infernum, a dark place for very powerful and dangerous supernaturals who are hard to kill."

I stare, awed. "You felled a god."

"I felled an archdemon who wanted to be a god, and now he wants retribution."

If the morning was cold before, it's frigid now.

I should say things like, "No, you can't fight him!" Or at least beg him to leave Havenwood Falls, but I don't.

In retrospect, sex kind of foiled things because now I feel something for him and that complicates everything.

I also keep my mouth shut because he's right. This is his battle with an old enemy, and I am simply the tool to make it happen.

"What can I do to help?" I ask. "You know, other than bleed everywhere?"

Respect fills his gaze. "Find a way past your fears. There is unimaginable power in you. I sense it."

The mace in my hand shudders, and I nearly drop it, a shriek escaping me.

"Desi senses it, too," Lucas adds, chuckling. "Now for a suggestion. Your bed was much, much warmer than this mountain. If you catch my meaning."

I throw him a look. "Do you even feel the cold?"

"No, but admit it." He leans close. "Bed has a nice poetic feel to it. Besides, it's Thanksgiving."

His words paralyze me. "What did you say?" Oh, God! My aunt! With everything going on, the date completely slipped my mind. "We need to go!" I wave the mace. "Make us do the whole blink in and blink out thing."

Lucas watches, amused. "I don't really do the holidays."

"Why?" I ask, aghast. "What's not to like? Food, fam—"

Family. My thoughts cut me off. Do Seraphs even have families?

"Harper," Lucas warns, grabbing for me.

I feel the gush before I see the blood pouring out of my face.

Ripping off his button-up shirt, Lucas stuffs it beneath my nose. I clutch at the material, and the mace falls to the blood-speckled snow at our feet.

"I'm sorry," I say to Desi, my voice nasal because of the shirt.

Resting a large hand on the back of my head, Lucas presses me against him. "Don't worry about the mace. He's been ordered to stay with you. Trust me, he finds his own way."

Blood soaks the shirt, and I sag against Lucas. "How has this not killed me?"

"You're weak because Levi is drawing on your energy. You're not dead because it's not your blood."

It takes a moment for his words to sink in, but when they do, I recoil, pure horror crashing down on me. "What?" I panic into the shirt, because who wouldn't? "What do you mean it's not my blood?"

"You stay calm when you think it's your blood, but you get all up in arms when it's someone else's?"

I push away from him, still clutching the shirt. "Lucas! That's like pissing out someone else's urine!"

He reaches for me. "Let's get you cleaned up."

"Whose blood is it?" I insist.

Lucas inhales, his gaze settling on mine. "The condemned. It's the blood of the condemned in the Infernum. Levi can't sacrifice humans, so he's sacrificing the condemned imprisoned with him so he can build enough strength through their deaths and your energy to escape. I don't know how he's doing it, but I know it's not your blood."

My knees go weak, but I hold my ground. "There's no way to stop him from doing this?"

"Not without going into the Infernum, and there are some places even Seraphs can't go. Escaping it is one thing; entering it is another."

"Has anyone ever escaped it before?" I don't think I want to know this answer.

"No."

My vision blurs, and I stumble away from him to lean against a tree. My hands are covered in blood, and it's not my own.

Lucas appears next to me. "The condemned suffer more than you could ever know. Death is relief. Even if it's brief. They won't stay dead. Remember what I told you about the Infernum, Harper. It's a prison for supernaturals who are nearly impossible to kill. Like archdemons." He pauses, letting that sink in before adding, "For creatures like me."

My gaze flashes to his face, Levi's words potent when I recall them. *You will have a place in Hell, Lucas Fox. Cast and chained in the Infernum of darkness. Death to the messenger. Death to those who give her sanctuary.*

"That's what he plans to do to you," I whisper.

Silence, and then, "Let's get you cleaned up."

A new resolve fills me. "Today, you're doing the holidays." He pulls back, surprised. "I may bleed everywhere, and it may be the most uncomfortable meal I have ever had, but you are damn well doing the holidays today, Lucas."

If I'm going to bleed other creatures' blood, and Lucas is prepping for a fight that may cost him more than he gains, then I'm damn sure going to show him what it means to be human.

CHAPTER 9

*A*fter returning to my cabin to clean up, Lucas blinks us to my aunt's basement apartment.

Below her shop, the apartment is an open and airy area with lots of recessed lighting to make up for the lack of windows. Stained concrete floors span the entire space, all of the rooms open to each other except for the two bedrooms. A vibrant multi-colored kitchen connects to a simple dining room with a farm table covered in artwork. The dining room joins a living room with wildly painted walls and a sofa and a recliner, each of the furniture pieces sporting gauzy scarves and strange-looking dolls. Two doors to the back of the space lead into the bedrooms. Candles are displayed on every available surface.

Eloise is in the middle of pulling a small turkey out of her oven when we appear, and she shrieks, dropping it.

Lucas catches the pan bare-handed in mid-air, places it on the kitchen's small counter, and smiles. Evidently, he's also immune to heat.

"You couldn't use the door?" Eloise asks, holding her chest.

"The angel doesn't have any manners," I tease.

Still shaken, Eloise glances from me to Lucas and then me again. "I wasn't sure you would come, but—"

I rush to embrace her, cutting off her words.

She stiffens in my arms, unused to me hugging or seeking comfort from her. Her scent of gingerbread and honey invades my senses. She smells like home. It doesn't matter that I was here only yesterday. Today, even though I am unsure about everything, I feel more confident than I have in years.

Relaxing, Eloise hugs me back, her hand stroking my hair. "Harper," she whispers in my ear.

Today, I am thankful for her.

Lucas pulls me away, regret coloring his eyes. "It's not safe," he reminds me. "I don't know how closely tied your psychic abilities are to hers."

Eloise clears her throat, turning away so she can swipe at her eyes, and guilt swamps me. I wasted too many years letting my fears and grief distance us. I doubt I'll ever feel natural around people, but my aunt is different.

Her, I should have tried harder with.

If all of this ends well, I *will* try harder.

Eloise faces us, all smiles again, although she casts a lot of ill-at-ease glances at Lucas. "I'm glad you came. I cooked enough for three meals. On purpose. Because who really wants to cook more than twice a year?"

She's lying. She loves to cook.

"Can I help?" I ask.

She ushers us into the dining room. "No! You sit." Her gaze slides to Lucas. "Both of you."

For years, every time Aunt Eloise would get stressed out about something, she would grab a box of paints and brushes, sit at the table, and create art until she was spent. The table is now a collage of anxiety-ridden graffiti. Pictures as simple as stars and as difficult as human faces fan out across the wooden surface. When she ran out of room on the table, she started on the walls.

The pictures *are* my aunt. They are her emotions, her thoughts, and her fears. My face is among the chaos, and I think it's a perfect place for it to be.

"How are things going?" Eloise asks.

Rushing back and forth, she fills plates before setting them down before us. My aunt may prefer making herbal concoctions, but she is an amazing cook. She says it's a way to express herself. Like the painted table.

"Stop," I demand. "Sit. If we need anything else, we'll get it."

She sits.

In a long, tiered peasant skirt, a strawberry-red top, and her auburn hair pulled up in a messy bun, Eloise looks young. Or *would*, if not for the circles under her eyes and the tight lines around her mouth.

"I made it through the night okay," I assure her.

She sinks her fork into her food and then stops. "Why my niece?" she asks, her gaze finding Lucas.

Because I wrote my name, I think.

Eloise stares at him hard, as if she's challenging him to a visual game of thumb war. It's not about who blinks first; it's about whose stare is stronger. "Angel?"

He leans back in his chair. He's too big for the farm table. It's like looking at an adult trying to sit at a kid's table, and yet he makes it look *not* ridiculous.

"Which question do you want me to answer first? The one about Levi or the one about her virginity?" Lucas asks.

"What?" I glance between them, horrified. Guilt takes up residence in Eloise's eyes. "You did a reading on me?" Realizing she hadn't asked the questions aloud, I throw in, "You know he can read thoughts?"

"Last night, I went to see Saundra," she replies, still staring at the angel. "It was educational to say the least. Afterward, I asked for a little guidance from the spirits."

Lucas raises his brows, impressed. "I'm developing a new respect for psychics and your tenacity."

"My niece?" Eloise persists.

"Levi is a tyrant. I don't get confused often, and when I do, it pisses me off. I don't know how he's doing what he is. I've seen a lot of demonic possessions over the years. This isn't a possession." He shakes his head. "It's like he's using her as a sacrificial altar, bleeding victims on her skin. That shouldn't be possible. He's slashing his victims. Each time he does it, it slashes her. Then he bleeds them."

My gaze falls to the table and to the food growing cold. Without looking at either of them, I eat. Stress wins out over the steal-my-appetite gruesome details. I already know I'm not bleeding my own blood. The other information is new to me, but I sense they're theories he must be throwing back and forth in his head.

"As for her virginity," he pauses, and I know he's looking at me. I refuse to look up. "She's a beautiful woman. Consenting adults. And—"

"You were protecting me," I finish for him. I should have known, and honestly, I did suspect it after he told me the story of Levi and his penchant for sacrificing virgins.

"Harper—" my aunt begins.

"I'm not surprised." I'm not. It doesn't shock me that she knows about what happened the night before. It doesn't surprise me that Lucas had sex with me as much to protect me as he did out of need and desire. Everything comes back to me—my curse and the things everyone around me has to do to fix it or protect me.

None of it surprises me.

I've been living under a microscope my entire life. What would surprise me is living *out* from under a microscope.

"You've got to know a good song for this one," I tell Eloise. "Come on, hit me with it."

When I look up, she's staring at me. Maybe she wants me to be fazed by all of this. Maybe she expects me to be upset. Maybe I should be. Thing is, I may not be doing cartwheels over all of the bad shit happening, but I'm glad I slept with Lucas. It let me connect with someone, and doing that is teaching me to connect with others. Maybe my first wasn't movie-of-the-week material, but it was an awakening. I can't regret that.

Slowly, she smiles. "Stranded."

The lyrics play in my head, and I smile back. "Now, *that* one feels like me." I glance at Lucas. "You're supposed to eat when there's a holiday. Like, a lot." He hasn't touched his food, and I add, "Even if you don't have to."

His gaze searches my face, his expression unreadable, and I'm thrown by how *deeply* he studies me.

A thousand years pass in one stare.

The sound of my aunt's chair scraping the floor drags me back into the present. "What the hell?" she exclaims. Abruptly, she stumbles away from the table, and then points to the end of it. "What the hell is that?"

There, resting in a seat, is Desi, the weird pet that turns into a badass baseball bat. Lucas *did* say it would find its way to me.

I sigh. "Just accept that my life is really weird right now."

Eloise circles the table, giving Desi a wide berth while eyeing the bronze protrusions on the weapon. "There's weird, and then there's a club with thorns."

"Weird," I repeat.

"Club," she points out.

"A mace actually," Lucas inserts. "With spikes."

Eloise pauses, leans forward, and then narrows her eyes. "A mace? Why does it feel alive?"

Her psychic abilities go much deeper than just spiritual reading. She's also an empath and extremely sensitive to auras and energy. Trying to lie to her as a teenager was a bitch. Hence, why I never tried more than once.

"It's sentient," Lucas replies. "Think a guardian inside of a weapon."

Stunned, Eloise glances at me.

I shrug. "Apparently, that's what you get when you channel an archdemon, and then have a one-night stand with a fallen angel."

Eloise shakes her head. "You are *so* my kid."

A sharp laugh escapes me, mainly because I did not expect that response.

"Let's eat," I suggest.

We barely make it through the meal when my chair slides backward away from the table, completely on its own. Blood trickles out of my nose, and my hand flies to my face to staunch a gush that never comes.

Eloise cries out.

For once, Lucas doesn't rush to help. He simply turns his chair, leans his elbows on his knees, and watches me.

I'm trying to breathe, not because I can't, but because I feel swollen, my body full of something extremely dark and terrifying. Like a doll stuffed with super-charged cotton.

"He can't do it," Lucas says.

Breathing through the panic crippling me, I look at him. "Can't do what?"

"Possess you." He stares, amazed. "He keeps trying. I can feel it. He's drawing on your energy, but he's not *entering* you."

"I'd say that sounds like a dirty joke, but," nausea slams into me, "this really hurts."

Lucas finally comes to me, kneels, and touches my chin. "You're not going to throw up."

Bile rises in my throat, metallic and hot, and I swallow past it. "Those are pretty words—"

"Fight it, Harper." He drops his hand.

I clutch my stomach and double over. "Fight it," I repeat. *You're not going to throw up.*

Inside my head, I start to scream, loud and shrill. Over and over again. The sound chases back the nausea.

My hands start to shake. Even pressed against my stomach, I can feel the tremors.

I lift them.

Aunt Eloise gasps. "Paper."

Rushing into her bedroom, she returns with pencils and a notepad. I shake my head, even as my chair slides back toward the table. Once again, all on its own.

"I can't do this," I insist.

Lucas joins me. "Yes, you can. Use your gifts. If a lesser demon tries to interfere, I've got you. There's not a damn thing they can do if I'm here."

Pushing the food aside, Eloise places the notebook and pencils in front of me, the cover flipped open.

"Aunt Eloise," I beg.

My hands are shaking so violently now, they hurt.

"It's okay," she promises, even though I can tell by the waver in her voice, she's not sure it is.

As soon as I lift my hand, it flies to the pencils. Gripping one of them, my fingers jerk to the notebook, and I feel my eyes rolling up inside of my head.

My world goes dark.

When I come to, Lucas is leaning over the table, furrows marring his forehead.

Beneath my fingers are the words, *You can't protect her, Luke. She's mine. Power. Time to suffer.*

Dropping the pencil, my hands fly to my throat, but there's no choking sensation like there was in Jeanine Turner's office. "Luke?" I rasp.

Lucas stares at the message. Small drops of blood are smeared over the ink. "Levi and I have known each other for a very, very long time." It's the only explanation he gives for the nickname.

"You can't protect her? She's mine?" Eloise massages her forehead. "I don't understand. This isn't about Harper, *is* it?"

Lucas touches the notebook. "We're talking about an archdemon who has had a very long time to build a grudge and make plans. I'm sure he has multiple agendas." Picking up one of the pencils, he taps it against the sheet. "Will you write for me again, Harper?"

My blood runs cold. "Lucas . . ."

Coming up behind me, he cages me in with his arms, the pencil in his fingers goading me. "Trust me. Write. Except this time, I want you to *think* about a name. Meri. She's a demon of fate in the underworld and an old friend."

"An ex-lover?" I ask, immediately kicking myself for the question and the terse way it comes out.

Lucas's head lowers, his mouth near my ear. "Jealous?" He sounds amused.

"No."

His breath whispers against my skin. "Not an ex-lover. I've dabbled with demons, but not this one. She's too prickly." He chuckles. "No one wants to tangle with a demon of fate." Holding out the pencil, he offers it to me. "Meri. Think about her name and ask her about Lucas and Leviathan."

When I don't move, he cups my shoulder with his hand. "Open yourself up, Harper. Take back control of your power."

My back stiffens.

Out of everything he could have said, *this* is what pushes me forward. Because there's nothing I want more than control over something I've been robbed of.

"Are you sure about this?" Eloise asks. She sounds nervous, and that settles it.

She's been robbed, too.

Meri's name echoing through my head, I take the pencil. *Leviathan,* I think. *Lucas.*

The response is immediate.

My hand swerves onto the notebook, the lines that appear surprisingly flowery and feminine.

Well, if it isn't the golden boy himself. Hello, honey.

As crazy as it sounds, joy races through me, the feeling replacing the horrible fatigue I felt when Levi forced my hand. *This* is what I'm supposed to do. This is what Eloise does for others, channeling spirits and the deceased for her customers. I may be channeling a demon, but I feel in control. Me. In control. I hope, anyway, and if I'm not, I don't want to know, because this feels good.

Lucas snorts. "Give me the rundown, Meri," he demands aloud.

My hand scribbles. *No sweet nothings? No, "It's been a long time and I miss you, Meri?"*

"I want answers," Lucas replies.

The pencil pauses, and then, *You imprison an archdemon with little more than a symbol of water and you expect that to hold?*

Lucas's hand fists on the table. "That was before my fall. I've learned a lot about your world since then. Firsthand. Even so, the symbol was strong enough."

I swear I hear Meri laugh in my head. *You are so cute, angel. The symbol has crumbled. The only thing keeping him there now is weakness. It only takes two things for a demon like him to rise.*

"Blood and energy," Lucas murmurs.

If you know, why contact me?

"Don't play games with me, Meri. He has secrets, and you're in a position to know that. You owe me. Remember those souls you let escape into—"

My elbow shoots out, catching Lucas just under the ribs. He grins.

The pencil scratches. *I'm disappointed in you. Why bring up old wounds?*

"The information, Meri," Lucas prompts.

Look to your psychic. Levi has been planning this since her birth. He has allies. Do you not feel the woman? Curses. Black magic. Blood. Power. Now, our debt is repaid. Leave me.

I lose my grip on the pencil, and it falls onto the table, bouncing off of the notebook before rolling onto the floor. My body sags in the chair.

Eloise slides a steaming cup of tea in front of me. "Green tea with ginseng." She'd been busy while I was transcribing. "For energy. Sessions take a lot out of the messenger. I'm proud of you, Harper."

Tears threaten to choke me.

Lucas tugs the notebook toward him. "Tell me about your parents again," he says.

Eloise answers for me. "There isn't much to know. A psychic and a mortal fell in love, fought for years to have a baby together, and then went to a black arts practitioner for help when the Court refused to do dark magic to save the child. Surely, you don't need it said aloud when you can hear it in our thoughts."

He glances at me. "I can't hear it in hers. There is nothing except silence in Harper's head."

Eloise looks at me. I sip the tea.

"I think we need to try this again," Lucas suggests.

Eloise recoils. "What? Do you know what channeling does to a person?"

"Unless I'm missing my guess, it just gave your niece a second wind."

He's right. Unlike the times I'd been controlled in the past and unlike the times Levi had used me, this felt different. Empowering. I sag in the chair not because I'm tired, but because I'm relieved.

Is it because I called on the demon rather than the demon calling on me?

"Harper?" Aunt Eloise asks.

"He's right," I admit. "I feel stronger."

Confusion eats at Eloise's face, leaving gnawed lines of concentration. "You should feel weaker."

Lucas leans toward me, completely focused on my face. "I think you need to try channeling your mother."

I don't know if the whimper that echoes through the room is mine or Eloise's.

CHAPTER 10

"You can't be serious," Eloise cries. "No. Absolutely not."

I'm frozen.

I never knew my mother. She is a myth, this idea I've built up like a wall inside of my head.

She is memories I created for myself from nothing. She is warm arms that never actually held me. She is brave words I never got a chance to hear. She is loud, angry lectures I never got the chance to endure.

Memories built out of imagination.

Okay, I tell myself. Because giving myself permission first somehow makes it easier to say it out loud.

"Why would you even ask this of her?" Eloise cries. Her question opens into a long string of rants, protests, and objections, and even though I hear what she's saying, it's like white noise behind louder thoughts. I'm focused on only one word.

"Okay." My voice isn't loud when I say it, but it has the power to quiet the room.

After a long moment of silence, Eloise reaches for me, aghast. "Harper, you don't have to do this. It's not the same, channeling family. It's," she closes her eyes, and then opens them again, "It's just not the same. You have no idea."

The thing is, I've already given myself permission to be okay with this. Because, in the grander scheme of things, my feelings are small compared to the knowledge we need.

My head rises, my eyes finding the angel looming above me. "Okay."

Lucas smiles. "Okay," he replies. He touches my face, and I'm prepared for him to back away, my mind and body primed to turn to the table and face my fears, when he suddenly slides his hand into my hair, startling me. His eyes darken, his fingers tangling with the strands. Lifting my face, he lowers his head, takes a moment to search my gaze, and then kisses me. Deeply. Briefly.

He tastes like spring feels.

"For being brave," he says when he pulls back.

The kiss stuns my aunt into silence. In truth, it does the same for me, not because I don't know what it's like to kiss Lucas, but because I sense something in the way he kissed me. Understanding, maybe?

Something feels different when I turn back to the table.

Flipping to a new page in the notebook, I reach for another pencil, mentally steeling myself against the destruction of something momentous. My mother is a fairy tale I created.

Memories built out of imagination. A house of cards dangerously close to toppling.

I inhale through my nose, the breath deep and fortifying. *Mom,* I call, and when I get no immediate response, I add, *Karen Sinclair.*

The house of cards crumbles.

The pencil slides across the page. *Harpists harp harping. My Harper.*

The words are everything I hoped for and everything I feared. Tears cloud my vision, and even though I want to walk away from this, I maintain my grip on the pencil. Unlike Lucas with the demon of fate, I don't talk to my mother out loud. I do it in my head. I'm not brave enough to share everything. Not yet.

Why did you do it? I ask Mom.

The pencil leaves loops and elegant word slopes on the page. A handwriting as beautiful on paper as she is in my head.

My dear child. My hopes. My dreams, she replies.

I am her everything.

Words I've thought a million times over the years, but never had the courage to say, flow out into the spirit realm, slow and unsure. *I shouldn't have been born, Mom.*

Meant to be, she protests. *You were meant to be.*

She's wrong. I was *made* to be.

Mom! I cry in my head, the wail loud and full of frustration. I'm not even sure why I say it. Maybe it's because I haven't had the opportunity to do it before, to wail with annoying repetition the way I know I would have done had she lived. *Mom. Mom. Mom.*

My pencil suddenly races over the paper, frenzied and all over the place. *She's coming,* Mom says. *She will come. He owns her. She will come, and you will destroy her. You will break your curse. A curse that was never a curse. A moment that was never bad. A childhood that was robbed too soon.*

She's not making any sense.

My curse? I ask.

Harpists harp harping. Angels airily dancing. On clouds, casting glances. Their eyes glowing brightly. Guarding. Guiding. And that's how you got your name. So says me.

She's a madwoman, even in death. I quit fighting the tears, and they slip unchecked down my cheeks. Quiet and deadly. *I killed you, Mother.*

There, I admitted it. Long before I was even born, I destroyed her mentally. Her need to have me was much stronger than her mind.

The pencil stiffens, as if angry, before scratching out, *No, you gave me purpose. She killed me, but she gave you what you needed to live. She's coming. Written in the stars.*

I can't make sense of anything she's saying, but I can feel my connection with her growing weaker, and out of desperation, I say the one thing I've been waiting a long time to tell her. "I'm sorry."

This time, I say it out loud.

Harpists harp harping. Angels airily dancing. On clouds, casting glances. Their eyes glowing brightly. Guarding. Guiding. And that's how you got your name. So says me. The pencil falls.

My eyes fall shut with it, closing out the world, my imagination trying desperately to rebuild the house of cards I had held onto so tightly all of these years.

"You shouldn't have asked her to do that," Eloise says shortly to Lucas.

She's wrong.

Despite losing the innocent childhood fairy tale I'd conjured up for myself, I am glad I connected with my mother. It let me face the grief I haven't been able to let go of until now.

I feel more confident. Strong.

My eyes reopen. Mom's words glare up at me from the notebook, and I just *know*. Flipping from Meri's words to my mother's, my mind pieces together what was left unsaid. "The woman who cursed our family is a demon. Not a witch. A demon."

Aunt Eloise places a hand on the table, bracing herself, and the temptation to go to her is strong. This isn't any easier on her than it is on me.

"Harper." Tugging me out of the chair, Lucas pulls me into his embrace, and I know by the way he hugs me that he senses my need to hug my aunt.

He's giving me what I can't give her right now.

"The woman is a demon," I repeat.

Lucas's arms tighten around me. "It makes sense. Meri's information. Your mother's words. The other demon I've been feeling . . . she's the sorceress your parents sought out. Meri's right. Levi has had this planned for a long time." Pulling back, he looks down into my face. "The demoness your parents went to must have felt your father's psychic powers and your psychic potential. If Levi had already reached out to her, she would have been looking for a way to help him break free. Your family would have been a breath of fresh air for her."

"Why?" Eloise asks, her voice rough with emotion. "Why would she help an archdemon?"

Lucas glances at her. "Because, while there are good demons in this world—somewhat—there are others who prefer the evil they were born from. In the underworld, there is no greater position than becoming an archdemon. To achieve it, you fight your way to the top, you make alliances with more powerful demons, and if you are a lesser demon, you find a way into an archdemon's good graces."

It all makes sense. The message Levi sent. His need to leave the Infernum. His vendetta against Lucas. My issues with writing.

The theory Lucas had earlier about Levi using me as a sacrificial altar rears its ugly head, and I gasp when a horrible thought suddenly occurs to me.

If the demoness used me as a way to open a connection with Levi, then . . . "No!"

My eyes widen in horror. "The man I gave the message to when I was a child . . ." The words trail off because they are too terrible to say out loud.

My aunt inhales, and I know she's thinking it, too, which means Lucas must know. He would see it in her thoughts.

Blood and energy.

No!

Fisting my hands in Lucas's shirt, I peer up at him, desperate. "Please tell me I didn't sacrifice him to Levi. Please. You know these kinds of things, right? You know how they work. Please, please tell me I didn't."

The angel can't meet my gaze. "You wouldn't have known. You were a child, Harper."

I back away from him, horrified. "No, please tell me he wouldn't." My words break on horrible sobs. "He wouldn't use a child for something like that, would he?"

"He's an archdemon desperate to escape a prison. A sacrifice made in his name would weaken the gateway. The fact that you went so long avoiding your gift afterward held him in check. Until now."

Hope flares, and I grasp at it. "But I did write. In school. At first."

Lucas frowns. "He would have been weaker then, and you had the Court's help. You didn't write completely exposed without any protection again until recently."

"Oh, my God!" I stumble across the room until the living room wall stops me. My body slides down it. "No!" I say the word over and over again, and still it's not enough. It's unforgiveable.

My gaze, clouded by grief and horror, finds Lucas. "How? How did Levi kill him?"

"Ask your aunt."

I can't breathe. My eyes fly to Aunt Eloise's grief-stricken face. Her expression says more than words ever could, and still I ask, "What? How?"

She steps toward me, her hand out, placating. "Harper, we didn't tell you because we thought it was best. We—"

"Tell me what?"

Her eyes fall shut, the lids squeezing a tear down her cheek. "The man . . . they ruled it a suicide, but they found the message you gave him stuffed inside of his mouth. He—"

"Stop," I sob. I don't want to know any more. I can't breathe. It's completely impossible to breathe. I am not a coward for not wanting to know. I am *not* a coward.

I don't need to know the details. What I need is to keep my sanity. Some secrets are better left with the Court and its members. How many secrets are they hiding for others in the town? How many of us are they protecting? How many of us are they trying to save?

The importance of Havenwood Falls—what this place means to me—is bigger than any word. This town is my mother. This town is the fairy tale my mother couldn't be. They kept me safe, even when I couldn't always keep myself or others safe.

My head hangs.

"Harper," my aunt pleads.

I was a child. I have to keep reminding myself of that. I have to.

A steely determination settles over me, and when I lift my face, I know my eyes are full of fire and hatred. The archdemon and his lackey will be destroyed. I'll make sure of it.

When I look at Lucas, my gaze locking with his stormy eyes, I think I know what it's like to live where he does. In the gray area among blurred lines.

CHAPTER 11

"*We* have a visitor," Lucas says.

A few minutes later, a series of knocks sounds on the shop door.

Aunt Eloise rushes upstairs. Voices murmur. Footsteps sound on the stairs.

Saundra Beaumont is the first to appear, Eloise fast on her heels.

Serious brown eyes scope out the room before settling on Lucas. "Our wards were tripped. According to some of the shifters, it's a demon. A female. I'm guessing yours." Saundra's gaze swings my way, her eyes softening when she sees me sitting on the floor, my face swollen from tears. "Oh, Harper."

Her eyes return to Lucas. "She's stirring up the shifters, and I've had calls from some of the demons in town who've sensed her, too. They're about as happy about this as we are. They've found peace here in Havenwood Falls, and I'm not letting an asshole among their kind ruin it. We're all prepared to stop her. What's it going to be, angel?"

"She won't come into town," Lucas replies confidently, his gaze finding me. "She wants Harper, and I want Levi." Gesturing at me, he adds, "We'll take this into the mountains."

"Don't be stubborn, angel. Your arrogance gets you nothing when dealing with evil. You're going to need some help."

"Only if it gets desperate. This is my fight. And hers."

She's obviously not happy with Lucas's response, but there's a strange respectful relationship between the witch and the angel, and I don't know if it's because they knew each other before this incident or if they'd heard about each other through supernatural channels.

"We'll be ready to step in," Saundra warns, turning, her gaze falling on the table. On Desi. She freezes, her eyes widening. "I thought I sensed something. What the hell is that?"

"A weapon," Lucas answers, grinning.

Sighing, Saundra presses a hand to her chest. "I think it's better I don't ask. Especially today. No one has ever accused this town of being dull." She gives Lucas a firm look. "If that thing does more than stay a bat, you better get it registered with the Court."

"It's a mace," he corrects.

"Hmm." With one final bewildered look, Saundra rushes up the stairs.

I can't quit staring at my aunt's apartment. At the wild walls and strange dolls. I hear things—my aunt talking with Saundra in the shop, Lucas moving around the room upstairs, and the heat blasting from my aunt's furnace—but my scope of the world has narrowed to me and the pictures on the wall.

I find myself among the painted sketches.

"Harper?"

Lucas is talking to me, but I can't look at him. My body feels like a ship caught on rough seas, in danger of capsizing.

My portrait—a rendition of me at least ten years younger than I am now—frowns at me on the wall, the eyes blinking. Around it, the other pictures come to life. Some of them reach for me. Others dance.

I am hallucinating.

"Harper."

My body catches fire.

Voices consume me.

Someone screams, the sound shrill and desperate, the wild wail full of pain and hopelessness. Grief and anguish.

The screams belong to me.

"All right," I hear Lucas say, "I'm going to need your help after all. The demon is already calling on Levi. We've got to move fast."

Someone looms over me. Saundra, maybe, but she doesn't look like Saundra. She looks like a watercolor version of herself, all fuzzy and blurred around the edges.

I taste blood in my mouth.

Pain lances through my stomach.

Someone lifts me. "It's going to be okay," Lucas whispers against my ear.

I wonder if he can promise me that. I wonder if sacrifices are ever meant to be okay. I wonder if *I* was ever meant to be okay.

My world slips away into nothingness.

CHAPTER 12

I am lost to a world of dreams.

"*I'VE BEEN WAITING a long time for you," a deep voice says.*

Even though I've never heard his voice, I know who it is, and I hate him. Levi.

A forked tongue dances in front of my face. "Do you feel it?" Levi asks. "Power." He inhales. "Ah, it feels good."

A serpent large enough to be a dragon slithers into view. Straight out of darkness. There is only him and a black backdrop.

"We finally meet, Harper Sinclair."

"Where am I?" I ask.

"Dreams," he answers. "The horror of the Infernum without actually being here. Maddeningly dark, isn't it?"

There's nowhere to go. Nowhere to hide. Only blackness.

"Why?"

He laughs, circling me, his tongue hissing. "Because you have the power to pull me free."

"I don't," I protest. "My family . . . we don't have that kind of power."

"You do." He sounds so sure of himself.

Anger wells up inside of me, and I spin, trying my best to keep up with him as he moves. Faster and faster we go.

"You made me do terrible things," *I call out, my voice shaking. I have a bad habit of crying when I'm angry.*

"You could be so much more than what you are, Harper," *Levi tells me. He stops so abruptly, I almost fall into him, his large, reptilian eyes glowing red. He has silver scales, and they shine even though there's no light to make them glow.* "You were born from darkness. Just like the demons here. A human born to the underworld. Your soul for power," *he offers.* "Give me your humanity, and you'll never feel pain again. You'll never know it."

"Harper."

Somewhere beyond the darkness, someone calls my name.

Levi hisses, his fangs flashing. "Choose!" *he yells, all patience gone.*

"You will die," *I tell him, my voice frosty.* "For what you've done to that man when I was small. For what you've done to people. You will die."

I suddenly wish I knew the man I'd given the message to. What his name was and whether or not he had a family. Maybe it's better he stays unknown to me, but there is power in knowing a name. A power that lets people put things to rest, and I want to put him to rest. I need to put him to rest.

"You will die," *I promise.*

Levi's eyes glow. "You would have been magnificent."

Fangs dripping, he lunges for me.

I FALL INTO ANOTHER DREAM.

I AM INSIDE A TENT. Other than a circle of lit candles, an athame, and a snake—a large dark boa constrictor—there is nothing in the space except a cloaked elderly woman sitting cross-legged in the center of the candles. The snake slithers around her, easing his body through her legs and over her clothes. Squeezing her. Loving her.

Long, stringy silver hair surrounds a face as craggy as a mountain. The woman's eyes are closed.

It's hot inside the space, the air so thick and heavy, it's hard to breathe. I catch a whiff of stagnant mud and sulfur.

A rustling at the tent's entrance draws my attention.

Two figures duck inside.

I gasp. My parents.

The woman's eyes pop open. "Why have you come to me?"

My mother—a woman I've only seen in pictures—steps forward. Her stomach is swollen, her long brown hair pulled protectively around her shoulders, her green eyes glowing. She looks too young to be my mother. She looks like me. I look like her.

My dad is a study in opposites. Auburn hair. Brown eyes. Slender and athletic. A pair of glasses sits perched on his nose, the spectacles softening a face that would otherwise be rugged.

"We need help," my mother pleads.

The woman waves at her candle-lit circle, and my parents join her. Heads bent, they whisper frantic words I'm not meant to hear.

"Stop!" I beg them. "She's going to hurt you."

I am nothing and no one.

The elderly woman lifts the athame, pulls the ceremonial knife free from its sheath, and places it against my mother's stomach.

I can't look.

I can't look away.

Lifting my mother's shirt, the woman grins, baring rotten teeth and gums glistening with spittle.

"Don't!" I beg.

She plunges the athame into my mother's pregnant belly.

If she screams, it's lost to me.

"Help me," I cry.

CHAPTER 13

"You've got to quit thrashing, Harper," Lucas murmurs.

I wake inside of his arms on top of the mountains, a waxing crescent moon hanging among a backdrop of tiny sequins. Air puffs from my lungs into a dark sky, the world below white and brilliant.

"What happened?" I am cold. So very, very cold.

Setting me down, Lucas pulls my coat tighter, his body supporting mine when I stumble, my legs weak. "Gillian did a ritual on the mountain."

"Gillian?"

He frowns. "That's the name of the demoness your parents approached. She moves fast. By the time the Court realized she was here and Saundra got to us, she was already in a trance and drawing blood. She needed your energy to pull Levi from the Infernum." He lifts my shirt, and even though I don't see any claw marks, I know they were there. I felt the pain inside my aunt's apartment.

"Did the Court send someone to stop her?"

"A few shifters came, mainly to keep an eye on her. We didn't want to stop her. We needed her to finish it. Levi needs to be destroyed before he can cause any more danger here or anywhere." Slipping his arm around my waist, he assists me through the snow and up onto a ridge. Pine trees look like looming monsters in the night, their angry shadows prowling on wind and frozen ground.

There, sitting comfortably among the white powder, is a young woman. Midnight hair flows down her back, the strands framing a pale face, red lips, and eyes as black as her hair. She's covered in dark leather, from the pants encasing her slender legs to the crop top wrapping her chest. Evidently, the cold doesn't bother her.

Glancing up, she grins, her eyes taking on a red hue. "It's about time you joined me," she greets.

"You're not her," I say.

Gillian looks nothing like the woman I saw in the dream. She looks nothing like the woman who plunged a dagger through my mother's pregnant belly.

"Glamours are beautiful things," she replies. "I was a lot more repugnant when I stole you from your parents."

Anger writhes like a flame inside of me. She senses it, her gaze lifting to mine.

"Oh my, you are precious." Standing, the demon saunters toward us, confidence lending an exaggerated sway to her hips. "Do you know how long I've waited to see how you would turn out?"

Pausing a short distance away, she studies me. "I'm not disappointed. What a beautiful creation I've made." She glances at Lucas. "You're too late. I've already summoned him."

"No," Lucas replies, surprising her. "I am just in time." He steps toward her. "You see, I don't play games. I was flying with angels and fighting with demons long before you ever blinked into existence." Lucas's gaze searches the ridge. "Come to me, Levi. You called. This time, I won't send you back to the Infernum. I will destroy you."

From the edge of the woods, the massive silver serpent from my dream slithers into view, his scales flashing as he moves. The only thing human about him are two arms protruding from his reptilian frame.

His forked tongue tastes the air, his red eyes finding me. "It's a pity you wouldn't offer me your soul."

"What did you do to me?" I ask, and I don't mean the ritual Gillian performed or the dreams I had because of it. We've known since the first mark appeared on my skin that Levi planned to use my psychic energy to manifest into the mortal world.

I mean other things. I mean dark things. I mean plunging a knife into my mother's belly kind of things.

Levi lunges for me, fangs glistening, so fast I don't have any time to react.

Lucas blurs past me, his hand catching the beast by the neck, his body suddenly glowing, a golden light surrounding him. Massive wings spill out of his back. Six of them altogether. All of them on fire. His pupils lighten, his angry eyes going colorless, white and terrifying.

"This is between you and me, demon," Lucas growls.

He throws Levi. The serpent rolls in the snow, his body coiling.

Hissing, Levi rights himself, his snake-like form growing in the night. Fire shoots out of his mouth. "The audacity you have is astounding. You have friends among my kind, and yet you felt the need to lock me away. You will pay for that."

"I could have killed you, Levi. I showed too much mercy by letting you live." From somewhere I can't see, Lucas produces a long, flaming sword, a feral grin spreading across his face. "Let's dance."

An object whizzes past me, and I barely have time to sidestep it when Desi appears, the mace slamming into Gillian's surprised face.

I shriek, taken aback.

"Never turn your back on a battlefield," Desi sings.

Gillian came for me while the demon and the fallen angel were fighting, my distraction a weakness I can't afford.

I am way out of my league. They all move too fast for me, they're stronger, and they have more power. I am a puppet being forced to join a battle I don't know how to win.

Gillian stumbles backward, her hand swiping at her face. Blood beads up from a gash on her forehead, the crimson fluid smearing where she's touched it.

Furiously, she kicks at the mace, and it rushes away from her in the snow, leaving a trail of turned up white powder. "Damn you, Destroyer," she hisses.

Her gaze finds mine, and I know, even before she sends me flying, that I'm no match for this fight. I'm no match for the massive serpent, flaming wings, and glamour-spelled woman.

I know even before I go flying that I'm going to die.

Power hits me like a brick wall, the force of it throwing me into the air before shoving me into the snow, the weight of it stealing my breath and pressing me into the ground.

A howl rises from the forest, and a wolf emerges from the woods. Ric Kasun. Even from a distance, I know it's him. Behind him, Saundra Beaumont steps free of the trees, her face angry. Other faces emerge with them, but my vision blurs as I struggle to breathe.

Gillian ignores them, her laughter loud on the echoing ridge as she approaches me.

Desi rushes through the snow, plowing a line directly under the power shield holding me captive, and a bright light flares. Sparks rain down around us, and I cover my head. The power's weight no longer suffocates me.

"Remember where you came from," the mace growls.

Something lands in the snow beyond our small circle, the force of it shaking the ground. Fire flames outward, so bright I have to look away, and I know by the golden hue coating the ground that it's Lucas.

Shaking snow off of himself, the fallen angel rises, a glorious sight, the size and breadth of him too much for human eyes. He's discarded his shirt, his fiery wings coating his skin in undulating flames.

As a bare-chested Seraph in full battle mode, Lucas is magnificent.

He launches himself into the sky, his blazing wings barely moving as he glides up, his face fierce when he roars, the sound filling the mountains. It sounds like thunder in the night, and I wonder if that's how the Court will tell this story one day.

The night when thunder fought thunder in the mountains.

I stumble to my feet.

"Remember what you are!" Desi yells.

Gillian stalks me, circling me like a predator.

What am I?

Raising her hand, Gillian clenches her fist. Once again, I fly into the air, my back slamming against the trunk of a bare oak tree, before being dragged up the rough bark.

Pain rips through me, and even though I try not to scream, it comes out anyway.

Desi soars into the scene, flitting from side to side like an annoying house fly before swiping at the demon's feet and knocking her onto the ground.

My back slides down the tree.

Snarling, Gillian grabs the mace and throws it into the night, and I watch, horrified, as it sails over the side of the mountain.

When she turns back to look at me, Gillian's eyes are the color of blood. "Pledge your soul to Levi and this ends, Harper. All of it."

"What did you do to my mother?" I ask, losing sight of the fight in the sky.

Gillian smiles. "I gave her what she wanted. I sank my blade into her womb, destroying what was killing you, before using my power to give you new life. You should thank me. You are here because of me."

"I lost everything because of you."

"I could take away your pain," she offers. "Pledge your soul to Levi and this ends."

Burning heat sears my back from the scrapes and gashes left behind by the tree, and I grit my teeth against the hurt. "I'd rather die," I finally manage.

Gillian marches toward me, a ball of red flame forming in her hands. "Maybe you'd rather die, but would you trade your soul for your angel's?"

Stepping aside, she gestures at the heavens, the red blaze dancing in her palm.

Terror engulfs me.

In the night, a great firestorm appears in the sky. It's a conflagration of unnatural light hanging unchecked in the atmosphere. Blue and red sparks shoot up and down a tower of orange flames like fireworks.

Lucas hovers beneath it, his colorless gaze on the fire. He doesn't look afraid, but I know by the gleeful grin on Levi's face and the way the archdemon circles in the air above Lucas, that the blaze between them is Lucas's weakness.

Sailing to the side, Lucas avoids the flames, his fiery sword swinging. It connects with Levi's tail, and the beast roars.

The firestorm barrels toward Lucas.

Gillian smiles. "That's my cue."

In a blur, she's closed the distance between us, her breath on my face, her fingers circling my neck. A familiar athame materializes in her free hand, and she places the point against my stomach.

Howls rip the air.

Behind Gillian, wolves gather, Ric Kasun leading the pack. Flanking him are his sons, Conall and Tate Kasun. Even in wolf form, I can tell them apart. By spending most of my days hiking or camping in the mountains and woods, I have developed a respectful relationship with the shifters in Havenwood Falls. We've barely talked in the years I've known them, but I've learned that shifters don't always need words. They protect me from a distance, and I don't take any pictures of them.

Members of the Luna Coven gather with the wolves. Roman Bishop, a lean, tall warlock and a member of the coven's High Council, watches with narrowed eyes and crossed arms. Flanking him are Ronya Augustine and Addie Beaumont. Both are witches. Addie is the closest to my age, and she nods at me, her brown eyes staring from behind black-framed glasses. She is the only girl who attempted to spend time with me in high school. Even though she says nothing now, her gaze yells, "Fight, Harper!"

Saundra Beaumont stands before them all, her gaze on me. There's something violent and powerful about the way she looks at me.

Lifting her hand, she shakes her head at the wolves and the witches, and I know she's ordering everyone not to interfere. I don't know if she has that much faith in me and Lucas or if she's just biding her time.

Remember what you are.

Gillian chants against my ear, the words foreign, and even though I don't understand what she's saying, I know when I see the black hole that opens in the air above us what she's doing.

She's opening a portal to the Infernum.

In the air, fire beats down on Lucas. He doesn't scream, but I know by the look on his face that the pain is agonizing.

He falls to the ground. Dead silence fills the area.

Struggling, I cry out, the sound strangled by Gillian's grip. He has to be okay.

Lucas's head rises in the snow, his gaze meeting mine across the distance, his eyes full of fury when he sees Gillian's hand wrapped around my neck.

Even wounded, he is mighty.

In a blink, he has Gillian in the snow, his flaming sword hovering above her head.

Remember what you are.

Growling, Desi suddenly appears, the mace gliding through the snow toward Lucas, no worse the wear for his trip over the side of the mountain.

My gaze falls on Lucas's back. One side of his six wings is badly damaged, an unnatural blue-tinted burn coating the surface beneath Lucas's celestial fire. Flames that can scorch an angel already ablaze is an eerie sight, and I realize it's a different kind of burn. An injury no earthly creature can define.

Hesitantly, I step forward, the pull of the wounds on my back making me grimace. "Lucas." He looks at me, and I reach for him. When he doesn't stop me, I run my hand down his good wing. Even though the wings are on fire, the flames don't sear my skin. It's a cool heat, and I realize it feels exactly like his hands felt when he healed me.

My fingers slide to the damaged section, and he hisses.

Above us, the black hole widens. Levi laughs, his serpentine body lowering in the night.

Lucas reaches back, produces three clear vials hidden somewhere in his wings, and pops off the tops. Before Levi even touches the ground, Lucas downs them all.

My eyes widen. I know those vials. My aunt sells them in her shop. "What the hell?" I gasp.

Lucas glances at me and winks.

Holy water. He's just downed three small bottles of holy water.

"I thought—"

"It does," Lucas answers, cutting me off.

The black hole above us shifts, sliding from the air above to the ground below. If I wasn't so unnerved by the portal and the place I know it leads to, I would have found the way it moved wicked cool.

Levi slithers from the sky to the ground, his fangs dripping, the fire that hurt Lucas gathered before him. He doesn't touch it, but he's able to manipulate it.

My eyes are drawn to the way it burns, the inferno dancing on the night air as if it's inside a fireplace rather than out in the open with no wood to fuel it.

The blaze throws streaks of light over my face.

"Brilliant, isn't it?" Levi asks. He leans forward, and I stumble back. "Holy fire. I brought it with me from the Infernum. It's one of the few weaknesses Seraphs have. Ironic, isn't it? Considering Seraphs are made of fire." He sneers. "Then again, the angel trapped me with water, and I was born from the waters of hell. What bears us is often our greatest enemy."

His words pummel me, and I hide the gasp that almost escapes my mouth.

Remember what you are.

What bears us is often our greatest enemy.

You were born from darkness. Just like the demons. A human born to the underworld.

My gaze flies to Gillian, the memory of her driving an athame into my mother's belly like a nail hammered into my subconscious.

Remember what you are.

There's a reason Lucas can't hear my thoughts.

Levi roars, shoving the holy fire at us. We scream, shielding our eyes. My body instinctively falls to the ground, but even though the fire covers me, it doesn't burn. Like everything else, it feels cool.

Not all of us are immune.

Lucas stumbles out of the blaze, his body covered in blue-tinted burns. The fire suddenly flares, and then vanishes, revealing a circling Levi as he edges Lucas closer and closer to the Infernum portal.

Crying out, I lunge for them, but Gillian grabs me by the ankle, dragging me backward, her hands clawing at me.

"You're mine!" she growls. Flipping me over, she crawls up my body, her fingers sliding up my sides. I feel more than see the claws that she digs into me.

Claws? Was she the one who left the marks on me? Not Levi. Was I simply a part of a ritual she and Levi were doing together? He bled prisoners. She used me as an altar, opening me up to bleed what he killed.

Her face transforms, her smooth pale skin aging before my eyes until she's the elderly woman from my nightmare.

Remember what you are.

My fingers curl into the snow. The cold is unbearable, but adrenaline pumps through my veins, heating limbs that would have given up already under normal circumstances.

"I am psychic," I say through gritted teeth.

She laughs.

"I am a spiritual writer," I continue.

My fingers begin to move in the snow, writing words I cannot see, power rushing into the ground. Shadows appear over the snow, and even though I am startled by their appearance, I keep writing.

"And I was born of darkness by a demoness who tied my psychic abilities to demons and the Infernum," I finish.

Lucas could never hear my thoughts because the Infernum is the one place a Seraph cannot enter unless he's imprisoned there.

I know even before the shadows descend on Gillian that I've won. Darkness cloaks her, invisible hands clawing at her skin, causing the same kind of wounds she and Levi had caused on me. She screams, and the shadows drag her away, pulling her toward the Infernum.

These shadows aren't prisoners. They're something else.

"Levi!" she screams.

He doesn't pay her any attention. He's too focused on Lucas.

"Wait!" I tell the shadows, my fingers still digging in the snow. Word after word after word. "Bring her to me."

Gillian slams into the ground before me.

I don't know what I'm doing. I don't even know how I'm doing it. All I know is that the only way to close the portal is to take out the woman who opened it. My chest burns, and it isn't that I'm sad. It's that death has become too much a part of me, and I'm afraid of what that means.

Desi slides through the snow toward me. "You've got a lot to learn about what you are, summoner."

What he calls me shocks me, and I stare at him. "Summoner?"

I'm talking to a supercharged baseball bat in the middle of a celestial battle. *This* has become my life.

"The spirits you channel, you can control them," Desi replies.

Levi and Lucas face off, and I know by the way Lucas staggers, both from pain and obvious drunkenness, he's in danger of falling into the portal.

"Can I close it?" I ask Desi.

"What?" the mace asks.

"If I kill the demoness, will it close the portal?"

Desi slides closer to me. "I don't know. She used your energy and her blood to open it."

Lucas falters, and even though I know this fight with Levi is his, I rush to him.

He tries sidestepping me and goes down in the snow. "Go," he orders, not unkindly.

"Get ready!" Saundra calls. Wolves and witches circle.

In a blur, Levi shoves me aside, and I slide into the snow, just as the archdemon grabs Lucas by the neck. "Do you know what it's like living inside a place full of so much immense power, and yet you can't touch it? Do you know what it's like being surrounded by beings you can't fight with or destroy? Do you know what it's like existing in darkness?"

Lucas simply stares at him.

Lifting the angel, Levi holds him over the hole to the Infernum.

I scream.

Lucas laughs.

Levi falters, his body coiling, the sudden movement drawing Lucas toward safety. "You have years of unimaginable torture ahead of you, and you laugh?" the archdemon asks angrily.

For one brief moment, I feel pity for Levi. Because, as ridiculous as his anger seems over a little laughter, I understand where it comes from. I harbor the same hatred for Levi and Gillian after what they did to my parents. After what they did to me. After what they did to innocent lives.

Lucas laughs again. "You will never win, Levi. Not when there are towns like Havenwood Falls. Not when there are creatures, gods, and monsters who want to coexist together peacefully."

Levi throws him against the snow, wraps his hands around Lucas's neck, bares his fangs, and strikes.

I don't have time to get to him. No one has time to get to him. Everything happens way too fast.

One moment, Levi's fangs are buried in Lucas's neck. The next, the archdemon is coiled up in the snow, struggling to breathe, his face as badly burned as Lucas's body.

It's the holy water, I think, astounded. That's why Lucas drank it.

Lucas tries to stand and falls. He's way too close to the portal.

I scramble through the snow, searching frantically for the one thing I know will help.

Levi rises, his anger even more palpable than it was before. He lunges.

A blur stops him, and I freeze. In the snow, a figure stands between Lucas and the archdemon determined to imprison him. This figure isn't human, although he looks it. Broad and burly, he is every inch the quintessential mountain man, his face covered in a dark, wiry beard.

I know this man. It's the man I saw the day I went to Jeanine Turner's real estate office. The same man who had been watching me outside Coffee Haven.

"I ought to have known you'd be the reason for all of this fuss in the mountains," the man says, glancing back at Lucas.

I continue my search in the snow.

When my hands close over the athame, I clutch it to me and scurry to the spot where the shadowy creatures I summoned hold down a weakened Gillian.

Standing over her, I lift the dagger.

"Don't," Lucas calls out. His voice is weak, his gaze locking with mine.

Levi uses the moment of distraction to plow through the stranger, knocking him aside before taking Lucas and shoving him into the Infernum.

Anger and grief overwhelm me.

I'm not fast enough to save him, but the stranger is.

The mountain man moves too quickly to be anything other than supernatural. With a roar, he reaches in and catches Lucas by the hand, his muscles bulging.

"I'm not strong enough to keep you for long, you old bastard," the man growls. "You'd better do this fast or you're going to be leaving that archdemon in this town, and I can't have that."

Lucas wastes no time. A bright light flashes, glaring and then receding to reveal Lucas and the other man sprawled out in the snow.

"God, I hate you," Lucas says, only it's *not* Lucas speaking. It's his body, but not his voice. "Do this fast, Seraph."

The mountain man's body rises, and I know by the way he moves that Lucas is inhabiting it. "You've been working out, Elias," the mountain man teases in Lucas's voice.

"Close the portal," Desi tells me.

Resuming my position over Gillian, I stand, the athame poised to strike, my hands shaking. The demoness stares up at me, her gaze wide and unflinching.

"Tell me how to close it," I command.

She glares. "You know how to close it, but I don't think you have the guts to do it."

Gillian is everything I could possibly hate in a demon, but she's right. Protecting myself and outright killing her are two entirely different things.

Blood and energy. She used my blood and my energy to open it.

With a cry, I bring the athame down. The blade slashes my stomach, and I watch as the blood drips to the snow below. Falling to my knees beside the demoness, I begin to write in the white powder, letting power run through my veins, spirits whispering in my head.

The portal begins to close.

A shriek shatters the stillness.

In the night, his broad frame standing over the serpent, the mountain man drives Lucas's flaming sword into Leviathan's heart. The gurgling sound of blood fills the air.

For a long moment, no one moves.

Placing his foot against the archdemon, the man pulls the blade free from Levi's chest, lifts the sword, and slices off the demon's head. Even in the darkness, no one misses the smile on the bearded man's face.

The portal vanishes.

An eerie relieved silence falls over the mountain. Wolves meld into the trees. Saundra nods at the mountain man, glances at me, and then motions at someone in the shadows. Men and women, some of them familiar, hurry onto the ridge. They don't speak when they approach me, their hard eyes on the demoness next to me on the ground.

Running my fingers through the snow, I watch as the shadows vanish. The men and women grab Gillian.

"The Court will take care of her," Saundra tells me from where she stands near the trees. Roman, Ronya, and Addie nod at me. My whole life I've known these people, but I've never seen them in this capacity. As warriors ready to fight if the need arose. Warriors ready to take down an archdemon if Lucas had failed. Warriors willing to die for the town they reside over.

The group sent by Saundra, a petulant but restrained Gillan between them, ducks into the forest. The demoness had been eerily silent near the end, and I wonder if she wishes I had killed her.

Death is too good for some people.

A bright light flashes, and I cover my eyes. When they open again, Lucas struggles to stand, his wings gone, their flaming beauty hidden away wherever wings hide.

The mountain man offers him a hand.

"Thank you, Elias," Lucas says, and I know by the sound of his voice, he's back in his own body.

"How did you do that?" I ask.

The men look at me.

Elias smirks, claps Lucas on the shoulder, and shakes his head. "As the highest order, your boy here can take over the body of any lower caste angel. He was quite the asshole about it years ago."

"I was a misguided youth," Lucas says.

"You're an angel?" I ask Elias.

"A Divine," he replies.

Outside Coffee Haven isn't the first time I've seen Elias around town, although I can't quite place where else we've run into each other. I've kept to myself too much over the years.

Lucas stumbles, and Elias steadies him.

"The both of you could use healing," Elias points out, his gaze falling to my stomach. It's probably a good thing he can't see my back. His eyes slide up, the bright blue depths softening when they fall on my face. "You did well."

I replace Elias at Lucas's side, my eyes holding the mountain man's gaze. "Thank you."

Pulling Lucas's arm over my shoulders, I wince when it slides across the sensitive skin of my back.

Elias studies me. "Can you make it home?"

"I'll get them there," a new voice pipes up, and I have to fight not to laugh when Elias looks down to find Desi at his feet in all of his badass baseball bat glory.

Only Elias surprises me by *not* being surprised. "It's been a long time since I've seen you, Destroyer. Fly safe." He glances over at Lucas. "And if you do stay in town, don't stir up trouble for those of us who like flying under the radar."

"Boring lot, all of you," Lucas grumbles, a teasing glint in his eyes.

Elias glances between us, a knowing look in his eyes, and then vanishes.

Taking some of his weight off of me, Lucas gazes down into my face. "Let's get you home and healed."

"What about you?"

He offers me a secret smile, and I'm tempted to kiss it away. "I've got a really long history of not dying."

In the night before us, Desi begins to vibrate, the mace quivering violently before transforming into the winged lion I first met in the mountains.

He kneels before us and drops his head.

"To home," Lucas says wearily. He assists me up onto the lion's back even with his injuries, and when he climbs up behind me, I don't mind that he leans on me for support.

"We're not going to fall, are we?" I *do* get rattled on occasion, and being on top of a winged lion right before taking off into the sky is more than enough reason to get rattled.

Lucas chuckles. "He's a fast and smooth flyer, but I won't let you fall, Harper."

CHAPTER 14

*I*t's funny to me how some stories end with more questions than there are answers. There was a time when that frustrated me. Now, it makes sense.

My aunt is the queen of strange stories. Most of the audiobooks she suggests I listen to—books I just *have* to read—are crazy, vivid, and full of more symbolism than answers.

Listening to them, I developed a love for philosophy. A love for looking at the world in a completely different way than most. Quite possibly, my curse has something to do with that, too.

Except I'm not sure I was ever truly cursed.

As soon as we land at my cabin, Desi transforms back into the mace, rolls himself up onto my porch, and settles there.

Inside, Lucas, who seems a little stronger than he did on the ridge, carefully peels away my shirt. Unsnapping my bra, he runs his hands over my skin. Cool heat flares beneath his touch as he heals me. From my back to my stomach.

He kisses the side of my neck.

This time, however, isn't about me.

Spinning in his embrace, I push him toward my bathroom. "I'd ask you to have sex with me, so this would be a lot less awkward for you, but we've already done that."

Lucas's lips twitch, his gaze stroking my face, but he doesn't say anything. Maybe he knows my courage only goes so far. If he speaks, I lose it.

I unbutton his pants, tugging them down over his hips before gently shoving him toward the beveled glass door. "Into the shower with you."

Undressing, I step into the space with him. Water blasts, steam rising, and for the first time in hours, I'm not cold.

I can't look at his face because I'm still learning to be more open, to be the kind of person who can meet someone's gaze without looking away.

Focusing on his skin instead, I run my hands over his chest, over muscle and sinew and healing wounds he seems not to feel. They heal too fast, the water turning a dark shade of blue with the unnatural soot as it washes down the drain. Lucas is too much of everything. Too strong. Too inhuman. He's even too much of an angel among angels. Water slips like rain, rivulets forming on his flesh, and I lean forward, my lips replacing my fingers.

His hand slips into my hair.

No words.

Steam, water, skin, and heavy breaths. This is how I will remember not dying. This is how I will remember pain and lust. This is how I will remember the moment when Lucas went from being a stranger to someone I could possibly fall for. If given the time.

I kiss every wound he has on his skin. I can't heal him the same way he heals me, so I give him what I can as he heals himself. Comfort. Friendship. Understanding.

He lifts me in the shower, pressing me against the wall, and even though I start to protest because I know his body is weakened, he fills me.

My hands slide into his hair, and he kisses me.

Who needs words when lips say things that are too awkward to say out loud? Who needs anything except sensation and fulfillment?

I've often wondered why books say the world explodes and stars rain down when an orgasm hits. Now, I know. It's not just the unmistakable pleasure ripping through me that makes stars dance before my eyes. It's the fact that the world really does feel different.

We leave the shower, dry off, and fall into bed.

Together.

Lucas doesn't sleep, but he does close his eyes. I find myself studying him, my gaze slipping from his golden hair to his rugged face and strong body. Even as muscular as he is, there is a sleek gracefulness to him when he moves. Confidence bred from an eternity of fighting.

Opening his eyes, Lucas smiles when he realizes I'm staring. "You really do have a nice home."

He couldn't have said anything more perfect.

"It really is, isn't it?" I reply.

He opens his arms, and I tuck myself into them. "You're making wise, independent choices."

I laugh. "I'm assuming that means you were a wise, first-choice decision of mine."

"The best."

"Long term or short term?" I ask, because it needs to be asked.

Lucas doesn't reply.

"What happened tonight?" I try again. I've puzzled out most of what I've learned. The revelations about who I am. "Shadows came to me, and Desi called me a summoner?"

Lucas turns his head, his gaze running over my face. "Those weren't shadows. Those were ghosts. Specifically, Hell ghosts, which are a little different from earth ghosts but essentially the same." Pulling me tighter against him, he breathes, "A summoner conjures demons and spirits. It's not unlike what psychics do. Except psychics only channel spirits while a summoner *controls* them. Summoners can even conjure lower caste fallen angels, although if you ask them to do your bidding, you may regret it."

I stare at him. "How am . . . I mean, I don't—"

"Gillian was a summoner," Lucas reveals. He runs his fingers down the side of my face. I've noticed he likes touching, and I don't know if it's because he's with me or because he doesn't get enough of it as a Seraph. "By saving your mother's pregnancy, Gillian made you a part of her. You share her gifts." His brows furrow. "And because Gillian was drawing so much on your energy for the ritual to help Levi escape, she created a connection between you and the Infernum. Which is why I can't read all of your thoughts."

My fingers capture his against my face. "I've had dreams. Most of them make sense now, but . . . but there was one . . ." I cringe. "There was one of me on top of a mountain, overlooking the town. A man, who I assumed was Levi, threatened Havenwood Falls. I'm not sure it was Levi now."

Leaning forward, Lucas kisses me gently on the lips, his face close when he answers, "Being a psychic summoner can either be dangerous or powerful. Now that you know, you can learn to control it. Without control, spirits can use you. You don't want that. You have a bright future, Harper. The dream is a warning that this town, because of what it is, is always in danger. That's why you have the Court. That's why having people like you they can call on is so important. You are going to be an asset here."

He smiles. "I have to admit, you confuse me. That takes power. Some of the things that happened to you were Levi. Some were your powers waking up. I have theories, but maybe all Levi needed was your energy and blood and Gillian's ritual. The Court is going to want to register you as a supernatural. Mortal blood flows through your veins, but you have the ability to call on spirits who would serve you. Who would kill for you if you asked."

"And Gillian?" I ask.

"I don't see them letting her live," Lucas replies. Discomfort lines my eyes and face with troubled thoughts, and Lucas leans his forehead against mine. "If it were up to me, *I* wouldn't let her live. Not only did she perform black magic on your mother, but she devised a way and a ritual to help a powerful demon escape a supernatural prison. That's dangerous information."

He pulls back and lifts my chin. "It took me and a legion of angels and demons to take down Levi hundreds of years ago. If I hadn't fought him here straight after he escaped the prison and while his powers were weak, this wouldn't have been an easy fight. Revenge blinded him. He wanted to imprison me in the Infernum, and he didn't have the patience to wait years for his power to grow. Lack of patience has always been Levi's downfall."

His fingers tighten on my chin. "I want you to remember something. I came into this town prepared for the worst because that's what truly great warriors do. It doesn't matter how easy a fight seems, it can always turn. There are too many variables in battle. Be confident, but don't let confidence blind you."

"You're going to leave, aren't you?"

The smile he gives me is sad. "I have a lot more enemies than just Levi. I am a risk the Court is not going to want to take, and I don't blame them."

My thoughts go immediately to the mountain man on the ridge. "There are other angels here."

"Not my kind. Not with my history."

I start to speak, but he stops me. "If you're going where I think you're going in your head, don't. You just bought your first house. You have a new beginning here. A place where you'll be safe, where you can finally be the psychic you were meant to be. There are people here you may finally be comfortable enough to get to know. People who need your help. Places you should go. Words won't be dangerous for you anymore. Not once you learn how to control them."

"Did you really think I was going to offer to go with you?" I ask, exaggerating the hurt expression I give him. "That's a really high opinion you have of yourself."

He cocks a brow.

"Okay," I smile, "maybe I was going to suggest it, but I don't think I would have meant it. I just hate," my gaze drops, "that there's no chance to see what this could have been. That there's no chance to get to know you."

"You've seen more of what I am outside of being an angel in the past couple of days than I've let anyone else see in a long time."

I look at him, and this time, I make myself hold his gaze. "You remind me of a falling star. Something beautiful I saw fall from the sky, and then *bam*, gone."

He grins, apparently okay with the analogy. "Did I make wishes come true before I left, at least?"

I nod.

He wraps me in his arms, our bodies pressed close. No barriers. Skin to skin. Beating heart against beating heart.

In the still room, he whispers, "Mortals can be falling stars, too."

CHAPTER 15

*W*hen I wake the next day, Lucas is gone, and even though I expected the absence, my heart clenches like a fist inside my chest.

The house is too silent.

After I dress, I make hot chocolate, the smell rich and deep when I lift the cup to my lips. It doesn't permeate the air quite the same way coffee does, the same way my aunt's apartment always smelled in the morning, but the chocolate is my smell. My scent in the morning.

The sun has already risen, leaving the world white and beautiful. Clean. Shadows climb the walls as the sun climbs in the sky, and I watch them over the rim of my cup. They remind me of the night before.

A psychic summoner. Someone who can both channel spirits and use them. My aunt is a conduit for spirits. She allows them to use her body to send messages to others, but she can't control them. I can. Not only can they use me to send messages, I can call them forth and use them to do my bidding. I can use them as an army, although I have no desire to do it.

A mortal supernatural.

I smile into my cup. Maybe Lucas is right. Mortals can be falling stars, too. I don't make sense as a person, but I do make sense as something in between human and make believe.

Maybe I'm the fairy tale I always tried to make my mother.

"Boy, he sure leaves a big empty feeling behind for having been here for such a short time," I tell the silence.

"That's Lucas for you."

I almost drop my cup of cocoa, my gaze flying to the floor. Desi. "What the hell?"

The mace shudders. "He told me to stay here with you until you're stronger."

The cocoa suddenly doesn't seem like a strong enough morning drink. "And how long will that be?"

"I'll know when," he replies cryptically.

"Great." Now I really *do* have a pet baseball bat. A talking one.

Despite my sarcastic tone, my heart melts. Lucas may have left, but he didn't leave me alone.

"You are not allowed to go into town with me," I tell Desi firmly. "There's no way I can explain you and your nasty looking bronze thorns."

"I don't have to be with you. All you have to do is call me. I'll hear you."

Thank God! I'm not sure I have a backpack big enough to hold him in public.

Speaking of public, I may not have gotten more than a sip from the cup Lucas brought me the other day, but I know Coffee Haven makes really good hot cocoa.

It's time to be brave.

CHAPTER 16

*M*y camera bag slung over my shoulder, I exit Coffee Haven onto the streets of Havenwood Falls with a smile on my face and a second cup of hot cocoa in my hands. In a cup with a *logo*. It's the small things.

On the sidewalk, an elderly woman with a walker meanders by in fancy sweatpants and a pair of sneakers. Big glasses cover most of her face, her lips painted a delicious shade of red. Irene Beckett, a retired schoolteacher and the town's biggest gossip. Even though she's a mortal woman, she knows all about the supernaturals in town, and it doesn't faze her a bit. Maybe that's why the Court lets her knowledge slide. Or maybe they're all as afraid of her as I am. There's something acutely honest and intimidating about Irene. As if, despite her age, she'd give anyone a good fight if challenged.

Even now, her head bent close to a lady I don't recognize, but who I *feel* is a supe, her words play on the breeze like naughty children looking to stir up trouble.

"The black bear kingdom has a new queen, and she . . ." Looking up, she lowers her voice, the words trailing into something too soft to hear. Excitement lights up her face, and her volume rises with it. "Oh, and that Xandru," she shakes her head, tsking, "he and Michaela are on the outs again. Tase is ruining yet another thing in that girl's life, but what can you expect from those Rocas?"

Irene catches me looking and shakes her finger at my face. "Don't be staring at me like that, Harper Sinclair. It's not as if you aren't in on the action in this town. I heard all about your little dalliance with an angel. Shame, shame. A one-night stand? What has the youth come to? There's no such thing as committed relationships anymore."

Technically, it was a two-night stand, but I don't correct her.

I smile. "Commitment would give you nothing to talk about, Mrs. Beckett."

She stops dead in her tracks, the tennis balls on the bottom of her walker resting in snow flurries. "Well . . . oh, my. I'll be damned! You just greeted me like a normal human being. Maybe the sexual awakening did you a little good." She grins. "I hear you may be a force to be reckoned with before long."

"I don't know what scares me the most," I reply. "The way you know things so quickly or hearing you talk about sexual awakenings."

She grunts. "I'm old, not dead, child."

With that, she continues past, head bent, whispering furiously once more.

On her heels, a familiar beard-covered face approaches the door, with shoulders hunched up near his ears and hands deep in the pockets of his pullover shirt. He stomps the snow off of his work boots onto the sidewalk, his eyes catching mine. Elias.

He nods.

I nod back.

He starts to brush past me, but then stops, his voice raspy and low when he asks, "He left?"

I swallow past the sudden lump in my throat.

"It's for the best," he tells me. "Especially with his kind. He'll never age, and he'll never die. You'll do both." He glances down at me. "He's marked you, though."

"Marked me?"

Elias smiles a slow smile. "Something angels do to let other angels know someone is under his protection." His gaze swings to the street, and then back to me. "It doesn't mean you're his. It means he will protect you and that other angels are expected to do the same."

I let his words process in my head before suddenly blurting, "You could be a friend, right? My friend."

Elias raises his brows. "Are you asking me to be one?"

"I'm trying out this list of 'first time for everything' stuff. So far, my friend pool has been limited to Court members and my aunt." I shrug. "I'm branching out."

Elias chuckles. "I'll be a first then." Nodding one final time, he enters Coffee Haven.

I hug my cup. Christmas music spills out of the shops down the street, the end of Thanksgiving a welcome reminder that jollier things are on the air. Big ribbons are tied on lampposts and lights are strung along the buildings, mostly unlit until night falls. This is my favorite time of year—the gap between the holiday spent giving thanks and the holiday spent sharing love and friendship.

This is a holiday season meant for magic . . . and maybe a little courage, too. Eggnog spiked with liquor from my aunt's collection would help, but I was never good at relying on liquid courage.

I rely on me.

Inhaling deeply, I turn and face the one place I've spent a lifetime avoiding—Shelf Indulgence. The bookstore is lit up, the inside a mixture of books and cushy furniture that invites customers to stay a while. The big showcase window is empty, a stack of decorations piled against it, and I know by the way the owner scurries back and forth beyond the glass that she has huge plans for her Christmas exhibit.

Books displayed at the front of the store glare at me, the words scrawled on their covers mocking me. Voices whisper in my head, and I clench my jaw.

Not without my permission, I growl inwardly.

"Squeeze any harder, and you're going to break your cup." Elias appears next to me, a fresh cup of coffee cradled in his hands. He's not as tall as Lucas, but he's broader. He has the frame of a bodybuilder with short, messy dark brown hair and full lips that would bring him a lot of attention if he didn't have the beard. Releasing his cup with one hand, he tugs on the brim of a baseball cap he wears pulled low, a

Havenwood Falls Ski-ventures logo printed on the front. "It will get easier over time. All powers are like that."

I glance at him. "Do you know anything about what I am?"

He stares at the bookstore. "We all have demons that haunt us. You are a scary person, Harper Sinclair. You can channel darkness and attack people with their own nightmares."

My breath catches in my throat. "I don't want to do that."

"I know." He looks at me. "That's what saves you."

The way he stands—his muscular arms making him look like a bear inside his pullover, his baseball cap casting a shadow over his face —makes me smile. "I hope I don't offend you when I say I own a scary-looking baseball bat that would look right at home in your hands."

He laughs, the sound as gravelly as his voice. Rock stars would weep. Yet, the *way* he laughs sounds new, too. Maybe untried?

"You don't do that enough, do you?" I ask.

He sobers. "What?"

"Laugh like that."

He smiles softly. "Maybe I don't."

"You should."

"I'll keep that in mind."

We stare at the bookstore.

"Do I smell like Hell to you?" I ask, turning to him.

He snorts. "Is everything out of your mouth always this unexpected?"

"Do I?"

He takes a sip of his coffee, and then says, "You smell good." There's nothing flowery about his words, and I find I like that.

Turning away, he gets ready to lope across the street.

"Do you come here often?" I ask out of nowhere. "For coffee, I mean?"

He glances back at me. "I do."

"Good . . . you know, you should switch to hot chocolate. It's more holiday-ish. As a matter of fact," my gaze flicks to Coffee Haven and then back to him, "the town Hot Cocoa and Cookie Crawl will be happening soon. That's as good a time as any to switch."

"Have you ever done the Crawl before?" Elias asks, his booted feet on the curb, a knowing glint in his eyes. "Or is this on your 'first time for everything' list?"

I shrug. "Branching out, remember?"

"You need a phone, Ms. Sinclair," he calls while crossing the street.

"Maybe I'll get one," I call in return.

Smiling, I turn back to the bookstore. New friends. A possible phone. Books I might attempt to read. People I want to try to talk to.

Christmas books start to pile up in the showcase window, and I briefly catch the title of one. *A Christmas Carol.*

My lips curl. My Aunt Eloise has forced me to listen to *A Christmas Carol* every Christmas for as far back as I can remember. First by reading it, and then in audio. It became tradition. I'm not sure why the book is her favorite, but by making me listen to it year after year, she's made it one of my favorites, too.

I suddenly feel the urge to hug Eloise. For nothing more than just being her. Now that I know my powers can be controlled, I can start building an even closer relationship with her, the kind of relationship I should have had before.

Who knows? Maybe, just maybe, I am Havenwood Falls' version of Scrooge. Only I'm not old or miserly. I'm a recluse imprisoned by fears rather than faults. My ghosts of Christmas past, present, and future are two villains, a fallen angel, and a sentient weapon.

A work truck roars to life, and I glance at the street just in time to see Elias driving off, his window rolled down. His hand lifts in a wave, and I wonder about his story.

But first . . .

Today is the first day in a new beginning.

CHAPTER 17

*N*ew beginnings mean less fear, right?

At least that's what I kept telling myself when I left Main Street for the one place I felt safe enough to practice my powers. After a hug fest with my aunt, which is less weird than it sounds, I hole myself up at her shop in a space I never even attempted to enter until now.

I am not afraid of my powers. I am not afraid of my powers. Over and over again, I repeat the mantra in my head, my eyes on the walls of the back room. The reading room, my aunt calls it.

There are notebooks and pencils everywhere. It looks like a wet dream for writers. For me, not so much.

I am not a coward.

The door to the shop dings. Customers enter, and then exit. Time ticks forward.

Eloise has a client scheduled for the afternoon, and I know by the impatient way she paces the floor beyond where I stare at the wall, that I'm running out of time.

"Hey, Eloise," a voice greets, her words chasing the door's bell. "Harper around?"

Relief and trepidation flood my veins. Addie Beaumont. Saundra's granddaughter.

The bead curtain behind me clicks together.

"Hey," Addie says gently. She walks in front of me, her studiously edgy appearance a welcome one. Light brown hair fans out over a red sweater, the shirt resting over ripped jeans. A diamond in her nose winks at me when she leans down, her eyes softening behind her glasses. "Bet you can't guess why I'm here."

"That fast, huh?"

In her arms is a leather satchel, the bag home to a tattoo kit. Adelaide Beaumont is here to mark me. All of the supernaturals in Havenwood Falls are marked when they come to town as a way to register with the Court. It keeps tabs on the supes. I'm one of them now. Always had been, I guess.

"They definitely don't take their time with things." She taps me on the arm. "Where and what?" She doesn't have to say more than that. I know how it works.

"My wrist. A quill pen."

She chuckles. "That makes sense."

Pulling a pad and pencil out of her bag, she gets to work sketching the design before tracing it with a purple pen and removing it.

Giving her my arm, I look away. Even if I was afraid of needles, the pain would be nothing compared to the pain I've already faced. To the way my heart feels now, torn between jubilation and heartbreak. New beginnings and loneliness.

Damp paper is pressed against my skin. "What you did last night was incredible," Addie tells me.

My eyes drop to the table. "Can you help me with something?"

Addie pauses. "Depends."

"I want to try to use my powers."

"Now?" she asks, startled.

"No." I shake my head, smiling. I know by the way I've stared at the wall for hours that I'm not ready. But I will be. "Not now. But soon." I look at her. "I'm going to be something big, Addie. I'm going to be a part of this town. A part of this community in a way I never was before. When I'm ready, will you come? I'd feel better if there was a witch there. You know . . . just in case."

Placing her hand against mine, she peers down at the design on my wrist, at the tattoo she's about to start on. "You've had a long, hard road, Harper. A lot of us admire what you've been through and how you've handled it. I'll be there."

As she's tattooing me, I stare at her. She's strong, too. I may not know a lot about what I can do yet, but I see and feel the strength in her.

"I want to be a part of what makes this town safe," I say suddenly.

Addie smiles. "Good. We'll both be a part of that."

Nodding, I shut my eyes. My time is coming.

CHAPTER 18

 *hristmas Eve*

THE WALK-IN UTILITY closet in my kitchen makes a perfect darkroom, and I outfitted it exactly the way I need it to be.

Landscape photography is a competitive business, but I've managed to make a name for myself and a decent paycheck—enough for a single woman—mainly by taking pictures no one else has been able to capture. It's easy to get unseen shots when I'm the only person snapping pictures of the mountains and landscape around Havenwood Falls for print in magazines. Most of my photographs are labeled as remote spots in Colorado with no specific name attached.

I'm careful not to snap shots of the shifters or other supernaturals that roam the hillsides. All of my photos have to be approved before I sell them, but I've been making a freelance cash flow from my work since my last year in high school.

A photographic safelight swings above my messy bun, the glow from the bulb turning the entire space red. My fingers clutch a pair of tongs, my eyes on a developing tray.

I get a thrill from this process because everything has to be perfect. From the water temperature to the exposure duration.

The picture I'm working on now is no different.

From developer to stop bath to fixer to the rinse, I take my time with it. Careful. Ever so careful.

The image that appears is exactly what I expected it to be.

"Why do you want that anyway?" Desi asks from my feet. For some reason, he's taken a real interest in my photography. Maybe sentient weapons need hobbies, too.

I stare at the picture. "Because there's nothing like framing a falling star."

Before me is a photograph of the mountain, pine trees and snow a backdrop to a walking wall of flames.

Lucas.

My falling star.

Maybe he'll be back. I certainly hope he returns, but if he doesn't, he gave me something I will never forget. He gave me confidence.

In a weird way, he also gave me purpose. He may have been the reason the archdemon Leviathan came into my life, but without the experience, I wouldn't have discovered what I am. I wouldn't have discovered what I can be.

I'd be living handicapped by words and held back by fear.

My thoughts stray to Gillian, and my stomach churns. Because of her magic, the demoness is as much my mother as my own flesh and blood mother. Two women. One evil, the other good. I am a part of both of them. One dead, the other's fate uncertain.

I'm not sure what that means for me now, but I'm willing to find out.

Hanging the picture up to dry, I exit the darkroom and pull out a new cell phone from my blue jeans pocket. Cell service may be terrible in the mountains, spotty at best on a good day, but at least I'm moving into the current century with modern technology.

Thumbing through my contacts, I click on a new name entered only recently.

Me: *Did you know that April is National Grilled Cheese Sandwich Month?*

Him: *No, I can't say I knew that.*

Me: *April twelfth is National Grilled Cheese Sandwich Day. I Googled it.*

Him: *Did you know that the term 'grilled cheese' made its first print appearance in the 1960s? I lived it.*

Me: *Overachiever.*

A few minutes pass, and then,

Him: *You're texting now?*

Me: *I'm trying.*

Those two words hold a lot of meaning. Words and I may never get along. I still feel the whispers when I try to read a book or when I try to write a word, but I'm getting better at pushing them back.

I have goals. Small ones. Each step a bigger one than the last. I started with a sentence. Next came a paragraph. Then a page. One day, I will finish a book. For now, I'll keep listening to them.

For now, I'll frame my falling star and remind myself that some wishes do come true.

EPILOGUE

 ew Year's Day

It is just after midnight on New Year's Day when Addie Beaumont knocks on the door of my aunt's shop. I'd stayed the night with Eloise, mainly to watch the fireworks in town from the room upstairs, a storage area full of boxes and insane clutter. Eloise is a closet hoarder.

"People should be kissing and doing, I don't know, things *other* than wanting to channel entities on New Year's," Addie complains when I open the door.

I grin. "This is my New Year's Resolution."

"What? Using your powers?" In black denim, a hoodie, and combat boots, Addie looks ready to take on the world. It makes me wonder what kind of New Year's resolutions she's made.

"To start *mastering* my powers."

"Harper's a go-getter," Aunt Eloise calls from the back of the shop. Pulling the hoodie up on her onesie unicorn pajamas, she waves at Addie before disappearing down the back basement stairs.

Addie laughs. "Only Eloise could pull that off."

"You should have seen her on Christmas." Locking the shop behind her, I lead the way to the reading room.

A small lamp is the only light in the space, and I turn it on, the dim glow casting as many shadows as it does light.

"The mortal clients must dig the dimness. It was a bitch tattooing you in this light," Addie says.

Two chairs rest at a small table, on opposite sides facing each other. I take one of them, and Addie takes the other. Paper and pencils rest on the surface between us.

She looks at me, her eyes wide behind her glasses. "You're sure about this."

"Are you?"

"Fuck it, let's do this."

Her words tug a smile out of me, and I place my hand on the table. A witch and a psychic summoner. That's what New Year's looks like in Havenwood Falls. For the two of us, anyway.

My hand starts to tremble, and I glare at it. "I want to know more about myself," I say aloud.

With a speed I don't expect, my fingers grab a pencil and move to the paper, scratching words faster than I can keep up with them. The light in the room flickers.

Darkness. Light. Darkness.

When it pops on again, shadows circle us, but these shadows aren't from the dim lighting. These are the ghosts from the ridge, the specters who held down Gillian until she was taken away.

"Holy shit!" Addie exclaims.

The shadows start to whisper, each of them edging toward me, expectant. I know if I told them to go somewhere or do something, they'd do it. Power fills me, the feeling so strong and amazing, I have to remind myself not to abuse it.

"Talk to me," I demand.

My hand continues to write. *Athame. Magic. Necromancer. Artifact. This is how you became.*

Addie leans over the paper. "Athame? The one Gillian used against you at the ridge?" Her eyes narrow. "Necromancer . . . a necromancer's athame."

Our eyes meet. The words don't flow as easily as they did on Thanksgiving, and I wonder if it's me being too cautious.

"A necromancer's athame. Life," I whisper. "She stabbed my mother with it. That would explain how it saved me."

Addie glances at the Hell ghosts. "And how you can do this. This is fucking creepy. I hope you know that, Harper."

Like her, I glance at them. "Bring us the scotch in the shop," I command.

One of the shadows departs the back room only to return seconds later, the bottle of liquor landing on the table in front of us. We both stare at it.

"Fucked up," Addie mumbles. Grabbing the bottle, she opens it, upends it, and takes a swig. "Yeah, this called for that."

My hand races back to the paper, scribbling furiously.

"Addie," I breathe.

She glances at the words, her face going white.

"Leave us," I cry.

The shadows vanish, and my pencil clatters to the table. Grabbing the scotch, I take a swig. I may not understand most of what I've written, but I know enough to realize it's not good.

"I'm sorry," I breathe. Addie takes the paper, stands, and stares down at me. She doesn't even have to say anything. I stop her before she can. "My lips are sealed."

"What you just did," she swallows hard, "it was crazy amazing, Harper. You're right. You do have incredible power."

Standing, I place a hand on her shoulder. "If you need anything . . . if I can do anything . . ."

Addie crumples the paper in her fist. "I'm going to kill that son of a bitch."

Picking up the scotch, I offer it to her. "Is that a New Year's resolution?"

"It's something," she says, upending the bottle once more before rushing to the front of the store. "Look—"

"Go," I tell her. "I understand. I just hate I'm the bearer of bad news."

"No, you're the opposite of that. You're shedding light on the truth." At the door, she gives me a small smile before slipping outside.

"Happy New Year's," I whisper, the door banging shut behind her.

For a long time I stand at the door, my eyes on the street, my hands tucked into the pockets of a navy hoodie. Pajama bottoms decorated with cameras cover my legs. My feet are stuffed into socks and unicorn slippers. The slippers are courtesy of my aunt.

A rumble rises down the street, headlights swinging as a truck pulls onto Eleventh Street, stopping in front of the shop. There's something reassuring about the man I know is driving it. He's strong in a silent, steady way that's fortifying.

The driver's side window rolls down.

My lips curve into a smile.

ABOUT THE AUTHOR

R.K. Ryals is the author of emotional and gripping young adult and new adult paranormal romance, contemporary romance, and fantasy. With a strong passion for charity and literacy, she works as a full-time writer encouraging people to "share the love of reading one book at a time." An avid animal lover and self-proclaimed coffee-holic, R.K. Ryals was born in Jackson, Mississippi, and makes her home in the Southern United States with her husband, three daughters, a playful cat named Delphi, and a coffeepot she honestly couldn't live without. Should she ever become the owner of a fire-breathing dragon (tame of course), her life would be complete. Visit her at www.authorrkryals.com.

ACKNOWLEDGMENTS

A book is a journey no one takes alone. I owe so much to the people who have followed me on this crazy adventure.

First, I have to thank my husband, whose patience and diligence in the face of my crazy coffee-induced long days should be reserved for saints. His tireless support means the world. Thanks to my daughters, who inspire me on a daily basis. I am truly blessed with amazing children. They have passion, determination, and resilience. Raising them to be the strong women I am watching them become humbles me.

A heartfelt thank you to my personal assistant, Christina Silcox. I am so very grateful for all of the late-night messages, motivating phone calls, and unerring friendship. I am proud to call you a part of my family. You amaze me.

To Jessica Johnson and Amanda Engelkes, who have spent the last two months letting me use them for a sounding board. This has been so important to me and *for* me. Thank you.

A special thank you to a group of loyal women who have followed me since the beginning of my career. To my Archive girls and my Scribes group, the dedication you have shown me is not taken for granted.

There are no words big enough to express how grateful I am to be a part of the Havenwood Falls family. Thank you, Kristie Cook, for creating this world and allowing all of us to play in it. It is no easy task to build a shared universe, and I am blown away by the hard work and diligence you put into everything you do. What an amazing and talented family you have allowed me to enter.

Huge thanks and crushing hugs to the Havenwood Falls authors who let me borrow the wonderful characters that make this story so strong. To Michele G. Miller, for the use of Elias. He is a wonderful character and was such a joy to work with. He has definitely left an impression on Harper and on me. To Kristie Cook, for the use of Saundra Beaumont. Her strength and firm loyalty to Havenwood Falls brings this novella full circle. Also for the use of Addie Beaumont. To E.J. Fechenda, for the use of Elsmed and Willow Fairchild. Having them involved in Ink & Fire brought Harper the strength and empathy she needed to move forward. To Kallie Ross, for the use of Ric Kasun. Havenwood Falls could not ask for a better sheriff. These characters lent so much to this story and to Harper's development. To the rest of the Havenwood Falls authors, for the characters they've created, some of which are mentioned in Harper's journey.

A massive shout out to Regina Wamba for the beautiful cover art. The Havenwood Falls novellas would not be the same without you. Your work astounds me.

To the Havenwood Falls family. Every day we grow bigger and stronger. A shared universe is born from the strength of its members. I respect all of you so very much. Your talent, dedication, and friendship is something I will always be grateful to know and be a part of.

To my Redemption fans who gave me the push to want to bring Lucas back to life even for a little while. He was a part of a series that birthed my career, and I can't thank all of you enough for being a part of that.

Finally, to my readers, you take my breath away. It means the world that you read my words. I am extremely grateful for your support on this insane journey full of crazy twists and turns. My love to you always.

TRAGIC INK

HEATHER HILDENBRAND

~ A Havenwood Falls New Adult Novella ~

Havenwood Falls

Tragic Ink

HEATHER
HILDENBRAND

ABOUT THIS BOOK

All's fair in war and unrequited love.

Tattoo artist Gwen Facharro prefers working alone in her Havenwood Falls shop. Coworkers want to be friends, and friends ask too many questions. The last thing Gwen wants to do is answer them. Especially when her inked images tend to take on lives of their own—and not everyone uses the fae magic for good. If the Court finds out, she'll be tossed in jail. Or worse, banished from town forever.

Although they grew up together, Seelie warrior Rhys Graywalk has been very careful to keep Gwen at a distance. Between the secrets he keeps *for* her and the ones he keeps *from* her, his plate is already full. Romance isn't on the menu. It can't be. He has his orders.

But when the people around her start turning up dead, Gwen's fears become reality. Someone has discovered her secret. Someone who wants Gwen's talents for themselves. And they won't stop until they get it.

To separate the truth from the lies she's been told about her fae heritage, Gwen is forced to work with the only friend she's ever really known. She's just not sure she can handle rejection a second time.

OTHER BOOKS BY HEATHER HILDENBRAND

Remembrance

Dirty Blood

Imitation

Bitter Rivalry

Whisper

On The Hunt for His Cougar

The Badge & The Bear

Wilde Bear

River Bear

Alpha Undercover

Guarded By The Alpha

A Risk Worth Taking

O Face

Austin & The Magical Jawbreaker

CHAPTER 1

The buzz of the tattoo gun vibrated against my skin until the bone in my hand ached from holding it steady. This was my third tattoo of the night—and the longest by at least two hours. I hadn't stopped to stretch, and now my neck and shoulders were paying for it. The way I hung over my work, hovering and squinting to get it just right, left me stiff and aching. It was a pain in the ass, really, the soreness that would inevitably follow tomorrow morning. But I loved it. The concentration required for the precision of the lines. Bringing an art piece to life on the canvas of someone's skin. It was a thrill every time, even if this one was so large and time-consuming. We were on our third and final session, but at least the patient was compliant. Strangely silent, actually. But it was better than when they complained.

When I was finally finished with the bright blues of the seascape, and the aqua scales of the mermaid's tail had been shaded in to the edge of the fine lines, I switched off the machine and set it aside. On the table before me, Sean stirred and sighed as if he'd just woken from a peaceful slumber.

"Is that a wrap, then?" His Irish accent was still thick despite the fact that he'd lived in Havenwood Falls for as long as I could remember. And I'd grown up here.

I nodded my head. Only Sean could sleep through a full-color back piece. "That's it," I confirmed.

He sat up slowly, his large back and broad shoulders probably just as stiff as mine. If the numbness had worn off enough to let the pain set in, he didn't show it as he swung easily to his feet from the table where he'd spent the last few hours facedown. His graying hair was disheveled, but then my short blond hair probably looked about the same. My own shirt clung to my back where the stuffiness in the room had left me coated in sweat. It wasn't something I minded. Not when it was the result of giving someone a fresh piece. A shower did sound heavenly right about now, though.

Sean stood and stretched and then fell still again, waiting for what we both knew came next. Standing behind him, I slathered a thick layer of Vaseline over the mural I'd given him and then wrapped it in plastic. When I tried reminding him of the care instructions, he waved me off. "Yeah, yeah, I got it. This ain't my first rodeo, girl."

He was right. This was his fourteenth, if I was counting correctly.

I let it go and slid my gloves off while he shrugged into his button-down. He left the buttons open on the top half, revealing a hairy chest and the edges of the older ink that covered his shoulders and flowed down his arms.

"You're catching up to me," I told him with a raised brow.

"Nah. None of mine are worth even half of those." He nodded to the various tattoos flowing up and out of my black tank. My arms were covered down to my wrists, and my chest was inked up to the edges of my collarbone. The only tattoo that I hadn't done myself was a small symbol on my left shoulder. Magical in its own way, but not like the rest. If the Court of the Sun and the Moon, our local leaders, only knew their mark wasn't the only one on my body that held spells . . . Thankfully, they didn't. Yet.

Sean studied the hawk on my forearm with sharp eyes. Something like fear jangled my gut at the way his attention caught on it. His words finally sank in, and I stiffened.

"What do you mean?" I asked.

Sean blinked, but the gleam in his eye remained. And the certainty in his tone was unmistakable. "Come on. You know what I mean, Gwen. They say your tattoos are more than just ink."

Motherfucker.

Fourteen times this guy had been in my chair, and he'd never once let on he knew about me. About what I could do. If he had, I damn sure wouldn't have inked him. Partly out of principle. Mostly, to avoid this exact conversation.

"Look, Sean," I began. "I think you're mistaken about what it—"

"No mistake. But don't worry, your secret's safe." He looked believable enough, and I had known Sean for a long time now, but even so, my gut roiled with fear and the guilt that always gnawed at the edges. "Honestly, I've just been hoping you'd pour a bit of that magic of yours into some of the ink you've put on me. I'd never tell a soul if you did."

And there it was.

The request that only the really plugged-in residents of this town bothered to make. They wanted the magic. Too bad for them I wasn't giving it out anymore. Not unless I was forced, but that was another issue altogether. And if the first thirteen pieces I'd done for him were any indication, Sean should have known that already.

I narrowed my eyes. Maybe he was sent here to test me. Maybe Ada was checking to be sure she was still my only customer when it came to the top-tier services Tragic Ink could provide.

"Look, you got what you paid for. That's all I'm offering," I said in a tone that left no room for argument—or more questions.

He shrugged and backed off, heading for the door. "Sure, no problem. Next time," he said.

The way the words hung there, even after he'd left and the door had clicked shut behind him, made it hard to tell what he meant. Did he mean he'd see me next time? Or that he'd expect the bonus package next time?

I made a mental note not to tattoo Sean, the Irish healer, ever again.

Then, shoving aside my anxiety, I straightened the studio and shut everything down for the night. I checked my phone, which had been set to silent while I worked, and read the five texts from Aelwyn, my foster mother. The first three were reminders about what time she was expecting me. The last two were warnings not to be late again. I texted her back to let her know I was on my way, hoping I wouldn't have to hear a lecture about how tardiness was a form of disrespect—Aelwyn wasn't strict, but on this she'd always been a dog with a bone—and hauled ass while I cleaned up. Hurrying as I shut off the lights and the neon "Open" sign, I locked up and took off into the frigid night for Aelwyn's house.

The few residents that were out walking on Main Street never even noticed me as I slipped out the front door of my second-floor tattoo shop and down the stairs, taking a hard right into the alley that ran between my shop's building and the next. From there, I cut through the back alleyway that ran behind Eighth Street until I reached the narrow space where I parked my truck.

Sliding in, I fired it up and slid my palms together to warm them while I waited for the engine to heat to something warmer than the frigid temperature outside. Winter in the mountains of Colorado was not exactly tropical. To ward off the chill, I let some of my human glamour slip. In the shadows of my truck, I felt my ears lengthen and come to a point at the top and the shape of my face narrow.

My human glamour made me appear shorter than I was, so without it my head brushed the roof of the truck. My suddenly longer legs bent more sharply at the knees, too cramped for the seat, but I dealt with it just long enough to let the fae blood inside me heat my skin. Between that and the heating vents, it was enough.

I waited until my hands and toes had warmed. Then, just as quickly as I'd let it fall away, I called my glamour back up, and by the time I blinked, I looked human again. Blonde, slender, and covered in ink, though that last part never changed, glamour or not. The tattooed star tingled a bit as the magic it was laced with settled back into place. I'd had it since I was a kid, a requirement for all the permanent supernatural residents of Havenwood Falls. It was also the symbol that housed my glamour and logged me with the Court of the Sun and the Moon so they could keep track of who was supposed to be here—and who wasn't human. It also helped lessen my weakness to iron, which was a nice benefit considering the stuff was literally everywhere these days, and all fae were sensitive to it.

As I'd grown older, the fact that I'd chosen such a common symbol had irritated me, but I knew if I had to choose all over again, I would still pick it. The stars had always called to me, even as a little girl. In fact, when Ethan had sprung to life that first time, it had almost made sense to me that I'd conjured a creature with wings. My heart had always craved flight.

Almost as if he knew I was thinking of him, the gray hawk inked on my arm seemed to twitch impatiently. "Easy, boy," I muttered and shoved the truck into gear, rumbling out into the empty alley and from there to the outskirts of town.

The drive wasn't long, but it was just treacherous enough this time of year to slow me down even more.

Aelwyn had always been supportive of my tattoo business. She'd been the one to encourage my art and to help me discover what sort of magic I was capable of using with it. She'd also been there to see Ethan come to life. And because of her support, I knew, once a week, she willingly ate dinner late just so we could have this time together after my work was finished. Still, keeping her waiting was a good way to be greeted with a lecture. I wanted to avoid that part if possible. A hot meal settled better when it wasn't preceded by a tongue-lashing.

My stomach twisted as I wondered if I would be the only dinner guest. Just as quickly as I thought it, I shoved it away. He hadn't been there in months, thanks to the bar he'd bought last year taking up so much time. And even when he did show, we barely spoke. It had been like that for years now. What was one more awkward dinner?

Nothing, I told myself. It was nothing. *He* was nothing.

It was utterly dark when I parked in front of the old Victorian where I'd grown up. Trees surrounded it, with only the winding drive ribboning in from the mountain road providing a view of the place. My headlights cast a narrow beam over the front entry, and I frowned as I pulled to a stop directly in front rather than off to the side where I usually parked. Something wasn't right. Trying to figure it out, I looked around to check the solar-powered lanterns that led the way across the lawn to the front door. None of them were lit. The porch light wasn't either. I looked closer and frowned. Even the lights inside were off.

Something anxious curled in my gut.

I left my headlights on and the engine running as I got out. Taking care to keep to the shadows, I crept around the shrubs as the gray hawk on my arm stirred and scratched. This time, I didn't hold back. The darkness would shield any prying eyes, and besides, I might need him. Despite the cold, I peeled my jacket away, revealing my tank top and bare arm underneath.

With silent permission, I let the magic call him forth. On a sigh, he raised his beak, already on alert, and in the next blink, the hawk had peeled itself away from my skin, its body filling in with form and feathers until it was much more than the ink outline I'd drawn on myself years ago.

With a sharp keening sound, my familiar took to the skies, soaring up and over the rooftop, doing a quick loop to investigate. I slid my jacket back into place and took a shallow breath, my eyes half-closed as I concentrated on the magic that allowed me to see the world through Ethan's eyes. I rarely allowed him loose like this so close to town where humans might see, but the darkness and the slithering unease that raced up my spine left me too anxious to resist.

When Ethan had done a full loop and found nothing out of the ordinary, I blinked, clearing my sight and refocusing on the yard in front of me. Slowly, with a silent stealth inherent to fae, I crept toward the front door.

I tried glancing in through the darkened window as I passed. Nothing moved inside.

My heart beat faster.

Aelwyn had been old when I'd been brought to her as a baby. Even by fae standards, which was saying something, because of how slowly we aged compared to humans. If she'd lost her balance and fallen . . .

But that still didn't explain the dark house.

With a steadying breath, I tried the knob, twisting it in my hand

and shoving inside. The hinges creaked, and I waited, listening. The scent of mistletoe hit me first. Not unusual. Aelwyn had an affinity for the stuff, and her garden out back was covered in it. But something was off. I just didn't know what.

Somewhere in the back of the house, there was the tiniest creak of a floorboard.

I flew into motion.

Racing for the kitchen, I tore down the narrow hall, skipping the living and dining rooms as I passed them on my right and left. It was dark as hell, but I knew my way around this house, lights or no.

When I reached the kitchen, I flipped the switch and was a little surprised to see the overhead light come on so easily. It washed the room in a yellowish tone, and I blinked at the sudden change. The back door stood wide open, the yawning darkness of the backyard beckoning me. I almost obeyed, but something out of the corner of my eye stopped me.

I whirled, searching.

A pot stood simmering on the stove, red sauce bubbling up the sides. Another pot sat in the sink. Spaghetti. She'd been making my favorite. When I caught sight of a chunk of white hair peeking out from behind the stove, I closed the distance, curving around the pantry and pulling up short.

My lips parted, but no sound came.

I dropped to my knees.

My mother lay on the floor, her legs curled at an awkward angle. Her white hair was splayed around her face, fanning out around her so that the ends were mixing with the pool of blood that was leaking fast from her abdomen and chest onto the floor underneath her.

"Ma," I choked out, my hands hovering over her uncertainly.

All I wanted to do was help her. But I had no idea how.

At the sound of my voice, her lids fluttered and then her blue eyes opened, squinting as if in pain. They widened when she saw me. "Gwenllian."

"What happened?" My voice cracked as I struggled to hold back a sob. "What can I do?"

"Nothing. It is too late to help me." She pressed her lips together, and her face contorted sharply.

A sob escaped. "Ma, please. You can't—"

I broke off, unable to say the word.

Die. She couldn't die. Not yet. Not like this.

"Listen to me now," she said quietly. "Hush and listen. I have kept this from you solely for your own safety. I thought I would have more time, but . . ."

"More time for what?" I asked through tears that blurred her face until I could barely make her out.

She drew a slow, pained breath. I squeezed her hand, willing her to go on. Part of me wanted to tell her to save her breath. To hang on while I ran for help. But something held me there. Something that knew these were our last moments, and I wasn't willing to waste them on pointless efforts. I blinked until I could see her weathered cheeks and light eyes once more.

"Gwen, you are special. Important. I've done all I can, but they have never stopped hunting you. You must not let them find you. Leave this house. Don't come back. Find Rhys. He will know what to do."

"What are you talking about, Aelwyn? Who is hunting me? Who did this to you?" Her words jumbled against each other in my mind—all of them taking a backseat to the puddle of blood I was now sitting in, while still more leaked from the fresh wounds on her chest. The horror of watching her bleed out this way overrode any sense I might have made of whatever secrets she was trying to spill.

She clutched my hand much too weakly, her eyes pleading with mine. "You are a bright star, Gwenllian. Much too bright to conceal. But you can't hide anymore. They have come for you. And you must not run from that. You must not run from who you are."

"I don't understand what you're saying," I sobbed. "Who am I hiding from?"

Aelwyn didn't answer, and for a terrifying moment, I thought she was already gone. My head bowed, and I leaned in to lay my head on her shoulder, my cries filling the silence.

"You will," she whispered, so low I might have missed it if I hadn't been lying so close to her lips. "Rhys will protect you. He always has."

"Rhys?" I sat up, confused and heartsick at the thought of asking him for anything.

"Promise me," she said, because Aelwyn knew. She'd always known. Somehow. "Please."

"I promise," I said, my voice breaking. My heart ached, because it was a promise I would keep no matter how much I didn't want to. The first stirrings of rage began in my gut. Even now, I could see the life fading in her, and I knew that when she was gone, I would have nothing else stopping me from my revenge. "Now tell me who did this."

"I love you, *nighean*."

Daughter.

It was what she called me when she was trying to comfort or reassure me, usually when my magic had gone awry or my heart had felt broken. And it was absolutely broken now. "I love you too, Ma. Don't go."

She didn't answer.

My shoulders shook as I lay with my cheek against her shoulder and my hand still squeezing hers. A coldness had seeped into her skin, and now, it felt odd, like I was holding onto a stranger. Thinking that only made me cry harder.

Outside, Ethan gave a sharp call, and I jerked my head up, blinking away the tears that blurred the kitchen cabinets as I looked toward the open door. For a split second, it all slid into place. The reality hit me that Aelwyn was gone and someone had taken her from me. And that someone might still be close by. For a moment, that was enough to dull the grief and sharpen my thoughts.

I looked down at Aelwyn. Her blue eyes were closed, and her chest no longer moved with the rise and fall of labored breaths. I swallowed back a scream as I searched for a pulse. I found none.

And just like that, my helplessness vanished. Instead, I had purpose. Not once in my life had I chosen violence to solve something. In fact, the only time violence had occurred at my hands, I'd spent the next few years punishing myself for it. But now, tonight, violence called to me. The idea of avenging Aelwyn made my blood sing.

No longer frozen in shock, I rose slowly to my feet. When I heard Ethan call again, I sucked in a breath and twisted toward the door. It was a battle cry. The call he used to let me know when he'd found his prey. Sometimes, when I loosed him in the woods behind the house, we'd hunt together. Him with his talons and sharp eyes as he soared overhead. Me with the bow and quiver I kept in my old room upstairs. Tonight, though, I had a feeling he wasn't signaling dinner.

I wiped my bloody palms on my dark jeans and ran to the knife block, yanking free the largest of the blades. I clutched it tight in my stained hand before racing out into the darkness in the direction of Ethan's call. If Aelwyn's murderer was still out there, I was going to find them. And when I did, I was going to kill them.

CHAPTER 2

*T*he backyard was small, bordered on all sides by woods. The trees were broken up by narrow walking paths I used to skip down as a kid. Tonight, the paths were lit by the moon's glow reflecting off the snow covering the ground. I used the light and Ethan's sharp cries to direct me as I ran.

Trees flew by as I sprinted, and branches scraped along my face and tangled in my hair. I would have kept going, too, lungs screaming, legs aching, but in the end, my chase only led me in a large loop. Eventually, I spilled out of the trees back where I'd started—and ran right into a broad chest.

"Ommph." I tried jumping backward, terrified I'd just thrown myself into the arms of a killer, but hands came up to squeeze my arms and held me still.

"Whoa, there. It's just me." The voice was masculine and rich, and I hated the sound the instant it invaded my head. As if I hadn't tortured myself enough with the memory of him on the drive over. Or every waking moment, if I was being honest. Now he was here, his presence mingling with my panic. And I hated how badly I wanted to let him save me.

"Let me go," I demanded, silently calling for Ethan to come and swoop down on my assaulter. The traitor remained airborne and silent.

"Gwen? Are you all right?" The voice came again, and I dragged my gaze upward, past a thick winter coat and shirt that I knew hid solid abs and broad shoulders, still struggling against the iron grip he had on me. But when I caught sight of that familiar set of dark eyes, I shivered at the rush of longing that always threatened to overwhelm me when I saw him.

"Aelwyn . . ." My bottom lip trembled, and before I could stop it, a sob escaped my throat. Desperate and panicked and at a loss for what to do next, I came apart, with tears and more sobs following quickly behind the first.

"I know." Strong arms came around me, pulling me close, and I clung to him, ashamed of my vulnerable display, but too embarrassed to pull away and let him see my tear-stained face. Not to mention the snot I knew was close behind if I didn't get my shit together pronto.

But every time I tried to take a deep breath, more tears leaked out and my shoulders only shook harder. Quiet murmurs comforted me, and a gloved hand ran over my neck and back, sending tingles down my spine. His flannel smelled like spilled whiskey and cigarette smoke —and him. There was nothing else in the world that smelled like him. Still, it wasn't worth this. Because I knew there would be no coming back from the mortification of crying in his arms.

After what had happened inside with Aelwyn and now this, tonight couldn't have been more of a nightmare. Even so, my heart thudded wildly in my chest at the feel of his arms around me. The truth was Rhys Graywalk hadn't been in nearly as many of my nightmares as he had my dreams. For that, I hated him.

With that thought in mind, grief and embarrassment turned quickly to rage. But I forced even that aside and somehow managed to conjure something resembling stony indifference. I sniffled one last time, used my jacket sleeve to swipe at my eyes and nose, and then stepped back, eyes downcast.

Overhead, Ethan circled, and I could feel his urge to return to me, but I willed him away with a command that probably came out rude rather than urgent. I wasn't in the mood to return him to my arm. Not with Rhys watching. He didn't get to know my secrets. Not anymore.

"What are you doing here?" I asked, my voice choked with the effort of trying to sound casual after all the snot I'd just left on his shirt.

"I came for dinner and then I saw—" He stopped, and I was glad he didn't finish that sentence. "Gwen," he said again, this time much softer. "Are you all right?"

"I'm fine. It's Ma. She—"

"I know." He wouldn't let me finish, and for that I was legitimately grateful. No part of me wanted to describe what I'd seen in the kitchen.

"She was . . . still alive when I got here," I said, my voice small. I steeled myself and looked up, meeting his eyes. I ignored the concern he gave off. My hands balled into fists, partly from the cold that was finally starting to settle in and partly to keep away the butterflies that batted my rib cage. I hated to look at him. No, that was a lie. I hated to look when he was watching.

"Did she say who did it?" he asked, his words hopeful enough that I felt bad when I shook my head.

"No. She said some other stuff, though." I frowned. "About you. And about me . . . being special—whatever that means. It didn't make a lot of sense."

He nodded, not at all surprised, like I expected he would be. "We can talk about all of that. Come on. The sheriff's on his way. And it's cold as shit out here."

I didn't question Rhys. Not about warming up inside—although I wasn't sure I wanted to wait in the kitchen. And not about offering to help me decipher Aelwyn's last words. Whatever he'd been or done to me, Rhys had always looked out for us ever since we were kids. Three years older than me, he'd come to Aelwyn when he was ten. She'd taken him in without question, just as she'd done for me years earlier. And from the day he arrived, Rhys had been everything to both of us. A friend and playmate for me. A handyman for Aelwyn. He'd moved out at eighteen, but even after things had fallen apart between us, he'd still taken care of her. I was grateful for that. But he didn't need to know it.

My heart thundered in my chest as I let Rhys lead the way into the house. When he stopped to hold the back door for me, my arm brushed his shirt as I passed, and my insides curled in traitorous enjoyment. Even now, in the middle of this nightmare, my body reacted to him on a chemical level I'd never been able to escape.

The lights were on now. Not just the kitchen, but the hall and a few lamps in the living and dining rooms as well. The pot on the stove had been moved and the burner turned off. Rhys, I assumed. I didn't bother to ask. Instead, I returned hesitantly to where Aelwyn lay on the floor. The pooled blood was larger than before, but her wounds no longer leaked with it. Her eyes were closed, and she might have looked peaceful even, if not for the blood and the wounds. I dropped to the floor beside her, my eyes filling with tears.

Rhys didn't speak, nor did he try to force me away, and I sat there, unmoving, until I heard the crunch of tires over the yard as a car pulled up. Doors opened, then closed. I did my best to quiet my own crying and sniffled hard as someone rapped on the front door. Footsteps behind me shuffled out and down the hall. I stayed where I was, listening as Rhys spoke quietly to the sheriff.

"You found her like that?" the sheriff asked when Rhys explained what they were about to walk in on.

"Yes. She was already dead when I got here," he said, and I flinched at the word. Dead. Yes, she'd already been dead. Because someone had killed her. And I'd let them get away.

"Did you call her other foster child? Gwen?" the sheriff asked.

"She's here," Rhys told him, and there was a beat of silence.

"Show me."

I waited while heavy boots made their way toward me. With a last swipe at my eyes, I looked up as they entered. Rhys came in first and crossed to stand beside me. The sheriff, a broad-shouldered werewolf with a permanent scowl, frowned when he caught sight of me kneeling over Aelwyn's body.

"Miss Facharro," the sheriff said, his expression grumpy.

"Sheriff," I said quietly.

But his eyes were on Rhys, and he looked pissed. "You let her touch the body?"

"She got here first. Damage was already done."

The sheriff huffed. A beat of silence passed. He stood stiffly with one hand propped on his weapon, and I watched that hand very carefully as he stared back at me. Distrust rolled off him. Nothing new there. No law enforcement official in this town trusted me. Not after—

"I'm going to need you to step away from the bod—from your mother." Sheriff Kasun moved aside, and I finally saw the second officer. Conall, Kasun's son, although younger and slightly shorter, was a carbon copy of his father, permanent scowl included. "This is Deputy Conall. You can give him your statement while I conduct an investigation of the scene."

I didn't answer. Instead, I turned back to my mother and leaned close, pressing a kiss to her cheek before climbing slowly to my feet. Rhys held out his hand, but I ignored him. I couldn't risk touching him in front of watchful eyes. Not when I knew my body would react so obviously.

When I was upright, I fastened the deputy with a look that I hoped made him wonder if I really was capable of whatever rumors he'd heard. I didn't know what those rumors might have been, and I didn't care. But if he was nervous about me, maybe that would motivate him to resolve this quickly. Behind me, Rhys shifted his weight, and I got the sense he was amused more than impatient. Still, I held the deputy's uncertain stare. The sheriff cleared his throat, and the deputy blinked, ending our standoff.

"Right. We can just go into the living room," he muttered, turning on his heel and leading the way.

I followed and was secretly glad when Rhys stayed behind.

In the living room, the deputy took one of the armchairs. I suspected it was a trick to get me to sit, too, but I remained on my feet. Too wired. Too on edge. My thoughts flicked to Ethan somewhere outside, and I frowned. My jacket covered the empty place on my arm, but I was antsy to get him put away again.

"Miss Facharro," he began, whipping a pad and pen out of his belt loop. "Why don't you tell me what happened. Start at the beginning."

So I did.

In a low voice that only shook when I came to the part about discovering my mother bleeding on the floor, I told him everything that had happened. When I'd finished, he was frowning. "You heard a noise, and instead of calling the police, you went racing after it into the dark woods?"

"Of course," I said. "If I'd waited for you guys, he would have definitely gotten away."

"He?" His brow rose. "So it was a male?"

"I . . . Well, I can't be sure, as I didn't see anyone, but I get a sense that . . . it was." Actually, it was Ethan who'd gotten that sense, but I couldn't exactly share the findings from my magical hawk or the fact that I had a familiar thanks to a magical tattoo that the Court of the Sun and the Moon currently knew nothing about.

"A sense," the deputy repeated in a tone that made me want to tattoo a thousand mosquitos on my skin and aim them all at him.

"That's right," I said through clenched teeth.

I braced myself, waiting for him to mock me outright. Instead, he said, "And can you think of anyone that might have wanted to hurt your foster mother?"

"My mother," I said.

"Excuse me?"

"She might have been a foster mother on paper, but she was a mom to me. The best mom anyone could ask for."

"Right. Of course. Your mother," he corrected. "Who might have wanted to hurt her?"

"No one," I said honestly. "She didn't have any enemies."

I waited while he wrote something down. When he was finished, he closed his pad and stood, sliding both pad and pen back into his belt loop.

"Thank you for your time," he said, and then walked out.

I stayed where I was, listening while he returned to the kitchen and assisted the sheriff in collecting evidence. Both of them moved slow as hell, and it was another hour before the coroner and an official evidence team even showed up.

By then, any expectations I'd had about the police actually giving a shit or doing anything productive here tonight to catch a killer had disappeared.

~

I stood alone in the dining room until a noise behind me made me turn. Rhys leaned against the doorframe, watching me.

"What?" I asked, but it lacked venom. I was exhausted, and the grief was starting to cloud out the shock that had been fueling me until now. I considered taking a shot from the espresso tattooed on my left forearm, but I didn't want to risk being seen. All I wanted was solitude—so I could fall apart.

"They'll find who did this," he said.

I turned back to the window, watching as a two-man crew loaded my mother's body into the back of a transport vehicle bound for the medical examiner's office in town.

"How?" I asked finally.

Rhys took a step forward.

I turned to glare at him, my face already hot with the words on my tongue. "How in the hell will they find her killer? They have no leads, and they didn't even send someone out to check the perimeter of the property?"

"Sheriff Kasun promised me he already has a team on it," he said.

"Whatever," I muttered. So far, Ethan hadn't been impressed by the wolves he'd seen investigating the property line.

"Gwen—"

"They don't believe me that someone was out there."

He took another step. "I do."

I looked away, back to the window where I saw the paramedics finishing up. The doors were closing now. The engines were turning over. This was it. After tonight, I would never see my mother again. This house would never feel the same. An irrational panic rose, clogging the back of my throat. A part of me wanted to fling open the front door and race out there to stop them. To keep my mother—or what was left of her—here. Even if it didn't make sense.

I forced my feet to remain where they were. "You believe me," I said dully. "What good does that do me?"

"A lot, if you'll let me help."

I turned to study him, unwilling to watch my mother be carted away from the only home I'd ever known with her. Instead, I put all of my attention and focus on the words Rhys had just spoken. And the ones he hadn't said out loud.

"Help with what?" I asked, wary and curious as I remembered Aelwyn's last words. The promise I'd made rang in my ears. I couldn't go back on that, but damn it, I couldn't ask Rhys for anything.

"We both know what," he said and then snorted. "The only mother either of us has ever known was murdered," he went on, and I flinched but didn't contradict him. Better to face the truth, no matter how hard, than live in denial. "And I know you're not going to rest until you figure out who killed her. I think you know that I won't either. And I can help you. If you let me."

"I thought that's what the police are for," I challenged.

Rhys sighed. "I heard Kasun speculating it could be related to the Bennett girl's disappearance last year."

"It could," I argued, with no real idea why I was suddenly sticking up for that asshat—except that I didn't want to side with Rhys.

He pinned me with a look, and in the dim lamplight, his eyes flashed. "You don't believe that for a second. Neither do I."

"I don't know—"

"Those woods—out there where I found you earlier—have traces of fae all over them, but it's unreadable. I've never seen anything like it. It's just . . . a ghost. The only real signature that's even remotely detectable out there is yours. Whoever was here used a glamour to cover his tracks."

That silenced me. I thought it had just been me. My own signature. Or Ethan was losing his touch, but . . .

"Does the sheriff know that?" I asked quietly.

"Yes."

"Does he also know that Aelwyn didn't let fae come to the house?" I asked, a strange sort of uncertainty sending a tingling down my spine. It had been a strange thing, Aelwyn's rule. She'd never explained it either, but it had been ironclad. No fae on her land. Period. If I hadn't known her so well, I'd have wondered if she was prejudiced or maybe bitter about something in her past, but she'd been friendly enough with everyone in town, fae included.

I'd never really thought about how strange her rule was until now. Or her unyielding routine of warding the house with fresh herbs and magic every month on the full moon.

Rhys didn't question it either, though, which only made it all the weirder. "I told him, but . . ."

He trailed off, and I caught his expression before he shifted away. Concerned. Hesitant. It set a warning bell off in my head, and I bit my lip as the pieces fell together. The police weren't very fond of me, thanks to a childhood spent as a loner and, on occasion, as a troublemaker. I'd broken into a building in high school and set up shop, using it as a temporary tattoo parlor. I'd made a few thousand dollars before they'd shut me down. I'd also made enemies out of Havenwood Falls' finest.

Apparently, they held a grudge.

I braced myself and asked quietly, "Am I a suspect?"

The beat of silence that followed told me all I needed to know. "Not officially."

I cursed. A long string of them that would have gotten my mouth washed with soap had I been younger. Aelwyn would have lectured me even now if she'd been here. And suddenly, the emptiness of the house washed over me. I had to get out.

"I have to go," I said, shoving past Rhys and crossing to the front door. I yanked it open, relieved now to see everyone else had gone, and strode out into the night. Overhead, Ethan circled. *Just a few more minutes.* I'd have to make a pit stop on the way home so I could put him away before I got back to town.

My truck was still where I'd parked it, but halfway there, I realized the headlights were off. They'd been on when I'd jumped out earlier. Before I could speculate why or who, Rhys was there, holding my keys out.

"I didn't want your battery to die," he explained.

"Thanks," I muttered, swiping the keys from him and heading for the truck.

"Aren't you forgetting something?"

I paused, one leg already in the truck. "What?"

Rhys pointed to the sky at the same time Ethan did a low loop overhead. I swallowed hard, debating whether to deny it. But what was the point anymore?

I sighed. "How did you know?"

"You shouldn't leave him loose for too long. Too many risks in this part of the woods," he said, ignoring my question.

I strode up to him until we were nose to nose in the darkness. Or nose to chin, since he was taller than me.

"How did you know?" I repeated. The temper that rolled off me was a welcome distraction to the grief building in my chest.

His eyes flashed with a knowing that rocked me. It was a look that suggested he knew a lot more about me than I might think. More than I ever told him, that was for sure. And I wondered if maybe my soul was the traitor, opening for him so willingly when he looked at me that way, so that he could just read it all for himself somehow. Like my heart just willingly gave up whatever he wanted from it.

I felt caught by his gaze, like a deer caught by oncoming headlights. One hundred percent of me was certain this was going to end with me wrecked.

"Let me help you, Gwen," he said softly.

His words were enough to break the spell.

I blinked, shaking my head to clear the fog that made it hard to remember why I didn't want his help in the first place. But the moment I remembered, my jaw hardened, and I stepped back, no longer trusting myself to stand so close to him.

"Aelwyn might have tied us together, but that common bond is gone now. Go home, Rhys. And leave me alone. For good this time."

I couldn't help the sadness that laced my words, but I told myself it was exhaustion and the loss I'd suffered tonight. Rhys didn't argue, and he didn't call out to me as I trudged back to my truck. I slid inside and turned the engine over, gunning it out of the yard and onto the main road. Just before the trees obscured my view, I glanced into my rearview. But the darkness was complete, and I saw nothing but shadows of the past in my wake.

CHAPTER 3

*E*than had whined all night and into the morning, and I knew
my own tears probably had a lot to do with his distress. Rhys
hadn't tried calling, though he'd texted that I should call him about
making arrangements when I was ready. I wasn't sure whether to be
glad or disappointed that he hadn't tried to come by. I'd made my
wishes clear with him, but still. He was the only person in the world
who knew Aelwyn. And me. The real me. The temptation to let him
comfort me was strong—until I remembered what that would cost me
in the end. Better not to go down that road.

Unfortunately, that left me no one else. In fact, when it came to
the rest of the world, I wanted to hide. But there was nowhere in the
world that I could go where Aelwyn was still alive. Not to mention
anywhere I wasn't a murder suspect. But I was determined not to think
about that until I absolutely had to. So, the next afternoon, when I'd
tossed and turned and then showered until the hot water ran cold, I
descended the stairs from my third-floor apartment to my second-floor
shop, Tragic Ink, and opened for business.

Twenty minutes later, I wished I hadn't.

The chime sounded, signaling the door opening, and I rounded
the corner while schooling my features into something that didn't
resemble a grief-stricken zombie. When I saw who it was, my blood

159

turned cold, and I stopped in my tracks. This was not what I'd had in mind when I'd intended to let work distract me from my grief.

"Hello, Gwen." A middle-aged woman waltzed in, her smile genuinely evil, calculating, and completely sure of herself as she rounded the counter with a thickly muscled man in tow.

"What do you want, Ada?" I asked, my eyes narrowing in disgust and wariness. Ethan scratched at my arm, but my own will kept him from making any real noise.

The man glanced up at me and then away again as he followed her around the corner and sat where she directed him. No question who was in charge here.

"You know what I want," she said so matter-of-factly, it was almost easy to miss the sharp edge to her tone. Almost.

But Ada wasn't someone I could afford to underestimate. Ada was the leader of the Green Coven, a group of witches suspected of practicing black magic. The Court of the Sun and the Moon overlooked Ada's methods for one reason only: because she would get her hands dirty when they wouldn't. No real accusations had ever been made, but I suspected that was all part of the backdoor dealings she had going on already—if the Court banished her, the town would lose one of their best hit men.

A quick-tempered witch with zero respect for the law, Ada Daryn was the worst of Havenwood Falls. So I didn't miss the way she always sugar-coated things when she was trying to hide her temper. Or the way her mood could shift on a dime.

A thousand times, I'd convinced myself to stand up to her. I'd even designed tattoos that might help me fight her off when she realized I wasn't going to do her bidding. But Ada wasn't someone to mess with. She was, however, in a position to mess with me. So in the end, I always gave in and did the work. I just hated myself for it later.

Tonight, though, my emotions were so frayed already, I wasn't sure I could deal with Ada and her shit.

"Tonight's not a good night," I said, willing to appeal to her compassion, if she had any.

Her eyes narrowed and then gleamed at my words, and I knew then the term *compassion* didn't exist in her vocabulary.

"Really?" She clucked her tongue. "That's unfortunate. I guess I could come back later. That would give me plenty of time to activate all the magic you've already inked for me. And when the police get those calls of mayhem and chaos unleashed on their lovely town, the only explanation I could give would be to admit where I'd gotten the magic from. Of course, that would mean you aren't available another night either. Not in this lifetime anyway."

"I'm not in the mood to be threatened, either," I warned, her words only serving to piss me off further. Maybe tonight was the night I'd finally tell her no.

But Ada's eyes sharpened, and she didn't look nearly as nervous at my rejection as I thought she would. "I would have thought you'd be a little more interested in self-preservation than this. What with last night's incident."

I went still. "What does Aelwyn have to do with any of this?"

Ada blinked. "Aelwyn?" She waved a hand. "Nothing at all. The mountain lion at the Village Apartments is something I assumed you'd be concerned about."

"Why the hell would I be concerned about that?" I tried to think back, but I'd been so caught up in getting to Aelwyn's last night. And then when I'd come home . . . I hadn't exactly sat down and watched the news.

"Because when it was done ransacking a first-floor apartment, it just vanished. Poof." She snapped her fingers, and I flinched. "Just like that. Strange, right?"

I pressed my lips together and tried to resist the urge to lift my shirt and check my own skin for the mountain lion I wore. Ada stood, waiting smugly, and I knew I had to call her bluff. If she was right and my tattoo had come to life—again—I was screwed.

Heart pounding, I turned away from her and the man who had sat patiently through all this, and lifted my shirt a few inches. I peered down at the collage of ink on my skin, searching. When my eyes landed on the spot where the mountain lion had been, I went still. A tiny patch of blank skin stared back at me, surrounded by the other images still sitting dormant on me—carbon copies of the magical tattoos I'd given out to others.

They all sat ready and waiting on my body until the magic was triggered. Then, they sprang to life just as the original was called to action by its wearer. The first time it had happened, I'd followed my own ink and arrived just in time to witness the chaos it caused. This time, I'd completely missed it. My grief had wiped me out last night, and when I'd finally passed out, apparently I'd slept hard.

Damn it. Ada was right. That mountain lion was my fault.

My gut twisted as I turned back to Ada. "Was anyone hurt?"

"No, the police were able to rescue the woman inside. Her ex-boyfriend was caught trying to flee the scene, however, and one eyewitness swears the boyfriend somehow conjured the mountain lion out of thin air. Quite a feat for a prairie dog shifter with no magic beyond his own shifting ability."

"Was he arrested?" I asked, trying to ignore the brick forming in my stomach, because I knew exactly which customer she referred to.

I'd given him the mountain lion a year and a half ago because he'd cried in my shop about how lame it was being a prairie dog shifter. Just once, he'd wanted to experience what it would be like as a predator and not prey. The mountain lion was supposed to be just for him. For a night of fun alone in the woods. Not to terrorize his ex-girlfriend.

"As a matter of fact, he's been called in for questioning," Ada said. "Conall, I think, was the officer on the scene. Isn't he the one investigating Aelwyn's murder? Small town, I guess." She smiled softly, and my shoulders slumped.

She had me.

"What do you want me to do?" I asked quietly.

"Nothing difficult." She beamed. "This one will be quick and easy for you."

"And in exchange, you'll make sure the mountain lion doesn't lead here?" I asked.

"Of course. You scratch my back, I scratch yours." Ada smirked at me.

I tried not to throw up. Ada still hadn't told me why she didn't just do these tattoos herself. She was much more powerful than me, and I was sure she could have figured it out, but she still came here. I suspected she just didn't want her own magic signature on them, but I wasn't sure why she'd even care. She got away with everything else.

Moving on autopilot, I went to retrieve my tools, and when I turned to face them again, the man had removed his shirt. He'd turned in the chair so that his back was exposed, and I winced at all the hair coating his skin. Werewolf, probably. Or bear shifter. And I didn't recognize him, which meant he was either new or a loner. Ada had probably chosen him to carry out some horrible deed for her. I tried not to imagine what that might be. Ada never told me what she intended with the tattoos she forced me to do for her minions, and I hadn't asked. If this ever came back on me, it was one less conspiracy charge. Or that's what I told myself.

"What'll it be?" I asked, wishing again that I'd just stayed in bed. Even calling Rhys back to discuss funeral arrangements sounded better than this.

"He needs an asp wrapped around his right bicep."

"An asp?" I blinked at her.

"Yes, it's a venomous snake that—"

"I know what it is." I felt the horror transform my features. "You can't be serious."

Her lips curved. "*Dead* serious."

"Ada, that's . . . I can't." In the pit of my stomach was an absolute certainty that this tattoo would bring someone harm. No part of me wanted to cause that ever again.

"You can and you will, or I'll tell the Court what you did. What you're capable of. Whom you've hurt with your *art*." The last word dripped with sarcasm.

"It was an accident," I said, but that didn't matter. Not to Ada. Not to the Court. And not to me. She was right. I'd hurt that woman. Didn't matter that her husband had housed the weapon. I'd been the one to ink him with it. I'd given him the loaded gun. He'd just pulled the trigger. "I can't let it happen again."

Ada rolled her eyes. "Your altruistic intentions will hardly matter to the Court," she snapped. "Your cursed tattoo took a woman's life, and that is all they will care about. You'll spend the rest of your life in a cell. And in the end, you will not have stopped me. With or without your tattoo, I will accomplish what I'm after."

She was right. About all of it.

But I still had one more card to play.

"Tell me about my mother's investigation," I said, levelling my gaze on hers and holding it steady even though my insides trembled. I'd never demanded anything of her before, and I wasn't entirely convinced it was the smart play now. But asking nicely wouldn't get me anywhere either.

"An ongoing investigation is classified." Ada scoffed. "How would I know anything about—"

"Classified information is your favorite kind, and we both know it. Besides, you have your snaky fingers in every pie this town has to offer. So I know you know something. Tell me what leads they have on Aelwyn's killer, and I'll do the tattoo."

Ada glared at me, and I wondered for a moment if she was capable of killing me with just her eyes. But finally, she blinked, and her lips curved upward in a sneer. "Why, I thought you knew," she said, too sweet. Too accommodating.

"Knew what?"

"The only suspect they have is you."

CHAPTER 4

*T*he moment Ada was gone, I closed the shop and went upstairs. With all of the lights still burning, I shed my clothes and climbed into bed, careful to keep my bow and arrows close. Aelwyn had taught me to use them in our backyard as a kid. Since then, it had been a fun hobby that helped explain the long periods I spent in the woods with Ethan. But tonight, it was a comfort. Not that I anticipated a need for self-defense, but my impromptu appointments with Ada always left me on edge. Her special requests were awful and draining, but this one had been worse. Coming to me when I was already off-balance and requesting a tattoo that was obviously meant to harm twisted my stomach in knots.

The new tattoo itched. I lifted my sleeve to scratch it and frowned when I caught sight of the snake's tongue where it blended with a vine of orchids that had already been there from another one I'd given out a few years back. My magical tattoos just sort of showed up on my skin. I didn't get to place them. They appeared in the same spot I'd inked them on the client. As a result, I had a collage of two or sometimes four or five tattoos overlaid, thanks to the fact that most people chose the same spot on their bodies for new ink. They also itched as if I'd actually inked them on my own skin, which was completely unfair in my opinion. Regardless, my upper arms, shoulder blades, and calves were covered. Some of them were so blended with past images, they were unrecognizable. I really wished that had been the case with the snake. Sadly, it was easy to spot among the orchids.

On my other arm, Ethan was still mostly unhindered, but I suspected that was because he somehow shoved aside anything that encroached on his territory. He'd been the first enchanted image I'd given myself when my gifts had developed, and it still thrilled me to know I'd created at least one creature that wasn't used for nefarious purposes. He was also the only enchantment on my body that was permanent. Mostly because I was too scared of getting caught to create more.

Aelwyn speculated that all of my own self-induced ink would always be that way: magical and permanent. The magic I gifted to others expired once they'd used it up. Thank goodness for that. People were so mean. It was the reason I stayed away from them. After witnessing the destruction my tattoos could cause, I hadn't given myself or anyone else a magical tattoo in a long time. Except for Ada's minions, of course. I hated her for those.

I lay in bed and thought of Rhys's offer to help me figure out who had murdered Aelwyn. Not to mention the fact that his senses had picked up on a strange fae behind the house. I couldn't believe the sheriff hadn't sensed that, but considering me as a suspect was insane. Sure, the cops didn't like me, but a murder suspect? It was beyond ridiculous.

With Aelwyn gone, Rhys was officially the only person in the entire world who was on my side.

He was also the one person in the world who could hurt me deeply. Who already had. And I wasn't sure I had the strength to survive it again. Not now. So I'd wait. See what I could uncover on my own. And hope the killer didn't strike again in the meantime. Or leave a trail that led back to me.

The problem was Aelwyn didn't have a single enemy in the world. Who would have wanted to hurt her? That question stumped me and, in the end, left me in tears as I tried to imagine moving forward without her wisdom, or her worry constantly hanging over me.

Ethan scratched at me. I wasn't sure if he was trying to comfort or distract me, but I ignored him.

I didn't sleep that night, and when the sun rose, I gave in and got up, too. A quick shower. A bite of stale toast. A rough comb through my hair. I was out the door earlier than I'd been in a long time. But I had to move quickly if I wanted to bypass Rhys and do some investigating myself. He wasn't going to be happy when he found out, but I wasn't ready to face him yet. My promise to Aelwyn rang in my ears. She'd insisted he could help me, protect me even. Maybe he could, but I wasn't ready.

Havenwood Falls in the morning was gorgeous. A three-hundred-sixty-degree view of mountain peaks with morning fog rolling off them and coating the air in tiny droplets. It was magical in a way that had nothing to do with the fact that this was a town full of supernaturals. In fact, with the sun reflecting off the mist, and the chilled air so clear you could taste it on your tongue, Havenwood Falls felt almost like any other normal ski town. And I felt like any other normal human. As long as said human had found her mother murdered and was the prime suspect in their joke of an investigation.

And just like that, reality crashed back down around me. I turned away from the view I'd been admiring from my second story balcony and made my way down the steps to the street. At the bottom, I jumped back to avoid a collision with a large cardboard cutout of a cartoon cupid drawing its arrow back. It was being carried by two men in handyman uniforms. The one in the back smiled at me and dipped his chin.

"Morning," he said brightly.

I eyed the pink and red hearts painted into the background behind the cardboard cupid and my brows knitted at the familiar coloring and design. "Isn't Valentine's Day still over a week away?" I asked, doing the math in my head.

But he was already gone.

A flash of red hair caught my eye, and I saw Rose Howe smiling wide as she headed for the square with another armful of pink décor. Rose managed Howe's Herbal Shoppe along with the help of her teenaged daughter, Scarlet. Ruby Howe still owned it, but the most she did for that place now was sweep the sidewalk out front while mumbling about talismans and enchantments. I didn't wander too close, mostly because I was afraid Ruby's sixth sense might detect my own ability to enchant.

Rose was harmless enough, aside from her excessive enjoyment for decorating. If a holiday was in sight, you could bet Rose was out here decorating for it. She'd cornered me in my shop two years back and tried to auction me off for a charity date event they'd included in the festivities that year. I'd narrowly avoided it by claiming I had a date of my own somewhere else that night. But then she'd just pried her way in, demanding to know who I was going out with.

I'd given the first name that had come to mind: Ethan. It had shut her up since she didn't know an Ethan, but she was still suspicious of me to this day for it. I couldn't blame her, since I didn't know any Ethan either. At least, not an Ethan that wasn't my magical hawk. But she left me alone after that. Still, I always made sure to steer clear of her this time of year in case she tried roping me in again. An event built around selling people to the highest bidder wasn't my idea of a good time.

"Hi, Gwen," Rose called out as she approached me. "How are you?" Her expression fell in worried concern.

"I'm okay," I said.

Her eyes brimmed with tears, and her chin wobbled. "I heard about Aelwyn, and I'm so very sorry about what happened. We will all miss her very much."

I nodded, suddenly distrustful of my voice at the sight of her watery eyes.

Rose grabbed my arm and squeezed affectionately. "If you need anything at all, please let us know," she added.

"Thanks," I said quietly and looked away. Losing Aelwyn was bad enough, but watching everyone else grieve for her too was too much for me right now.

I cleared my throat and nodded at the decorations Rose carried, forcing my voice lighter. "A little early for decorations, don't you think?" I asked.

"Never too early for romance, Gwen," Rose joked.

I grimaced.

Maybe not, but it was definitely too late.

Aelwyn's final words rang in my ears. She'd told me not to come back to the house, but here I was anyway, completely disregarding her warning. I didn't like going against her, but I was desperate for answers, and if there were any to be found here, I was going to find them. The house was dark, just like I'd left it two nights ago. Even from where I sat in my truck with the cheerful sunshine filtering through the bare branches overhead, it felt lonely. I told myself that was only because I knew she was gone, and then I climbed out of the truck.

The front door had been locked back up since the other night. Rhys, I assumed. I checked the planter by the porch and found the spare key still underneath it. Tucking it into my pocket, I let myself in with my own set. The hinges creaked, but it was a comfort, the familiarity of it.

My phone rang. I glanced down. It was Rhys. No way was I answering him now. If I somehow gave away my location, he'd probably just show up. Instead, I silenced it and ignored the text that followed.

Standing inside the foyer, I inhaled deeply, letting the familiar scent of the house wash over me. There was a bleach smell mixing with it, but I ignored that and concentrated on the scents from my childhood. Grapefruit, for cleaning, my mother would say. Mistletoe for health. And cedar wood. For home. It had always struck me as superstitious and strange—just like her rule about no fae on her property. She'd walk around on weekends sprinkling dried herbs in the corners and onto windowsills, muttering words like she was a witch. I'd rolled my eyes every time.

Now, the memory of it made my chest ache.

My eyes pricked with tears, but I blinked them back and strode through the house and up the stairs to the office. Very deliberately, I ignored the closed bedroom doors—hers and mine—and focused on what I'd come to do. If there was evidence of who could have done this, I would find it. I couldn't afford to give in to grief. Not yet.

For the next two hours, I lost myself in the work of going through all the papers and files Aelwyn had stuffed away up here. Baby pictures, old report cards, and recipes made up most of the desk drawers. Rhys had his own album, and I shoved that aside, determined not to distract myself by reminiscing about happier days. The photos weren't the real story. They didn't tell how he'd broken my heart and my spirit when he'd rejected me. It had never been the same between us after that, and it made me wonder if any of his caring had been real. Maybe I'd just imagined it. Maybe the pictures would prove that if I looked too closely.

I shoved the pictures away, absolutely sure I didn't want to know. Not today.

I poked through the rest of her desk quickly after that. The shelves behind the desk were another matter. Packed full of books, some of them with notes and photos stuffed between pages, the shelves boasted a thin layer of dust and took a lot longer to search through.

When the light coming in the window shifted as the sun climbed toward its high point, I considered breaking for lunch. But no part of me wanted to step foot in that kitchen yet. I went back to work, my stomach grumbling.

I'd nearly given in and decided to come back another day when a book caught my eye. Worn at the edges of the hardcover and blank on the spine, it wasn't familiar to me. I pulled at it gingerly until it slipped from the shelf and fell into my hands. But when I turned the cover, I blinked in surprise. The inside was hollow. It wasn't a book at all.

A hiding place, I realized.

Folded and ancient-looking, a small slip of paper lay inside.

I took it out and unfolded it, leaning on the book case as I opened it and read the scrawled words. The further I read, the colder I became. It was from a woman named Moonlaith. The language she used was formal, but the tone was so personal and emotional, I knew they must have been close.

Make sure she eats the mistletoe at least once a week. And the cedar wood. To protect the magic that lives inside her skin. I know you will protect our daughter with your life, Ael. We are eternally grateful for your sacrifice, dear friend. Should you need us, the Protector can send word. And if we do not meet again in this life, we will reunite in the next. She is special, Ael. Too gentle for them and too strong for the life we would give her here. When the time comes, she will not have to hide. They will hide from her. When the time is right, tell her what she is so she will understand all we have done.

With love,
Moonlaith

I read it over and over again, stunned. My entire life, I'd believed my parents had given me up, left me on Aelwyn's doorstep as an infant and never looked back. They were unknowns. Even when I'd grown old enough to try to dig up any information on my own, the town records left no trace of them. But this woman spoke as if she knew Aelwyn well. As if Aelwyn knew her.

And who was I supposed to be hiding from? Aelwyn had said they'd never stopped hunting me. My stomach tightened at the idea that someone might have killed Aelwyn to get to me.

The letter shook in my hands.

It took a long moment before I realized it wasn't the letter shaking. It was me.

I looked up, staring out the window, unseeing as the questions threatened to drown me. The woman had mentioned a protector. Whoever it was, they had access to my mother. I needed to find that person. To find the truth.

My arm itched as Ethan stirred, his claws scratching at my skin until I turned irritably toward him. "What?" I hissed.

There was no answer, but movement outside the window caught my eye, and I jerked my head to the glass just as a figure turned away. A blur of red cloth flashed boldly through the bare branches below. With a sharp breath, I shoved the letter into my cargo pocket and bolted down the stairs and out the door.

The moment we hit the open air, Ethan peeled away from my arm and swooped up and overhead. His sharp cry pierced the air, and I shushed him with my mind, listening for anything else that moved or spoke. Just like two nights ago, the house disappeared behind me and the woods closed in. This time, I had daylight to guide me.

I slowed and took better care to move quietly. Fae were good at stealth, but I'd been too panicked and too intent on catching up to whoever it was to take care. Now, I could only hope it hadn't been a trap, because I'd played right into it, announcing my presence like a steamroller. Or a human.

But that face . . . For a split second, it had almost looked like—

But it couldn't be. Aelwyn was gone.

A few minutes later, the woods were silent around me, and the only scent I caught came from the neighbor to the west. A human couple. Elderly. No children or pets. Even Ethan had come up empty. Whatever had been here earlier, it was gone now. And now I had to admit I'd lost the lead for a second time. I doubled back to the house, swearing to myself and to Aelwyn there wouldn't be a third.

CHAPTER 5

*T*wo days passed quietly. I worked and ate and slept—all the while waiting for Rhys or Ada or even the police to come sniffing around. But none of them did. I felt like I was being watched, but every time I turned to look or tried peeking out my windows, there was nothing there. Ethan remained uneasy, so I knew it wasn't all in my head, but I also had no idea what to do about it. Grief set in, causing me to tear up every time something small and stupid reminded me of my mother. I kept the tears at bay with a small tattoo I inked onto on my right hip. A box of tissues that, when directed properly, did the trick to keep my emotions at bay while I worked.

It was the first magical tattoo I'd given myself in years. Ada's claims about the mountain lion had spooked me, but after no visits from the police or any more news, I forced the issue from my mind. Besides, Aelwyn would have loved that I'd used my gift, and that made it okay somehow.

By the third day, I was starting to grow impatient with the police. They said they'd reach out when the investigation would allow me to pick up Aelwyn's body, and I needed to make arrangements for her burial.

I woke to my alarm and dressed quickly, intent on a cup of coffee before making my way to the police station that sat around the corner next to City Hall.

As I walked, the back of my neck prickled with a strange sort of awareness. Someone was watching me. No, scratch that. Everyone was watching me. Or maybe not watching but seeing. Three different people stopped to say hello and ask how I was doing as I passed them on my walk to Broastful Brew. That never happened.

In fact, ever since my Awakening a few years ago, when I'd come into my fae powers, most residents of Havenwood Falls had made it a point to avoid me completely. It was as if I wasn't even there. Unless they came looking for a tattoo. But that was another matter.

Today, something was different. The way Mabel, the coffee shop's owner, smiled at me as she said "good morning" was wrong somehow. It felt like too big a gesture. Or maybe I was just grumpy pre-coffee.

"Hot damn, where did you get those boots? They're awesome."

I turned slowly at the voice. "Are you talking to me?" I asked, shocked to find the girl behind me blinking expectantly.

She smiled. "Yeah, those boots are rad. I love the vintage vibe. Did you get them at Callie's?"

"Uh. No. Amazon."

She laughed. "That was my second guess." Before I could respond, she leaned in and whispered, "We'll let this be our secret, though. Wouldn't want to make Callie think she was losing her edge."

I nodded in agreement. Callie's Consignments was the local spot for anything vintage. She did get some cool pieces from time to time, but buying something would have required I interact with actual people. Something I tried to avoid at all costs. And usually it wasn't difficult—until now.

Did I know this girl? Maybe we'd met and I'd forgotten?

"I recognize you from your shop, Tragic Ink. You know, if you're looking for some help—"

"Listen, I hate to cut this short, but I have some place to be."

"Sure, yeah, no problem." She waved me off with a bright smile. "Nice to meet you."

"You, too," I managed before slipping out the door and into the sunshine, coffee in hand. A twinge of guilt twisted in my gut at how rude I'd been to the girl. She seemed nice, actually, in that overly friendly way that could sometimes be annoying. It would have been great with the customers. But I'd had an intern once, last summer, and while Cole was talented, it hadn't gone well, despite the convenience of having someone else do my coffee runs. I wasn't ready to take on another.

I let the cardboard cup warm my fingers as I walked, using my free hand to pull my hat low over my forehead. Head down, I blazed a trail across the street and inside the police station, determined to get there without another "friendly" encounter.

What was wrong with people today?

THE RECEPTIONIST at the front desk took my name and information and disappeared through a door behind her glass window. When she didn't return right away, I wandered into the waiting area and took a seat.

Several minutes passed.

And then several more.

I tapped my fingers against my thigh and drank my coffee. When it was gone, I got up, tossed the cup, and began pacing. Finally, I sat again.

By the time the door opened, my mood had turned dark and my patience was wearing thin.

Deputy Conall stood in the open doorway that separated the seating area from the receptionist's desk. His eyes were distant and his smile forced. Overly polite. "Miss Facharro. What can I do for you?"

I stood up. "I'd like a status update on my foster mother's case. I was supposed to hear back when it was clear for me to have her picked up. I need to make arrangements with the funeral home and a transport to take her to—"

"I'm sorry, Miss Facharro," he cut me off, frowning now. The smile —and the politeness—were gone. "Your foster mother's remains have already been released."

I grimaced at his casual reference to her "remains," but then his words sank in, and I blinked. "Released? When? To who?"

He consulted the scrap of paper again, but it didn't seem to hold the answers he was looking for. "I, uh, I'm not sure exactly. I was off yesterday, so I would have to put in a request to check."

"A request to . . . Are you kidding me? I'm her family. There's no one else you could have possibly released her to!" Well, me and Rhys, but he would have told me. Right? I thought of the unanswered calls and texts from him, but then shoved that thought away. The only thing that mattered was Aelwyn's last rites and wishes—and the fact that I should have been involved in facilitating both.

"All due respect, ma'am, you're not really her relative. The law dictates a relative is bloodline—"

"I don't give a shit what the law dictates." On my arm, Ethan clawed and whined at the heat that crept over me as my temper spiked and flared. I ignored both my familiar and my own conscience that whispered against losing my shit on an officer of the law. In the police station. Especially when it was very likely I was still a suspect. But I couldn't stop myself. The woman who had been a mother to me was gone. They'd given her body to someone who wasn't me. And now I would never see her again.

"Be that as it may—" Deputy Conall began.

"She was my legal guardian, and as such, I have every right to her. Including the information about her killer—who, by the way, is not me." My voice rose, and it was all I could do not to unleash enough magic along with my words to send a real message. Several of the tattoos etched along my skin burned and tingled, practically begging to be used. I noted it absently, and in the back of my mind, surprise registered. Those tattoos had never stirred before. "Now, you run back to Sheriff Kasun and tell him I want a phone call by end of day with whatever information he has on her case and the name of the person her body was released to. Otherwise, I'll take up the legalities with the Court. You got that?"

"I . . . Yes, ma'am. I've got it." His expression was tight-lipped, but he didn't argue.

I spun on my heel and stormed out.

CHAPTER 6

*B*y the time I walked off the worst of my temper, the sun was high in the sky and traffic in the square was bustling. In preparation for Valentine's Day, the gazebo had already been decorated with fresh red roses and climbing vines that had been woven through the railing. The lattice I'd seen being delivered yesterday had been set up and more climbing roses decorated that, creating a selfie station for pedestrians to stop at. Despite the chill in the air, the color and energy was cheerful. Too cheerful. It only made my dark mood feel even more tempestuous.

To top it off, people were still nodding and smiling softly at me as I passed by. Some of them even whispered a hello or an "I'm sorry for your loss." Miss Mary Beth stopped me and asked what time I'd be home later, so she could drop off a casserole. She was too nice to argue with, so I made the arrangements, secretly a little comforted that so many people wanted to show how much they'd cared about Aelwyn. But it also served as a nonstop reminder that she was gone.

My own grief was heavier by the time Miss Mary Beth had disappeared and I'd turned toward my shop. These people were grieving for Aelwyn, same as I was, but watching them do it only made my own pain worse. To keep from crying, I let it piss me off. God, what the hell was wrong with people today? When did everyone become so damn friendly?

My phone rang, and I answered with a clipped, "Hello?"

"Miss Facharro, Sheriff Kasun here. You asked for a phone call." He didn't sound happy to be fulfilling my request, and that could only mean he knew why I'd asked him to call—and how I felt about it.

"Yes. I'd like to know who you released Aelwyn to and why you think you could just—"

"She was released to Rhys Graywalk, her oldest living relative per the legal code on guardianship."

I blinked. "What?"

"Rhys Graywalk. Aelwyn was his legal guardian, right?" He spoke slower now, like he was waiting for his words to sink in.

"Yes."

He sighed. "And he's older than you, correct?"

I didn't answer. We both knew that he was.

"Miss Facharro, I am sorry you were in the dark on this, but that's something you'll have to take up with Rhys." When I still didn't answer, he cleared his throat. "I am sorry for your loss."

"Thanks," I said in a wavering voice and then hung up.

A quick scroll through my texts confirmed what I'd already suspected. Rhys had tried to reach out, several times actually. Two of the texts he'd sent had specifically asked me to call about making Aelwyn's arrangements, and I'd ignored them all. This was my own fault.

I reached the alley and shoved my way through the throng of people that loitered on the stairs leading up to my shop.

It wasn't until I reached the front door to Tragic Ink that I realized the loiterers on the stairs weren't just hanging out for fun. This was a line. And they were all waiting to enter my shop.

"Oh, there she is," said one of the men near the front. "That's Gwen. The owner." Ricky, a bear shifter I remembered from high school, pointed me out to the crowd from where he stood second in line. "You have any appointments available today?" he asked eagerly.

"Um. I . . . need to . . ." I didn't finish answering him before I shoved him and the man in front of him out of the way and unlocked the door. Then I slipped inside and closed the door behind me before they could follow. A few called out protests and whined at being kept waiting.

I locked the deadbolt and didn't bother with the lights as I strode to the back cabinet where I kept a stash of whiskey. The first shot went down harsh, burning a trail down my throat and into my empty stomach. The second was smoother and calmed the worst of the storm inside me.

I did my best to shove aside thoughts of Aelwyn—and what I wanted to do to the person who had murdered her. For the first time in years, the temptation to ink myself with a magical tat made for harm was strong. A vat of acid, a plate of rat poison—a bullet would have been too good for whoever it was. But then I pulled myself up short. Killing was not the answer. And I was not a murderer.

Someone else was, though.

I had no idea who in Havenwood Falls was capable of that, and it was nearly impossible for an outsider to gain that kind of access to the town without tripping an alarm—all of the boundaries were spelled for that kind of thing and the Court's magic was strong. Surely, they would know if someone had breached their wards and snuck inside the borders. Regardless, I would be the last to know if something like that happened.

I sighed.

Rhys was right. I couldn't do this alone. I needed help. And someone who had access to information. I had no idea if he did, but he was the only one who believed in my innocence. In fact, without Aelwyn, Rhys was the only person I had left in the world, and that, I realized, was depressing as hell.

Ten minutes later, the whiskey had served its purpose. I was calm enough to realize I needed help and just depressed enough about that fact to realize the line outside my shop was a perfect distraction until I could talk to Rhys. I knew for a fact his working hours nearly matched mine exactly thanks to the bar he owned and ran near the ski area. Resigned and more than a little cautious, I pulled my appointment book out and unlocked the front door.

The next four hours passed quickly. The first hour was nothing but scheduling as I worked my way through the line of people outside. It was a first, having my calendar full like this. I told myself it was a good thing, that having the bills paid on time would be a nice change, but this sudden influx of attention still had me suspicious. Four people had the balls to ask me how much I charged for the magical ink. The first three left easily enough when I told them to get the hell out without confirming or denying my ability. The fourth wasn't so easy.

The man stood with hands out, pleading at me from the other side of the front counter. "Look, I'll pay whatever you ask. I just need—"

"I said I don't do that." I leaned over the counter, planting my hands for more leverage as I got in his face. "And if you don't leave now, the only magic I'll infuse into your tattoo is the blood I'll draw when I stab you with my favorite pen."

He left quickly after that, still muttering. I crossed my fingers he wasn't the type to report bodily threats. That wouldn't go over well with the police right now.

The next few hours were spent inking new customers. The first wanted a ladder with initials carved into each of the rungs. I had no idea why, and I didn't question it. Probably a family or lineage thing; I'd seen my share of those. It was a cool idea, but after the morning I'd had, conversation was the last thing I wanted.

When the next customer wouldn't stop attempting small talk, I told him I worked best in silence. He finally shut up, and the rest of the evening passed quickly.

At ten, I closed the door behind the last client and flipped the sign, turning the deadbolt just in case. By the time I'd cleaned up, the couple of shots I'd taken had long since worn off, and my stomach growled and twisted in defiance at being left empty. A diet of coffee and booze didn't sit well. Or maybe it was the knowledge that I was about to willingly visit the Dirty Knuckle.

I needed food.

And time to figure out how to approach Rhys.

THE DIRTY KNUCKLE was a brick building with soft lighting and lots of dark leather. I'd been inside once. A personal test two years ago to see if I was really over Rhys like I'd been telling myself for so long. Thirty minutes in a corner booth that obscured me from the bar and the back offices had proved otherwise. I hadn't been back since, though I was ashamed to admit that I knew for a fact he was there now. Just like I knew he was there every day during the same hours I was at Tragic. I knew more about Rhys Graywalk than I'd ever let on. But, this time at least, it worked to my advantage.

I sat in the same booth as last time, needing the view of the bar and offices it provided. The dark leather was cold against my jeans, so I took my jacket off and slid it underneath me to warm my legs.

Across the room, I spotted Michaela Petran sitting with her fiancé, Xandru, and her best friend, Addie Beaumont. The three of them had been practically inseparable since Michaela had returned to Havenwood Falls almost a year ago. I'd gone to high school with them, and Addie and I were still friends.

Addie was the official tattoo artist for the Court, a job I wouldn't want in a million years because it meant taking orders, but Addie seemed to enjoy it. She was also an amazing artist, and her friendliness could somehow cut through my layers of grumpy self-defense. She was actually a fun drinking buddy when I felt like getting out, but I wasn't in the mood to socialize tonight. When Addie glanced my way, I made sure to keep my eyes averted and my ski cap pulled low. She must have taken the hint because, thankfully, none of them came over to say hello.

A moment later, a server with a nametag that read Casten took my order. He was fae, older than me by maybe ten years. I didn't know more than that, but like recognized like; it was easy to spot my own kind around here.

And he was friendly—just like the rest of the damned town today.

I grunted answers, making it clear I didn't want to chat, then wolfed down a burger and fries. While I ate, I watched for Rhys and eventually lost myself in the hum of voices and laughter as the human tourist crowd piled in from the ski resort just down the road. It felt good to be anonymous again. Maybe I'd come here more often if the locals didn't let up on their new friendly routine. Unless Rhys chased me away again.

Casten had just cleared my plate and brought me a beer when I spotted him. Rhys emerged from the offices behind the bar area, smiling and chatting with a couple of men seated on leather stools. I recognized one of them as Everett Weston, a gargoyle who'd moved to town about a year ago. Rhys was great at making new friends and maintaining them, not like me with my former classmates. I'd always liked that about him, like we balanced each other out somehow. Yin and yang.

But now . . . I'd never felt less close to him.

From here, I could see his dark hair falling over his forehead nearly to his eyes. I had no idea when he'd started growing it out, but I liked it better that way. It made him look younger but still dangerous. Sexy. The thought brought me up short. This visit was not about the way Rhys wore his hair. It couldn't be. It was about mutual cooperation. It was about finding a killer.

It was about justice, and that was it.

As if I'd called his name aloud, Rhys suddenly looked up, the easy smile he'd worn a moment ago frozen on his face as he spotted me. Our eyes met and held. The smile vanished. In its place was a storm that reminded me of my own dark mood from this morning.

Good. My temper was going to come in handy now that it had a target. I latched on to my anger, still simmering underneath the surface, and slid to my feet. When Rhys cocked his head at me, I grabbed my jacket and made my way over, leaving my empty beer glass behind.

"Hey," he said. Relief, surprise, and a lot of what might have been hope was packed into the single word.

"Hi." My response was short. Hopefully impossible to read.

He gestured toward the office door behind him, and I slipped inside, my expression arranged into something hard as I scanned the space before me. I'd never been in here before, nor had I seen Rhys in his personal space in several years now, but it was somehow exactly what I pictured for him. The office was done in dark leather and warm earth tones. Deep-cushioned chairs that complemented a dark-stained desk took up the center of the room. Along the wall was a leather sofa worn into soft creases. Landscape prints of the forest hung above it. Across from the sofa, a fire blazed in the hearth. The effect was masculine and still somehow cozy.

I wanted to hate it out of spite, and because I didn't, that fueled my temper too.

When the door clicked shut behind me, I whirled and found Rhys watching me, his dark eyes warming when they settled on mine.

"Gwen," he said simply, but the single word sent a thousand emotions rippling through me. It was so warm and personal, like an invitation. Like he was telling me a secret. "It's good to see you here."

I could tell he meant it, and that hurt. My temper flared, thanks to the pang of hurt. "I wish I could say the same."

He didn't react to the harshness of my words except to nod as if he'd expected nothing less. I bristled at the easy way he gestured to the sofa. "Would you like to sit?"

"What I would like are answers," I said.

"We have that in common, then."

I blinked. Whatever I'd expected him to say, that wasn't it. "All right," I said uncertainly.

"You've thought over my offer?"

"I have." My shoulders sagged, and I couldn't shake the feeling that I was admitting a loss. "And we should do it. Work together, I mean."

I blinked, realizing he'd wandered closer. When I took a step back, he frowned. The heat of the fire warmed the back of my legs.

"What?" I demanded when he didn't say anything.

He cocked his head, peering at me. "Are you still taking the mistletoe—your vitamins, I mean?"

"My— What the hell does that have to do with anything?"

"You look a little tired. I just want to be sure you're taking care of yourself."

I didn't miss the fact that he'd mentioned mistletoe—the same thing that mysterious letter had mentioned—or the way he'd just changed the subject, like he'd said too much.

"Of course I'm tired," I snap back at him. "I've just lost the only mother I've ever known. And what the hell do you know about mistletoe?"

He took a step closer again, this time invading my space, and my pulse thrummed wildly. But Rhys was scanning me head to toe as if on alert, completely oblivious to the fact that his smell had invaded my senses and made it hard to remember what the hell we were even talking about.

"Something happened," he said, his brows dipping in concern.

I lifted my chin, determined not to react to his closeness. "I went to the police today to ask about collecting Aelwyn's remains. They said she's gone. Apparently, they released her to you already, so I'm here now to discuss her arrangements. I think we should bury her in the cemetery behind—"

"Gwen, stop for a second."

"What?"

Rhys looked away, and there was something about his expression that sent alarm bells off in my head.

"Do you have something else in mind?" I asked.

"We can't bury Aelwyn in town," he said quietly.

"What are you talking about? Where else would we bury her?"

"Nowhere. She'll be cremated," he said.

"What?" I stepped back. "You can't just decide something like that without me. Look, I know I didn't return your texts about the arrangements, but you could have told me you'd already picked her up. I had to find out from Deputy Conall, who by the way, has a shitty bedside manner."

Rhys sighed. "I'm sorry. You weren't returning my texts or calls, and I couldn't wait any longer."

"Wait for what?" I demanded. My heart thudded hard in my chest as I stared at his tight expression. There was something he wasn't telling me here, something more. "What have you done with Aelwyn, Rhys?"

"She's been returned to the Seelie Court," he said gently.

"What do you mean 'returned' to the Seelie Court?"

Rhys spoke gently. "It was her wish to return to her homeland when she . . ."

He didn't say the words, but I couldn't appreciate his sensitivity. Not when I was still processing what he'd just said. Like he knew for sure that's where she'd gone because he'd been a part of it. And I didn't just mean now that she was gone. He'd known about this all along, and he'd kept it from me. No wonder Aelwyn had told me to go to Rhys. They'd been in on whatever this was together.

My pulse raced faster now, but it had nothing to do with attraction and everything to do with fear. Rhys was holding back. And if there was some lie, some secret he was keeping, I needed to know. I damn sure couldn't let him betray me twice.

"How do you know all this?" I demanded, my voice low to keep it from shaking.

"Because," he said, "I took her there myself last night. I used the portal that brought her here almost twenty years ago. The same portal that brought you here with her. The same portal that brought me when I was ten." His voice was sad, and I knew he was bracing himself for the truth he was about to admit. "We're all three from Faerie, Gwen. And we're connected in ways you don't yet know. But I think . . . it's time to tell you. Aelwyn would want that, and I can't keep you safe any longer without admitting the truth."

"What truth?" I asked.

"The truth about who you really are."

"And who am I?" I asked.

Rhys took a deep breath. "You're Gwenllian, a member of the Seelie royal court. Your father was a warrior, a Protector. You inherited your gift with the ink from your mother. She uses her gift to fight for the Seelie Court in the war against the Unseelie. The dark fae have been after her for years, hoping to take her power for themselves. Hoping to take you. Your parents sent you here as a baby in order to hide you from Unseelie spies."

"How do you know all of this?" I asked.

"It was part of my mission to know."

"Your mission . . ." I repeated, my voice breaking underneath the weight of my grief. Aelwyn was gone, but Rhys was here, and he was breaking my heart all over again. Everything I thought I knew about myself, about her, about him, was a lie.

CHAPTER 7

"*S*ay something," Rhys said quietly.

But I couldn't. All I could do was blink back the tears and put one foot in front of the other, my gaze locked on the door behind him. But a hand on my wrist stopped me just before I reached the knob. Rhys squeezed and yanked, twisting me back to face him. Instead of anger, I found desperation in his eyes.

"Say something," he repeated, this time pleading.

"There's nothing left to say." My voice sounded strangely ragged, even to me.

"There's everything left to say," he argued stubbornly.

"And you've had my entire life to say it."

He flinched. "Let me explain."

"I don't want to hear it." My shoulders sagged with real defeat this time. Rhys had won again, though the prize was twisted: my broken heart.

"You do," he insisted, tugging on my hand—and I let him because it struck me that I couldn't remember the last time I'd touched his skin. Even after all the lies, that's what I noticed. "Five minutes, Gwen. Give me five minutes, and after that, if you want to walk out of here, I won't stop you."

I eyed him. A beat of silence passed.

"You're not the only one who lost her, you know." His voice broke.

I watched as a single tear leaked from the corner of his eye, and my heart ached at the sight of it. He was right. Lies or not, he'd lost Aelwyn too, and I knew he'd loved her just as much as I had.

"Five minutes," I whispered.

Rhys nodded and blew out a breath. "Okay. The truth is that your parents sent Aelwyn here, with you, from Faerie. The dark fae had tracked you all, and your parents knew you weren't safe with them anymore. They used their fae contacts here on the Court to get approval and help erase any paper trail of your arrival or the names of your real family. Aelwyn gave you her last name as another way to throw the dark fae off your trail. She was vigilant with her wards and careful to keep out any fae she hadn't personally vetted. Everything she did was to keep you safe all these years."

I felt my knees wobble and threaten to buckle as I thought back to how adamant Aelwyn had always been about strange fae coming around. "How do you know so much? Did Aelwyn tell you all of this?"

"She did, but that's not the reason I know." He hesitated, his gaze flicking from my face to my legs. "You should sit."

Without waiting for a response, he walked behind his desk and opened a drawer. He drew out a couple of glasses and a bottle of amber liquid decorated with a label I didn't recognize. Not bothering to ask first, he poured a shot and handed it to me. I took it and sank onto the edge of the couch without a word, watching as he poured one for himself and then knocked it back. When it was gone, he immediately refilled the glass.

After a long moment, Rhys continued, "I was born in Faerie. Both of my parents were soldiers for the Seelie Court there. When I was five, they were both killed in a skirmish with Unseelie mercenaries."

"God, Rhys, I'm sorry. I didn't know." The words were out before I could stop them. The feeling of loss was too raw and too familiar not to feel empathy for him. All this time I'd known him and he'd never told me this. So many other things, but not this.

He nodded slowly, and I could see the grief it still caused him. "Thank you. After that, I was drafted into the junior academy. A training program for future fae soldiers. I worked hard, determined to avenge my parents, and because of that, my performance stood out. When I was ten, I was chosen for a smaller team, and I graduated from that as a Protector."

Protector. Just like the letter from my mother had described. I took a deep breath, my heart pounding. "What's a Protector?"

"We're what you might call a bodyguard. We're tasked with keeping a specific fae safe. Our missions are usually more dangerous than a soldier's, because we're on our own without backup. We're the only one standing between our assignment and the threat."

"Kind of like Secret Service then?"

He nodded and hesitated before adding, "I was tasked with protecting you."

"Me?" Shock, confusion, and anger were a chaotic cloud inside me. Quickly, I did the math, counting back to how old he'd been when he'd come to Aelwyn. He'd only been ten years old when they'd given him the assignment? I vaguely remembered him moving in with us around that time, and we'd become fast friends. In fact, by the time I'd grown into my power, he'd been my only friend.

All this time, and he'd never let on . . .

Rhys set his glass aside and knelt in front of me. "Your gift, Gwen, with the ink. The tattoos . . . You're very special. There are enemies of the Seelie Court that want that gift so they can use it for their own gain."

"Those enemies, the dark fae you were talking about," I said grimly. "That's who Aelwyn was hiding me from."

"Yes."

"The night she died, she mentioned it. But I was only a baby when I left. How would they know I have this gift?"

Rhys grimaced. "We suspect they didn't know for sure. But since your mother has it and your father was a seer, they're betting you're going to be valuable to them in some way."

"And now that they found Aelwyn, they know for sure," I finished.

Rhys didn't answer.

"My gift," I repeated, twisting the word with as much cynicism as I could muster. "More like a curse." Rhys opened his mouth to respond, but I redirected—mostly because I was not ready to address any of the crazy, unbelievable things he'd just said about who I was and where I really came from. "Tell me where you took Aelwyn. Tell me how to get there."

"There's a portal about three miles northwest of Aelwyn's house. It leads directly to the outskirts of the Seelie Court's territory, where Aelwyn is from. Last night, I took her through it and delivered her to the Seelie guard on the other side."

"You actually went to Faerie . . ." I wanted to ask about my real mother, but I held back. I couldn't let my emotions run away with me. Not now. Not while I still needed answers. "How? Wouldn't the Court here sense the portal opening?"

He nodded. "They did. I had authorization, so it wasn't a problem."

I stared at him, but it was like staring at a stranger now. He'd gotten special permission from the Court to open a portal? The only way he could have managed that was if everything he had said were true. He was a Protector. A special agent from beyond the veil sent here for the sole purpose of protecting me from the worst of the worst. Like Ada. I snorted. No, whoever was after me was worse than Ada. That made me shudder.

"What happened to make them send you here?" I asked.

"What do you mean?"

"For ten years, it was just Aelwyn and me. So, did something happen for them to think we needed you? Did someone come after me?"

"No. You had another Protector. An older fae named Leif. He lived just past Fred and Betsy, the human couple next door."

"Oh." I let that sink in, remembering the older man Aelwyn had mentioned when I was younger. A friend of hers who liked to bring us fresh vegetables from the farmer's market in town, until one day he just stopped coming around. I barely remembered him now.

"When you were six, Leif retired, and I was sent in his place."

"You were only ten," I said, still a little stunned that he'd received a mission so young.

"My age was an advantage they believed outweighed my inexperience."

I snarled, the betrayal twisting further. "Because they knew you and I would be friends."

His expression mirrored the pain I felt. "Gwen—"

"Was any of it real?"

"What?" he asked.

"Our friendship. Was it all part of your mission to make me trust you? To make me spend time with you. Or was any of it real?"

"Gwen." He softened. "Of course it was real. Every second of it was absolutely real. You are everything to me."

His words sounded so sincere, but I couldn't reconcile them with his rejection. I gripped the glass tightly in my hand, desperate not to relive the moment that had ended our friendship three years earlier. "What was my mother's name?"

"What?" Rhys blinked at me.

I scowled. "If you want me to believe what you're saying is true, then you need to give me something I can verify. What was my real mother's name?"

"I don't see how that will help you verify anything. It's not on any records here."

"Humor me."

Rhys sighed. "Her name is Moonlaith."

The words were so soft. So certain. And an exact match to the name on the strange letter I'd uncovered in Aelwyn's study. Which meant Rhys wasn't lying. Not about any of it. Knowing that didn't make this any easier.

"Wow. The letter was real," I whispered.

Rhys rose from where he'd crouched and slid onto the sofa next to me. "What letter?"

"I found a letter when I was going through Aelwyn's things . . ." In a halting voice, I told him what it had said. And the name that was scrawled at the bottom.

"It's true. Moonlaith is your mother," he confirmed.

"Is?" I tensed. "You mean she's still alive?"

"Yes."

"And my father? You said he was a seer?"

Rhys looked away.

"Rhys?"

When he turned back to me, his expression was pained. "Gwen, he . . ."

I swallowed hard. "Just tell me the truth, Rhys."

"He was a seer," Rhys agreed quietly. "He was also your mother's Protector. According to the report, he saw the dark fae coming for you. You weren't going to make it out, so he stayed behind to buy you some time. He was killed defending you and Aelwyn on the day you were both smuggled into Havenwood Falls. I'm sorry."

"It's okay. I . . . Thank you for telling me," I said. He nodded, and I bit my lip. "But my mother . . . you could contact her? Could we maybe go through the portal and see her?"

"Yes, I—" He frowned at the sight of my face. "Gwen, hold on. It's not safe right now, okay? When this is all over, I promise you, I'll take you to see her, but not until then."

"Okay." I forced myself to relax and focus on the rest of what my mother had written. "So it's true about the mistletoe?"

Rhys nodded. "The mistletoe keeps others from detecting your gift. Actually, according to Aelwyn, it also keeps people from really noticing you or becoming too interested. Another protection."

I gaped at him. "Is that why everyone's being so damn friendly lately? Because I stopped taking the mistletoe?"

He shrugged, but the half smirk he gave confirmed my suspicions. "You have something against folks being neighborly?"

I leaned back, stunned. "All this time, I thought she was just a health nut. Always shoving herbal supplements at me and insisting they were vitamins."

"Well, they are good for you."

I glared. "You knew all this time, and you never told me. And neither did she." More than anything, I wished Aelwyn was still here to defend herself. To hug me. To let me forgive her. How did you forgive a dead person?

"After your Awakening, Aelwyn wanted to tell you, but I had orders. I took an oath, Gwen. I couldn't break that without permission. It was too dangerous. And Aelwyn respected that, even if she didn't like it. That's why she didn't tell you about her burial wishes.

I'm sorry I went behind your back about that, but I couldn't do anything that would break my oath."

"And now? Why are you telling me now?"

"Because your safety trumps everything. Even the oath. Even . . . my feelings."

I hadn't expected him to go there—and because he'd surprised me, I faltered. For a split second, I knew my emotions showed on my face. By the time I'd rearranged my features, Rhys had leaned in, his warm hand resting on my knee. His dark eyes were intense and stormy and full of . . . whatever it was that had made me ever think he cared about me like I'd cared about him.

"I don't want to talk about it," I mumbled.

"Gwen, I know I hurt you. I'm so sorry for that. But . . . I couldn't let it go that far. My oath forbade—"

I shook my head. "You don't have to explain."

"I do. I should have explained a long time ago. The kiss . . ."

"Was a mistake," I finished for both of us, and in one swig, I knocked back the liquid in my glass, welcoming the burn that followed. It was sharp enough to drown out the twinge of pain in my chest my own words had caused.

"No." Rhys grabbed my leg and pulled me closer, shifting me so that we were knee to knee—and eye to eye. His swirled with emotion. Mine . . . I wasn't sure what I looked like now, except that I was terrified and breathless and completely mesmerized by him. Again. I swallowed hard against the pounding in my chest. He could hear it, I was sure of that. "Gwen, that kiss was so much better than any of the times I'd imagined it happening."

"You . . . imagined it?"

"Of course." His expression softened. His lips curved into a smile, and I couldn't tear my gaze away from his mouth. "I've wanted you probably since the moment I saw you. Even at ten, when girls weren't on my radar, you always managed to get my attention. You were my favorite person before the end of that first week at Aelwyn's house. By high school, I was a lost cause. You were way too skinny, with legs too long for the rest of you. But you had this passion and fire that lit you from the inside out. You were all I thought about. Still are."

His hand came up to cup my face, and I tried not to lean into his calloused fingertips as they stroked my cheek. I shuddered as he leaned in.

"What about the oath?" I whispered.

"Screw the oath." His lips were only a breath away now. "I shouldn't have let it ruin this. I want you back in my life. It's been hell without you."

I wasn't even sure I was breathing anymore.

A sharp cramp in my hip sent me jerking, my spine curving until my entire body was pulled taut. I gasped as one of my tattoos came to life, stretching and growling as it animated against my skin.

"Damn it," I said between clenched teeth.

Rhys's brows dipped, and he leaned away as I spasmed again. "What's wrong?"

"The fucking hellhound." I shoved to my feet, peeling my shirt back to reveal the canine I suspected would be shifting and shimmering as it moved against the canvas of my right ribcage. I didn't need to remove my clothes for the ink to break free, but I needed to be sure which tattoo had begun to wake up.

Rhys stared, eyes wide, and his breath whooshed out as he watched the tattoo come to life on my skin. "Holy shit, Gwen. I mean, I knew you could . . . that they were . . . I've just never actually seen your ink come to life," he finally finished.

I gritted my teeth against the pain as the hound scratched and tore, trying to break free from where it had been stretched from my side to my back—an exact replica of the one I'd inked on a client almost four years ago now. It was one of the scarier magical tats I'd done before I'd realized how deadly the consequences could be if activated in the wrong hands. There were only a few still floating around unused out there that could actually do serious harm. The rest were either for Ada—and I didn't like to think about those—or harmless. I'd hoped after this long, maybe the hellhound would never actually be used.

I was wrong.

"What is it?" Rhys asked, his grin vanishing as he took in the horror-struck expression I gave him.

"I gave that tattoo to Walter Glass a couple of years ago."

"Looks like someone pissed him off pretty bad tonight." Rhys looked back at me, his expression grave. "Will it be like last time?"

My body hummed in dread at the thought. "Maybe. We have to go," I said, grabbing my jacket and heading for the door.

Rhys jumped up, and rather than stop me, he followed on my heels. "I'm driving."

I steeled myself against the pain, hoping like hell I'd make it outside before this thing peeled away from me.

"Fine," I said, breathless with the effort of holding the ink inside my skin. I was too distracted to care when Rhys pressed his hand to the small of my back, leading me though the busy bar and into the night.

When he steered me to his truck rather than my own, I let him. Mentally, I listed out all the reasons why this time wasn't the same as last time. There weren't nearly enough to convince me, though. We were together, we'd been about to kiss, and I was still just as much in love with Rhys Graywalk as I'd ever been. I could only pray history wasn't about to repeat itself; that whoever was on the receiving end of this hellhound would live through it.

Inside the truck, Rhys cranked the engine and peeled out, asking, "Where to?"

"I don't know yet. The tattoo is going to . . . peel off my skin," I said through gritted teeth. "When it does, it will try to find its way to the other half."

"Will it obey you like the bird does?"

"No. This one's different. It doesn't belong to me, so I don't control it. I just get a carbon copy."

"What will it do once it's free?"

"It will try to join itself. We need to follow it wherever it goes and try to stop it from hurting someone."

"Will it be solid?" he asked.

I understood his question and shook my head. "No. It will be life size, but only the original is solid. That's the one we have to stop." *Kill.* I meant kill, but I couldn't say the word. Not so soon after Aelwyn.

"Okay," Rhys said, his gaze hard. His eyes glinted in the darkness of the truck, and I didn't miss the edge of danger he wore now like a second skin. I'd never seen him fight, but I knew instinctively in that moment that Rhys could take down anyone or anything that threatened me.

Anything but my own magic, anyway. No one could save me from that.

The thought depressed me. But then the pain took over again, and everything else faded. The hellhound was seconds away from separating itself from my body. Which meant the magic being used to activate it was almost complete. This time, I let it happen. When the ink on my side disappeared, I blinked and looked up. Through the window of the truck, I saw it pass through the passenger door beside me and out onto the empty street beyond. Nothing more than a gray shadow of a creature, but I knew better than anyone how lethal it would be against whatever it was aimed at.

"There," I said. "He's headed for the west side of town."

"Shit," Rhys breathed again as he stared at the ghostly form of the hellhound. "He's fast."

"We have to hurry, Rhys," I urged.

Rhys blinked, then punched the gas, and we shot off.

If we were lucky, we'd get there in time to stop history from repeating itself. If we weren't . . . someone else might die tonight. And it was all my fault. My gift had once again become a curse.

My heart constricted with fear and confusion as the hound led us closer and closer to the edge of town—straight toward Aelwyn's old Victorian. Rhys didn't speak a word, but I saw his jaw tense up as we neared. I held my breath when the driveway came into view, but the creature didn't turn and instead streaked right past, finally turning in almost half a mile later and sprinting straight for the little cottage that belonged to Fred and Betsy, Aelwyn's closest neighbors. Very human neighbors—which meant they didn't stand a chance against something like a hellhound.

"Shit," Rhys swore as we pulled to a quick stop in their yard.

I didn't answer. The hound had already disappeared inside, passing straight through the closed front door. I jumped out of the truck and sprinted across the yard in pursuit. Rhys was right beside me.

Fred and Betsy were retired. No kids. Not a very active social life. Fred liked to garden. Betsy liked to can. They made preserves for us every Christmas, but that was about as far as my knowledge of them went. If they were in danger now because of some tattoo I'd done—

A hand on my arm yanked me sideways. I let Rhys drag me along, surprised by his strength, until we were both tucked around the corner of the house.

"What the hell are you doing?" he whispered. "You can't just march in there. If that hellhound is being used for something violent—"

"It's my creation, Rhys. My fault. If they're in there, I have to help them."

"Fine, but be smart about it." He pulled a knife from somewhere inside his coat. Its pointed tip gleamed in the dim light.

Silently, I eyed it, then him, and he blew out a breath. "I go first," he said.

I nodded, ignoring the flashback to three years ago. Another night. Another husband and wife. A heart squeezed and squeezed until it just stopped. Tonight's spell might be even worse, considering the sharp teeth on the monster in there.

Rhys crept toward the door, and I stayed close, listening and watching as a light breeze ruffled through the bare branches overhead. It was cold, but it was still—the kind of stillness that always seemed to accompany a freeze. It was also the kind of stillness that made every little noise sound even louder. I forced my breathing to go quiet, taking in a long, deep breath to help steady my pulse.

Ahead of me, Rhys climbed the steps and tried the knob. It turned easily in his hand. The door swung open. I held my breath, still close on his heels as we crept silently inside. A rustling sounded from somewhere in the back. Rhys adjusted direction and headed toward it.

On my arm, Ethan stirred. I was about to let him loose when something squished underneath my boot.

I looked down and cringed at the pool of blood. No, not a pool. A trail. I followed it with my eyes until it disappeared around the corner of the kitchen. Not the kitchen again. Rhys and I exchanged a glance. Somehow he managed to look both concerned for me and violent at the same time. My chest ached for him, but I ignored it and instead focused on the magic that was tugging at me. The magic I'd created and that had called me here tonight.

With slow steps, we made our way around the corner and into the tiny galley kitchen. I stared at the blood on the floor in confusion.

"There's no one here," I said finally.

Rhys bent low, studying the pool of blood more closely now. I stepped around him, caught up in the scene before me as I edged closer and closer. Beside me, Rhys was careful not to touch anything, but by the time I remembered to pay attention, my boots had already wandered too close. When I backed away, I left a set of bloody prints in my wake.

"Damn it," I muttered.

The rustling came again, this time from just outside the back door.

Rhys jumped up, brandishing the knife as he leapt clear of the pooled blood and threw open the back door. I made the same jump, peering around his shoulder just in time to see the two hellhounds merge into one another and become a single solid form.

The hound looked up from where it had bent low over a pile of leaves on one side of the yard, its snout and jaw covered in blood. Fangs protruded from its open mouth, and yellow eyes glowed as it glared down at whatever lay before it. Black fur covered its giant body, and long claws extended from its huge paws. When it spotted us, it gave a sharp howl and then turned for the woods.

I hissed, knowing we were about to lose it for good. Rhys fumbled in his jacket, hopefully for a weapon, but we were out of time. Without stopping to think, I let Ethan peel himself free through the layers of my clothes and coat. He tore free from my skin faster than he'd ever done before, and with a single flap of his powerful wings, he swooped across the yard and dug his claws into the hind parts of the four-legged creature. The hellhound cried out and tried twisting away, but Ethan held fast, and they both jerked sideways as Ethan pecked and clawed at the thing.

I looked back to where the hound had been crouching. Two forms lay half-covered in leaves. I peered closer, unsure of what I was seeing, but after willing my eyes to adjust to the darkness, two faces came into focus. Wrinkled with age and coated in blood, Fred and Betsy stared upward, both of their stark expressions frozen in lifeless terror. I let out a strangled gasp and took a step toward them, but Rhys stopped me with a hand around my waist.

"I see them," I choked, desperation clawing its way up my throat. "I have to help."

"It's too late," he said in a rough voice.

In the distance, a siren wailed.

Rhys and I locked eyes. "Motherfu—" Rhys began.

Ethan screeched sharply.

I swung my gaze back to him as he went flailing and hit the ground several feet away from the hound. I sucked in a sharp breath, every single thought vanishing at the sight of my familiar in danger. I wrenched free from Rhys and ran for my hawk, kicking up a spray of mud in my wake. I was vaguely aware of the hound's howl and its new track—aimed right for me. But I didn't care. I couldn't stop. I had to save Ethan no matter what else happened.

The sirens grew louder, drowning out the sound of my own cry and Rhys yelling my name. For a moment, everything faded, and all I saw was Ethan shuffling toward me in the half-melted snow. Sounds faded.

When I was a foot away, I called up every ounce of magic inside me and sped up. When I collided with Ethan, instead of slamming into me or bouncing off, he melted into a thin layer of magic and ink, and by the time I blinked again, he was nothing more than an image on my arm.

Safe.

He was safe.

Already, I could feel him gathering his energy and healing himself to become the whole creature I'd spelled when I'd created him.

I sank to my knees, gasping for breath and thanking whatever forces had helped me salvage at least one life from this night.

Behind me, something growled.

My stomach tightened as reality came crashing down around me. The hellhound.

I twisted in time to see it lurch for me, its bloody jowls open and sharpened teeth aimed for my face. I screamed.

Over the hound's head, I watched as Rhys sprinted for me. In mid-stride, he flicked his wrist, a quick back and forth that was nearly too fast to follow. Silver glinted through the air. A second later, the knife he'd held a moment ago buried itself in the back of the hound's head. The creature let out a yelp that ended abruptly, and then it fell less than a foot from where I sat, unmoving against the leaves.

Rhys rushed over, yanking me to my feet. I leaned on him, letting him hold me tightly against his chest, stunned by how fast Rhys had moved. How ruthless and true his aim had been and how little he seemed affected by it all. Had he always been able to do that? How had I missed it? What else was he hiding? I started to ask, but the siren reached a crescendo and tires rolled over gravel.

Rhys stiffened and then grabbed my shoulders, peering down at me. "Are you hurt?"

I shook my head. "No, but Betsy and Fred—"

"There's nothing we can do now. Gwen, listen to me. Your footprints are all over that kitchen. It won't look good." My stomach tightened as understanding dawned. Had this been a setup? If so, I'd walked right into it. From the look on his face, Rhys knew it too. His mouth tightened at the edges. "Can you run?"

I nodded. "Yes."

"Do not go to Aelwyn's. Run a mile west past the falls. There's a rock peak there. Do you know it?"

"At the base of Mt. Alexa. Yes, I—"

"Wait for me there. Hide yourself and do not make a sound. Use your familiar to guard yourself. Do not come out for anyone else," he said quietly. "Do you understand?"

"Yes."

He pressed a cold kiss to my forehead, then my lips, but the pressure was gone before I could react. He shoved me toward the trees as a car door opened and closed out front.

"Go," he insisted.

I didn't question his order. Instead, I turned and ran, letting the forest swallow me up, leaving the murdering magic I'd created behind me once again.

CHAPTER 9

*H*uddled inside the alcove of a large outcropping of rocks, I shivered for an hour before Ethan alerted me through our bond that someone was coming up the dirt road. A moment later, headlights came into view. I tensed, ready to run if necessary. Park Ranger Rusty Higgins patrolled the woods around town every night, although he should have been in wolf form instead of driving. I'd been lucky to avoid him so far, and I couldn't afford to be found by him now. Rhys had said he would come, and I had no doubt he would keep his promise, but in the meantime, I was exposed. Cold. Without a single form of defense if whoever was doing all this found me first. I had no doubt now that someone out there was trying to screw with me. Not kill me. They could have done that already. No, instead they wanted to ruin me first. And so far, they were doing a damned good job of it, too.

The headlights swung sideways as a truck pulled into the visitor lot down the hill from where I'd hidden. The base of the great falls was a popular hiking meetup for tourists and even locals. Not at two in the morning, though.

The headlights swung away, and I finally got a look at the vehicle from my vantage point. A sigh escaped me, interrupted by the shuddering of my body. Ethan swooped low enough that Rhys ducked as he got out. It seemed I wasn't the only impatient one out here tonight.

"Gwen?" Rhys called quietly as he started up the hill.

I pushed to my feet and slid out into the open. Rhys breathed out when he spotted me, his shoulders relaxing as he closed the distance between us and gathered me into his arms.

"I was so damn worried. Are you all right?" he asked, wrapping his arms around me and rubbing hard.

Some of my shivering subsided. "I'm okay," I said in a voice that was nowhere near convincing.

"Come on. Let's get you warm and safe."

I didn't argue as he led the way back to the truck. In fact, I didn't say a word as he tucked me inside, spreading a blanket over me before blasting the heat as high as it would go. I sat back to let him shut the door, but he paused, brow creasing.

"Your hawk . . . I'd like to leave him up there for a while to help scout our way. Is that okay?"

Ethan practically screamed at me mentally, and I nodded, a wry smile tipping one side of my numbed lips. "I think you two are on the same side."

"Good." Rhys shut the door and walked around, climbing inside. When he reached across the space and grabbed me, I jumped. He ignored that as he slid me across the bench seat until my thigh was pressed tightly against his.

"What are you doing?" I asked, though I didn't protest the contact. I already felt warmer than I had before.

"Warming you up for one thing," he said, tucking the blanket carefully around me. "And doing a little to help restore my own sanity."

"What are you talking about?"

"I was out of my mind for the last hour," he admitted. "Terrified I'd get here and you'd be gone . . . or worse."

"Did you find Walter?" I asked.

"No, I didn't see anyone else, and the cops are . . . there'll be a full investigation."

I nodded, still too numbed to think too hard about that.

"I don't understand why Walter would have wanted to use his tattoo on innocent people," Rhys said.

"He's not exactly the world's most cheerful person," I admitted.

Rhys shook his head. "Still. Why get it in the first place? A hellhound is a pretty aggressive choice, right?"

I shrugged. "He said he was worried about his safety on the job. He worked for Waste Management and said he frequently had to outrun aggressive dogs and that he'd once stumbled on a bear digging through someone's trash."

"Yeah, I guess I could see that," Rhys said.

We were silent for a minute. "Maybe it was someone else," I said quietly.

Rhys turned to me so quickly, I knew he'd been considering the same thing. "You think someone else activated it? Is that even possible?"

I didn't know what to think, but that didn't change the fact that the hellhound had been here and done some real harm. "Sure, I mean, with the right magic, anything's possible, right?" I shrugged. "All I know is someone wanted to hurt innocent humans and they used my tattoo to do it. Again."

Rhys bit his lip. "Gwen, we're going to figure this out. It's going to be okay."

I nodded, my eyes stinging with tears. "Rhys, I . . . Thank you."

"For what?" he asked.

"For all of it. Protecting me and caring for Aelwyn and for saving my life tonight. I'm sorry I've been so selfish when you— I should have thought more about your feelings in all of it. I should have realized everything you gave up just to keep me safe."

"I'm sorry I walked away, Gwen. It's the single biggest regret of my life." His voice was hoarse with emotion, and I felt my own eyes sting as I blinked back hot tears. "You're the most important thing in the world. Making you happy is all I've ever wanted."

I swallowed hard as he stared down at me, aware of our closeness. And suddenly it wasn't all about warmth or worry. His chest heaved, and I leaned closer, my body straining for more of him. The air around us thickened, and the world outside faded.

There was only this—the two of us. And how badly I wanted him to kiss me.

"Gwen," he whispered, his gaze dropping to my mouth.

Like a mind reader, he lowered his head, his lips brushing over mine in a feathery kiss. I sighed, and my reaction spurred a growl from deep in his throat. His lips crashed over mine, suddenly demanding and desperate. I threw off the blanket and wrapped my arms around his neck, holding him as close as I could and willing this moment not to end.

His hard chest pressed against my own, his breath washing over me and doing more to warm me than any blanket so far. But it wasn't enough. I needed to be closer. After all this time, the reality was so much better than I ever imagined.

I grabbed his shoulders and shoved him back, climbing onto his lap with my knees digging into the seat belt holster and the armrest along the door. Rhys held my hips tightly, helping me adjust as I settled on top of him. His mouth never left mine, and when I lowered my center to his, he pressed against me, his tongue shoving against mine until I moaned softly.

I felt Rhys harden against his jeans.

My hands tangled in his hair, pulling and pleading for more.

He kissed me like we were drowning, but it was the opposite. This was the first moment I'd felt like breathing in three years.

"Wait."

I tried not to feel a pang of disappointment and fear when Rhys eased back. He squeezed his eyes shut and dropped his head, and I braced myself for the rejection that was about to come. But when he opened his eyes, a smile tugged at his lips. "You are ridiculously sexy, you know that?"

"I . . ." I blinked.

"We need to get you somewhere safe before we can . . . finish this. But we will finish this. I just . . . Protecting you comes first, okay?"

"Okay," I said shakily.

He held onto me as I slid back to my seat, tugging me close again when I ventured too far. I waited while he readjusted the blanket, tucking it in around my legs—and then adjusted himself. When he looked up, I sent him a small smile of my own at my handiwork. He responded by planting a quick kiss on my mouth before straightening and backing us out of the empty lot.

Neither of us spoke on the ride back to town, but Rhys held my hand tightly the entire way. I was sure I'd have more to say when I was warm and coherent again. For now, the silence felt nice. Rhys's hand in mine felt even better. Right here, I was completely safe. I just hoped it would last.

*B*y the time we arrived at Rhys's apartment, I was ready to burst with questions. Between making out with Rhys and the truck's heat, the cold had been chased away, and the fog had lifted. My thoughts were clear—and overwhelming. I had too many questions to know where to begin. And the grief of seeing Fred and Betsy like that . . . I tried not to blame myself, but it was hard. The biggest question, though, was Walter.

The Dirty Knuckle was empty and dark when we pulled around back. Rhys showed me inside and up the back stairs, unlocking the door and then stepping back to let me go first. I walked cautiously. My eyesight was sharp enough to keep me from running into things, but my slow steps had nothing to do with that. This was Rhys Graywalk's private space. And I was standing here with the scent of his body still on my skin. It was a lot—even with the whole nearly dying thing, it was a lot.

My heart thudded extra hard as I stood in the center of the living room and waited while Rhys went around turning on lights. He disappeared around a corner, and I heard cabinet doors and then a fridge. A moment later, he returned with two dark bottles already opened.

"Drink this," he said. "It'll calm your nerves while we talk."

I took the beer gratefully and sipped, mostly to keep from having to talk. I didn't know what to say about the apartment. It was all dark wood and leather, like his office. But it was lived in. A sweatshirt thrown over the arm of the couch. A newspaper and stack of magazines spread over the coffee table. Dirty socks by the door. It was so personal. I didn't want to admit how many times I'd ached for him to bring me here over the past few years.

So I drank until the moment passed.

Rhys downed half his beer and then set it aside. He strode to a rolltop desk in the corner of the room, slid it open, and pulled out a pad of paper and a pen. He returned to where I stood and tugged me down on the couch beside him.

"Okay," he said, the pen poised and ready, "tell me what else you know about this Walter guy."

"First tell me what happened after I left the house." Fred and Betsy's. That's what I would have normally said. But saying their name now . . . I couldn't.

Rhys frowned, but nodded. "It was a setup, that's for damned sure. Deputy Conall said he got an anonymous call to come check out a disturbance, but no one else even lives close enough to be disturbed, even with the racket that beast made. So that doesn't add up. And the blood in the kitchen—that was a message."

"You think whoever unleashed the hellhound was the same person that killed Aelwyn?"

Rhys nodded. "I do. And I think they wanted us to know that, too. I didn't have much time to look over the bodies before Conall chased me off, but I think whoever left that blood in the kitchen did it before the hellhound got there. And the energy signature was the same as the one at Aelwyn's that night."

"Ethan didn't sense anyone else out there with us," I agreed. "So they must have already left when we got there."

"Ethan?" Rhys blinked.

"My hawk."

Rhys stared at me, brows raised. "You named him Ethan?"

"Yeah."

"Ethan Hawk?" He laughed out loud, and my lips curved at my

own private joke. Aelwyn had been the only other person who knew, so I'd almost forgotten the humor of it.

"It was Aelwyn's idea," I admitted.

He smiled warmly. "Sounds like her."

My smile vanished too quickly as I remembered what we were doing here in the first place. "Do you think . . . I mean, whoever killed her is messing with me now. Do you think they killed her to get to me?"

Rhys took a deep breath. "Honest truth? I do. And I'm sorry. For what it's worth, I managed to wipe out your footprints in the kitchen, so they failed tonight."

"Failed?" I felt the blood drain from my face. "Fred and Betsy are dead because of me. Because of my tattoo. That's not a fail, that's—"

"I know. Bad word choice. I'm sorry. Gwen, how do you know Walter couldn't have activated his tattoo?"

"Because I check up on him. On all of the ones who have magic in their ink. After last time, I realized I had a responsibility."

"Last time wasn't your fault."

"That couple would still be alive if it weren't for me."

"Gwen, that asshole was going to hurt his wife with or without your help. The tattoo was a heart, for goodness' sake. There was no way you could have known he'd find a way to twist that into violence."

"You're right. He could have done something different, but he didn't. And then his death—"

"Was his own damned fault. He should have come out and surrendered when the police told him to. Instead, he ignored their warnings and shut himself in that house. If not for him, she could have gotten medical attention in time. He let her die and then let himself get shot when they stormed the house. None of that is on you."

His voice was firm and almost angry now. Aelwyn used to talk to me about it the same way. They wanted to assure me. But my own guilt was so much bigger than their ability to convince me I wasn't to blame.

"I know that," I said, but we both knew I didn't. Not really.

Rhys sighed. Finally, he spoke again, changing the subject. "So you know for a fact Walter couldn't have activated that hound."

"Yes."

"Hmm."

"What?" I studied his face as a shadow passed over his features.

"That means someone else knows about your gift and how to activate the magic. Is that possible to do on someone else's ink?"

"I've never tried, so I'm not sure. What are you thinking?"

"I just . . . Conall showing up tonight was weird. I want to check on that anonymous call. Verify it really happened."

"You think Deputy Conall is the one doing this?"

"I don't know. But he seems all too eager to point fingers at you for Aelwyn. Besides, we don't exactly have a long list of possible suspects."

I hesitated and then said, "Well, there's one."

"Who?"

"Ada."

"Ada Daryn?" His eyes narrowed. "What makes you think she would do this?"

"She's been blackmailing me into giving enchanted tattoos," I admitted.

"Gwen, what the . . . Why didn't you say anything?"

He didn't sound nearly as surprised as I'd expected. I cocked my head. "Something tells me there's not much to tell."

His mouth tightened, and he set the pen and paper aside. "I've seen her coming and going from your place."

"You've seen her?" I repeated, my eyes widening. "Have you been watching me?"

"I'm your Protector, Gwen. I have to keep an eye. But since . . . I've kept my distance for a while now. I knew you didn't want me to come around, so I stayed out of sight. But I had a job to do, and I wasn't going to let anything happen to you just because we weren't—" He broke off, and my temper flared.

"Because we weren't speaking," I finished for him. "You mean because you rejected me?"

He winced. "Don't say it like that."

"How else should I say it? That's what happened, Rhys." I waited for the hot fury that usually rose when I thought about his rejection. But this time, all I felt was sadness. His apologies were getting to me, and I could feel myself edging closer to giving in to his pretty words. But the fear of being hurt twice hadn't gone away entirely.

"Gwen." Rhys grabbed my hand and squeezed. I turned to meet his eyes, and my stomach flipped just like it always did when his gaze turned so intense. "I hate that I did that to you. I never should have let it go this long. But the oath—"

"I know," I said. "You already explained. I just . . . it's a lot to let go of." Too much, maybe. But I didn't say that.

He nodded and then pressed a kiss to my lips. His mouth was warm, a solid comfort after everything that had happened tonight. I kissed him back lightly, expecting him to stop it just like he had in the truck. And I couldn't blame him. We did have a killer to catch. Besides that, I wasn't sure what this was yet. I'd wanted it for so long, but now that I had it, I had no idea how to process it against the years of thinking he didn't want me.

But he slid closer, reaching for me and pulling me swiftly into his lap, his tongue exploring my mouth and leaving my skin prickling where his fingers trailed.

"Rhys . . ." I whispered against his mouth.

He responded by pulling me closer, his hands roaming everywhere before slipping underneath my shirt. I panted against him, arching into his palm as he cupped my breast.

Outside, a hawk called sharply, and we both went still.

My shoulders sagged as Rhys eased me away. He rose and went to the window. I followed reluctantly, adjusting my shirt and bra and then running a hand through my hair, which was probably already a nightmare.

"Is he okay?" Rhys asked, throwing the window open and peering out into the night sky.

"He's fine," I said wryly, bracing myself against the gust of cold air that blew in. "Just letting us know it's all clear."

Rhys turned back to me, his confusion melting into amusement. "He can sense us . . .? I mean, he knew we were . . ."

"He's my familiar. I see through his eyes, and sometimes he sees through mine."

"I see." Rhys smiled mischievously. "No pun intended."

"Funny."

"You should call him back before the sun comes up," Rhys said, and I nodded, knowing he was right, but wishing Ethan had kept his mouth shut for a while longer. I still wasn't entirely ready to trust Rhys, but I couldn't deny how badly I wanted to try.

"And when the sun does come up?" I asked, already sticking my arm out the window to call Ethan back to me.

"We'll pay a visit to a friend at the Court," he said. "See what we can uncover about Ada. And the deputy. And figure out where to look next." He turned and began building a fire in the cold hearth near the couch.

I called Ethan back to me and then sank onto the soft couch as the fire crackled to life. We sat in silence for a few minutes, finishing our beers. When mine was empty, I leaned my head back against the soft leather. Between the warmth of the flames and the crackle of the wood, I couldn't keep my eyes open.

Soon, I drifted.

I woke to the jostle of being lifted by a pair of strong arms. When I opened my eyes and saw Rhys staring down at me in the firelight, I protested against his firm grip. "I can walk," I insisted.

"You looked so peaceful. And tired," he said quietly. The firelight danced strangely over his features. "Let me carry you."

Struck by the hard planes and strong lines, I looked away and let him carry me to the spare room without further argument. He tucked me into bed with gentle hands that contradicted his sharp edges, and didn't help the pitter-patter of my traitor heart. When he was gone, I tried not to register the disappointment that he hadn't carried me to his bed instead.

I woke to the smell of coffee and the sense that I wasn't alone. When I rolled over, my breath caught, and I gasped. Rhys jumped back, nearly spilling the coffee he'd just set on the nightstand. I blew out a breath, clutching my chest and willing my pulse to steady as I sat up. "Shit. You scared me."

"Sorry. I wanted to offer caffeine before I started overloading you with information."

"What time is it?" I asked, inching toward the steaming mug and trying to blink the rest of the exhaustion away.

"Almost ten."

"In the morning?" I squawked.

Rhys winced. "My contact called me back a few minutes ago, and I think we should meet with a couple of people today. I didn't want to wait too long to get moving."

"Why? Who? What did he say?" I grabbed the mug and took a sip, mostly so I could comprehend whatever details he was about to give.

Rhys hesitated. "Take another sip of coffee first."

"Rhys," I warned, irritable and wary. "Tell me."

He didn't respond, and finally I took a large gulp of coffee. Then I raised my brows. "Now tell me," I said.

"They found Walter's body this morning."

"What?" It was the last thing I'd expected, and for that reason, it confused me more than upset me. For about five seconds. Then my eyes stung with tears that I blinked back. In an effort to hold it together, I gulped more coffee. "How did he die?"

"Natural causes. That's the official finding so far. But . . ."

"We both know it wasn't natural. Not with the hellhound getting loose."

Rhys' brow furrowed. "Is it possible his tattoo could have activated when he died?"

"No. The magic only lives as long as the wearer."

He let out a breath, but he didn't look relieved.

"What?" I asked.

"Remember the call Deputy Conall claimed to get about the disturbance last night?" I nodded. "My contact says Walter was the anonymous caller."

"That doesn't make sense. Walter let his hellhound loose and aimed it at innocent people he likely didn't even know, and then he called the police?"

"It doesn't make sense," Rhys agreed, his gaze far away as he stared at the curtains covering the sunlit window. Finally, he blinked and looked at me, focusing on my body for what felt like the first time since he'd come in.

Suddenly, I remembered I'd taken off everything but my black tank top and panties last night. My exposed skin tingled where his gaze touched.

"I should get dressed," I said hastily, reaching for the sheet, coffee still clutched in one hand, but Rhys stopped me. Carefully, he took the mug out of my hand and set it on the nightstand. Then he scooted closer until we were almost nose to nose. His eyes blazed with a hunger that I'd only ever experienced in my own body. Desire—no, need— reflected back at me.

Slowly, he reached for me, his hand cupped tightly against the back of my neck, his thumb stroking my jawline. He held me there, his expression daring me to object.

"If you think for one second that I'm done with you," he said, and then rather than finish that statement with words, he kissed me.

The second his mouth met mine, heat exploded inside me. His kiss wasn't gentle or soft or anything resembling asking my permission— not like it had been last night in the truck. Instead, he took, his mouth hot and heavy, his hands demanding as they explored. And damn if I didn't let him.

Screw enchanted tattoos—this right here was the real magic.

His hands roamed my body, down my arms and then over my hips, all while pressing into me with his mouth and his erection. My skin thrummed where his fingers touched—my collarbone, my throat, tangling in my hair. He leaned against me, easing us both down so that I was on my back against the bed and Rhys was pressed against me in all the right places. My blood heated, and I rocked my hips against his, lost in the feel of him. Of knowing he wanted me. Finally.

My left hip tingled extra hard, but I ignored it, too caught up in the moment to do anything but appreciate my body's reaction.

When his tongue darted inside my mouth and tangled with my

own, I clutched at his shirt, fisting my hands in the fabric in desperation. His hand dropped from my hair long enough to hook behind my knee, drawing my leg up and wrapping it around his waist. He rocked into me, and I lost it, my head falling back against the pillow as Rhys pressed a trail of hot kisses down my throat before nipping at my ear. His fingers found the edge of my panties, and my insides sizzled in anticipation as his hand slipped inside the thin fabric, inching toward my center.

It was everything I'd wanted for so long.

Without warning, Rhys broke off, his eyes wide, his mouth open in a shocked expression.

"What the hell?" he demanded, jumping clear of me and the bed in one leap.

Iron clanged against iron as the tattoo that had peeled itself away from my hip took shape, color, and then dimension, and finally fastened itself to Rhys's body. He stared down at it, dumbstruck as it welded itself together—tight from the looks of it. Painfully tight.

Dazed, I stared up at where he stood with his back to the bedroom door. It took a moment for the fog to clear and the tingling to subside enough for me to notice what was happening. When I finally did, I had to press my lips together to keep from laughing. The twinge in my hip suddenly made sense. After all this time, I'd almost forgotten.

Rhys glared back at me, indignation hard to accomplish in his current state. But he managed. "What the fuck is this?" he demanded.

"Um, I believe it's called a chastity belt," I supplied, sitting up so I could get a better look at my own creation.

"Are you kidding me?"

I decided not to answer, fairly certain anything I said would unleash the laughter I was holding back. Rhys glared at me, the iron clanking as he shifted his weight. "You did this—your tattoo . . . Why the hell would you do this?"

"I honestly forgot about it," I told him, guilt creeping in as I watched him struggle to unlock the thing.

His eyes narrowed, clearly unconvinced.

I tilted my head as the memory returned. "That day in my

backyard when we were— The day we first kissed . . . I was hurt when you broke it off and walked away."

"I hurt you, I get that, but a chastity belt, Gwen?"

I shook my head, caught up in the memory that had scarred me so deeply that I'd inked this protection into my skin to keep it from ever happening again. "I was nearly naked, and you just stopped. Then you walked away and left me there, Rhys. Standing there like an idiot. That was right around the time of my Awakening, and I was starting to understand how my ability worked. So, I inked myself with a defense mechanism. If you ever tried anything with me again, it would activate the spell behind the tattoo and, well, this would happen . . . Thus, saving me from you."

"What about last night?"

"Last night was a kiss. This was . . ." I felt my cheeks heat. "About to be more."

He stared at me. "If it's to keep you safe from me, shouldn't you be the one wearing it?"

I folded my arms over my chest, smiling haughtily. "Why should I be punished if you were the one who started it?"

He shook his head, muttering to himself. I caught enough of it to glare back at him, but the sight of him saying anything while standing before me trapped in a medieval chastity belt was too amusing. Before long, I was biting back more laughter.

"I bet you think this is funny," he said, taking a step closer so that the iron clanged again.

A small laugh escaped. "It's pretty hilarious," I admitted.

He stepped even closer, sending me back against the headboard as he sat so close that he crowded me. His brows had dipped so that his expression was serious, intense. I couldn't quite read whether he was still pissed, but the heat in my stomach was curling again.

"You're only laughing because you haven't really thought this through," he said, his voice dropping low as he leaned in.

"Oh?" I blinked, trying to stay focused on what he was saying rather than how hot he looked while saying it.

"If I'm all locked away, it's going to make the outcome pretty frustrating for you." His hand came up to cup my breast, and I bit my lip against the moan that built. His voice dropped to a whisper, his lips grazing my chin as his fingers found my nipple and tugged slightly. "Especially when I'm touching you like this . . . Don't you think?"

Damn it. He was good.

With a sigh and a small flick of my wrist, the iron vanished.

The second the iron was gone, Rhys sighed in relief. "You're more diabolical than I ever knew, you know that?"

"Now you know why I don't walk around inking everyone with this sort of magic," I said.

"Damn right." He shuddered. "I'm terrified to imagine what the hell is going to happen to me when we actually have sex."

My lips curved just as his mouth covered mine.

CHAPTER 11

 upids & Cuties, the annual celebration that always took over Havenwood Falls, was three days away, and the evidence was all over town. I didn't necessarily hate Valentine's Day. Hating it would have required giving a shit in some way, which I didn't. Normally, I had no problem ignoring the whole thing, though I did roll my eyes at the cliché hearts and cupids I ended up tattooing on couples this time of year. Still, I couldn't hate on a holiday—or a town event—that was so good for business.

This year was different, though.

Business was already booming, thanks to the herbs wearing off. And Rhys Graywalk was currently walking next to me—a simple thing that made my heart race and my palms sweat. He was also eyeing the pink and red décor currently coating the town square.

"Wow, that's a lot of pink," he said.

"Ugh. It's stupid is what it is."

We'd had to park around the corner thanks to all the service vehicles delivering décor for the square. I wove through the swarm of them on our way from Rhys' truck to my apartment. As if it wasn't weird enough that Rhys Graywalk was about to see where I lived, now we had to navigate there through an entire herd of cardboard cupids being carried by delivery workers who wouldn't stop smiling at me and offering a hello.

My life had become really fucking weird.

"When you say 'stupid' are you referring to Cupids & Cuties?" Rhys asked, increasing his pace to keep up with me. "Or the entire concept of Valentine's Day?"

"All of it, yes, but mostly the event itself. The idea that an enchanted arrow can lead you to your true love and when it does, you have to kiss the person right there in front of a ballroom full of people? It's bullshit."

"Spoken like a true Grinch."

I caught his teasing grin and scowled as I turned to climb the steps that led to the shop. "Are you saying you're a fan?" I asked, suddenly nervous that he'd tell me he'd been there every year and made out with a different girl each time.

But he shook his head. "Actually, I've never been." He bumped my shoulder. "I had a feeling the arrow wouldn't work without you there, so I've always skipped it."

My face heated, but I ducked my head, grumbling to cover up my pleasure at his words. "Well, I think love takes a lot more work to find than an enchanted arrow."

"Can't disagree there."

At the top of the stairs, I unlocked the door of my shop and headed inside. I didn't stop in the dark shop, but kept walking straight through to the next set of stairs that led up to my apartment. "You can just wait down here if you want," I said, not bothering to look back in case it gave away just how nervous I was to have Rhys in my living quarters.

But his footsteps didn't slow or stop, and his voice came from close behind me as I shoved open the door at the top of the steps. "No way. I'm not letting you out of my sight after last night."

I bit back a quick retort, mostly because I didn't want to ruin the agreement I'd managed to get out of him at all. I'd had a hell of a time convincing him to let me come here in the first place. And part of me would have been happy to stay away until all this was resolved, but I couldn't afford not to be here when my first client showed. Not with the packed schedule I had thanks to the herbs wearing off and the people in this town actually wanting to be around me. Rhys had argued, but I'd convinced him to give me ten minutes. Not eleven. Ten. That was it. The plan was to grab a few things, reschedule all my appointments for the next couple of days, and get out again. Fast.

It should have been more than enough, but then I stepped through my front door, and the energy signature in my tiny one-bedroom hit me. It was fae, but it wasn't mine.

I took a quick step back, but Rhys was even faster, grabbing me by the waist and yanking me behind him. I huddled behind him, my heart pounding. Rhys didn't move a muscle as we both listened.

Outside, there was a thud, and my head whipped to the window. Rhys bolted, beating me there, and together we peered at the street below. I caught sight of a man's shoulders and head just before the figure's feet hit the ground. Once he'd landed, he looked up at us, and it took me a moment to register what I was seeing.

Walter Glass stood staring up at us from where he'd just swung himself down two floors using the rafters and railings. The only thing different about him from the last time I'd seen him, other than the fact that he was supposed to be dead, were his eyes. The brown color had changed to a bright yellow, glowing to an impossible hue before dimming again. He blinked, and the yellow vanished, replaced once again by the dull brown that I remembered.

"Impossible," I said, but even as I breathed the word, his eyes flashed with fury, and a ripple of magic passed over his face. It was only a split second, but it was enough, and I realized why we hadn't been able to identify the signature before.

"It's a glamour," Rhys said flatly.

I didn't argue. I knew Rhys had received this particular gift during his Awakening, and now he could see through any fae's glamour, Seelie or Unseelie, no matter how old or powerful.

"That's not Walter," I said, the hushed words coming out more like a question.

"No, it's a fae glamoured to look like Walter. It's also the same energy signature I sensed at Aelwyn's. And again last night," Rhys added. His voice was quiet now, like a simmering rage that he was keeping under tight control.

"Can you see his face?" I asked. "Do you recognize him?"

"Yes. I've never seen him before, but his markings suggest he's an Unseelie soldier of some kind."

"Seriously?" How in the hell would an Unseelie soldier get into Havenwood Falls unchecked?

Dead Walter stared up at us, and the full weight of the glamour resettled over his features before he took off at a full sprint. Rhys moved to follow, then stopped just short of the window that led to the fire escape.

"Why aren't you going after him?" I asked.

He didn't look up as he slid his phone out and started typing. "We need to know more about who and what we're dealing with first."

He had a good point, but still, letting a dead man run off through town didn't seem like the smartest play. I eyed Rhys warily as he keyed in a few lines and sent a message. "You want to call the police?"

"Yes, but first, I want to reach out to my police contact to see if he can dig up anything else on Dead Walter. Then we'll go see someone at the Court. Maybe one of them can tell us anything about that glamour we just saw."

"And in the meantime?" I asked, already impatient as he set his phone aside and leaned against the counter.

"We wait."

"I thought you said we weren't safe here."

"We're safer than roaming the streets until we know more. If Walter wanted a fight here, he could have had it—and the element of surprise. Instead, he ran. I think we should lay low here until we know what our next move is."

"Fine." I sighed, resigning myself to sitting around for a bit when all I wanted to do was run outside and chase Walter down.

"Tell me about Walter's other tattoos."

"Walter doesn't have any other tattoos," I said slowly.

Rhys looked over at me. "Well, Dead Walter does, but they have a lot more magic in them then that hellhound did."

I frowned at that. If Dead Walter was really an Unseelie fae, and he was covered in magical tattoos that I certainly hadn't given him, that meant I wasn't the only one with this ability.

"Do you think he found my mother?" I asked. "That he made her give him those tattoos?"

"No."

He sounded so sure.

"How do you know?" I asked. "If he already has magic tattoos, he had to get them somewhere."

"If something had happened to your mother, I would have heard, trust me. Besides, if he wants you badly enough to risk coming here, glamoured or not, it means he needs your gift. It means he doesn't have it already. I think those tattoos were done by witch-magic. They felt different than yours."

"Different how? What did they look like?" I asked.

"I only saw one of them clearly. It was an azurite stone." He hit send and slid his phone away again before responding. "Azurite is a divination stone. It would . . . possibly allow him to see past the shields you have. To find you—if he knew what or who he was looking for."

"What shields?" I asked.

"The mistletoe." He nodded to the room around us. "And the cedar wood."

"The cedar wood's a shield?" That was news to me. Then again, hadn't that letter from my birth mother mentioned cedar wood? Most of my furniture had been a gift from Aelwyn, but I didn't think—

"It protects your house. Aelwyn spelled it to work against fae. Especially anyone not from Havenwood Falls."

"Oh." I blinked, stunned.

Rhys' theory made sense. If the azurite tattoo had allowed him to pick up on what I really was, he would have ended up at Aelwyn's for sure. Between her energy and mine, that house was laced with fae magic and enough cedar wood, or shielding, to make it clear we didn't want to be found. I swallowed the lump in my throat, blinking back hot tears as I realized Aelwyn really had died because of me.

Rather than dwell on that here, now, under Rhys' sharp eyes, I forced myself to focus on what Rhys was proposing about the azurite.

"Wait." I blinked. "You think he came through one of the portals? But wouldn't the Court have sensed that?"

"They would. They have," he amended, looking only slightly guilty as he admitted, "I got a text from my contact yesterday morning. There was a breach a few days ago that they still haven't identified."

My eyes widened. "And you were planning on telling me this when exactly?"

He sighed. "It's not like we've had time to really sit down and catch up on every little thing. We started to last night before your tattoo alarm system went off."

I stalked to the chair beside my sagging couch. "Point taken. Let's go ahead and do that now."

"Gwen . . ." Rhys looked tired despite the fact that it wasn't even lunchtime yet. I couldn't blame him. We were both night owls, and I couldn't remember the last time I'd been up before brunch.

"You wanted me to come to you for help, Rhys. And you told me that whole story last night about you being a Protector and where I really come from because you wanted me to trust you. Why ruin it now by keeping things from me?"

He shook his head. "I'm not hiding anything from you, Gwen. There's a lot happening here, and I'm trying to keep up and keep you alive."

I sighed. "You're right. Sorry, I'm just stressed."

"I know. Just . . . take your herbs," he said, and I pushed to my feet. "We'll start there. Get the shields back in place so people don't see you so easily."

I winced, and his eyes widened. "Shit, I'm sorry. That came out wrong. You know what I mean."

"It's fine." I waved him off and turned toward the kitchen, where I kept my herbal supplements.

"It's not fine," he said, following me. "You're scared, and you're counting on me, and I don't mean to insult you."

"I . . ." What could I say? I *was* counting on him, but I wasn't ready to admit that out loud. "I'd like to find a way to be of use in this whole thing," I admitted instead.

"You will," he said, with enough certainty I decided not to admit how much I doubted that right now. "Your magic is strong, Gwen. More than enough to stop this guy from taking it or from hurting you." He stepped closer, grabbing my hand with his own and spinning me to face him. "I believe in you."

He barely applied pressure, but the contact alone was enough to halt me in place. I turned slowly and met his eyes, the look he gave going straight to my stomach. Butterflies flipped and flitted inside me. And the heat that curled there shot low, straight to my thighs. "Rhys," I began.

He stepped closer, and I remembered the way he'd felt pressed against me when we'd first arrived. Not to mention kissing in his truck last night. And earlier this morning. The heat inside me seemed to warm the space between us, charging the air with a spark. Without consciously deciding to, I curled my fingers tighter around his, willing the moment to last. Suddenly, sitting and waiting for our next move didn't seem so bad.

Rhys bowed his head, leaning in, and I held my breath. Every single thought of the danger and the uncertainty vanished. All that mattered was this moment.

A small voice deep down warned me against getting distracted right now. And Ethan scratched at my arm, reminding me of the very real danger we were both in until we found answers to why a dead man had been inside my apartment. But none of it penetrated the fog of my own desire. And for a moment, neither did the insistent buzzing of a phone that broke the silence between us.

The buzzing continued, and Rhys sighed, his breath warm as it washed over my face.

When he pulled away, I came crashing back to reality. We did not have time for this right now. Not with a glamoured fae on the loose and out to get me.

Rhys pulled out his phone, checking the screen before looking back at me, apology written all over his expression as he stepped away.

"It's my contact at the Court," he explained. "We need to go. Now."

CHAPTER 12

From the cab of the truck, Rhys frowned as we both studied the empty spaces where tattoos had once covered my side and hip. The hellhound had left a large blank spot on the right, and then the chastity belt had disappeared on the left. Then there was the missing heart from where it had lived for a short time on my chest. It was strange seeing so much smooth, unmarked skin when the rest of me was practically covered in ink. Guilt pricked at me for the hound. And even more so for the heart. Not so much for the belt. Rhys had definitely deserved that one.

"So they can only be used once, right?" Rhys asked, even though I'd already explained it all. Twice.

"Right," I said, exhausted.

The light ahead turned green, and Rhys hit the gas. He hadn't told me yet where we were going, and he'd already turned away from the Court's headquarters in town. But he was also keeping me talking, which made it hard to wonder too much about it.

"So the hellhound," Rhys said as he made a right turn. "What would have happened to it if we hadn't killed it?"

"I'm not exactly sure. I mean, when the spell had run its course, it would have vanished. Its only power lies in executing its order. But . . ."

"It had already killed Fred and Betsy, and it was still coming after you," he finished for me.

"I've never seen that before," I admitted. "Unless the spell was more complicated than we thought."

"What do you mean?" Rhys pulled to a stop at a four-way intersection. When it was clear, he went straight through. This part of town was mostly industrial. I wasn't sure where we could possibly be meeting a Court member in this area, but he pulled into a half-empty warehouse lot, wound around behind a row of buildings, and cut the engine.

"Well, the words used to activate it are simple. It's all about the intention of the person wearing it. If his intention was to have it kill Fred and Betsy, it should have blinked out. But . . ." I trailed off, unwilling to say the words out loud.

"But if it's intention was to, say, pin a murder-suicide on you, it would still be kicking when we arrived," Rhys said grimly.

"Yeah." My voice was hoarse.

For a moment, we were both quiet as we digested this new theory.

"Gwen, we have to report this to the Court."

My head snapped up, my gaze whipping to his. "What? How can you ask that of me? I'll be arrested or banished."

Rhys shook his head. "I can speak for you. I—"

"What the hell good would that do? The facts are all there. My tattoos have helped kill four people so far. There's nothing you could say."

He growled. "If you'd just told me about the magic, that it wasn't over with that one tattoo, I could have helped you."

Touchy. We were both touchy as we forced ourselves to dance around the issues between us. My issue was that we had a killer to find, and all I wanted to do was make out with him on the couch like a high schooler. I sort of hoped that was his issue, too.

I huffed. "And whose fault is it that we weren't on speaking terms all this time?" He opened his mouth. Closed it again. "And don't act like you didn't know. You were watching me, remember? You know more than I probably want you to know right now."

"It was my job, Gwen."

He was right. And his job had kept me and Aelwyn alive and safe until now. I couldn't bring myself to keep arguing.

I sighed. "To answer your question, yes. The magical tattoos I give can only be used once. As soon as the magic has run its course, my copy merges with theirs, and they both disappear forever," I explained.

"But Ethan is different," he said.

"Yes." I hesitated. I'd never actually told anyone any of this. Except for Aelwyn. And she was gone. "Ethan is . . . I realized a couple of years ago, that if I want to, I can create something more permanent."

"But you've never done that with the spelled tattoos," he said.

I shook my head. "It only works on myself anyway."

He grunted. "Thank the gods you didn't decide to do it with that damned chastity belt."

I smirked.

"Does anyone else know about Ethan? About the permanent aspect?"

"Just Aelwyn," I said quietly.

Rhys didn't answer, but his expression was thoughtful and dark.

"What?" I prompted.

"I think it's obvious our guy is using your tattoos to get to you. He won't come directly at you, though. And I think we need to try to figure out why. It could be that he knows about your true ability. That he feels you're enough of a threat to play it careful."

I nodded. "But what is his end game? What does he really want from me?"

"I don't know yet." Rhys yanked the key out of the ignition and reached for his door handle. "Come on. Let's go inside and see if we can find some answers."

He got out of the truck, and I followed, looking around at the nondescript building. No signage or markers were displayed. The handful of buildings in this area served as mostly storage facilities for local business and delivery companies. I couldn't understand who or what could possibly help us here.

"What are we doing here?" I asked.

"Meeting a friend," he said. I gave him a pointed look at his vague answer, and he sighed. "A friend who works for the Court."

I scowled up at the two-story building where it rose in front of us, blocking the sunlight. "If that's true, I don't have any friends in there."

Rhys ignored that, trudging on ahead toward the door.

In the end, I followed. Maybe I didn't have any friends on the Court, but if Rhys did, it couldn't hurt to try to get them on my side. Especially when Ada came sniffing around again for another piece of ink and found me all closed up.

Inside, I stayed close as we wound our way through the halls. No one else was around, though I could hear machinery running somewhere deeper in the building. Rhys seemed to know where he was headed, and I wasn't about to tell him differently, so I let him lead. Ten minutes later, we'd found a receptionist of sorts. A tall, broad-shouldered man with white hair and black, leather gloves greeted us with a simple nod before herding us into a small conference room with a scarred table and four wooden chairs. No windows. No other equipment.

Rhys immediately sat, stretching his legs out and slinging his arm over the adjacent chair. Relaxed. I might have paced if there had been room. "Relax, Gwen. No one is going to mess with you."

I spun, irritated that he'd read me so easily. "Easy for you to say," I muttered. "That guy looked more like a hit man than a secretary."

Rhys smiled in amusement. "He's neither. Calm down. He's just a driver."

"A driver for whom?"

Before Rhys could answer, the door opened, and an old man with silver hair strode in. My muscles tensed as recognition dawned. I'd seen him before, always at a distance. Aelwyn hadn't been close with him, though she'd visited with him from time to time over the years, and she'd always described him as stern, so I'd steered clear. But this close, I could feel the aura around him that spoke of his age. Elsmed Fairchild was a member of the Court. He was also the oldest living fae I'd ever met. And between my own blurred line with the law and those piercing blue eyes he now fixed on me, he was intimidating as hell.

"Miss Facharro," he said in a clipped and vaguely polite tone. He gestured to a chair. "Please. Sit. Rhys, good to see you, son."

I lifted a brow at Rhys and sat.

"Good to see you too, sir," Rhys said, leaning forward and folding his hands together on the scuffed tabletop.

Elsmed sat too, somehow folding his long body into the small chair. I wondered at the way he let more of his true height show. Way too tall to pass for human. Did he add glamour only when he was out in public? Or was he only letting it all show now to scare me on purpose?

If so, it was working.

If Rhys had asked me the member of the Court I least wanted to be put in a room with, it would have been Elsmed. The man was rumored to have a gift for mind reading. And that was the last thing I needed now. My eyes narrowed as I recalled Rhys imploring me to be honest today. Was this why? Because he knew I'd have no choice but to admit what I'd done.

My mouth went dry.

"Your messages said you had new information about Aelwyn's case," Elsmed said.

Rhys nodded.

"Tell me what you know," Elsmed said.

I shot Rhys a look, absolutely not okay with sharing everything with a man that, for all I knew, was the fae behind the attacks. But Rhys ignored me, clearly more trusting of this guy, and began laying it all out. "We know Aelwyn was killed by a fae. So were Fred and Betsy."

"Do you have proof of this? What do the police say?" Elsmed asked.

"No physical proof," Rhys admitted. "But the energy signature was the same at both houses, and today, I saw a dead Havenwood Falls resident leaping from Gwen's apartment window. He was glamoured and underneath I saw the markings of an Unseelie soldier."

"You saw him?" Elsmed said, much more interested now.

"Yes. He escaped as Gwen and I entered, but I saw through his glamour, and he is definitely Unseelie fae."

"Hmm. And this dead resident," Elsmed said, glancing at me. "You knew him?"

"I tattooed him a while back," I said, nodding.

228

"So Gwen is at the center of this after all," Elsmed said to Rhys.

Rhys nodded with a grimace. The truth wasn't exactly good news. "Aelwyn was killed moments before Gwen arrived. I don't think that was a coincidence."

"You think they wanted to torture her? Make sure she found Aelwyn as it happened?" Elsmed asked.

Rhys nodded. "And maybe pin it on her. That much was clear at Fred and Betsy's."

Elsmed frowned. "I wasn't aware Gwen was present at the second scene. The police report didn't mention her."

Rhys shot me a glance, but pretended not to notice the death stare I was giving him as he continued. "She left before the police showed up. I . . . thought it best until we can gather a list of viable suspects."

To my surprise, Elsmed nodded, rubbing his chin thoughtfully. "I can't disagree. The sheriff seems to have tunnel vision here."

"He has his head up his ass," I muttered.

Elsmed's gaze swung my way, and I wished I hadn't let that slip. "What do you think this person wants from you, Gwen?"

That silenced me. I debated my answer—partly out of genuine speculation. And partly out of self-preservation.

When I didn't answer, Elsmed nodded knowingly. "I realize you have no reason to trust me," he said. "For what it's worth, Aelwyn was a dear friend to me, though in recent years we kept our distance for . . . various reasons." Something about the way he said that caught my attention. "Rhys has kept in close touch, letting me know how your family is doing and whether you need anything that I can provide. I want to help you, whether you can believe that or not, but in order to do that, you will have to be honest with me."

"I . . . What reasons?" I demanded.

Elsmed blinked.

"Trust goes both ways." I lifted my chin. "What were the reasons that kept you from Aelwyn?"

"Gwen," Rhys warned.

Elsmed lifted a hand and waved him off. "Valid question and fair point." He looked at me, studying. "You were the reason, Gwen. We wanted no contact or interference with fae for your own safety. So I kept my distance. We didn't want someone using me to get to you. I'm too high profile in this town to ignore that possibility. And as I said before, I do want to help you."

I chewed my lip, debating. Finally, I blew out a breath. "They want my magic."

Elsmed gave no visible reaction to that, which only made my anxiety worse. "Your fae magic?" he asked.

I nodded, swallowed hard, and then answered. "My tattoos," I said, gesturing to the ink peeking out from the collar of my shirt. "They . . . I can make them come to life. Some people have used them for violence, so I don't offer the service up anymore, but . . ."

"Someone has discovered your talent anyway," he finished. I nodded. "And they are using it against you with these murders?"

Rhys shook his head. "Aelwyn's death wasn't magical—"

"Except that they knew about the mistletoe and the cedar wood wards," I pointed out.

"And Fred and Betsy?" Elsmed asked.

"A hellhound," I said quietly. "I inked it a couple of years back."

"And do you remember the person who purchased that tattoo from you?" Elsmed asked.

Purchased. He made it sound like nothing more than buying a sweater. I snorted.

Rhys was the one who answered. When he did, his voice was grim. "It was Walter Glass. The deceased Seelie fae I mentioned earlier."

"He's the one who ran from Gwen's apartment," Elsmed said. "The glamoured Unseelie soldier?"

"Yes," Rhys said.

The room fell silent.

"I see," Elsmed said finally. He looked at Rhys. "So we know that a dark fae is here to exploit Gwen's gifts."

"How do you know he's dark?" I asked sharply.

"Because the signature on the portal shows an unauthorized fae entry," Rhys explained. "And no Seelie fae would glamour themselves to look like a dead guy in order to go unnoticed."

I scowled, but said nothing. I knew the whole light and dark argument when it came to fae. I also knew most of them lived up to their reputations, thanks to the Unseelie apprentice I'd taken on last year. But I wasn't a fan of prejudgment based on one's genes. Then again, the guy that had killed Aelwyn, and maybe even Walter, was Unseelie, so maybe it was that simple after all.

"Hmm. But we also know he doesn't want to kill her. At least not yet," Elsmed said.

I shuddered at the casual tone he used to talk about someone trying to murder me.

"And we know this dark fae can glamour himself to look like anyone he chooses," Rhys added.

"Yes, but so far, he's only appeared as the dead," I said. Both men looked at me, and I went on. "So far, he's appeared as Walter—who was already dead at the time—and I think . . ." My forehead crinkled as I thought back. "The day after Aelwyn was— I was there going through her things, and I saw something out the window. It was only a split second, but it looked so much like her. It was enough to startle me, and by the time I got outside, they were gone."

Rhys just stared at me.

"What?" I demanded irritably. "You're not the only one withholding information."

Elsmed's lips twitched. "Interesting. Well, that does present a problem, either way."

"It's going to make him damn near impossible to catch," Rhys agreed. "If Gwen won't hand over her gift—"

"He'll just take it," I finished for him, my voice hushed with horror.

Elsmed nodded somberly. "My guess is he needs you alive in order to soak up what you have to offer. That's why he continues to lure you out. He needs to get you alone long enough to steal your magic. He can't kill you until that's done."

Rhys huffed. "The question is, what can we do to identify him? I can sense his energy signature, but I can't penetrate his glamour enough to recognize his face."

Elsmed rubbed his jaw. "The Court is working with the police already on the portal breach. What you've learned about his ability to disguise himself will be valuable toward that. I can put the word out—"

"We can't go through the Court," I cut in.

"Do you have something against justice?" Elsmed asked, one brow rising in challenge.

I could feel Rhys's eyes on me, probably a glare that was meant to shut me up, but I purposely ignored him. "Considering I'm the prime suspect in my own mother's murder, I don't see how justice has much to do with it."

Elsmed considered me for a moment and then threw a glance at Rhys. "She makes a fair point." Before I could say anything else, he added, "But since revealing this new information would remove you from the suspect list, I'm assuming you're mostly just worried about Ada's preoccupation with your ability."

I gaped at him and then tried to cover it with forced innocence. "I don't know what you're—"

"Gwen, your secret is safe here, in this room." He cocked his head. "And just to reassure you, I have no intention of using your gifts for my own gain."

I just stared at him, at a loss. Apparently, the rumors about Elsmed being some sort of mind reader were true. Judging from the surprised look Rhys wore, he hadn't betrayed me. Elsmed had to have picked all that out of my mind—I'd been thinking about it hard enough since we'd arrived.

"It's not an exact science, you know," he said—again, reading my thoughts. "But you do make it easy."

"I . . ." I had no idea what to say to any of that, but I forced my back straighter, heart pounding.

"Your gift is incredible," he added.

No intonation. No clue if that was a good thing or a death sentence.

"It's dangerous," I corrected. "And not something I want becoming public knowledge."

"I've kept your secret for twenty-two years already. I have no intention of revealing it now."

Really?

"Sir, I'd like permission to put Gwen into protective custody," Rhys said, and my head snapped up.

"Wait. What?" I demanded.

"I can't say I disagree," Elsmed said slowly.

Rhys looked relieved.

"Now just hold on, damn it." My temper flared. "I'm right here. You don't have to talk about me like I'm not in the room. Or like I don't get a vote."

"Unfortunately," Elsmed went on like I hadn't spoken, "the police are diverting all of their resources to their ongoing investigations."

"Diverted where?" Rhys asked.

"The Bennett case, for one. Not to mention the ongoing investigation into Aelwyn's death and the unauthorized portal use we're still looking into."

"I think it's pretty clear all these things are connected," Rhys said.

"While that is probably true, between these and a few internal matters, we simply don't have the manpower to assign an official protective detail at this time."

"I have a friend I can call," Rhys said.

Elsmed tilted his head as if listening into the silence, then his eyes lit. "Gargoyles?" he asked, and Rhys nodded.

"I'll call Everett before we leave," Rhys said. "He can have two of them here in a couple of hours or less."

I was a little surprised at how easily Elsmed accepted that Rhys was taking matters into his own hands. Clearly, this wasn't the first time he and Rhys had worked together. I considered arguing about the protective detail, but knowing there were others watching out for me did make me feel better right now.

Elsmed turned to me. "I do recommend you resume your herbal supplements."

"My . . ." The mistletoe and the cedar wood. "You knew about that?"

"I was the one who suggested it," he said.

"But my mother gave those instructions before she sent me here from Faerie."

"Exactly."

My jaw opened. "You were there? When I was sent here?"

"I've had an eye on you for a long time, Gwen. You are very special and important to your people."

My people. He spoke as if they belonged to me. Or I to them. Like I should have felt a connection somehow. But how could I connect with a people I'd never even met?

"Funny. I don't feel very special. Or important."

"That's because Havenwood Falls is about equality. Blending in. Many of our citizens come here to get off the radar. The ones who are on it don't particularly like the sort of attention that comes with it."

"When this is all over, I'd very much like to visit Faerie," I said. The words were out before I'd thought much about them. But as they settled in the space between us, I knew I'd meant them. Without Aelwyn, I had nothing tying me here. There was Rhys, but . . . I didn't want to think about how complicated that felt just now. Or how uncertain.

Elsmed nodded. "Take a few days. Lay low. Stay with Rhys. We're doing all we can to look into the portal and the deaths. The wards in this town won't allow an intruder to go undetected for long, glamoured or not. Once this is resolved, we'll discuss your trip."

He rose, and Rhys did the same. Finally, I did too, thoughts racing at the idea that I might get to see where I came from. More importantly, I would get to meet my mother.

Elsmed opened the door and stood just outside in the hall. A clear signal this meeting was over.

Rhys nodded at the elder as he passed through, heading back the way we'd come with heavy steps. I moved to do the same, but Elsmed stopped me, bending close.

"The hellhound was quite the creation, you know."

I went still. Again, trying to decipher his true meaning. "I . . . It's awful the way it was used," I said.

"True. Still . . . very creative. And impressive."

"Thank you?" I couldn't help that it came out like a question. No one had ever complimented me like this before. Like it was a gift rather than a curse. Like I should be proud.

"Don't worry. She won't bother you much longer," he added, and I blinked, hope blossoming immediately.

"How do you know?" I asked, too desperate for answers to care too much about implicating myself any further.

He patted my arm before dipping his head and striding off, his steps completely silent against the stained hardwood. His driver-slash-secretary fell into line behind him. I stared after them, hoping like hell he was right.

I slammed the cabinet doors, stomping around the kitchen as I eavesdropped on Rhys' phone call with Sheriff Kasun. I didn't even know what I was looking for, exactly; something to take the edge off, maybe. When I finally settled on a beer and a bag of chips and stomped out again, I found Rhys leaning against the doorframe, watching me. He offered a small smile as he tossed his phone on the narrow breakfast bar.

"What did that cabinet ever do to you?" he joked.

I scowled and shoved past him, flopping onto his leather couch.

Behind me, I heard the fridge open and close. A moment later, Rhys joined me on the couch with a drink of his own. It dawned on me then how rude I'd just been to help myself to his alcohol and not offer him one, too. I sighed, cracked my beer, and reminded myself I was a guest here. And Rhys was actually trying to help me. He didn't deserve my temper.

"Sorry," I muttered, and since I didn't say the word often, it grated on me. "I just want to strangle the sheriff for not taking this seriously."

Rhys took a long drink and nodded. "I can't disagree about the strangling part. But they're doing what they can on the investigation."

Elsmed had warned us the police wouldn't share any information on the case, but Rhys had tried anyway, hoping for a different answer. No such luck.

"I heard the conversation just now," I admitted.

"Then you heard Kasun explain they can't comment on an ongoing investigation."

I pinned him with a look. "Why do you think I'm irritated? Come to think of it, why aren't you irritated?"

"Simple." Rhys shrugged. "If Kasun isn't willing to comment, it means you're not the only suspect. It means they're actually looking into this from all angles. Following all leads. It means they're going to help us catch this guy."

"Or I am the suspect and he knows that puts you guys on opposite sides," I pointed out.

"Kasun doesn't know what I am to you," Rhys said.

"Oh." I sat back, unsure what to say. Did I know what Rhys was to me? Did he?

We drank in silence for a moment. Our earlier meeting with Elsmed Fairchild played on a loop in my mind—especially his promise at the end to take care of Ada for me. If he managed to do that, I wouldn't have to give any more magical tattoos. Maybe ever. Just the thought of it made my shoulders a little less heavy. That and knowing two gargoyles had arrived to sit outside and keep an eye out for glamoured fae.

"She would be proud of you, you know."

The words jarred me, yanking me out of my hopeful daydreams of a very boring life as a very normal tattoo artist. I blinked up and found Rhys watching me closely. His words sank in slowly, and my chest ached as I thought of her. Aelwyn.

"I don't know. She was always pushing me to embrace the magic. To find a different side, to see it as a blessing instead of a curse." I shook my head. "If she were here now, she'd probably just lecture me some more about having faith in the universe or something."

"You don't?" he prompted.

"What?"

"Have faith?"

"I have faith that what you put out comes back. And that there are a lot of bad people in the world—and more of them seem to be drawn to my gift than anyone good." I couldn't help the bitterness that coated that last word.

"You expect bad things to happen to you."

I shrugged. "Expect the worst, hope for the best."

Rhys looked away, his face falling and his expression clouding over into something unreadable. I swallowed hard, not sure why I was suddenly struck with the urge to comfort him.

"I hate that," he said finally, his voice raw and coarse in the silence.

"What—" I began, but he shocked me into silence by getting up and coming to sit beside me on the couch. He set his beer aside and folded his leg, sitting sideways so he could face me. His knee jutted gently against my thigh, and my leg tingled at the small contact.

"It's my fault. For shutting you out and making it hard for you to trust people. I'm so sorry for that. I hope you can forgive me, Gwen. I hope . . . Aelwyn would want us to be there for each other."

My stomach tightened. "So all of this . . ." I waved my hand around at his living room. "It's for her?"

"What? No. Of course not."

"Because you weren't going to tell me the truth about yourself otherwise, were you?"

"Gwen, I—"

"How long are your orders for?"

He sat back. "What do you mean?"

"Your oath to protect me," I said. "Will it end when this threat is over? Or will it continue?"

"I have sworn to protect you for as long as you are alive," he said, and the way he said the words sent tingles down my spine.

"And are there . . . rules about getting involved with me? Will you get in trouble if we . . .?"

"No trouble," he said softly. "But there is one rule."

"What is it?" I asked, not even sure I wanted to know based on the intense expression he wore.

Gently, Rhys took the bag of chips and set both it and my drink on the coffee table. Then he scooted in again.

He took a deep breath before he spoke. "Once we're together, we can never break up. It's all or nothing for Protectors. Our choice has to be final."

"Oh." I licked my lips, not quite daring to tell him that's how it already was for me.

His eyes burned into mine. "That's why I stopped our kiss and walked away from you before. What I felt for you was so deep, and I knew what would happen if we continued. I knew there would be no going back for me, and I couldn't let that happen without you fully understanding what you were getting into."

"What do you mean?" I asked. "What would have happened?"

"My soul would have forged a connection with yours, and that's not something I can break," he admitted. "You would have been trapped."

I blinked, staring into his dark eyes, searching to be sure he was serious. "Oh," I said again. I was so smooth.

"I understand if you need to think about it now. Take all the time—"

"I don't need to think about it," I said quickly, then blew out a breath. "Sorry, I guess this is unexpected. I didn't think you'd ever . . ." I searched for words that hopefully wouldn't sound as awkward as they did in my head. "Rhys, you've had my heart since the moment I saw you."

He scooted closer. "You have no idea how long I've wanted to hear you say that."

"Yes, I do," I said, the words no louder than a whisper. "Because I've wanted it all along too." My heart thudded wildly, and I swallowed hard against the nerves I felt admitting all of it aloud, but he'd already apologized—more than once—and made it clear how he felt about me. All while I'd thrown it back in his face. And for what? To punish him? Except all it did was punish me, too. And I was tired of doing that. If Rhys was offering himself up, I was going to take him. Rhys was my Protector, but he was also my one and only love.

"I'm sorry for being so angry all the time," I said.

"You had a right," he began, but I shook my head.

"I use anger to cover my hurt so that people can't really see me, but all that does is make the pain worse. I want you to see the real me, Rhys."

"Gwen, you have to know how sorry I am about hurting you before." His voice was rough with emotion. "But I couldn't risk breaking my oath, and I had to protect you first and foremost. That kiss . . ." He trailed off, his expression twisting into regret.

"It's in the past." I reached for his face and ran a hand down his stubbled cheek. "I loved you when I was six and I love you now, Rhys Graywalk. You are my choice, always."

His lips spread into a slow smile that lit his eyes. "I love you, too, Gwen Facharro. I always have, and I always will."

Slowly, he reached out and let his fingers trail down my cheek and around my neck. The air around us felt tense, like the universe was just waiting for us to make the next move.

Rhys leaned in. His lips brushed over mine, and just that soft, quick contact was enough to make me tremble. I squeezed my hands together, praying he hadn't noticed the way my arms shook at his touch. But then I opened my eyes and caught sight of his wary expression. My eyes widened. "What's wrong?"

"I just want to make absolutely sure," he said uncertainly.

"Sure of what?" I asked, but he was eyeing my arms, his glance skittering over my torso and up to the ink that peeked out from underneath the collar of my shirt. "What are you doing?" I asked when he reached for the hem of my shirt and yanked it up, scanning the tattoos covering my abdomen and hips.

"After the chastity belt incident, I'm not taking any more chances," he said, frowning as he inspected my skin. "I need to know if you have any more magic ink up your sleeve." He grinned up at me, still holding my shirt up. "No pun intended."

"Hilarious," I said, yanking my shirt down again. "And no, you're safe."

The wariness turned to a calculating gleam full of mischief. This was a side of Rhys I hadn't seen in ages. "Am I now?"

I leaned away, cocking my head as he crawled closer, forcing me back until I was lying flat and he hovered over me. The romantic moment had vanished, but in its place was a playfulness I'd missed.

"Well, I don't know about safe. But nothing is going to attack you if you kiss me," I said.

He grinned, his teeth flashing at me just before his lips feathered across my own. "That's too bad," he said, lowering his body to mine. He paused long enough to wink as he added, "I've always secretly hoped it would be you doing the attacking in the end."

I wasn't one to disappoint.

A buzzing sound stirred me from sleep. The following *thud* jolted me awake. I looked around, half panicked until I realized the sound was just a cell phone vibrating with an incoming call. Rhys looked up at me from the floor, where he'd rolled off the couch thanks to our still-entwined ankles. He blinked dazedly before reaching for his phone on the coffee table. I sat up and ran a hand through my tangled hair as I struggled to get my bearings. It was early —too early for sunlight judging from the darkness that framed the edges of the closed blinds. I tried to remember how we'd both ended up tangled and half-naked on the couch. Empty beer bottles littered the coffee table along with cartons of rice and noodles.

Last night came crashing back to me in a renewed wave of heat, leaving my body tingling as I remembered the way it had felt with Rhys pressed against me, bared skin to bared skin.

"Yeah." Rhys greeted whoever was on the other end in a gravelly voice that drew my eyes to his. He stared back at me as he listened, his dark hair wild from sleep. His hand reached for my arm and stroked lazily—until he suddenly stopped moving, all of his attention focused on the caller. "Are you shitting me?"

I glanced up from where my gaze had wandered down his bare chest. He frowned, the expression sending his brows furrowing. He listened for another moment and then grunted a goodbye before hanging up and tossing the phone back to the coffee table. It slid and bumped a Napoli's takeout container before coming to a stop.

"Who was that?" I asked.

"Emile. The bar manager," he said, and judging by his tone, I knew that wasn't a good thing. He rose, fumbling through the pile of clothes on the floor and picking out his jeans. He tugged them on quickly, which only made me more alert.

"He was calling you now?" I asked.

"He just locked up and left. Late night," he added, when my eyes widened as I noted the time.

"What did he say?"

"He found something outside he thought we should see."

Before I could ask what it was, there was a sharp knock on the apartment door. Rhys jumped up, his jeans slung low on his hips as he padded down the hall. I listened as the front door to the apartment opened. Low voices rumbled, too quiet for me to make out more than a few words.

"Thanks, man," I heard Rhys say before the door clicked shut.

A second later, he reappeared, a manila folder in hand. His expression was tight, and my stomach clenched at what could possibly be inside.

I waited while Rhys opened the flap and pulled out a handful of photos, fanning them out on his lap. My chest tightened, and my stomach dropped straight to my knees. I went still, staring at the photos as Rhys picked up each one and examined it for a long moment.

"This asshole's a real piece of work," he muttered.

I couldn't believe he was so calm about it all. But then, it wasn't his future on the line here. And maybe that made less of an impact somehow.

I could only stare, openmouthed and speechless, as Rhys flipped through them all. A candid of me standing in Aelwyn's backyard the night she died, Ethan peeling away from my skin, half-inked and half-formed as he took flight. Another of the hellhound, a shimmering, translucent monster, passing through the door of Rhys's truck as it led us on the chase. And a third—this one showing Rhys and me locked in a heated kiss with me straddling him in the cab of his truck.

All of them were invasive and threatening in a different way. And all of them made it clear that whoever had taken them knew my deepest secrets. Not just my gift for ink, but my feelings. Rhys. They knew about Rhys. And the message was clear: they could get to me, to him, anytime they wanted. One way or another, eventually, they were going to hurt me.

"I think I'm going to be sick." I clutched my stomach, willing it to settle against the churning panic. I rose, pacing and shoving a hand through my hair over and over again.

"Calm down, Gwen. He's just trying to intimidate you—"

"Well, it's working!"

Rhys frowned.

I blew out a breath. "He knows my secret, Rhys." I gestured to the photo of Ethan. "He knows what I can do."

"That's why we have to show these to Sheriff Kasun."

"Are you kidding? Hell, no. Forget the sheriff. If he sees these, I'll be a suspect of totally different crimes. We need to handle this ourselves."

"Gwen, they need to know who we're—"

"You show them those photos and the first thing they'll do is lock me up."

"Elsmed then."

I hesitated, part of me wanting to resist even that. But I nodded, knowing I had to give him something. "Fine."

"I'll make the call." He was already grabbing his phone from the coffee table as he spoke.

I stood stiffly, watching Rhys move as he punched in things on his phone. I noticed his glamour tattoo inked onto his right shoulder and went still.

"Rhys, what's your tattoo?" I asked, sharply enough that he looked up from the phone.

"An arrow," he said. "Why?"

I licked my lips, thoughts whirring. Arrows. My weapon of choice.

Rhys liked knives, but I could do that too. And rope—to bind him. And—

"Gwen?" Rhys wandered closer, his eyes studying me, his brows knitting at my silence. "If you're upset, don't be. I got it for you. For your love of archery and because it reminded me when I came here that I needed to stay focused on my target—"

"I'm not upset," I said. "I just . . ."

"Gwen, what is it?"

I hesitated, wondering whether I was being too impulsive or reckless. That maybe I should stand back and let Rhys ask Elsmed for help. Hide inside this apartment and wait for the Court to find this guy and take him out. But the reality was that whatever semblance of personal safety I'd had had vanished the moment I'd seen those photos. Even inside this apartment, we were just waiting for this guy to decide he was ready. It was all on his terms, and I hated that most of all.

Fear held me back. Rhys believed in me. In my ability to use my own magic to defeat this guy. But could I really? My mother thought so, I realized, remembering the letter.

When the time comes, she will not have to hide. They will hide from her.

"I don't know yet. I need a second to think," I said slowly. I bit my lip, adding, "I have an idea but . . . Go make your call and then we can talk about it."

"Okay," he said uncertainly, but he backed off and went about sending the message he'd been typing. A moment later, his phone buzzed with an incoming call.

I waited while Rhys spoke to Elsmed or his bodyguard-slash-driver, thinking again about that arrow tattoo. I had no idea if my plan would work, but I did know that making a damned phone call was not enough. It was time to take action. It was time to finish this once and for all. On our terms. And I finally knew a way to do it.

CHAPTER 15

$\mathcal{I}$ was lost in a sea of ghostly masks, and for a split second, I couldn't breathe at the sight of all the people filling the ballroom at Whisper Falls Inn. Coming to the party was a huge risk—which was sort of the point. It was also grating on my rebellion against every commercial thing about this stupid holiday. And to top it off, I'd somehow been convinced to wear a formal dress. "For the mission," Rhys had insisted. "To really sell this we have to blend in," he'd added. I'd shot back that if we really were doing this for the mission, it meant full sleeves to hide my tattoos and a wig to cover my hair. But even with all that, Rhys had stared at me the entire drive over, and I wondered if his reasons hadn't been more selfish. Either way, we were here now. With any luck, we wouldn't need to stay long.

Beside me, Rhys was silent as he surveyed the crowded room from the entryway. We were what Aelwyn would have called "fashionably late," which meant soft music was already playing from the orchestra in the corner. Couples were already swaying to the song. And well-dressed waiters wandered between milling guests, offering hors d'oeuvres. A familiar face caught my eye—the only face not wearing a full white mask. Our hostess, Michaela Petran, was fast approaching us. She wore a forced smile wide enough I thought her face would crack.

"Gwen Facharro, holy shit! I can't believe you're here! And Rhys. So glad you guys could make it. Nice to see you two together." She added more emphasis on the last word than was necessary, but I didn't argue.

"Thanks for having us," Rhys said, a lot less enthusiastically than Michaela. "What do we need to do, exactly?"

"Well, first off, you both need masks." She thrust white masks at each of us, still grinning.

"And why is that, exactly?" I asked.

Rhys shot me a scowl. I knew I shouldn't question this. It was one of the reasons we'd chosen this venue to lure our dark fae out of hiding —the masks. The anonymity. But I couldn't go quietly, apparently.

"Love goes beyond what we can see on the outside," Michaela explained. "Cupid's aim strikes at the heart—that's how you know it's true love."

I did my best to hold in the snort. I didn't disagree with the sentiment; true love was about much more than looks. But the idea that these silly arrows could help someone find their soul mate was such a gimmick. Everyone knew love spells weren't real.

"Got it," I mumbled.

Rhys stayed silent.

We each took our masks and slid them on. I adjusted mine carefully so that I could see out of the tiny eye-holes, but the visibility wasn't great. My muscles tensed as I realized spotting our guy before he attacked was going to be even harder without peripheral vision.

"And here are your arrows." Michaela held out two white arrows trimmed in gold, one for each of us.

Rhys grabbed his and nodded at Michaela. "Thanks."

I took mine gingerly. Michaela smiled at that and winked. "When their aim is true, they'll light up for you. Follow the arrow's tip to your special lover's lips."

I blinked. Was she for real?

Rhys shifted. "Um, thanks."

Michaela herded us inside. "Happy kissing," she called as we walked off.

I decided to pretend I hadn't heard her. She was becoming more and more like her old bubbly high-school self, whom I'd never been a fan of.

Rhys let me lead the way, and I wove through the guests toward the bar at the far end of the room. If I had to be here, I needed a stiff drink, that was for sure. Skirts swished at my feet, and people in masks murmured hellos as we weaved in and out of the bodies. Rhys stayed close on my heels, and I knew he was nervous about the anonymity. But it was the best idea we'd had, and Elsmed had actually endorsed it when I'd insisted on pitching it to him last night. In fact, he had assured us he'd have a security team stationed around the room, too, including two gargoyles I'd never met, but who made excellent protectors, according to Rhys. And, of course, Michaela had been alerted that there was a possibility of an arrest tonight. She didn't know we were involved, and I was glad for that. I'd hate to be the one to ruin her party. From the looks of it, she'd put a lot of effort into this night, her first big event since taking over the inn.

If I thought the town square had been lavish, this was opulent. White roses were everywhere. In the centerpieces for the standing tables, draped from the stage, and hovering above us along the walls, held in place by some sort of magic—or really strong duct tape. And carefully placed among all the white were pops of red. Roses, silks, and even mixed in among the glassware, everywhere I looked, the red grabbed at me. It was supposed to be classy romance, I was sure. But it reminded me too much of the blood dripping from my hands as I'd kneeled over Aelwyn's body.

"Gwen?"

I blinked, snapping back to the party as if the whole thing had reappeared out of thin air. Rhys was waiting, and I wracked my brain, trying to recall what he'd just said. "Um, wine?"

It was, thankfully, the right answer.

Rhys nodded and turned back to the bartender. I scanned the room, forcing myself to breathe evenly and focus on the moment at hand. Elsmed promised his men would be here, but so far, no one was standing out as possible undercover agent. Everyone seemed to be here for drinks and kisses—and there were plenty of both to go around.

I thought of the weapons we'd smuggled inside—several of them worn in the form of fresh ink against our skin—and hoped they would be enough. Or that our dark fae would show up at all. Maybe kissing strangers wasn't his thing.

We got our drinks and then wandered to the edge of the room. I felt a lot better with my back against the wall, and I suspected Rhys would too.

"Do you think he'll come?" I asked, facing the crowd, constantly searching the anonymous faces for some sign of our killer.

"I think if he does, we'll be ready for him," Rhys said quietly. I'd been amazed at the sheer amount of knives he'd managed to attach and conceal on his body before we'd left. How he could walk like that, while still bending his knees, was pretty impressive. Still, I'd seen enough damage left by this guy to be nervous for Rhys. For both of us.

"I thought I'd recognize more people. I thought they'd have their masks off by now," I said, irritated by the lack of recognition for people I'd literally grown up around.

"You just have to look for other markers," Rhys assured me. "See there? The woman with short, silver hair?" He pointed. "That's Jetta Mills. And there? The purple hair? That's Julianna Fairchild."

"Yeah. Okay, that makes sense. I see it now." I forced a deep breath in, then out slowly.

"Look for those clues," Rhys encouraged. "And if you see anything strange, let me know."

For a few minutes, we watched and quietly pointed out when we each recognized someone in the crowd. The sight of the familiar figures made me feel a little better until I remembered our guy could literally be any of them now.

Rhys finished his drink, and a waiter appeared to take his empty glass. I handed him mine, still half-full. I couldn't drink when I was already so tightly wound.

"Don't scratch it," I said quietly when the waiter was gone. "It'll draw attention."

Rhys dropped his hand from where he'd been rubbing at a spot on his arm through his suit jacket. I watched his hand fall to his side and then let my gaze trail up his arms to his chest and back down again.

My thoughts wandered to last night; the ink I'd given him and then the part that came after . . .

"Are you checking me out again?"

I jerked my gaze back to his and could just barely make out his eyes through his mask's holes. They were crinkled in silent amusement.

"I'm checking to make sure your bandages haven't leaked through to your shirt," I said stiffly.

"Uh-huh. We both know your ink didn't draw enough blood for that," he said, clearly trying to bait me. "You're too good at what you do."

"Fine. I was checking you out," I admitted, softened by the compliment. "You look pretty nice in a suit."

"You look pretty nice all the time," he shot back. "Especially naked on my couch. But tonight, in that—" He nodded at the white gown I wore. "You look like an angel."

I snorted. "Are you trying to insult me?"

He blinked and then rolled his eyes. "I didn't mean a literal angel. Havenwood Falls has plenty of those. I meant . . . you look hot," he finally finished.

I smiled behind my mask, glad he couldn't see how stupidly large my grin was. "Thanks."

On my right, someone cleared their throat, and I jumped, nearly dropping my arrow.

"Hello," said a male voice, somewhat amused as I tried to breathe through the adrenaline pumping through me.

"Hello," I countered uncertainly.

I didn't recognize the voice, which meant it wasn't Walter—or anyone else I knew. Rhys and I had already discussed this. Our dark fae could still be running around as Walter—but probably not. In fact, chances were he'd already moved on to another glamoured disguise. Especially now that everyone knew Walter was supposed to be dead. He could literally be anyone. Which was exactly why we'd chosen Cupids & Cuties as our backdrop. If he was going to be anonymous, so were we. I just hoped between the masks that hid our faces and our freshly inked tattoos serving as weapons, it would be enough.

"I was just wondering if . . ." The mystery man beside me held up his arrow, pointing it awkwardly at me.

We both waited. Nothing happened.

Finally, he sighed. "Well, it was worth a shot. Have a good night," he said and wandered off, still clutching his unlit arrow.

I looked over at Rhys and found him watching our mystery man with narrowed eyes.

"What?" I asked.

"He thought his arrow might light for you," Rhys said in a strange voice.

"Ridiculous." I huffed.

"Are you referring to the arrow pointing toward true love or the idea that anyone could want you to be theirs?" Rhys asked.

"Take your pick," I muttered.

"Gwen, he's not the first person whose attention you've attracted tonight," Rhys said.

I felt my cheeks heating. "But . . . it's not like any of them talk to me normally."

"You're a little . . . hard to approach when you're not disguised," he pointed out.

I scowled.

"Not to mention the mistletoe you take."

"Point taken."

Rhys continued watching the human mystery man, and I bit my lip, still trying to decipher his strange tone. Was he actually jealous of some human with a spelled arrow? I'd been a little distant since we'd slept together on Rhys's couch. It wasn't so much the sex as what came afterward that had me unsettled. Rhys said he wanted me—not just for today but forever. And goddess knew I wanted him. But with a dark fae killer after me and the future so uncertain, I wasn't sure whether I could let myself believe him just yet. Maybe when all this was over. Maybe then I could really open myself to Rhys and his promises.

I let my thoughts wander, both of us still watching and scanning the guests. But everyone looked like they were supposed to be here. A few arrows lit up here and there, and people giggled or just tore off their masks, smiling—all too happy to lock lips with their other half.

"These arrows are really stupid," I muttered, feeling like a Scrooge more than ever. I wasn't even sure why.

"Really? I think they're kind of nice."

I rolled my eyes, still watching the latest couple to match arrows. They'd removed their masks and pressed their lips together, both of them unconcerned at the room full of onlookers.

"How can you think it's nice? The magic is obviously fake," I scoffed. "It's like a classy orgy that—" I pulled up short as I turned to Rhys, my eyes locked on his arrow. It was lit a bright white. And the point was aimed at me.

When I didn't react, Rhys reached for my arrow and gently spun it in my hand. He set it back against my palm so I was the one holding it, the point aimed at his stomach. Immediately, the entire thing lit up to a bright white.

"Well, shit," I muttered.

Even with the mask, I knew Rhys was grinning as he closed the distance between us. "Looks like we get our own orgy right here in the corner."

"Rhys, we have to stay focused," I began but he'd already ripped his mask aside, leaning toward me, lips puckered. He grabbed the edge of my mask, lifting it just enough to expose my mouth—and pressed his lips to mine.

CHAPTER 16

*V*aguely, I was aware of someone clearing their throat. It took me a moment to come out of the haze of the kiss. When a hand closed over my elbow—and I realized both of Rhys' were wrapped around my hips—I jumped, yanking back and whirling on the third hand. A man stood there, masked and dressed in a tux with a red bow tie. His hair was slicked back, and his skin was pale. A vampire, maybe? His dark eyes were sharp enough as he studied me. I dropped my very human glamour long enough to let my senses read him properly.

I stiffened. A vampire, yes. Not that I was concerned. But he had another scent on him. One I recognized all too well now. The dark fae we were hunting.

Rhys took a step forward so that he was blocking me from the man. I could only guess he'd noticed it too. "Can we help you with something?"

The vamp rolled his eyes, not bothering to react to Rhys or the way he'd drawn up his chest and shoulders.

"Here," the vamp said in a bored voice. He thrust a slip of paper at Rhys and wandered off.

While Rhys unfolded it, my eyes tracked the vamp, but he made a straight line to the door and ducked out of the ballroom. Huh. Someone whose aversion to this party outweighed my own.

Rhys growled, and I snapped back to the note he'd been handed.

"What does it say?" I asked.

"It's from Elsmed. He has new information. Wants us to meet him out back." Rhys didn't move, though.

I bit my lip. "Do you think it's a trap?"

"If it is, that means our guy knows Elsmed is helping us. It also means—I hate to say it, but . . ."

"He could *be* Elsmed by now," I finished.

Rhys grimaced.

"The only thing we know for sure is that he isn't you or me," I said, trying to stay calm even though my heart was threatening to pound right out of my chest.

Suddenly, the partygoers filling the ornate ballroom before us were more threatening than festive. And I wanted nothing more than to be gone from this room.

"Right, but . . ." Rhys trailed off.

"But what?" I asked, because if Rhys was nervous, I was nervous.

He hesitated. "In order to protect ourselves from whatever's waiting out there, the smart thing would be to split up. I go out to meet Elsmed and you—"

"Do not say 'stay behind,'" I warned.

"Actually, I was going to say you should watch my back," he said. "Let's slip into one of the rooms upstairs with a balcony. You can let Ethan loose and watch me from there. If anything looks wrong, you have your tattoos and can help get me out of there."

I mulled that over, but he had a point. Our entire plan tonight had hinged on improvising once we knew where "Walter" was hiding. I'd already assumed part of that would include splitting off to appear weaker to the dark fae we wanted to draw out. So, I couldn't complain about this detour. Well, I could, but it wouldn't do much good.

"Deal," I said.

"Let's go."

I let him take my hand, and together we navigated our way back to the door. Thankfully, Michaela was nowhere to be found, so we didn't have to explain our early exit. In fact, the lobby and stairs were all deserted, and we found our way upstairs without much trouble.

Out on the balcony, Rhys waited while I let Ethan out, and we watched as he took flight, soaring up and out of sight quickly. Then we both stared down at the east side of the inn's property.

Immediately to my right, a third-floor turret rose and I had to lean around it to scan the rest of the lawn. From the balcony's view, the large lawn was bordered by a narrow driveway that led down to a row of cottages on the right. On the other side of the cottages, a line of trees separated the inn's property from the rest of the block.

To my left, the street and shop lights of Main Street sparkled in the distance, reflecting off the snow below, bright enough to see for a long way out.

Even with my fae sight and the brightly-lit night, I couldn't spot Elsmed or anyone else among the trees that lay beyond the property's edge.

"Something moved down there," I said, "But I can't tell who."

"Same here." Rhys turned to me. "If it turns out to be a trap, I want you to—"

"Rhys," I warned sharply. "Don't say something that makes me sound like a damned damsel in distress. If it's a trap, I'm saving your ass. If it's not, I'm still saving your ass."

His lips twitched, and he laid a hand gently against my cheek. "Deal. If you need me—"

"I'll send Ethan. And Rhys? If this guy shows up and he's . . . I don't know, got his claws in my power or something, get Elsmed."

"Why?"

"I don't know, but something tells me he'll know what to do."

"Were you always this bossy and interrupting?"

"Were you always this overprotective?"

"Yes," he said without pause.

I shrugged. "Guess we haven't changed then."

He grinned and pressed a quick kiss to my lips that left me panting despite the fact that it was over nearly before it began. Then he strode to the door, and with a final glance back that said everything with a single, smoldering look, he walked out.

I waited, biting my thumbnail until Rhys appeared on the lawn below. He didn't look up or acknowledge that he knew I was watching him. I hadn't expected him to. I watched in silence as he made his way around the cottages and toward the thick trees that lined the back of the property. He stopped just short of entering them, and I called to Ethan, trying to pick up on any hidden dangers he'd found.

But Ethan was quiet.

A moment later, my familiar returned, swooping low and coming to land on the railing of the balcony where I stood.

"Nothing to see out there, huh?" I asked him quietly.

Ethan offered a jerky motion that I knew was meant to be a nod.

I looked down again, but Rhys still stood at the edge of the trees, clearly debating something. Slowly, Rhys took a few steps forward until I could no longer see him from where I stood.

The moment he was out of sight, Ethan began to shriek. I gripped the railing, wondering if I should call out as well, urging Rhys back to the safety of the lawn. Too late, I realized the danger wasn't down there after all. It was here. With me.

CHAPTER 17

*T*he door at my back creaked as it opened, and I whirled. Ethan screeched, which only added to the rush of adrenaline that poured into my veins, rooting my feet to where I stood. Deputy Conall stood in the doorway, and I didn't know whether to be relieved or terrified. Either way, my reflexes were working faster than ever. I'd already called up the magical tattoo and now held a bow in one hand and an arrow in the other. I dropped my hands to my sides at the sight of Conall.

"Gwen?" He made no move to approach me, probably because of the terror already written on my features.

I struggled to find my voice—and to make it work.

"What do you want?" I asked. The spot on my thigh where I'd inked the arrows—to hide them—still tingled from how quickly I'd spelled them into solid objects.

"We received a tip that Walter Glass has been spotted in the area. We'd like you to come down to the station until he's found."

I studied him, debating whether or not to trust him. But despite his apparent dislike for me, I had no reason to doubt his story. Doubting his identity was another matter. I kept my gaze locked on his, searching for that flash I'd seen in Dead Walter when he'd jumped from my apartment. If this was a glamour, that flash of color behind his eyes would give it away, but so far his eyes were normal.

"And Rhys?" I asked, taking a step toward him—which only made Ethan shriek louder. "Is that what Elsmed wanted? To bring him in until this blows over?"

"Elsmed Fairchild?" Deputy Conall frowned. "Uh. I didn't realize he was involved, so I can't answer that."

I halted. "I think I'll just wait right here, if it's all the same to you."

Ethan still gave a warning sound, but the shrieking quieted.

Deputy Conall looked annoyed.

"Fine." He closed the door behind him and took up a position in the corner, leaning against the wall next to a photo print of Havenwood Falls circa fifty years ago.

"You don't have to stay," I told him.

"Actually, I do. Sheriff Kasun's orders."

I huffed.

So did he.

A moment of silence ticked by slowly.

Finally, I turned to glance back outside, scanning quickly for Rhys. He hadn't reemerged from the trees, and with every minute that he was gone, my worry grew. Something wasn't right. Not with Elsmed's cryptic summons and not with Deputy Douchebag hovering behind me.

I spun, ready to chew Conall out for whatever he'd just done. But he was still in his place in the corner.

Beside him stood Walter.

He glared at me, and I had to blink several times before I realized it wasn't my eyesight that was washing him out.

Walter was a ghost.

That was a trick I hadn't anticipated.

"Hello, Miss Facharro. It's been a while," Walter said.

Behind Walter, Deputy Conall went pale, and I could only assume being confronted with the backside of a dead guy was a first for him.

"What the hell are you doing here?" I demanded.

On the railing behind me, Ethan shrieked wildly.

"Shh," I hissed at him, so that I could hear over his shrill call.

Silent now, Ethan was practically molting. Walter watched him warily.

"I'm back to see this through," he said defiantly.

His feet never moved, but somehow he was closer now. I took a step back, wishing Rhys would hurry the hell up. Across the room, Deputy Conall toyed with the cuffs attached to his belt. His brows were wrinkled, and I knew he was contemplating how the hell to cuff a ghost. So was I.

"See what through?" I asked.

"My deal with the Unseelie mercenary, of course." He sighed. "Trusting an Unseelie, and a Greater Fae more powerful than me, might have been my fatal mistake, but I still get my revenge . . . and I can't complain." He held up his hands and did a little dance in place. "I'm mobile again!"

I raised my brows at that. "Walter," I said, speaking as if to an ignorant child. "What the hell are you talking about?"

Walter's eyes narrowed, and his good mood vanished. "I'm talking about getting revenge on you for killing my sister."

"I didn't kill anyone."

"Maybe not directly. But your tattoos have. And that means her blood is on your hands."

My body went cold. "Your sister is . . .?"

"Sarah. My sister *was* Sarah," he corrected, "until her husband used his magical tattoo to cause her heart to fail. A tattoo that you inked and then infused with a spell. Her death is on you, and I vowed that even if it killed me, I'd see you suffer for what you'd done. It took time and a lot of planning, let me tell you, but I finally found someone who wanted you dead more than I did." He barked out a laugh. "Who knew it would be someone even more capable than me—and someone even more dangerous."

I couldn't answer, not when I could barely breathe. Walter's sister had been Sarah? The fae woman whose husband had . . .

My first magical tattoo gone awry.

I felt numb underneath the crushing weight of the familiar guilt. Aelwyn's death I could avenge. But this . . . this was justified. Whether I liked it or not, Walter was right. I deserved to suffer.

"Walter, what happened to your sister was a tragedy. I can't tell you how sorry—"

"Save it," Walter snapped. "The time for talking is over. You're my only unfinished business here, and I'd really like some god damned peace and quiet now, so just hurry up and die already."

"You're wrong," Deputy Conall said.

Walter rounded on him. "What the hell do you know about it?" he boomed.

"I know that, according to the coroner's report, iron poisoning was listed as her cause of death." Deputy Conall's voice was clear, his words certain.

I blinked.

Walter went silent.

"Are you sure?" I asked.

"Positive. I never forget a case file I sign off on."

He held my gaze, unflinching, and for the first time, his was free from annoyance.

If what he was saying was true . . .

"No, I don't believe it. Doctored the evidence. I saw the heart tattoo missing from my brother-in-law's body, and I know—"

"According to the note Lyle left, he activated that heart spell to try to save her when he'd realized what happened," Deputy Conall said.

Walter's lip curled. "Lies." He whipped around to me. "All lies to try to stop this. But it's not going to work. I will avenge Sarah."

He roared, and although I wasn't sure what he could do to me as a ghost, I backed up as he came. In a swift move, I notched the arrow in my hand and pulled it taut. When Walter still came, I let it fly.

It passed straight through Walter's ghostly form and narrowly missed Deputy Conall's shoulder as it buried itself in the wall. "Shit!" He glared at me. "Watch it."

"Sorry," I managed, but Walter was still coming.

I lowered the bow, and it clattered from my hand, useless. Damn.

Walter reached for me, and I jerked backward faster than I'd meant to when I realized his fingers had actually caught hold of my dress. They wrapped firmly around the strap and pulled. I yanked against his grip, startled. How could he touch me if I couldn't kill him? Most ghosts couldn't summon the energy necessary to manipulate the physical world, but then most ghosts weren't carrying a grudge like Walter's.

The fabric ripped away, freeing me, and I went stumbling backward onto the balcony. My heel caught on my dress, but the momentum was too strong to stop.

A sharp pain lit up my back and hips as I hit the railing. Ethan flapped his wings, desperate to move out of the way as my arms flailed. Walter still came, his ghostly eyes crazed. I felt my body give over the railing and knew I wasn't going to be able to stop myself.

I was going over.

The last thing I saw before I tumbled was another figure—ghostly and old and just as crazed as Walter, as she raced for him with her arms outstretched.

Then I fell.

I grunted, the wind whooshing out of me as two arms caught me roughly. The impact delayed the scream building in my throat, but when I opened my eyes and saw Rhys hovering over me, my relief outweighed the pain, and I sighed.

"Impeccable timing," I managed to say.

Rhys was not amused. "Are you hurt?"

I shook my head, glancing up toward the balcony. Sounds came from there—something shattering and then a moan—but I couldn't see anything. Ethan had left his perch and was circling, relieved that I was all right.

"I can walk," I said.

Rhys set me upright and held me steady until he was sure I wouldn't fall. "What happened?"

"Walter happened."

Rhys started to move, but I stopped him. "Not Walter the dark fae. Walter the ghost."

"What?"

I sighed. "It's a long story but, believe it or not, I think Madame Luiza has him under control."

Madame Luiza, Michaela's aunt who'd managed the inn for a brief time, had passed away last year. Aelwyn had spoken of rumors that she'd returned as a ghost and now spent her time watching over her family. I believed the rumors after what I'd just seen. She was not a bad security system, really.

"Luiza Petran?" Rhys asked. "Isn't she dead?"

I shrugged. "So is Walter. Sounds like a good match to me. What happened in the woods?"

He hesitated. "It was a trap."

"Where's Elsmed?"

"No idea."

"Where's your tattoo?" I asked, suddenly struck by the fact that his shirt had been peeled back to reveal smooth skin where I'd inked him last night.

"I had to use it."

"Was there something in the woods? Did you see him?"

He shook his head. "Not him. Another hellhound."

"Where would he get another hellhound?" I asked.

"No idea. I think this asshole anticipated how we would have armed ourselves and found a way to conjure his own monster to try to use up our weapons."

"But you didn't see him?" I asked, suddenly aware of how exposed we were out here.

"No. Did you?"

"I think . . . I might have."

"Where?"

"I don't know for sure but . . . follow me."

We didn't make it more than three steps before a figure appeared. Rhys and I stopped. Ethan screeched, but the figure ignored it, all his attention focused on us.

"I know who you are," I said in a voice that I hoped sounded more confident than I felt. When I'd warned Rhys earlier that the dark fae could be disguised as anyone, I hadn't realized just how true that would prove to be.

Between us and him, the darkness seemed to grow its own shadows.

The figure took a step toward us, his broad shoulders and muscled arms so familiar to me. Even the swoop of the hair over his forehead—

it really had grown long—was like a comfortable blanket or the scent of herbs in the foyer at home. Something I'd know anywhere.

"Rhys," I said quietly.

Both figures answered. "Yes?"

I didn't wait for the imposter next to me to notice he'd just been outed. Instead, I rammed my elbow into his ribs and sprinted for the figure up ahead.

The real Rhys Graywalk.

CHAPTER 18

Fake Rhys roared and pushed forward, arms outstretched as he chased me. Up ahead, Real Rhys was whispering furiously at the tattoos I'd given him, willing them to form into three dimensional weapons. The knives Fake Rhys had claimed were gone suddenly sprang to life and found their way into Real Rhys's hands as he ran for us. I gathered my own magic faster than I ever had before, and the ropes I'd tattooed on my own skin sprang forth. I whispered the phrase I knew would activate the magic, nothing more than a few broken words paired with my own strength of intention, and the ropes spun out into the air, wrapping themselves almost instantly around Fake Rhys' ankles. They tightened into a lasso and then yanked hard.

He went down with a loud grunt.

Real Rhys reached me and pulled me against him in a fierce hug. He ran a hand over my hair and down my neck then pulled back long enough to search my face. "You're all right?"

"I'm good."

"How did you know it was me?" he asked while Fake Rhys thrashed on the ground nearby.

I rolled my eyes. "You weren't nearly as paranoid with worry for me as usual. And when I told you to follow me, you did it without question. That was a dead giveaway."

Real Rhys grinned and planted a hard kiss on my mouth. "Don't ever change."

It was all we had time for before Fake Rhys was groaning and pushing up on his hands. When he raised his head, his eyes were ringed in a bright yellow that was definitely not a trait he'd stolen from Rhys.

"Gwen, get back," Rhys said, already shoving me aside as he brandished his knives.

Fake Rhys was already working at untangling the ropes, but my magic held them in place. Still, it wasn't enough to stand against whatever he had. When his hands couldn't untie them, he wrapped his fingers around the rope and whispered words I didn't understand. The ropes slipped free, their spell broken.

He sprang to his feet as the ropes melted into thin air, the spellwork having run its course. Real Rhys was ready. In a move too fast for me to see, Fake Rhys drew his own set of knives, and the two men launched themselves into a violent dance accompanied by the sound of clanking metal and soft grunts.

They moved almost too fast for me to keep up with, and I knew if a human happened along, we were all going to be in a world of trouble for it. The only glamour left was the magic that held our human disguise in place. But reflexes, strength, speed, magic—it was all out there. And it was only a matter of time before the police or Elsmed or someone came along and noticed.

The longer they fought, the more I realized what an even match they were. Leaps, stabs, and parries—they moved like carbon copies of one another. Probably because they were. My anxiety left my palms clammy and Ethan practically wringing his wings in helplessness.

I had to end this. Now.

The first specks of magic on my arm sprang to life at my coaxing. Translucent images of knives and bindings, more rope like the coil I'd already unleashed and even zip ties. I kept concentrating, my impatience threatening to weaken the whole thing. But Rhys needed me, and I finally understood—and gave myself permission to use—what was really available to me. For so long, I'd held back on this part of myself, because I'd been terrified it would be used to hurt others, but I couldn't hold back anymore. It was time to use all of it.

I kept calling on the magic that was laced into the ink I wore. The weapons materialized in my hands, but it wasn't enough. Not nearly.

Before my eyes, Fake Rhys began to change form. First, his skin tone darkened until his hands and face were a darker brown than they'd been before.

While they fought, the rest of the dark fae's features changed until he no longer looked like Rhys at all. His big eyes glowed that same strange yellow as I'd seen before. His nose grew longer, and his lips thinned. His cheeks sank in, revealing a much leaner form than he'd had as Fake Rhys. His ears elongated until they came to a point, and he rose in height until he towered over the real Rhys.

I gasped as the rest of the dark fae's glamour dropped and his magic filled the air around me. It felt like invisible hands grabbing at my throat and choking me until I couldn't breathe. I coughed, then dropped to my knees as the invisible hands tightened to cut off my air completely. Dark spots danced in front of my eyes, but no matter how hard I pried, I couldn't pull the pressure away. I couldn't even get a hold on the invisible force.

Rhys heard my wheezing and turned, but the dark fae used the distraction to his advantage, and I watched in silent horror as the dark fae's knife sliced a gash in Rhys's cheek. Blood rose to the surface and then began to drip down Rhys's face.

I tried to scream but no sound came.

Rhys stumbled back, wincing and trying to regain his focus as he pressed his free hand to his cheek. The dark fae didn't chase him, and instead, he stared intently at where I knelt on the snow. His forehead creased in concentration, and I knew he was putting all his effort into attacking me now.

Desperate, I fought harder against the invisible hands at my throat, but it was no use. I waited for the moment the hands would tighten and I'd suffocate completely, but the pressure remained the same.

Slowly, my energy began to drain and my body sagged as if something or someone were siphoning my strength. One by one, the magic in the tattoos I wore began to blink out. I could feel the moment they left my body, and more than that, I could feel my own well of untapped magic growing smaller and smaller. I tried calling out to Ethan, but there was only silence where our bond had been before.

More tattoos began to appear on the dark fae, until his skin was just as covered with them as I was. Some of them glowed and some pulsed, and his eyes gleamed brighter as if the tattoos themselves were energizing him now.

Rhys roared and ran at the dark fae with his knives raised, but the dark fae parried easily and swiped the knives away. It was clear that whatever magic the dark fae was taking from me now was fueling him. If we wanted to beat him, I had to break free of his attempt to rob me of my magic

I had to take his instead.

The invisible hands around my throat remained, and the pressure was just enough to let me take small sips of air. He wanted me conscious, for now anyway. I didn't have much time, but I was determined not to let this asshole win.

My mother had said in her letter that someday they would hide from me. Today was going to be that day.

I gave up fighting against the invisible force around my throat, and instead, I put all my energy into the magic the dark fae was sucking out of me.

The magic resisted at first, and I felt like I'd been caught in a massive game of tug of war. I was sweating with the effort of calling my magic back to me, but a moment later, the pressure around my throat eased slightly. Rhys continued to circle and stab at the dark fae, and even though he wasn't making much progress with his weapons, I knew he was saving me by keeping the asshole distracted.

It was exactly what I needed now.

I kept pulling.

With a groan, I yanked one final time and took back the last of my magic. The tattoos remained on the dark fae's skin, but they no longer pulsed for him, and I knew they would answer only to me.

Using every ounce of magic I had inside me, I called out loud to the tattoos that covered the dark fae's skin. "Answer me! I am your master. Not him. Activate!"

Like I was the pied piper of ink, the tattoos peeled away from the stranger's skin and began to take form. I held my breath, hoping like hell my magic was capable of everything I suspected.

Rhys cried out, and I almost lost my hold on the magic as I jerked my attention to the two men. Both of them were winded now, their chests heaving as they stood several feet apart and eyed each other. Rhys bent over, cradling his arm. The dark fae stood tall, eyeing the injury with a look of triumph.

Fear, more real than anything I'd experienced so far, stilled me. If anything happened to Rhys . . . it wouldn't matter if I won. Not if I couldn't share the victory with him.

"Your warrior is no match for me." The dark fae sneered and then started for me.

Fear almost drowned me as I noticed how much the real Rhys was struggling to stay on his feet.

"And your magic is no match for mine," I shot back.

"My tattoos have been inked by some of the most powerful fae in the world," he said. "You are nothing compared to them. I took their power for my own, and I'll do the same to you. It is time to give your magic over to me."

The invisible hands brushed my throat again, and I scrambled back. If he was telling the truth, that meant I wasn't the first fae he'd come across with my particular gift. If he weren't trying to kill me for it, I might have been tempted to ask him about them, but those answers would have to wait.

Rhys lunged forward, knife out, distracting the dark fae once again. But I knew this burst of energy was temporary for him. If he was wounded . . . I didn't want to think about that. Or whether my preparations would be enough.

"Hang on," I called out, and then refocused everything I had back to the magic I'd called up.

Like ripping off a Band-Aid, all of the tattoos suddenly peeled away from the dark fae's skin. Not just the ones I'd felt him steal from me, but all of them. Even the ancient ink, probably from the fae he'd mentioned, ripped away from his flesh at my command.

The dark fae screamed, and I smiled grimly in satisfaction.

One by one, the tattoos floated up into the air, and then I used my magic to snuff them out. It wasn't nearly as hard as I'd imagined it to be. In fact, so much of their magic had already been poured out, they snapped like twigs against my will. When a particularly dark symbol lifted and vanished alongside the others, the dark fae stumbled. The glow in his creepy eyes dimmed.

"Whatever you're doing, keep it up," Rhys yelled.

I worked harder at snuffing out the magic of the tattoos he wore. With each one, he looked visibly weaker and slower, and I realized he stored everything in the ink. His ability to steal an appearance, the invisible hands he'd used to choke me, and finally, an intricate rune offering healing from any physical injury. Spells. They'd all been spells he'd stolen from other fae he'd hunted. One by one, I stripped them all until I could feel his magic waning.

When I got to the healing rune, I glanced over at Rhys and nodded.

"Now, Rhys," I yelled as I crushed the rune's magic with my own.

It shattered and then vanished like a dust cloud above my head.

"This is for Aelwyn," Rhys yelled, and I shivered at the depth of feeling in his words.

A second later, Rhys sent his knife flying through the air and the blade sank into the dark fae's stomach, sending the asshole to his knees.

The tendrils of invisible pressure vanished. I scrambled to my feet and rushed over to the dark fae now lying on the ground, my Rhys standing over him, his knife dripping with the fae's blood.

"Who are you?" I demanded.

He remained silent.

I crushed two more of his magical tattoos, and he winced. It gave me a sense of satisfaction to know it hurt him.

"Who are you?" I repeated.

"I am Cael, warrior for the Unseelie Court."

"You're a thief," Rhys spat as he wiped the blood from the cut on his cheek.

"You were sent by the Unseelie Court to steal my magic?" I asked.

Cael nodded, then winced, clutching at the wound on his

stomach, which was bleeding a lot more heavily now than before I'd removed his healing rune.

"Why do you have tattoos?" I demanded.

"You are not the only fae who can bring their art to life," he said. "The Unseelie see the value in this gift, even if your own people do not."

"You mean you see how it can be used to hurt people," I said.

"Yes, I am aware of the Seelie's distaste for doing what must be done. It is why I am not here to recruit you."

"You act like you're doing me a favor by trying to steal my magic and then kill me," I said.

Cael sighed, but he didn't bother to argue. "We've been looking for you for a long time, but you were undetectable for years. Then Walter . . ." He broke off and started coughing.

"Walter hired you to take revenge on me because he thought I'd helped kill his sister," I finished.

Cael nodded. "His need for vengeance brought you to me on a silver platter. It also made him weak and easy to kill when it served me."

I resisted the urge to kick him for that. "But then you got a little carried away, didn't you?"

He coughed again. "Your magic is unlike anything we've ever seen. Even your mother—" He broke off, and I knelt, grabbing him by the collar. Suddenly, any hesitation I'd had over actually causing another creature harm vanished.

"What do you know about my mother?" I demanded.

"I know you're already more powerful than her if you've just destroyed my healing rune." He coughed.

Rhys looked up at me sharply, questions in his eyes, and I realized he had no idea what I'd done, because he'd been too busy fighting Cael. I ignored his confusion, my questions burning a hole right through me.

"What did you do to her?" I demanded.

"Moonlaith is well hidden. Well protected," Cael muttered, as if he hated that fact.

He blinked, and when he opened his eyes, I saw that they were no longer glowing. Probably a product of his life force draining. My shoulders sagged in quiet relief. My mother was alive. Wherever she was, she was alive.

"Her warrior was fierce," he added. "Like yours. He gave himself up to protect her and she escaped our grasp. We have not been able to get close to her since then."

In an instant, my relief vanished and was replaced by fury.

Rhys had said my mother's warrior had died protecting her, and that meant—

"You killed my father," I said through clenched teeth.

"I was following orders," Cael said, and his dismissive tone only made me angrier.

"Gwen, someone's coming," Rhys warned, and I looked up to see a couple of men approaching from across the property. They were still pretty far off, but I couldn't afford anyone to notice the amount of magic I was wielding just now. "Whatever you're going to do, do it now," Rhys added.

I didn't hesitate.

Sparks flew in more ways than one. All around me, magic snapped and crackled and left tiny sparks in its wake. Like sharpened flint grating against stone, heat surged in the air between the three of us, filling the space with electricity. My fingertips tingled even before I reached for Rhys. When my hand slid into his, my body thrummed.

One by one, Cael's tattoos shattered, and the magic was stripped from his skin. Tiny specks of light blinked on and off over our heads while I worked, and I knew it was the last of the magic snuffing out of each one of his inked spells. I could only hope those approaching were too far off to notice.

Rhys stood watching in silent wonder.

At my feet, I felt the last of Cael's life force drain away. The remnants of his tattoos and any spells inside them drained right along with his final breath. On a gasp, he shuddered and then fell still, dead.

I waited to see if any of the familiar guilt would come, but I felt only relief, and a small sense of justice. Aelwyn's killer was dead. I had killed him, but in doing so, I'd avenged both her and a father I would never meet. I was probably going to have nightmares from the entire thing, but I didn't regret what I'd done.

Beside me, Rhys squeezed my hand, and I looked up at him. His cheek was still bloody, and I remembered one last magical tattoo we still needed. With a muttering of words, the bandages on my inner wrist came to life. They took shape and dimension and then landed, wrapping around Rhys's injured arm and cheek.

He looked over at me in amusement. "Hardly important, considering."

"You are always important," I told him.

His eyes held mine, and I felt a thousand promises pass between us, unspoken. It should have felt new, this . . . thing between us. The way he rooted me to this spot with just a look and an unspoken commitment in his eyes. But it wasn't new. It had existed from the moment we'd met. The only difference between then and now was that we'd decided to acknowledge it and to let it in. We'd stopped running from it.

"It's over," I said, my voice hushed. I knew, logically, talking aloud wouldn't break the spell, because there was no spell. Not anymore. There was just us. The magic that was my love for him and his for me. But I whispered anyway.

Rhys watched me, eyes glittering. "You did it," he answered, stepping closer so that there was no more space between us.

I ran my finger over his tattoo, the still-healing lines raised into ridges on his skin. "I can't believe . . . I can't believe it's over."

"You were amazing."

I shook my head. "Not just me," I said. "You were . . . You didn't leave."

His brow shot up. "You thought I'd leave you?"

"You were supposed to get Elsmed if—"

"The only thing I'm supposed to do is kiss my girl."

"Right now? In front of all these people?" I became aware of the crowd we'd drawn, and my cheeks heated at the awareness. The figures we'd seen approaching were a few of the partygoers who had wandered far enough outside to notice the commotion we'd caused. Women in flowing gowns clutched at the arms of their dates, necks craning toward us to get a good look. No one approached, and I could only assume none of them had grown bold enough yet. But they would eventually.

"Damn straight," Rhys shot back, tightening his arm around me. "They need to know you're not available." His kiss was hard and fast and full of flourish; a message—like he'd just said.

We earned a few whistles before I pulled away, laughing softly before I could stop myself. "Show-off," I muttered.

"You just killed an Unseelie warrior without laying a finger on him, and I'm the show-off?"

"Point taken." My half-formed smile disappeared. "Oh, God. Here comes Sheriff Kasun."

Sure enough, a growling sheriff was shoving through the crowd. Deputy Conall was at his heels, still picking what looked like spider webs from his uniform.

I tensed, turning to face the sheriff so that Rhys and I stood shoulder to shoulder. Rhys squeezed my hand, but he didn't say a word as the sheriff nodded curtly at us both. His sharp blue eyes were unreadable other than the glances he threw at the cleanup crew gathering to my left. The team was a mixture of witches who I knew stood ready to investigate whether any humans had witnessed the supernatural events that had taken place here tonight. If anyone had, the witches would make sure no one remembered any of it by the time they walked away.

"Thank you all for your concern here tonight, but everything's under control," the sheriff said authoritatively. "If you'll all please step to the left and give a statement to someone from our team, we'd appreciate it. Once you're done there, you'll be free to return to the party."

The crowd took off in pairs and small groups, marching toward the team that waited for them.

When they were out of earshot, the sheriff turned back to face us, his gaze lingering on the dead man behind us. "So, either you've upped your body count, Miss Facharro, or the two of you have done me a solid and caught a killer tonight."

"Uh, definitely the second thing," I said.

"Not bad for our first date," Rhys said with a smile.

The sheriff eyed him, then me, noting our formalwear. "How romantic."

I glared at him. "You're not seriously still going to treat me like a suspect, are you?" I demanded.

"You never were a suspect, Miss Facharro. You did obstruct justice by tampering with evidence that first night, which put you at the top of my shit list for a while."

I gaped at him, but in the end, I couldn't argue with his claim. I'd definitely made a mess of that crime scene—unknowingly, but still.

"Sorry," I mumbled.

"I thought you said—" Rhys began with a frown.

"Son, I think it's time we had a talk about your access to confidential case information where Miss Facharro's concerned," Sherriff Kasun interrupted.

"I'm authorized, as her Protector, to—"

"You're a lot more than that, though, aren't you?" Sherriff Kasun gave him a look and he looked back at me, a soft smile playing on his lips.

"Yes, sir," he said quietly.

"Precisely. Anyway, I've got a team on the way to process the body you've brought me tonight," the sheriff went on. "And I suspect the energy signature will match the unauthorized portal entry from a while back. While we wait, why don't you tell me what happened here tonight."

"Sir, you're also going to want to send a team upstairs," Deputy Conall said.

Sheriff Kasun followed Conall's glance up to the balcony I'd fallen from earlier. "We got another body up there?"

"Not a body per se," Deputy Conall said slowly.

"What the hell is it?" Sheriff Kasun demanded.

"A ghost," Deputy Conall said on a sigh. "He'll need to be charged with conspiracy to commit murder—among other things."

"A . . .?" Sheriff Kasun stared at him and then finally drew a long breath, shaking his head. "Can we ever have a normal night? All right. Call in a second team."

Deputy Conall nodded and hurried off, pulling his phone out.

At the same moment, Elsmed appeared, clearly rattled. "Well?" he demanded.

"What?" Sheriff Kasun frowned.

"Is someone here going to tell me why I received a note from a salty vampire to meet you all at the tattoo shop when you're all clearly still here?"

Sheriff Kasun pinned me with a look. "You. Tragic Ink. Start talking."

CHAPTER 19

Snug and warm in my thick coat and wool gloves, I adjusted my pack, slowing to navigate a stream that had frozen over months back. The only sound our party made now was the crunch of our boots. Up ahead, Rhys cut a path as straight as he could, considering there was no real trail to our destination, not in the snow anyway. I couldn't believe I was leaving this winter wonderland behind. I'd never been beyond the town limits, and here I was leaving this realm altogether. At least it hadn't required a passport. I almost snorted at that, because it had been nearly as complicated working out our travel details as a rushed passport would have been.

Behind me, Elsmed muttered words that sounded like crooning compliments. Ethan perched on his shoulder, his beady, black eyes constantly scanning. I still couldn't understand what drew him to Elsmed of all people; I could barely get him to sit like that for me. I wondered if it had something to do with Elsmed's telepathic abilities.

Rhys stopped and waited for the rest of us to catch up.

I hurried forward, excited—and more than a little nervous—to get a look at the portal.

"Um, am I missing something?" I asked, turning a complete three-sixty before frowning. "There's nothing here but a bunch of rocks."

Rhys raised a brow. "Be patient. We have to activate it first. It's not like we can leave the door open all the time. Any sort of creature could slip right in."

I gave him a look.

"Again," he added ruefully.

I shook my head.

Cael's body had been transported and sent through the portal a few days back. A different portal than the one we were using now. I was more than okay with that. Sharing my arrival into the faerie realm with a dead criminal wasn't exactly my ideal impression.

"Right, makes sense." I took a deep breath to steady my nerves.

Rhys grabbed my elbow and bent closer, lowering his voice even though Elsmed was still a ways off. "You don't need to be nervous," Rhys said. "She already loves you."

"I know. I just . . . It's a lot."

He nodded. "I can imagine." Then he put his arms around me and pulled me close, propping his chin on my head while he held me. "But we both know it's not nearly as heavy as that misplaced guilt you've been carrying around."

"True." It was a huge relief to know my tattoo hadn't killed Walter's sister. My magical tats were still capable of a lot of damage. The hellhound was proof of that, and I still battled with that guilt a bit. But learning the truth about Sarah had made me realize everyone was responsible for their own actions. My tattoos could be used for good—or for evil. It wasn't up to me once the ink had dried.

Rhys seemed more relieved than I was to hear I'd let some of that shit go. It had also allowed us to reconnect, catching up on the years we'd been apart. Standing here in the circle of his arms made me think of some of those reconnections now. I was snug and warm like this, and I almost didn't want to let go, but we had a portal to catch.

Elsmed joined us, still chatting to Ethan. He looked at us expectantly as he came close. "Well?" he asked. "Are you both ready then?"

I shot a glance at Rhys. "I think so."

"Good. Now remember, once you're settled, the Seelie Court would like to meet you both. Rhys will need to make a statement about his mission here, and I suspect they'll want to get to know you, too, Gwen. If you want help setting that up, get in contact with Chase MacElvoy."

"Who is he?" I asked.

"Chase is our Seelie representative. He travels back and forth from here to Tír na nÓg regularly, so he can help coordinate your appearance with the Court there."

"Tír na nÓg?" I repeated, trying to place the name from everything I'd heard of the Seelie Court.

"It's a small island off the coast, and it's the capital of the Seelie Court. Chase has an office there, so just contact him when you're ready, and he can bring you home. But take your time." His gaze settled on me. "When you return or how long you stay is completely up to you. Just remember—time passes differently in Faerie. A couple of weeks could equal months here."

"Thank you," I told him, startled to realize how far we'd come in a short time. Elsmed had been completely terrifying to me when we'd first met—what? Two weeks ago? And now, at least to me anyway, he was one of the friendliest faces in this town. Not that any of the others were unfriendly. Not anymore.

"You're welcome. As for your personal affairs while you're gone . . ." Elsmed said the words like a question.

Rhys jumped in. "Everything's in order, sir. My bar manager is in charge with complete autonomy while I'm gone. Gwen's shop is closed until further notice."

"I'm told Aelwyn's house belongs to both of you now," Elsmed said.

We both nodded. We'd been over this with Sheriff Kasun and a lawyer during the past week. The sheriff had been a lot friendlier after we'd caught Cael for him—a strike against him that meant I probably wouldn't be sending him a Christmas card anytime soon. But at least I wasn't on his short list of "chicks capable of murder" anymore. Deputy Conall had actually hugged me when I'd given my statement. *Weirdo.*

I planned to resume my mistletoe supplements the moment we stepped foot back in Havenwood Falls.

Thanks to Aelwyn's savvy financial foresight, the taxes and mortgage were both paid for the next few years. Which meant we were keeping the house until after our trip. I didn't want to think about it right now, but I'd probably never sell it. It was home in a way Faerie could never be. Rhys agreed.

"All right, I think that's everything. Oh," Elsmed held his arm out. "You'll want him back I suppose."

I returned Ethan safely back to my skin, and then Elsmed surprised me by offering his gloved hand for a shake. A handshake wasn't all that foreign, but I'd never really seen him touch anyone before. Another thing I could blame on the mistletoe. Maybe this was what it felt like to be normal?

I shook and gave him a smile. "Thank you for arranging all this," I told him earnestly.

"It's the least I could do." He bent lower, his voice dropping as if he were sharing private information. "Speaking of arrangements, I wanted to let you know that there are . . . circumstances at work regarding your blackmailing problem. I think, by the time you return, that particular problem will have worked itself out."

I blinked. "Wow. Thank you so much."

Elsmed's eyes seemed to twinkle, and then he moved on to Rhys. "Son." They shook stiffly. "You don't need me to tell you, but keep our girl safe, will you? Bring her back."

"Will do."

Rhys was so solemn, their handshake so formal, I rolled my eyes.

But then Elsmed stepped back. He closed his eyes and murmured words in a language I'd never heard before. A moment later, the rock façade that loomed before me began to move. Small ripples started in the center and ringed outward, like the surface of a lake after throwing a rock into it.

I watched in awe as the ripples spread and the liquid grew lighter—until I wasn't looking at a surface so much as seeing through it.

Rhys slid his hand into mine and squeezed.

My stomach tightened with nerves again as a figure came into view on the other side. A woman, tall and slender with flowing hair, stood just beyond the veil.

"Is that—?"

"Moonlaith," Elsmed said from behind me. "Sure looks like. Give her my regards, would you?"

I didn't answer. I couldn't speak around the lump in my throat. My hands were clammy inside my gloves.

Rhys looked over at me. "Are you ready?"

I nodded, knowing full well I wasn't ready. How could anyone ever be ready for something they were positive would never happen? My whole life, I'd believed my mother was dead. Never coming back. Gone. And now, here she was, standing just on the other side of this portal. A few steps away.

Hell no, I wasn't ready for that.

But I also wasn't going to stand still any longer. I was going to live my life moving forward. No more hiding what I was and what I could do.

With feet that felt like lead, I took one step. Then another. With each footfall, they became easier. Until I was passing through the strange gel of the portal and through the magic to the other side. The woman waiting smiled at me, her hair white like the moon. Her smile soft and warm. Like a mother's. I kept walking—straight into her open arms. And I knew I'd always look back on this moment and think, *This is when it all began.*

～

ABOUT THE AUTHOR

Heather Hildenbrand was born and raised in a small town in northern Virginia, where she was homeschooled through high school. (She's only slightly socially awkward as a result.) She writes paranormal and contemporary romance with plenty of abs and angst. Her most frequent hobbies are riding motorcycles and avoiding killer slugs.

You can find out more about Heather and her books at heatherhildenbrand.com or sign up for email updates.

ACKNOWLEDGMENTS

First, I have to say a big thank you to Kristie for inviting me into the world of Havenwood Falls. I am so honored to be a part of something so unique and alive! Thanks to the entire team at Ang'dora. It's because of you, this story actually shines! Special thanks to Randi Cooley Wilson, Kallie Ross, and E.J. Fechenda for helping me include some of their characters in these pages. It's such a cool thing to be able to share in this way—also, I'm a huge Everett fan so I am kind of swooning that I got to write him into a few corners of my own story. (If you haven't read *Covetousness* by Randi Cooley Wilson, what are you even doing with your life?)

To my early—and emergency—beta readers: Amber Shepherd and Rebecca Pruner Kimmel, you guys made this story WAY better, and I am so lucky that you're always willing to read my stories on short notice. I still have no idea how you are able to do that. I swear, it's like a superpower.

And to my readers, my Love Birds, thank you guys for always reading with such excitement! Your ideas helped shape this story early on, and I can always count on our Facebook tribe to help me out when I get stuck. I appreciate all of you! See you in the next book!

NOWHERE TO HIDE

BELINDA BORING

~ A Havenwood Falls New Adult Novella ~

HavenWood Falls

Nowhere to Hide

Belinda Boring

ABOUT THIS BOOK

Fact One: A flock of crows is called a murder.

Fact Two: Cherophobia is the fear of fun.

Fact Three: It's impossible to sneeze with your eyes open.

For Sedona Mathews, facts and knowledge act as a buffer between her and the outside world. Born as an empath, others' emotions bombard her senses, complicating any relationship she's tried to enjoy. When she becomes sole owner of Shelf Indulgence, she happily devotes her life to the Havenwood Falls bookstore, hiding away amongst books she loves. Because there's another fact Sedona is painfully aware of . . .

Fact Four: In a town where nothing and no one is as they seem, falling in love can be treacherous.

Micah Westbrook has no time for love. Cloaked in secrecy, he brings his niece, Holly, to Havenwood Falls, hoping they can hide amongst the other supernaturals. He's charged with keeping Holly safe and will risk everything to ensure those hunting them can't pick up their trail. The last thing Micah needs is to be blindsided by a danger he didn't see coming . . . Sedona.

Micah struggles to keep her at arm's length, forgetting one important fact: When it comes to loving an empath, there's nowhere to hide.

ALSO BY BELINDA BORING

THE MYSTIC WOLVES SERIES

The Mystic Wolves

Forget Me Not

Testing Fate

Forever Changed

Savage Possession

Darkness Unleashed

Last Wolf Standing

Blood Oath

A Very Mystic Christmas

DAMAGED SOULS SERIES: BITTERSWEET MELODY

Bittersweet Symphony

BRIANNA LANE SERIES

Broken Promises

Enchanted Hearts

Loving Liberty

Angel Kissed

To my late father-in-law, Donnie Boring.
You are loved and you are missed.

CHAPTER 1

*Y*ou can do it, Sedona. There's no need to panic. Everything will be okay. Just put on your big girl panties, smile, and pretend that you can't feel everything he is thinking.

If I had a dollar for every time I'd rehearsed this small mantra, standing here at the window of my bookstore, Shelf Indulgence, I'd have enough to leave Havenwood Falls and explore the world for the rest of my life.

Not that I truly wanted to leave the only place I'd ever felt safe enough to call my home, but you get the idea.

I sounded like a broken record that kept skipping and repeating the same old tired words. Part of me wished I could toss aside my reservations each time I decided to bravely face the possibilities of dating.

The problem was there was nothing normal about beginning a new relationship, especially when you held the special gifts I did. My mother used to tell me how unique being an empath was, and that when my ability was paired together with my other inherent powers, I would become a force to be reckoned with.

Those pep talks ended by the time I reached my teens, replaced by the now familiar fear that echoed in her heart. She was careful to prevent it from ever shining out through her eyes or filling her voice when she spoke. I didn't need those nonverbal cues to know what she was feeling.

The empathy I'd been raised to believe was a gift morphed quickly into a curse—one that kept my peers at arm's length, their soft whispers following behind me as I walked down Havenwood Falls High's hallways. I didn't blame them for not wanting to invite me to sit with them at lunch or bond over fun sleepovers.

Even though many of them were part of the hidden supernatural community, somehow their fangs, claws, and weirdness weren't nearly as dangerous as being able to reach into them and pluck out their secret feelings.

It wasn't until I found comfort in running Shelf Indulgence and escaping into the beloved books I cherished that I made my peace with who I was—am.

"I could always cancel," I murmured, my stomach churning with nerves. "It's only a first date . . . nothing important." My throat dried the second I spotted Robert crossing the street, headed in my direction. "God, I hate this."

A deep, familiar voice answered. "One of us needs to leave this store and have a life, Sedona. And considering I can't, that leaves the burden firmly on your shoulders."

Maxwell appeared beside me, his fingers twirling the end of his mustache. I often wondered if he realized he did that—if it was a nervous habit he'd failed to break. I couldn't quite cross out an alternative thought that it was his way of impersonating a villain because right now, my dearest friend wasn't enabling my cowardice at all. He was supposed to agree wholeheartedly with me and suggest I spend the evening secluded quietly in my apartment with a delicious glass of wine and a book.

"I still think you made that up, Maxwell. I'm sure if you tried hard enough, you could leave and go haunt Willow over at Coffee Haven. You know . . . expand your horizons and all."

A look of horror and disapproval blazed across his ghostly features.

Did I forget to mention Maxwell was a ghost?

"I'll pretend I didn't hear you suggest that, young lady. Do you really think I'd stay here and witness your weekly neurotic diatribe about the woes of dating if I could simply waltz out of here?"

I knew Maxwell well enough to remember that beneath his offended pout, he was teasing me. Like he said, we pretty much went through this conversation each time I foolishly agreed to go out with someone. We both had our parts to play.

Clenching my hands into fists, I straightened and drew in a deep breath. "How do I look? Am I presentable enough?"

Despite my blasé attitude toward dating, I still found myself making an effort, a small sliver of hope surfacing that maybe, just maybe, this time would be different.

"You look beautiful as always. Although," he paused for a moment, casting a glance outside as Robert drew closer. The corners of his lips twitched into an almost smile. In stepping off the curb, my date had misjudged the slickness of the ground, his feet slipping over ice. To some, winter in Havenwood Falls was far from the magical wonderland that I viewed it as. Robert's mouth formed a silent curse word.

Maxwell cleared his throat, bringing my attention back to our conversation. "I believe your beauty is wasted on this human."

There was no mistaking the sneer in his tone. My dear friend didn't approve of my dating someone outside our supernatural community.

"You know why I agreed," I retorted, steeling myself to once again remind him that there were slim pickings for me no matter how hard I tried.

Who would want to date an empath?

"Heathens," Maxwell exhaled in disgust. "In my day, men would be lining up around the town square for a chance to be with you."

"Well, pity we can't just hop in a time machine and find me these rare males." I laughed, desperately hoping it disguised the sadness I couldn't always bury. Truth be told, I was lonely. Just once, I wanted to experience the toe-curling, heart-racing, giddy swooning love I read about.

My gaze remained with Robert now—the moment I'd been waiting for. The closer he came, the sooner I would sense his intentions. Over the years, I'd become pretty good at protecting myself from the overwhelming crush of emotions that surrounded me. It was one of the first spells I perfected when I came of age and could practice magic on my own. Invisible to the naked eye, a silvery aura encased me, thinning only when I purposely lowered my guard to get a reading of someone.

He must've sensed I was watching because a huge smile lit his face when our eyes met. Everything seemed normal as his intentions mentally reached me—nerves over whether he could impress me, a list of topics to cover over dinner just in case we ran out of things to say, and that he believed I was one of the prettiest girls he'd ever laid eyes on.

That last one made my own smile grow. What girl didn't like knowing others thought she was attractive?

Robert was only a few steps away from the store's door when I caught the briefest of flashes of another feeling—one that instantly brought the shutters around my heart. Sighing sadly, I knew I couldn't forget and pretend he hadn't just cast aside those other emotions for one that made my skin crawl.

Lust. The lewd kind that left you feeling stripped bare and vulnerable in front of a group of men catcalling and yelling for you to shake what the good lord gave you.

I was far from being a prude, so lust in general wasn't something to make me retreat. There was nothing wrong with finding someone good-looking and noticing how they made your body respond.

That wasn't how Robert was feeling right now. If anything, he was contemplating how long it would take him to get me flat on my back, legs in the air, as I screamed his name in worship.

"Blech," I uttered, already heading to the door. "Be right back, Maxwell." Not giving him a chance to reply, to convince me I didn't have the luxury of turning yet another man down, or to list the million reasons he worried I would become the Cat Lady of Havenwood Falls, I was out on the street. I was the queen of excuses, and I didn't feel guilty for the lies I told Robert, or the fake disappointment I expressed over having to cancel the plans he had for us.

It took everything I had not to shudder when he rubbed my arm, his touch lingering longer than was appropriate. Another blast of lust shot out from him, and I took a few steps backward.

I couldn't run back inside the bookstore fast enough, leaving Robert standing on the sidewalk, confused over how I could possibly choose something over him. His arrogance was another turnoff—something he'd managed to hide when he'd asked me out earlier in the week.

"What was the reason this time?" Maxwell asked, exasperated. If he rolled his eyes any harder, they would've fallen to the back of his head and down his body, before coming to a stop in his feet. Snarky ghost.

"Unexpected inventory audit," I answered weakly. Even I could hear what a lousy reason it was. "In my defense, he was a pig."

His brows furrowed in concern. "You can't keep doing this, Sedona. Do you honestly want to end up like me?"

"I could think of worse things to become." In trying to lighten the conversation and perhaps deflect the lecture I sensed brewing within him, I couldn't deny he had a point. "Next time I'll go, okay? Just not with him."

He snorted. "What was wrong with this one?"

My face flushed. "Let's just say, if given the chance, he'd rather have skipped dinner and dived right into dessert."

A deep baritone laugh burst from Maxwell. "He found you attractive and that upset you? You do know what happens when two people like each other, Sedona? Please tell me I don't have to inform you about the birds and the bees."

The very thought made me squirm uncomfortably. "I already know about sex, smart-ass." I shook my head at him. "I just don't like it when the guy I'm with is more interested in getting between my legs than really getting to know me."

"And here I thought I was the old-fashioned one," he retorted quickly. "You can't hide away in here forever, Sedona. Sexual sparks are a good thing. You need chemistry." His voice grew louder and more passionate. "The heroes in those romance books you love won't keep you warm at night. You need someone real."

"Says the ghost that won't leave either." It was a low blow, but I was feeling defensive.

In the years since I'd taken over my grandfather's bookstore and made it my own, I'd never once seen Maxwell leave. He'd simply appeared one day, and no amount of questioning would get him to reveal where he'd come from.

"My circumstances are different." His response was gruff. As an empath, I couldn't get a fix on his emotions, my gifts reserved solely for the living, but in this case, I didn't need to rely on my gift to know what he was feeling.

We were both defensive.

"I'll try harder next time," I promised, wishing I could reach out and touch him without my hand passing through. "He just wasn't right for me."

"You can't afford to be so selective. You need to seize the moment before time slips through your fingers. Take it from me." His voice trailed off.

It was on the tip of my tongue to ask him why, to perhaps prod a little to see if he would finally open up and share.

I didn't get the chance, however, as the door to the store opened, startling me. Maxwell disappeared, leaving me standing there like a fool, talking to myself. Most times that wouldn't bother me. Most of the town believed I was weird anyway, so nothing really surprised them.

As my heart began racing and my mouth instantly dried, all I could think was two things:

One, I hoped this guy didn't think I was a freak too.

Two, the stranger standing in the doorway, his gorgeous blue eyes fixed completely on me, was by far the sexiest man I had ever seen.

And when he spoke, I knew I was in trouble.

CHAPTER 2

"*H*ello."

  They say that words hold power, and living in the small town I did, they could also be very dangerous. Witches used them to invoke magic, shifting energy through the ether in order to do their bidding. One wrong syllable or nuance could cause an outbreak of aggression with the werewolf packs, and vampires . . . well, they were notorious for using their silken tones to bend others to their will.

But this one word—hello—it had the power to completely undo me. I'd heard it countless times throughout the day as customers came into Shelf Indulgence, but never was the greeting connected to the man that personified sexy goodness simply from uttering it.

I gulped.

Don't you dare stammer and embarrass yourself, Sedona. Just take a deep breath and act as if it's every day a gorgeous stranger stops by to say hi.

I gulped, again, my palms already beginning to sweat from nerves.

"How can I do you?" I blurted out, instantly cringing over the jumbled sentence falling out of my mouth. Inwardly, I wanted the floor to open up and swallow me whole.

HOW. CAN. I. DO. YOU?

What the heck!

If I thought him speaking melted my insides, his laughter was pure sin. The twinkle in his deep blue eyes set me at ease and, despite the heat blistering my cheeks, I knew his grin was a sign that he had a sense of humor.

"Is that how you greet all your customers?" He cocked his eyebrow as he asked, and my heartbeat thundered.

This man was going to be the death of me.

"Only the good-looking ones." It came out all breathy. Then, as if the Fates needed proof I'd lost my ever-loving mind, I winked. *Winked.*

Awkward silence followed.

Even Maxwell showing up and scaring the bejeezus out of me would've been more welcome.

In the space between seconds, I automatically reached out with my empathic gift, searching for those telltale signs that he was one of us—supernatural. I hadn't seen him before, and perhaps he was simply passing through. Something in the back of my mind whispered that I hoped that wasn't the case.

Electric tingles brushed over my skin, setting those nerve endings aflame with magic. He was definitely supernatural, but what species? Each group had a certain flavor that belonged solely to their kind. It made it easy for people like me to uncover.

The Court of the Sun and the Moon often called on me with tasks to subtly dig into someone's psyche to see whether or not their intentions were true and honorable. Havenwood Falls was fiercely protected from unwanted attention, and although I didn't want to get involved with the town's politics, I couldn't resist my aunt's requests.

Just my luck. She knew that it bothered me, but didn't hesitate to remind me it was my duty as her niece and an empath to use my gifts for the common good.

Sometimes that line got pretty murky. I didn't like invading people's privacy and had spent years trying to master my own control.

After a hellacious childhood of blurting out people's emotions, revealing their innermost feelings without permission, I'd retreated into the world of fiction, where it was safe.

Characters I understood.

People were just . . . complicated.

I pushed outward again, imagining tendrils of light reaching toward the quiet stranger, who was now eyeing me with curiosity. I couldn't quite get a reading on what he was—my mind was fogging over and keeping the answer just out of reach.

Testing to see what feelings he was protecting turned up even more questions.

Nothing. He was the perfect balance of calmness, like a blank sheet of paper. If it weren't for the fact I could read his facial expressions and body language, I would wonder whether he was actually there.

It was tempting to push harder. I was inquisitive in nature, and this was a puzzle I wanted to solve.

Again something whispered that he was someone I definitely wanted to know more about.

Just as my innate magic touched him, a sizzle of energy snapped out, causing me to take an actual step back.

His eyebrow rose again.

Did he know what I was doing?

Covering my tracks in case he did, I cleared my throat and offered a shaky smile. "What I meant to say was how can I help you?"

There was a quick wrinkling of his brow before it smoothed over and he nodded. "I'm needing a book for my niece. She's studying history, in specific the Tudor era with King Henry the Eighth. There is a reference book she needs." Digging into his pocket, he pulled out a folded piece of paper before continuing, "*The Life and Loves of the Infamous King Henry Eighth.*"

Excitement fizzled up inside me. This was one of my favorite subjects to read about.

"Not that I condone putting aside reading for watching television," I started, making my way through the shelves to where I kept historical books, "but she may want to watch *The Tudors*." It was on the tip of my tongue to gush about how incredibly swoony Jonathan Rhys Meyers and Henry Cavill were in the addictive series, but I didn't think he'd appreciate the sudden surge in estrogen.

"I don't think that would be a wise parental choice, considering she's only fourteen." He leaned in, and I caught a whiff of the most delicious scent. Whether it was him or his cologne, I didn't know, but it took everything in me to move away.

"My name's Sedona Mathews, by the way. I'm the owner of Shelf Indulgence."

"I know," he replied in that deep baritone voice that liquefied everything. This reaction was beyond strange, because the only time I'd *ever* felt such a strong reaction to a guy before was when I was reading one of my beloved novels.

They were safe, however. He was not.

What I meant to say was "You do?" but what erupted out next was nothing short than a ridiculous squeak. A huge part of me hoped against hope that Maxwell had retreated to wherever he goes when he's not annoying the hell out of me.

With all the grace I could muster, I answered the only way I knew how.

"Did you know that King Henry was well known for how incredible his legs were? That's how men's beauty was described back in the 1500s. Apparently he had attractive calves."

Facts were my life. They brought me comfort in stressful moments because they didn't ever change. I'd heard some say the same about mathematics, which I thought was completely bonkers, but facts were like a lodestone I could touch and ground myself with. I kept them all filed away in my head on the off chance there would be a situation I could share them.

Like with this stranger.

And the king who had six wives, two of whom he beheaded.

I rested my hand lightly on the shelf containing the books about the English monarchy.

"Well, it would be ironic if he was known for having a beautiful neck, wouldn't it?" He placed his finger on one of the spines, mouthing the title silently. "My name's Micah, in case you were wondering."

I blinked. I seriously felt like some starry-eyed teenager in the presence of her idol. Shaking my head, I berated myself for not being more professional.

"It's a pleasure to meet you, Micah." Turning to face the shelves again, I scanned the section briefly and let out a disappointed sigh. "Looks like I don't have it in stock. When does she need it by?"

Micah was still studying the books, slipping a few out before returning them to their place. "Why?"

There was a flicker of emotion—suspicion.

"Because if you don't mind waiting, I can order it in for you. Shouldn't take more than three to four days." Thank goodness for Amazon shipping.

He seemed to ponder that for a moment before nodding. "I'm sure she'll make do with what she has until then. I've never seen anyone read as much as she does. Every time I turn around, she either has her nose stuck in a book or she's sharing what she's learning."

So she was a kindred spirit and fellow bookworm.

"How is she liking Havenwood Falls High?" I asked, guiding him back to the front of the store, where my computer was. He followed behind quietly, and it wasn't until I was typing in the web address that I realized he hadn't answered.

He was studying me with the same intensity he gave the books back there. It was almost like he was an empath too and was trying to push beyond the barriers I kept raised for protection.

But I hadn't detected that gift.

"Sorry." I offered an apologetic smile, and my hands paused above the keyboard. "I forget that not everyone is as nosey as I am. My mother told me that one particular trait would get me into trouble one day."

Micah's features softened. "You're fine. I'm just not used to meeting someone who doesn't seem to have an agenda." Before I could ask him what he meant, he pulled out his wallet. "Did you want me to pay for the book now or later when it comes in?"

"You can pay now." Accepting his card, I began entering the information into the computer.

"Do you need to see my I.D. as well? To make sure I am who I say I am?" He extended his driver's license out between his two fingers.

One look at his earnest expression and I shook my head. "I trust you. Besides, I know where you live." Smirking, I pointed to the screen where his order was still displayed.

"You shouldn't be so willing to trust strangers, Miss Mathews. Not everyone is so easy to read."

Damn, was that him saying he knew I was empathic? The hair on the back of my neck rose.

I decided to take a page out of his book and change the subject. "Is there a number where I can reach you when the book arrives?"

"How about I stop by at the end of week and check in with you? That might be best." Micah was already at the door. "Until then." And with a slight head nod, the most intriguing man I'd ever met was gone.

My fingers flew over the keyboard, the book for his niece ordered within moments. I let out a weary breath as I sat back on the stool I kept at the front counter and stared out at the town square outside. Micah had already disappeared from view.

"Well, that was interesting!" Maxwell boomed, his smile all teeth. "I must say I've seen you flustered before, Sedona, but that was something else."

"How much did you see?" I asked, knowing the answer already. The ghost had witnessed the entire thing.

"Enough to wonder what people would've thought about my fine legs."

A groan escaped my lips, and it was tempting to bang my head against the countertop. Why couldn't I be like everyone else and not embarrass myself at every turn?

"Cheer up, my dear. There is a ray of sunshine peeking out from behind those clouds of gloom." He gestured above my head like he could actually see them.

"And what's that?"

"You've got the next couple of days to rehearse what you can say to him when he comes back for the book. Perhaps you could study up on some American history facts to dazzle him with."

"Have I told you how much I hate you?" I retorted halfheartedly. The truth of the matter was he was right—my head was already ticking over what to say next. There was no way I would be caught off guard again.

"Maxwell," I asked, taking one last glance out the window, "have you ever met someone who you couldn't read, or heard of someone an empath felt little emotion from?"

"Usually they're people with secrets to hide. Why?"

I shrugged and put on another smile. "No reason. Just curious."

The rest of the evening passed quickly, but Micah was never far from my thoughts. While I usually honored people's privacy, there was something about him that I couldn't put my finger on, and I was determined to figure it out.

There was one thing I did know—when it came to my gifts, when I focused all my intent, there would be nowhere to hide.

CHAPTER 3

"*I*ncoming!"

Austin's quick-fire warning could mean only one thing.

Before I even had a chance to prepare myself for the approaching storm, the bell jingled as the door opened.

Thanks for the heads up, I mentally groaned, making a quick note to give the high school student a stern talking-to if I survived the next few moments. I loved Austin with all my heart. Hiring him a year ago had been one of the best decisions I'd made with regard to the store, because his love for learning rivaled my own. He also was a natural whiz kid when it came to computers. In fact, the current system we used was his recommendation. The kid definitely had his finger on the latest technology pulse.

Frankly, I'd have been somewhat lost without him, but I would never tell him that.

"Sedona." Her greeting was short and to the point. She glanced around the quiet store, a frown creasing her forehead. "I trust business is good?"

My aunt didn't bother to try hiding her disappointment that I'd eagerly chosen to take over my grandfather's beloved bookstore instead of following in her footsteps and working for the coven. She didn't understand how appealing a life surrounded by literature could be.

Instead, all she saw was dust and shelves, pages upon pages of tedious reading. I'd spent many evenings desperately trying to help her see, to somehow help her feel what I did, to no avail. She may have been a witch, but she was no empath.

My mother had been one—a powerful one, judging by the stories others had shared with me. My heart hurt whenever I thought about all the many missed opportunities of being guided by her as my gifts emerged.

That was before the tragic accident that had stolen my father away from us. Within a few months, my mother had joined him—dying from a broken heart.

Love could be deadly for empaths.

"How are you today, Aunt Millicent?" There was no point in commenting on her original question. No answer would please her.

A black head of hair peered around from behind one of the bookshelves. The expression Austin wore as he mouthed *sorry* was almost comical. Part of me wanted to beckon him out so he could act as a buffer between us.

"Is there somewhere private we can talk, niece?"

It always amazed me how effortlessly my aunt could reduce me to a little child being scolded. With a long haughty glance around my store, I knew she was looking to see if we were alone.

"If you'd rather we talk in the back storeroom with my inventory," I stated, my heart already sinking with all the possibilities of why she wanted to have whatever conversation she'd planned away from prying eyes and curious ears. "Or you're more than welcome to come by tonight and we can chat."

Secretly, I wished she'd opt for neither and leave. Her unexpected visits were rarely meetings I cherished. That could be because the majority of the time I felt she saw me more as a pawn to do her bidding than as family.

While she didn't exactly enjoy the inner circle of the coven, we had ties to the Beaumont family, and she ranked high in the coven. She absolutely enjoyed being useful to those in power.

She let out a snort of disgust. "My time is precious. I'm sure your back room will suffice." Without waiting, she sashayed past me like she owned the place. "Better yet, send the boy out on an errand."

I knew better than to argue, because that would only result in her lingering longer. I loved my aunt and was grateful for the way she'd taken me in after my parents' deaths, but when she got this particular look in her eye, I knew this wasn't a social call.

I quickly dispatched Austin on a java run, telling him to take his time coming back. The instant flash of gratitude in his eyes spoke volumes.

She scared the crap out of him—something about how he was terrified she could peer into the deepest recesses of his soul or curse him to become a toad. I always chuckled whenever he said that, because what kind of secrets could a seventeen-year-old boy be hiding?

When I finally returned to her, Aunt Millicent let out a loud, overly dramatic breath. "As you know, coven business keeps me busy, not that I'm complaining." And here it came. "You know. Your gifts are being squandered in this . . ." Again, she didn't bother disguising the disdain she felt as she glanced about Shelf Indulgence. "Quaint little store. Why he left it to you is beyond anyone's understanding. He knew I had bigger, more impressive plans for you, Sedona."

With my parents dead, it had fallen on my aunt to continue raising me and seeing to my education—both academically and supernaturally. The obvious choice would've been my grandfather, but with his advanced age and reclusive tendencies, the task had been left to my mother's older sister.

It was my turn to sigh. "Did you really come here to argue, aunt?" I asked, feeling my own sense of sadness that she couldn't see how happy my life made me.

Sometimes feeling her emotions weighed on me like a concrete-encrusted blanket. It was suppressive and overwhelming. It totally eclipsed the bond of love and family buried beneath. It was *that* version of Millicent that I longed to be nurtured by.

She sniffed. "I only want what's best for you, my dear niece." A flyer on the front counter caught her attention, giving me a temporary reprieve. "What a shame. Heidi had so much potential. If they don't find her soon, I believe it will destroy her poor family."

My gaze strayed over to the photograph I'd memorized.

Heidi Bennett had disappeared during the Cold Moon Ball back in December, and no amount of searching had led the authorities to her whereabouts.

"Is there still no news?" I asked, genuinely hoping there were at least a few leads to go on.

Aunt Millicent shook her head and placed the flyer back with the others on the counter. She then turned her steely gaze back to me. There'd been a flicker of compassion there—of some long ago memory that had surfaced—but it evaporated the moment she started talking again.

"Can you not see why I push so hard for you to come work for the coven?"

I closed my eyes briefly, my shoulders sagging a little before I repeated the same words I always answered her with. "We all have our own paths to walk. This is mine." I stepped away, as if joining with the shelves behind me, my private comrades. "Why can't you see how happy I am?"

"Duty doesn't always equate to happiness, Sedona."

And there was the truth—the reason why I believed my aunt was so fixated in converting me over to her way of thinking. For her, everything was about duty and control. She was willing to sacrifice happiness, and even love, if it meant she held power and could be of use.

She couldn't comprehend that there was a myriad of ways of fulfilling your life's purpose that didn't result in being miserable.

"Was there something in particular you wanted?" It was time to focus on the real reason she'd stopped by the store. Aunt Millicent wasn't one for idle chitchat.

Her gaze narrowed, and her lips turned up at the edges in a half smile. "Can't I simply visit with my niece?"

I remained silent. We'd played this game many, many times over the years.

With a sigh of exasperation, she finally nodded. "Well, now that you mention it, I heard you had a visit from a newcomer yesterday . . . a Micah Westbrook."

Thank goodness she didn't share in my gifts, because the blast of longing and heat that coursed through me at the mere mention of his name would've shocked her.

"Yessss . . ." I drew out, cautious.

"What were your impressions of him?"

There it was, the reason why she'd come, and not because she felt any sense of obligation toward me as a family member.

She was fishing for information. Sometimes being one of the few empaths in town was exhausting. It made conversations like this a tangle of weird intentions.

"He seemed like a nice guy," I answered. "Why, is he of interest to the coven or the Court?"

Everything was about the Luna Coven, in my aunt's eyes.

"As you know, whenever someone comes to live in Havenwood Falls, they must meet with us and state their purpose. He registered when he first arrived, but the coven's High Council is still . . . curious." The way she spoke that last word sent an involuntary shiver up my spine.

"Something set off a red flag?" Unintentionally, I'd stepped forward as if being drawn into the intrigue.

The movement wasn't lost on her.

"You know I can't discuss the High Council's business with you, Sedona." There was a *but* in there somewhere. "But, while he appeared to be honest and upfront, there was something not quite right about him that they couldn't put their collective finger on."

Here it was.

The request I always dreaded.

"I need you to get a reading on him, Sedona." She quickly held up her hand to stop the refusal she knew was coming. "And before you get on your moral high horse, remember that you are my niece, and the position comes with certain responsibilities. While I barely condone you hiding away in this musty bookstore, I won't continue to support you constantly neglecting your gift. You were given empathy for a reason. You will do this task for me—and your High Council—without complaint."

"And if I find nothing of consequence?"

Her lips pursed. "I will be the judge of that. Do this for me, Sedona. Do this, and it will be last time I will ever ask."

It was the same promise she always offered and one I knew she'd never keep.

"He seems like a great guy, Aunt Millicent." I replied carefully, because while I believed he was hiding something, the last thing I wanted to do was tell her she was right. Once unleashed, my aunt could be relentless in pursuing answers. I needed to know for myself before I confirmed her suspicions.

She pushed again. "Is that all you felt? You didn't feel anything out of the ordinary?"

I shrugged, suddenly tired of this whole conversation. Why couldn't things be simple between us? "He was polite when he came into the store . . . perhaps just gaining his bearings as a newcomer."

"You will do this for me." It was more of an order than a request. She gave one last look at the missing person flyer. "For all we know, he's connected to Heidi's disappearance."

She'd found my Achilles heel. As much as I wanted to respect people's privacy, and regardless of the temptation I felt over uncovering why Micah was like a blank slate, I couldn't ignore this.

I finally relented. "Okay, one more time, and then you won't ever ask again."

The smug look of satisfaction across her face made my stomach dip. "Thank you, niece. The Council thanks you as well."

In a flurry of cheek kisses and a request for me to stop by on Sunday for dinner, she left me standing, staring out after her.

Fifteen minutes later, Austin reappeared, two large coffees in his hands. "Is it safe to come back?" Austin's whispered question broke through my daze.

"Yes, she's gone," I retorted, shifting slowly before turning around to face him. "You couldn't have warned me sooner? I thought we had an unspoken code that whoever saw her coming would let the other know?"

Austin's gaze dropped to the ground, softening whatever annoyance I felt. "There wasn't enough time, I promise." He walked over to the large bay windows. It would be time soon to change over the display. "So what did she want?"

I gave him a look that told him I wasn't going to be confessing anything anytime soon. "Just family stuff. Nothing that warranted the cloak-and-dagger routine."

This only made him laugh. "With her flair for the dramatic, she'd be perfect in the theater." Austin handed me my drink before taking the lid off his own and blowing across the heated surface. "Although God help the fool that hires her." He shuddered before realizing what he'd said. "Sorry, Sedona, I know she's your aunt."

That was the perfect cue to change the subject. "So, Austin, what's the word on the street?"

His eyes lit up. "Did you know there's a new girl in town? Everyone at school was excited to meet her, but she never showed up because she's homeschooled. Rumor has it she lives with her uncle in a house they're renting by the Kasuns'." The fact that this was his gossip reminded me that my young friend paid more attention than I gave him credit for.

But he did share something interesting. Micah was living out by pack property. I was surprised the alpha, who was also our sheriff, had okayed it without knowing everything about Micah—from a thorough background history to what type of toothpaste he used and how he liked his coffee.

"Makes sense that her uncle came in here looking for a book for her, then," I commented, finally moving to the computer at the front counter so I could check on the order status.

"He did?" Austin's eyes went wide with interest. "You met him? When will he be back to pick it up?"

My finger traced a line on the screen. "Looks like it should be delivered here in a few days. Perhaps I could drop it off at his home. It'll give me a chance to meet his niece."

"Uh-huh." His teasing grin told me he could see right through me. "Maybe I should join you, and then I can convince her to come to school. The drama department is always looking for fresh meat. Speaking of which," Austin's voice raised an octave in excitement. "You're officially looking at the recipient of a full-ride scholarship!"

All thoughts of Micah were temporarily forgotten. "You got it!" I squealed and threw my arms around him. "Austin, I'm so excited for you! What does this mean?"

"It means I get a free ride to any college I choose." He was positively beaming with pride. "I heard I was a shoo-in for it, but you know . . . there's always a part of you that reminds you of all the ways you suck."

"You? Insecure? Really?" I gently teased back. Despite the cocky confidence he seemed to ooze, it wasn't surprising that he also doubted himself. "I can't think of anyone more deserving." I quickly gave him a warm hug. "So will you be majoring in theater?"

His answer surprised me.

"I'll be minoring in it. I figured I shouldn't let my tech skills go to waste, so I'll be majoring in computer science." And with that, a huge toothy grin spread across his face. "You know, something to fall back on in case my career on Broadway doesn't pan out."

Suddenly a wave of sadness washed over me. "So you're leaving after you graduate." It was more a statement than a question.

Austin nodded. "As soon as I figure out where I want to go, I'm out of here."

Most supernaturals stayed in town and enjoyed the protection it provided. But with Austin being human, the world truly was his oyster.

"You do know that I shouldn't be too happy for you. After all, I've invested so much time in training you, and now I'm going to have to start that process all over again. You're pretty irreplaceable." I tried to look disappointed. I turned the corners of my mouth downward, but couldn't hold it. A smile quickly broke out and revealed my true feelings.

He had the decency to look at least a little remorseful. "I can ask around to see if anyone would be interested in replacing me. I could even train them for you." Austin's expression was one of pure earnestness.

"I'm just kidding you. It will all work out. For now—" I gave him another quick hug. "Enjoy your accomplishments and let me know a good time for us to go out and celebrate. This isn't something to ignore."

The rest of the day passed by uneventfully, giving me a lot of time to ponder the discussion with my aunt. As much as I hated it, she'd roused my curiosity once more.

I took one last look at the order screen before closing it out.

Mr. Westbrook, what are you hiding, and do you understand how much danger you're in now that my aunt's picked up a scent?

Chances were he was about to find out.

CHAPTER 4

The days seemed to drag on slowly. I hadn't seen Micah at all, and part of me wondered if I'd simply imagined the dark-haired stranger in my store. I knew I'd often been accused of having my head in the clouds, daydreaming about the romantic stories I devoured by the page, but he'd been very real. The order page I kept stalking by the hour proved that.

"Look what just came in," Austin declared, holding up a package triumphantly. "Maybe I should go deliver this, or better yet, we should call Mr. Westbrook and have him personally come to pick it up himself."

There was a muffled cough and chuckle from the back of the store. Maxwell had also taken to teasing me about my sudden fascination with Micah, something very unbecoming of a ghost his age. When I'd mentioned that, he'd grinned, rolling the end of his mustache between his fingers like some conspirator.

From what I understood, I was the only one who saw the store's deceased occupant. I considered that a blessing, because there was no way I could ward off both Maxwell's and Austin's digs at how flustered I became at the mention of Micah's name.

Austin's latest game was seeing how many times he could make me jump by mentioning the newcomer's approach to Shelf Indulgence. It was only when I threatened to fire him, or worse, make him do the next six months of inventory by himself, that he simmered down.

Snatching the parcel from his hands, I scoffed as if I truly wasn't affected by the book's arrival.

"Don't you have something to do? Shelves to dust? Someone else to annoy?" The more I spoke, the softer my questions became.

Carefully opening the package, I slid out the book. Yep, *The Life and Loves of the Infamous King Henry Eighth, Fourth Edition.*

"You're okay to watch the store while I run this over to the customer, aren't you, Austin?" I already had my phone and the book in hand as I headed toward the door. "If you need anything, you can reach me on my cell."

"You look fine, by the way," he called out after me. Damn kid was too smart for his own good.

"There's no way Austin knew where you'd go first," I murmured, looking about to see if anyone was watching before turning around and heading back toward the Havenwood Village apartments. It was stupid that I felt the need to hide what I did, but if there was one thing the past had taught me about living here, it was that you couldn't be too careful. This town was founded on secrets—whether you were human or supernatural. Someone was always watching, taking note of everyone's activity. While I had nothing to hide, it didn't hurt to show caution anyway.

One false move and you could be the center of your very own Havenwood Falls scandal, the town's chief gossip the ever-reliable ringleader.

"Sedona? Sedona, my dear, just the young lady I was hoping to bump into!"

Speak of the devil.

One moment the street was empty, and the next, Irene Beckett stepped out of Pyntz Butcher Shoppe.

Here was one other person, besides my aunt, who had a sixth sense when it came to anything newsworthy and hidden agendas. Irene currently stood in the middle of the sidewalk, forcing me to stop and acknowledge her.

"Hi, Mrs. Beckett," I answered politely, forcing a jovial smile across my features. She was the last person I wanted to see today. "How are you?"

In one sweeping glance, she took in my appearance, and her dark eyes twinkled. "I hope once you visit with the mysterious Mr. Westbrook that you'll stop by the salon and let me know all about him. He's quite the catch, from what I've been told, but way too elusive for my liking. I should've known he would've sought you out, my pretty friend." She reached out and brushed a stray strand of hair to the side of my face.

Did I also mention that she had absolutely no respect for personal space?

"How did you—" I began, before she spoke up and answered.

"Why, the book, dear." She pointed at the package I was holding. Without thinking, I raised it to my chest, hugging it tighter as though it was a shield that could somehow protect me from her scrutiny. "Tell me, what kind of books does he read? Suspense or mystery, perhaps." Irene paused long enough to catch her breath. "Something tells me a man like him would be more into works of nonfiction than fiction."

It was often hard to keep up with Mrs. Beckett, but even this made me laugh. "What makes you think it's for him? Seems you've given him a lot of thought."

She waved her hand through the air, dismissively. "Of course I would. While I'm no longer in the market for a husband, that doesn't mean I don't look out for my younger friends. In fact . . ."

I inwardly groaned over what I knew would pass through her lips. Taking a page from her own book, I held up my hand to stop her. "I can find my own boyfriend, Mrs. Beckett. I'm perfectly capable."

I took a step back, glancing around to see if anyone could come rescue me. Like a blessed angel of mercy, Callie stepped out of her consignment store for a moment of fresh air. She also scanned the street, and as our eyes met briefly, I wanted to scream for her to come help.

As if by magic, she nodded and called out. "Oh, Mrs. Beckett. I had some new items come in this morning that I think you'd like."

The town gossip looked back and forth between us, silently trying to determine which conversation she wanted to continue.

Please, go to Callie. Please, please, please.

She placed her hand on my forearm, gently squeezing it. "Stop by the salon later and fill me in on all the details, will you?" Before I could let out a sigh of relief and mouth a quick *thank you* to Callie, Irene added one more opinion. "And there's no need to hurry home and change. You look beautiful already, Sedona. He would have to have rocks for brains if he doesn't recognize that."

"I promise," I answered, lying through my teeth. Waving her off, I stood for a moment, my nerves rattled. I guess you could say that was one of Irene's special gifts as well.

Turning around again, I headed toward the address I collected from Micah earlier in the week. There would be no stopping home quickly to check my appearance. If I did, it would just add fuel to the fire, leaving Irene to gossip with someone else about me changing clothes to deliver a book.

"You're going to die a spinster at this rate, Sedona," I grumbled.

And the thought of that was more depressing than usual.

CHAPTER 5

One of the things I loved most about living in Havenwood Falls was that it truly was a gorgeous place. Set in the midst of lush greenery that still caught my breath in the morning, my childhood home was surrounded by beautiful, majestic mountains. If there were ever a place that could cater to the many needs of the supernatural, it would be this town. It lacked the constant hustle and bustle of larger cities, but the residents liked it that way. As it was, the many prying human eyes always seemed to be on the verge of discovering how closely they brushed shoulders with the supernatural.

Not that the humans we lived alongside were completely oblivious, but it was much easier for the Court to govern and watch over a small town like ours. As for me, I loved the quaint charm Havenwood Falls held, and while there were definitely times I wished I could be invisible and simply blend in with the crowd, the small population was less chaotic against my empathic nerves.

I'd carved out a piece of heaven for myself and didn't really see myself leaving. Taking in a lungful of clean, fresh air, I could feel the energy that often thrummed quietly around me gently caress over my senses.

Spring was coming. While each season held its own brand of appeal, I loved watching the world wake up and the coming of new life

—the trees leaving behind the bareness of their branches as green leaves flourished and flowers blossomed. The rivers and creeks would grow fuller as the snow melted. Creatures would emerge from their wintry slumber, and the days would grow longer and warmer.

Something inside me whispered that this spring would bring something more personal and fulfilling than the picturesque scenery waking up. A new feeling was brewing deep within my spirit—a promise of growth and something I couldn't quite put my finger on. All I knew was it caused butterflies to flutter in my stomach and a pulse of excitement to quicken my breath.

Leaving the main streets of town, I followed the familiar path that would lead me to where Micah and his niece were currently residing. I was a little envious as I paused long enough to sidestep a heavy branch hanging over the trail. Small snowflakes glittered onto my hair from the pine needles above.

While I loved the magical feel of winter and Christmas, I was ready to say goodbye to wet boots and cold fingers.

It didn't bother me so much today, though, and I knew it had to do with seeing Micah. The man had taken over my thoughts and refused to budge. Over and over, I relived our encounter, questions filtering through my mind of possible reasons for him moving to Havenwood Falls.

With his modest home finally in sight, those butterflies kicked up a notch into a full-blown flurry and storm. My mouth dried from nerves, yet I kept on walking, as though drawn to him like a magnet.

The books that I read described this feeling as falling in love, and while I was a romantic at heart, being an empath had layered that feeling with a healthy dose of practical reality. There was no such thing as insta-love, at least not for me. Unfortunately, I wasn't some gorgeous heroine being swept off her feet by some tall, dark, and handsome stranger, and as mysterious as Micah was, I was pretty sure he wasn't my knight in shining armor.

I swung the small wooden fence open and approached his front door. With each step, my anticipation grew, and for the briefest of seconds, I prayed that he wasn't inside. I was being a coward. Yes, I often felt uncomfortable around people and would much rather be back in my bookstore with a cup of hot chocolate and my nose in a book, but life was about risk.

As scary as it was for an introvert like me, it was good to step out of my comfort zone. Besides, it wasn't like Micah was a werewolf or vampire. He wouldn't be biting me anytime soon.

Rapping my gloved knuckles against the thick door, I bounced on my toes to keep warm, my breath making white fog in the air.

"Hello?"

The door opened a crack, and from what I could tell, a teenager stood peering at me.

"Hi." I smiled, lifting the book in my hand. "I'm Sedona, and I'm looking for Micah Westbrook. He ordered something from my bookstore."

Whatever hesitancy she'd felt evaporated instantly as the door flew open, revealing a cute brunette wearing white fluffy unicorn slippers.

"You brought me my book!" she exclaimed, pulling the package from my arms and hugging it to her chest. "Micah said that he ordered it, but I was afraid it was never, ever, ever going to get here!"

"Holly?" came a deep voice from within the house. "What did I tell you about answering the—" And then he appeared—the man I'd had a hard time forgetting. Not that I wanted to. "—door?"

Much to my mortification, I let out a small gasp as I drank in the sight of him. Wearing dark blue jeans with a regular green flannel shirt, the man was attractive, but that wasn't what elicited such a reaction from me.

It was the glorious yellow shimmer that glowed around his entire body. I'd never seen anything so bright or so beautiful. There was a purity about it that stole my breath.

"Hi, Mr. Westbrook," I stammered, desperately trying to gather my thoughts.

So much for being professional.

"Your book came in early, so I thought I'd drop it by instead of waiting for you to come to the store. From the looks of it, I made the right call." I chuckled lightly and pointed to his niece. "I think I saved her from the torment of waiting forever, and ever, and ever."

"Don't be angry, Micah. She's right. You know how hard it is for me to wait when I want something badly!" Heaven help the poor man, but the puppy dog eyes she gave him were powerful enough to melt even the coldest of hearts. Hell, she wasn't even leveling that gaze my way and I wanted to take her back to Shelf Indulgence and tell her to go crazy.

The glow that had encased him vanished. Whatever wall he kept up between him and the world returned. But I still caught a glimmer of gratitude and, dare I say, interest.

My cheeks heated. I could only wish that someone like him would find someone like me interesting.

"Then it seems I'm in your debt, Miss Mathews. Thank you." He'd come to stand by Holly, placing himself slightly in front of her body as if to shield her from something. I didn't have to understand their relationship or read him to know she was someone he felt incredibly protective of.

Her small hand tugged on his shirtsleeve. "Aren't you forgetting something, Micah?" Holly asked, her smile wide and eyes twinkling. She adored him.

His expression grew confused as he looked at me. "I paid for the book when I placed the order, didn't I?"

I nodded, and before I could reassure him he had, Holly piped in again. "You forgot your manners." Then, pushing gently past her uncle, she stared up at me. "Do you have time for a cup of hot apple cider? It's pretty cold outside, and you look like you're part snowman!"

It was on the tip of my tongue to refuse, not wanting to invade their privacy. I could only begin to imagine the interrogation I'd get from Aunt Millicent once she found out I'd been in Micah's home.

He beat me to the punch, however. "My apologies, Sedona." The sound of my name on his lips sent a shiver through me that had nothing to do with the cool temperature. "Please, come in."

The door swung open wider, and I banged my boots on the side of the step before entering. I instantly went on sensory overload, and my gaze swept across the room, taking everything in. If I expected to uncover all his secrets by inspecting his home and the things he collected, then I'd be sorely disappointed. The living room was functional, holding all the appropriate furniture and décor, but it lacked his personal stamp and style. Holly's was all over the cozy room, from the laptop on the table where some website was currently opened up to the several piles of books scattered over the different surfaces. Just the sight of so many volumes brought a smile to my face.

"Can I say how happy I am to have another bookworm here in town?"

Micah was watching me from the entryway that I assumed led to the kitchen. His stare seemed to press against my aura, like he was trying to figure me out as well. I stared at him openly, showing him I wasn't someone to fear or worry over. Whatever he was looking for, he must've found, because the next moment he ducked out of the room and left Holly and me alone.

"I love books. All kinds of books. I love how they smell and the stories they share." Her words gushed out with an excitement akin to my own whenever I talked about my passion for reading. "One day I'm going to be a writer because words are my life!"

"Then, as one reader to another, you are more than welcome to come to Shelf Indulgence and read to your heart's content."

Her eyes widened to the size of saucers. "Seriously? I can read whatever I want?"

I nodded and drew an X over my chest with my finger. "Cross my heart."

You'd have thought I'd given her the moon when she threw her arms around my neck and squeezed tightly. "Thank you! I need to convince Uncle Micah, but I'm sure I can. He likes to think he's all tough and mean, but he's really a soft marshmallow."

"Are you sure of that?"

Micah's appearance caused Holly to squeak in surprise, her face flushing a mottled shade of red. "You can't say no! If you do, I'll run out of books and die!" And to her credit, she gripped her chest and fell dramatically to the floor, one eye peeking to see if he was watching.

"How could I possibly refuse?" Micah's voice was full of love and humor. He adored his niece just as much as she adored him. "There will be ground rules, though. Like always. Miss Mathews and I will discuss them, and if . . ." Holly sat up, holding her breath as she hung on his words. "If I feel it's okay, then we'll arrange for you to visit."

The young girl bounced on the ground, her smile so big that it brightened the whole room. "You are the *best*!"

"Yeah, yeah," he replied, shaking his head slowly. "I hope you remember that next time I tell you no."

Scooping up the book I'd delivered, Holly rushed over to Micah, threw her arms around his waist, and hugged him hard. "I won't ever argue with you again. I promise. Thank you!" And with that, she blew out of the living room like a whirlwind of adolescent hormones.

That left us alone together.

With him studying me as if I was a puzzle to solve.

"I hope you have good intentions, Sedona," he finally said. He hadn't moved closer and instead folded his arms across his chest, leaning against the doorframe. "I love my niece very much, and there's nothing I won't do to protect her."

An ominous chill swept over me, causing the hairs on my arm to rise.

"I'm not sure who you think I am, but I assure you, I'm no one to worry about." I lifted my hand up. "I'm just a girl who owns a bookstore."

His gaze narrowed. "No offense, but looks can be deceiving. I guess we'll just have to see."

His demeanor and response roused my curiosity. I once again sent out my senses in the hopes of picking up something—anything—from him.

He was still a blank slate.

I pushed again, determined to leave with at least some kind of clue.

"You'll have to try much harder than that, Sedona," he bristled. His stare held such intensity that it was hard not to flinch. This was a man I would never want to cross or anger.

"Than what?" I replied, feigning innocence.

"I know about your gifts, and by now, you should know they don't work on me. I hope that's sufficient for you to stop trying to read me." While his tone wasn't cold or unfriendly, it didn't hold the warmth it had before. I missed it.

Bowing my head, I nodded. "I'm sorry to invade your privacy," I murmured softly. "I guess you could say it's an occupational hazard."

His voice thawed slightly, and his gaze softened. "Not all secrets should be uncovered. Trust me. It's more for your benefit than my own." Then with a focus that felt like it pierced my core, Micah added, "Pass that on to your aunt. I am not her enemy, nor will I bring trouble to the Court or Havenwood Falls. I am simply an uncle trying to raise his niece the best he can."

Words failed me. There was an honesty that rung out—truthfulness that whispered he wasn't lying. It was more than I deserved after being caught using my gifts.

"Okay. Hopefully we can be friends, Micah." I stood from where I was sitting, suddenly needing to be anywhere but here. His presence filled the room—pressing back against my senses. "I need to get back to the store, so I'll take a raincheck on that apple cider, okay?"

He nodded. "Perhaps when I bring Holly into town we could go to one of the coffee shops."

He followed silently behind me as I headed toward the front door, pausing long enough to look over my shoulder, one hand already on the doorknob. "Let Holly know that I hope she enjoys King Henry."

"I will."

We stood there—looking at each other—a thousand unspoken words between us.

Just as I reached the end of the walkway, Micah called out. "Be safe, Sedona. Things aren't always as they seem."

Before I could ask him what he meant, he closed the door.

As snow began falling from the heavy clouds above, I gave his home one last look and started back into town, more confused than ever.

CHAPTER 6

$\mathcal{F}$ridays were my absolute favorite because as soon as it turned three o'clock in the afternoon, Shelf Indulgence would be filled with the sounds of children's excited chatter and giggles. I'd started the tradition of story time the previous year, and it had proven to be a huge success.

Usually it was just me, wearing my special "reading hat" and spectacles, making sure each character had its own distinct voice, much to the merriment of each of my little visitors.

Today's book had reduced us to fits of laughter. *Hugs and Kisses* was a cute story of a little girl catching her parents sharing a sweet kiss and wanting to make sure she knew how to when she grew up. Belle, the confused heroine of the tale, had then gone around her house, kissing her stuffed animals, the mirror, and even her sleeping grandfather's bald head. In her mind, she wanted to be happy just like her mom and dad, and the book ended in a loud symphony of lip smacks—and groans from those who worried about catching cooties from others.

The doorbell sounded, and everyone turned around to see who'd come to join in. I was a little surprised to find Holly standing there, alone, glancing about the store before her gaze met mine.

"Oops," she quickly said, her eyes taking in the small group of children sitting around me. "I don't want to interrupt. I was just hoping to maybe look through some of the shelves . . . like you were talking about earlier with my uncle."

Speaking of Micah, there was no sign of Mr. Tall, Dark, and Broody.

I hoped the smile I gave her helped ease her uncertainty. "Sure. If you find something interesting, there's an oversized chair in the back that is super comfy."

There was a tug at my sleeve. "Miss Sedona, can she read us another story?" Big, round chocolate-brown eyes looked up at me. Even though I told myself I shouldn't have favorites, this little boy knew how to tug hard at my heartstrings.

"I think you need to ask her, sweetheart."

Everyone turned again, watching Holly expectantly.

A huge grin spread across her adolescent features, and she brushed her long, thick brown hair back over her shoulder.

"Of course!" she exclaimed, before coming to join us on the rainbow-colored rug I used for story time.

Not missing a beat, the boy hurried over to the overflowing stack of books I always kept close by. I was pretty sure we'd read through most of them, but it didn't seem to bother anyone. For me, it was about seeing their imaginations expand and blossom. By capturing their hearts now, I hoped they would become forever readers.

"Read this one! It's funny, but you've got to do all the voices. It's only good if you do that." The earnest expression in his gaze had me stifling a chuckle, because I knew he was being as serious as his four-year-old mind could be.

"You sure you don't mind?" Holly asked me. There was no mistaking her excitement. While I didn't know too much about her and Micah, something whispered that she wanted to do this just as much as the children did.

Standing up, I leaned in and quietly added, "Just be careful. If they have their way, they'll have you reading all night."

Of course, when I looked back down at them, each child reflected an image of perfect innocence. The little stinkers!

"Oh, I don't mind. I was getting a little stir crazy anyway." There was no mistaking the sharp twang of loneliness I felt from her. Poor kid was probably bored from constantly staring at the four walls of her home.

Holly took the vacated seat in front of her attentive audience, and I took that as my cue to return to the work I'd left sitting under the register at the front.

Lavender was curled up in her favorite spot by the window, soaking up the warm rays of the sun shining through. I'd discovered the tiny ball of fur late one night, abandoned by the dumpsters outside, shivering with cold. After a brief inspection, I saw that the poor kitten had been born with a deformed, infected leg that made it difficult for her to get about and search for food.

It had taken a few trips to the vet clinic before the doctor deemed it necessary for her to lose the limb. I instantly handed over my credit card, assuring him that Lavender would have a forever home with me and that we were kindred spirits of sorts.

He'd given me a weird look at that, but he was used to it, living in Havenwood Falls. Nothing was ever what it seemed, so why wouldn't a twenty-four-year-old bookstore owner take a disabled kitten into her life? It wouldn't be the strangest thing he'd see in his career.

When I looked into Lavender's eyes, I felt a deep, resounding connection. Both of us knew what it was like to be misunderstood. All we wanted was to be loved for who we were, and not judged solely on our limitations—or in my case, my ability to see into the hearts and minds of those around me.

It was with that peace and calmness that I named the sweet tabby after the purple herb lavender. Had I known her true temperament, I may have chosen Diva instead, or Queen Sassy Pants. But she made me smile, and her early morning meowing for food was more endearing than annoying.

Most days.

"Enjoying the view, Lavender?" I asked, gently brushing my fingers over her soft fur. "See anything interesting happening out there?"

I peered out the bay windows, wishing for the time when the town square would return to its gorgeous manicured green lawns and gardens.

They'd finally taken down the Valentine's Day decorations in preparation for the upcoming spring equinox celebrations. There was always something happening—some party, fair, or festival.

I especially liked the Into the Mystic New Age & Psychic Fair Eloise planned each year that ran during the equinox. It was one of those occasions where some of the supernaturals in town could be themselves, sharing their gifts and talents with the unsuspecting, yet enthusiastic, human population. Eloise had tried to convince me to buy a booth and use my empath skills with some kind of love theme. So far I'd managed to sidestep her insistent asking. It seemed a sham to help others find love when I couldn't do it for myself.

Lavender purred beneath my touch, her fur rippling as she leisurely stretched.

Austin came rushing through the door, sending a cold draft of air in and ruffling the flyers on the counter. I didn't know who was more annoyed—me or my pampered cat. She threw him a disdainful look before closing her eyes again.

"Sorry I'm late. I ran all the way from school." Dumping his heavy backpack behind the counter, he kissed my cheek, grabbing his name badge at the same time. "I was beginning to think I was going to die in that last period. Why the hell did I take AP Statistics again?"

I rolled my eyes at him. "Because, and I quote, what's life for except to live a little dangerously." I lowered my hands after making quotation marks in the air. "I believe you also mentioned that it would be fun."

I still had a hard time accepting my part-time employee took hard subjects like math because he thought it would be fun. The only entertaining thing about that would be watching how many brains exploded from mental calculations and test anxiety. My own time in school was purposely blocked out, so I never remembered the trauma of trying to memorize equations and formulas.

Words I loved.

The alphabet had no business in math.

"Well, I'm seriously rethinking that theory and questioning how reliable my common sense is. Why didn't I take some fluff class like pottery making or papier mâché? I could've graduated *and* made a cool Christmas present for my annoying cousin, Ling." Austin smoothed down his wind-blown hair and glanced around. "So, who's the new girl?"

There was a glint of interest in his eyes and a ping in his aura.

"She's fourteen," I answered, sharply. Austin was a good kid, but he was also a flirt. The last thing I wanted was Micah storming in because his niece was suffering from a broken heart. "So go easy on the poor girl. Not everyone is immune to your charm."

His boyish grin made it hard to remain stern. He really did have a good heart, from what I could tell. He did what he wanted. He wore what he wanted. There wasn't much he couldn't talk himself out of or into. That was how he came to work for me. He wanted a part-time job and had decided Shelf Indulgence was in dire need of his services. After five minutes of listening to him, I was shoving the new-hire paperwork at him.

Austin placed his hand over his chest while feigning shock and offense. "You wound me, Sedona. You truly do. I was simply asking who she was. No other motives. Pinky swear."

I rolled my eyes at him again. "Just get to work and leave her alone. Go through the books and make sure everything's in order and where it should be."

He bowed dramatically, rolling his hand out in front of him. "As you wish."

And just because he could, he took a slight detour by the small group of attentive listeners and winked at Holly. She forgot her place in the story for the briefest of seconds, but it was enough to earn a response from the children. Stammering, she returned her focus to the book and continued on.

I wanted to throttle Austin.

"I'll gladly do it for you, Sedona. He won't feel it, but I would take great pleasure in the mere action of it."

My life was utterly crazy, with a diva cat, a Casanova employee, and a ghost who never gave a warning when he popped in and out from wherever he went when he wasn't bothering me.

"You know, it's not healthy to keep all that suppressed anger bottled up, Maxwell. You should learn to relax." I gave him a sidelong glance before reaching under the counter for the small pile of order forms and bills. "Maybe you should channel your inner Casper."

The snort of indignation that erupted from him made my teasing worth it. "You would mourn me if I ever decided to leave this establishment. Don't try to deny it."

"Not if you keep threatening to inflict ghostly bodily harm on Austin. How many times is it this week? Eight? Ten?" I'd lost count.

"Twelve, but that's beside the point. You refuse to listen to me when I warn you something isn't quite right about him. Mark my words, you'll regret not listening to me, Sedona."

Austin could never see Maxwell when they were both in the same room, but sometimes I wondered if he really could. Now was one of those moments because, as if hearing his name, Austin looked back toward the front at me.

I refused to give any credence to Maxwell's paranoia. Austin was as hardworking as he was smart, and he had a sense of style that I admired. Today, he wore a pair of blue denim jeans with a red-and-yellow-striped T-shirt that had a Gryffindor patch on the breast. He loved to dress up for the different events in the community, wearing his fandom favorites with pride.

"He's harmless," I countered, repeating the same thing I did each time the topic came up. "Don't you think I'd sense if something was off about him?" I glared at him, tired of having to defend Austin. "Seriously. I think I'm a pretty good judge of character." I tried not to be offended when he cocked his eyebrows at me and scoffed. I continued, "Fine, besides some of the guys I've dated."

"You're still very young, Sedona, as are your gifts. And because of your youth and naiveté, you often ignore what's right before you."

"Well, right now, I have a grumpy old man standing in front of me. How's that for talent?" I hated arguing with Maxwell. I knew he had good intentions, but he wasn't my father. He didn't have a right to tell me how to live my life.

He instantly closed his mouth, pursing his lips. The edges around his form began to grow hazy. He was about to fade away. I didn't stop him this time. We would no doubt talk later, and all would be forgiven.

I guess he wasn't done lecturing me. Just as he was almost gone, I heard him say, "Mark my words, Sedona. Mark. My. Words."

I plopped back onto the counter stool and stared at the empty space where he had just been. Our conversation had left a weird taste in my mouth, and I felt myself nearing my limit. Being an empath could be exhausting, and there were days when I found myself suddenly overstimulated and in desperate need of solitude.

The clock on the wall behind me said it was already four. Parents would be coming for their children soon, and maybe I could close up early for the day. The safety of my home felt very appealing right now.

"What say you, Lavender? Shall we go home and spend the night watching *Kitchen Nightmares* on Hulu?"

She ignored me.

I guess it would just be me then.

Sorting through the papers, I took care of the most urgent and important, then placed the pile back under the counter for tomorrow. I was starting to get a headache, and the numbers on the bills had begun swimming on the page.

With my head resting in my hands, my eyes closed. I didn't see him coming until he was standing in the entryway, fists clenched, thunder echoing in his voice as he glared at me.

"Where is she?" Micah demanded, his anger filling the store until there was no room to even breathe. He was magnificent as much as he was terrifying.

Two of the children began to cry.

"Micah," I started, instantly choking as he advanced toward me.

It was then that I felt it—fear . . . panic . . . uncertainty.

It was in total contradiction to the body language he was displaying.

Micah Westbrook was terrified, and he looked like he would level the town in his wrath.

I tried again, gulping nervously before finding the courage to face him.

"She's here, Micah." That was when I realized she hadn't told him where she was going. She'd been here all this time, and I'd foolishly assumed he'd known.

It took a few moments for him to register what I said, and a few more for him to notice that Holly had come to stand beside him, her hand lying gently on his bicep.

"Uncle."

And in the space it took for him to finally see her and take a breath, his emotions were locked back behind the wall he always had erected. But I'd been prepared this time—quicker. I'd caught some images that had flashed in his mind before it all went blank.

He looked at me, knowing I'd seen something with my gift.

Wrapping his arms around Holly, he crushed her to him, all the while telling her to never, ever leave the house again without telling him. His eyes never left mine, even though he was talking to his niece. Part of me wanted to feign interest in my paperwork so they could have a little privacy, but I wasn't the only one watching the encounter.

"Perhaps you two would like to use the back storeroom to talk?" I suggested.

"No, we're leaving. Grab your things, Holly." There was a heavy dose of authority in his tone that most people would struggle to ignore. It demanded obedience and submission. It wouldn't tolerate defiance, which was exactly what Holly showed.

With her hands firmly on her waist, she glared up at her uncle. "I'm not ready to leave yet. I haven't finished reading the story. Plus, you're angry."

I could almost hear Micah count to ten in his mind. I wanted to laugh and remind him that it only got worse with teenagers—that if he thought he could win every battle with her, he was sadly deluded.

"Fine, let's talk." Gesturing for her to go ahead, he looked my way again. "The room is back there?"

"Yes," I nodded. "Take your time."

The storefront was eerily quiet once the two had left and the door closed swiftly behind them. The children shifted uneasily, and I threw on another smile just for them.

"How about we have another story while we wait for your parents?"

It was the longest ten minutes I'd ever spent in the store as I attempted to read, watching nervously where Micah and Holly had disappeared, and also the front door. Finally the last of the children were gone.

Austin snuck up beside me. "What the heck was that?" he murmured, letting out a low whistle.

"Good question," I answered.

Unfortunately, I didn't have a clue either.

CHAPTER 7

*J*t was difficult not to say anything as Micah and Holly walked past me on their way out of the store. Some of the intensity that had been rolling off Micah had subsided, and poor Holly meekly followed behind him.

She quickly apologized for any problems her coming had created, and before I could reassure her that she was more than welcome to visit, Micah tugged on her hand, and they were gone.

I closed up Shelf Indulgence shortly after that, exhausted. The whole afternoon had been one hell of an emotional roller coaster, and all I wanted was to hide away in my fortress of an apartment with Lavender and forget the world existed.

"I wonder what Gordon's up to tonight, Lavender?" I asked as I clicked on the television, scrolling through my DVR for the episodes of *Hell's Kitchen* I'd saved. Slowly stroking her soft fur, I smiled as her loud purrs filled the room. "What do you think my chances are of meeting him?" Relaxing back into the couch, I curled my feet up beneath me. "A girl can dream, right?"

Gradually, all the events of the day melted away, and I finally found my happy place. The specialty peppermint tea I'd purchased from Broastful Brew left a soothing path down my throat, and everything was perfect and in order.

Chaos often spelled disaster for an empath, because it was the quickest way to overstimulate the senses and send them spiraling into overload. It was why I made sure I was always protected with the charmed pendant I'd fashioned out of black tourmaline. It helped keep any negative energy out of my aura and prevented it from seeping into my own consciousness. Today I'd been caught off guard.

"Okay, my darling." The sexy British accent on the television pulled me back to the present, and I smiled. Goose bumps spread across my bare arms. If only I had someone to speak such endearments to me.

"I need to get a life, Lavender," I murmured, looking around my small apartment.

I'd been living at Havenwood Village for the past three years and spent most of it decorating my one-bedroom home with things that usually filled me with a calm sense of satisfaction. Tonight, however, it was merely a reminder of how alone I truly was—a loneliness I often hid from myself.

The spoiled cat opened one eye, as if to say she agreed, before shutting it again.

Suddenly, I didn't want to be hidden away in my apartment. I was tired of spending yet another night watching pre-recorded shows before trudging off to bed. I wanted to be where everyone else was—experiencing life in all its glory. It was time to shake off the introvert and embrace the part of me that loved being social.

I quickly slipped into jeans, a pretty top, and flats, then grabbed my keys and bag.

"Don't wait up, Lavender! I have no idea how long I'll be or when I'll be home." Throwing open the door with a huge grin on my face, my impromptu adventure was pulled to an abrupt stop.

Micah Westbrook stood on the other side, his hand poised as if he was about to knock. I didn't know who was more surprised—me or him.

Damn, he smells amazing!

He cleared his throat, looking unsure as he glanced over his shoulder to where he'd come from.

"Did I catch you at a bad time?" There was a sexy rasp in his voice

336

that I hadn't noticed before. It skimmed over my senses, leaving a trail of tingles in its wake.

I looked down at my hand to my keys. "I . . . well, I was . . ." *Damn, I sound like an idiot.* "I was thinking about going to the Haven Saloon."

Micah's eyes narrowed as he studied me. "I've never seen you there before."

My face heated, and I wanted to curse whoever's genes gave me this inclination to blush all the time. I was a grown woman, and yet, the way Micah's gaze bored into me, I wanted to confess all my secrets.

"Would you like to join me?" I blurted out.

A slow smile crawled across his handsome features. "Will you be meeting someone there?"

My stomach did a flip as I confessed that I was planning to go by myself.

"Then I'd be happy to escort you there."

Locking the door behind me, I walked silently beside him as we made our way down to the street. How had this happened? What made me think I even stood a chance with a man like him? He was so confident, while I preferred the company of books and animals. He held all the mystique of a newcomer, while I was someone people often kept their distance from because I might sense some dark and foreboding truth.

When he took my hand and placed it in the crook of his arm, I threw caution to the wind. I relaxed. I let out a breath. I released the anxiety knitting a knot in my stomach.

I'd said I needed to get a life, and the Fates had answered.

The question was . . . what kind of life had I just agreed to?

"DID you know that the tune of 'The Star-Spangled Banner' was borrowed from the melody of an old drinking song?"

Micah cocked his brow in interest. "Really?"

I could understand why he was skeptical. It was such a patriotic song, beloved by everyone.

"Yep," I answered. "The original was the song of a British gentlemen's music club some two hundred years ago." I took a small sip of the beer I'd ordered. I had no clue why I'd chosen it, but after a few mouthfuls, the hoppy taste didn't bother me as much.

Micah rested his head on his hand, the fingers of his other hand lightly curled around his own glass. "You're a wealth of information, Miss Mathews. What other tidbits do you know?"

I didn't know whether he was genuinely curious or teasing me, but I didn't care. The beer was warm in my body, and my energy was thrumming from all the people surrounding us. The saloon was busy tonight, and we almost didn't find a table. Fortunately for us, there were a few in the very back, and we'd rushed forward to claim one of them.

I raised my glass, tilting it slightly to the side as the amber liquid sloshed back and forth.

"Did you know that the world's oldest known recipe is for beer? Or that it's illegal to feed alcohol to moose in Alaska and fishes in Ohio?" When he went to respond, I took a quick sip before continuing, "Or that there is a cloud of alcohol in outer space that holds enough booze to make trillions of drinks?"

"You're making that last one up!" Micah exclaimed, incredulously.

"Nope, it's all true. Just one of many useful facts I have stored up here." I tapped the side of my head, grinning. "Or useless. I haven't quite decided on that yet."

He leaned forward on his elbows, close enough for me to catch another whiff of his spicy cologne. I absently licked my lips as my gaze dropped to his chest. I was a freaking lightweight when it came to alcohol. Half a glass, and I was contemplating what facts could convince him to take his shirt off.

"Why do you do that?"

It was my turn to wear a quizzical look. "Do what?"

His nails tapped gently against the surface of his glass. "Whenever you're nervous, you become a fount of knowledge. You did the same that first time we met."

I shrugged. "I don't know. I guess I find a certain comfort in facts . . . in truths. People often confuse me, especially when I can't figure out their intentions. It's why I love reading and books. The only surprises are the plot twists the author throws in."

The air seemed to still around us, dimming the music that played in the bar. "Do I confuse you, Sedona?"

I was tempted to lie and fake bravado, but I knew he'd see right through it. Micah was good at reading people . . . he'd known straight away about my gifts, and that I was trying to use them on him.

"Truthfully?" I held his gaze as he nodded.

"Naturally."

A small blast of heat went through me. "You don't confuse me as much as scare me a little."

He hadn't looked away. "How so?"

Licking my lips, I sat up a little straighter. "Well, for starters, I can't get a lock on your emotions. The only people I can't read are those who purposely shield themselves from me. As far as I know, you don't really know me, so why would you hide?"

His eyes were like the crystal blue waters of the Bahamas. "And is that what you want? To have me lower my guard and let you in?"

If I were to guess what kind of supernatural he was, I would say he was a warlock, because he'd somehow created this web of attraction between us.

"What are you hiding from me?" I countered, my voice low.

"We all have secrets, Sedona. It isn't always good to be so open with everyone."

There he was again with his cryptic talking. "But isn't that part of becoming friends with people? Of developing relationships? It's about give and take. It's about letting someone in and showing them pieces of yourself."

"Is that what you want from me? To be friends?"

"Don't you?" I fired back. "I may not know you too well, but I know another lonely soul when I meet one. You're extremely guarded. The only time I've felt any semblance of emotion from you is with Holly." Instantly, the shutters fell in his eyes, and I let him know I saw it. "See? I mention Holly, and suddenly you clam up tighter than a bank vault. I know you said to be careful with who you trust, but isn't life too short to keep everyone at arm's length?"

I let my question hang in the air between us. Resting back in my chair, I cradled the glass in front of me between my hands. "All I'm saying is it's okay to trust someone, Micah. It's okay to let people in. We're not all villains or whoever you seem to think we are."

He sat quietly, his lips closed as he mulled over my passionate rambling. As the seconds ticked slowly by, panic began to fill me. This was why I shouldn't ever go out in public. I wasn't good with people, and sometimes—well, often—I shoved both feet in my mouth.

I started feeling desperate, so I did what I always did in such occasions.

"Did you know chewing gum while peeling onions can keep you from crying?"

He remained still until he burst out laughing. It defused the tension, and I joined in.

Once he eventually stopped, Micah nodded. "I think I'd like to be your friend, too, Sedona. Perhaps you are someone I can trust."

"While I can't promise you I won't bore you with more facts, I can promise you that you won't regret it." Raising my glass in the air, I clinked it against his. "To being friends."

His voice was thick as he murmured the same.

I placed the glass back on the table, glad to have that all out of the way. "So, you never did tell me why you came over tonight."

His eyes widened when he realized the same. "I simply wanted to apologize for my poor behavior today at your store. I let my fear for Holly get the best of me when I couldn't find her. We talked about it, so knock on wood." He rapped his knuckles on the tabletop. "You won't ever see me acting like a raving lunatic again."

There it was again—that niggling thread that just begged for me to tug on. "You're a good uncle to worry about your niece. Havenwood Falls is pretty safe, though. Maybe you don't have to worry *as* much now."

His mouth twitched as he shook his head. "I'll always worry, but that's a story for another time. For the time being, she can continue coming to the store on the condition that she call me once she gets there."

"You're really protective of her, aren't you?" I said, hoping it would lead to him sharing why. There was no such luck, however. When he said it was a tale for another day, he meant it.

Giving him a sly look as I finished my drink, I warned Micah that sooner or later I would figure him out.

"Be careful what you wish for, Sedona. That's all I'm going to say. Be careful."

If only someone could tell that to my heart.

CHAPTER 8

*A*pparently what Micah had meant that night at the Haven Saloon was that he would watch Holly like a hawk regardless of whether she called him.

I still didn't know what hidden dangers lurked inside his head, and trust me, it irked me to no end that I couldn't seem to penetrate the wall he had around his mind, but it didn't take a rocket scientist to see why he suddenly became a fixture at Shelf Indulgence.

Just one word: Austin.

Holly had spent just one afternoon with my employee, and it was plain to see that she was well on her way to a full-blown case of teenage angst and puppy love. Whether Austin realized it or not, I noticed the longing stares she cast his way and how she twisted a strand of her hair between her fingers. But those signs paled in comparison to the rather large flashing neon sign that seemed to hang above her that screamed CRUSH.

I took care not to invade her emotions, knowing just how hard it was at that age, when you first discovered boys and that they were more than just cootie carriers. It had been tempting to pry a little and see if I could uncover Micah's secrets through her. I hated the sleazy feeling that skated over my senses as part of me warred with the other.

No one would know if I did decide to push just a little bit against Holly's defenses. Well, someone would know—me.

Besides, the more time I spent with the kid, the more I grew to like her. Her thirst for knowledge was refreshing, and it was satisfying watching her voraciously devouring each book she pulled from the shelf.

Then Austin sauntered through the door in all his shiny senior glory, and Holly found a new subject to enjoy. I had a quick word with Austin to remind him that she was off limits and that if I caught him leading her on, I would put him on toilet duty for a year. He scoffed at my attempt at a threat, replying that one toilet wasn't that big of a deal, considering he already took care of it. His face blanched a sickly shade of white, however, when I told him I hadn't quite finished. I would see that he cleaned every toilet on town square and the surrounding businesses, and that if he didn't believe me, I'd throw in the ski resort for good measure.

I didn't really have that kind of pull, but it was funny to watch the belief in his eyes. Austin was then on his best behavior and volunteered to tutor Holly with her schoolwork. She impressed him immediately with her knowledge, and they spent most afternoons with their heads down as they read from some textbook or another.

Harmless enough to me.

Worrisome to Micah.

"I don't like him," he murmured, not once taking his eyes off the pair. "Are you sure you threatened him enough? Perhaps I should have a talk with him."

I studied Micah as he stood leaning against the wall that led to the back storeroom. I was once again perched on my stool behind the counter, scrolling through a list of books I was hoping to order from. I clicked out of that window and opened another, this one the site where I often purchased the decorations for my window display. I'd finally narrowed the list down to a spring theme, considering the spring equinox was fast approaching.

Who was I kidding? I'd spent more time memorizing the leanness of his body and how his jaw tightened each time Austin moved closer to Holly. He was watching them, and I was watching him. My heart raced faster whenever he looked my way, and it became increasingly harder to focus. Suddenly I understood Holly a little better—we both had crushes on guys way out of our league.

"Are you seriously going to stand there ready to pounce on that poor boy?" I asked, laughing. "What do you think he's going to do? Whisk her away to Mexico and get married? Get her drunk at some frat party?"

I was only teasing, but for a second there, I worried the muscle in Micah's tight jaw might snap from pressure. His glare was positively lethal.

"He'll be dead before he takes his next breath," he muttered softly below his breath, poised to take a step toward the two unaware teens.

"Micah!" I exclaimed, my eyes widening. A sick sensation settled in the pit of my stomach, and a menacing, oppressive wave flowed over me. He wasn't joking around. Deep in my gut I knew that what he had spoken out loud was truth.

Moving away from where I was sitting, I cautiously approached him, trying to figure out what had flipped the anger switch inside him. Yes, most males got overly protective when members of the opposite sex so much as breathed too close to their female family members, but this was excessive.

I had to think quickly and defuse the situation. Catching him off guard, I shoved hard at him, pushing him back into the storage room, and slammed the door closed with my foot. I was getting ready to lay the law down with him.

"I may look small, Micah Westbrook, but believe me when I tell you that I won't hesitate to knock you on your ass if you don't start acting with better manners. I've known that kid out there for a year, so you can trust me when I say he's a good kid."

Micah began to speak, but I cut him off.

"I'm not finished." I jabbed at his chest with my finger, which earned me a soft grunt. The corners of his mouth trembled as he tried not to smile.

Great. He thought I was being cute.

"You've got two choices, mister. You can either leave, and I'll call you when their tutoring session is over, or you can quit acting like a caveman and be useful."

He cocked his eyebrow, intrigued. "Useful how?"

"Well, for starters you can stop acting like a helicopter parent, hovering in anticipation, and help me organize in here." I gestured to my neatly arranged shelves of inventory. "And before you make some sarcastic remark, this system no longer works for me." My hands rested on my hips as I stared him down.

"Are those the only two options I have?" For some reason, his gaze dropped to my mouth before rising again to meet my stare.

"Well," I began, wearing a smirk of my own. "You can always choose door number three and explain to me why you want to kill anyone who gets close to Holly. You know that's not normal, right? Keep acting this way, and I'm going to start thinking your secret is you're a serial killer on the run."

He had the audacity to bark out a loud laugh, tears forming at the corner of his eyes. "Is that what you think, Sedona?"

He took a step toward me, blocking the way out with his body.

I stood my ground, not intimidated in the least. "I don't know what to think, Micah. You refuse to answer any of my questions, remember?"

I tilted my head back slightly so I could still hold eye contact. Good lord, he was tall. I briefly closed my eyes. I could still feel him. *Damn it.*

"What if I told you I'm feeling generous today?" He stepped even closer, and the room suddenly felt too small, my own emotions bouncing off the walls. Instinctively, I searched for his, and once again felt the tall, hard wall he'd erected as a defense.

No, wait.

Somewhere in the few moments that had passed, my traitorous hand had reached out and now rested over his heart. The hardness that I felt was in fact . . . him.

"Sedona," he murmured, his tone now soft and gentle. I wanted to lean into him. "Tell me what you want."

A thousand responses raced through my mind—from all the

questions I had to the private fantasies I entertained late at night while I was safe at home.

He tilted my chin up with his finger. The look on his face melted me because it brought a different emotion for him into the forefront, one I hadn't expected.

Desire.

"Micah," I breathed, licking my lips. "Just let me in. Trust me." I was about to add *and don't kill my employee*, when he surprised me again.

"Okay." It was just one word, but I knew how much it meant for him to grant it. "Feel this."

I gasped out loud as I felt his walls come down, and the sweetest, most intense sensation spilled out from behind it.

Attraction.

Desire.

Interest.

A wild desperation at having to deny the one thing he wanted—me.

One word filled my mind that confused me.

Forbidden.

I parted my lips to ask him why he saw me that way, but he didn't give me a chance, because he crushed his mouth over mine, his tongue tracing the seam of my lips. My arms wrapped around his neck, and his hands spanned my waist, bringing my body up against his. I didn't know whether it was because I was up on my tiptoes or because he'd lifted me up off the ground, but we fit perfectly. His kiss was beyond perfect. In fact, it far exceeded anything I could've hoped for.

In that one kiss I knew he had ruined me for any that may follow. He savored each taste, each dip of his tongue as it met with mine, causing both of us to moan softly. It was both beautiful and savage— beautiful because he held me like I was precious and savage because there was a barely restrained hunger that lurked beneath the kiss.

I wanted to encourage him to let go of whatever kept him always on guard.

I wanted to tell him—scream—that it was okay and that nothing catastrophic would happen—that we were both consenting adults who wanted this. I felt myself melt in his arms and his embrace tighten, holding me closer. It was everything and more, and I begged that time could stand still so I could memorize every blissful second.

His hand skated up over my back and into my hair, his fingers curling in the strands. A thought flashed through my mind to never wear it down again because electricity sizzled through my nerves, setting them on fire.

I felt alive—painfully, blissfully aware of everything around me.

And then the moment was over, and I could feel him pull back. I kept my eyes closed as if to prolong the numbness of my lips, the touch of his hands on my body.

"Sedona," he whispered, his voice low and husky.

"Mmmm," I replied, and I slowly opened my eyes.

"Did you know King Henry the Sixth banned kissing in England as a way to prevent the spread of disease? Or that the average person spends two weeks of their life kissing?"

My eyes flew open as I burst out laughing. "Oh, really?"

His grin showed me more than tapping into his emotions would. He was very proud of himself. "I also read that scientists at the University in Tokyo believe our love of kissing comes from an ancient rat."

My brow furrowed, and I scrunched my nose. "Ewwww, I'm almost too scared to ask about that last one, but I have to know!"

I locked eyes with him again, enjoying his impromptu fact sharing.

"Yeah, I wasn't quite sure I wanted to share that with you, but I also knew your thirst for knowledge—the weirder the better." He brushed the hair away from the side of my face, his fingers slowly trailing down before cupping my cheek. "I'm hoping it will earn me brownie points in case that kiss was an epic fail."

My mouth watered, and I wanted to grab his face to kiss him back. Hard. "I never pegged you for someone who lacked confidence in that area, Micah," I teased. "But yes, you earned big points for those pieces of trivia. In fact, I have it on good authority that if you tell me more about that ancient rat, there will be another kiss." I sounded cheesy as hell, but I didn't care.

"Something about the rat rubbing noses with its mate to signal desire." Micah leaned in, placing his forehead against mine, our noses barely touching. "I didn't expect to find you, Sedona." His warm breath fanned across my lips.

"Yet here we are."

He leaned in again, whispering against my mouth, "I guess this changes everything."

And with that declaration, my heart soared.

CHAPTER 9

There was no denying the extra little bounce in my step or the huge smile plastered across my face was because of Micah. I was turning into one of the heroines in my beloved books who can finally claim the man they love.

Not that I loved Micah, but hell, I was definitely falling.

There was something about him that instantly drew my gaze whenever he was in the room—his presence filled the entire space. He took my breath away with the simplest things, those small considerations that showed he was paying attention.

If I thought he was protective of Holly, that awareness had now spread to cover me. In the weeks since our first kiss, I often wondered what had rattled him so badly and set his instincts on fire. He was always vigilant when we were together, even when I shared a meal with him and Holly in their home. Every noise caused him to pause momentarily, as if he was waiting for something to crash in and attack.

It was torturous not to blurt out my questions whenever he got that faraway look in his eye, a sign that he was thinking . . . listening. I fought the temptation to casually ask Holly if she understood her uncle's driving need to protect, but I knew in my heart that was crossing a line. It was something my aunt would do—something she encouraged me to use my gift for.

"Why would you be given such an important gift, dear niece, unless you were expected to serve the coven? Don't you want to help keep Havenwood Falls safe and free from nefarious creatures?"

It didn't matter how many times I argued that it went against my ethics. I was a tool to be used, plain and simple.

It was because of Aunt Millicent that I reined in my curiosity when it came to Micah. I wouldn't stoop to her level. I wouldn't prove her right when she said that one day I would regret not listening to her.

"You'll call me when you're done, right?" Micah asked as he lifted my hand to his mouth and kissed it. He'd insisted on walking me to my hair appointment at Shear Magic. His expression was kind of cute when I casually wondered out loud who he thought would attack me as I walked the short distance from the bookstore. He tutted beneath his breath and gripped my hand a little tighter.

"It might be late," I replied, bouncing slowly on the balls of my feet, looking up at him. "It's usually an all-day thing when I change hair color."

Micah twisted a strand of my hair around his finger. "Explain to me again why you're doing this? You're beautiful, sweetheart, and wouldn't it make you stand out?"

I nodded at the last of his response. I did want to stand out. I was finally ready to step back out into the world and participate. Maybe it was Micah who gave me this newfound sense of courage, because with him, I didn't feel so scared.

"I had to cancel my last appointment because I was sick, and this was the first opportunity I could get back in. Besides," I grinned playfully, "it's not every day a girl can get hair like a mermaid."

"And that's a good thing?" His quizzical expression was adorable.

"It's a very good thing." Rising back onto my tiptoes again, I pressed my mouth against his firmly. A sense of brief frustration flittered across my senses—his. "I promise you'll like it."

"Perhaps I should stay," he murmured, lips pursed.

"Are you imagining a fleet of ninjas rappelling from the salon's ceiling? Perhaps karate-chopping us into submission?" I gently teased him even though I knew his concerns were real to him. "Seriously, go glare at Austin for a few hours. He mentioned Holly coming in to work on some homework. You know how young men can be."

It was a mean thing to say, but Micah responded exactly how I thought he would. One mention of Holly, and all thoughts of my being assaulted while getting my hair colored were shoved onto the back burner.

I knew where I ranked compared to his niece, and it didn't bother me in the slightest.

He kissed me once more, chuckling under his breath when we pulled apart. Glancing over my shoulder, I caught the gaze of one of the ladies inside the salon.

"Looks like we have an audience, Micah." I couldn't hide my amusement. I didn't try to as I openly laughed.

He quickly hooked his arm back around my waist and tugged me up close.

"Then let's give them something to talk about."

And what a kiss it was.

I was afforded at least an hour before I heard his name mentioned. After entering Shear Magic, I'd made a beeline to the stack of magazines, randomly choosing one as I buried my nose in the thrilling gossip of some celebrity and their inner turmoil. I feigned complete interest, avoiding eye contact with anyone until finally my own name was called.

"We still doing the mermaid look, Sedona?" Charlotte asked, peering at my reflection in the mirror I now sat before. Charlie, for short, was a genius when it came to hair, and the only person in Havenwood Falls I would trust with mine. She'd squealed with excitement when I showed her a photo I'd found online and vowed she wouldn't let me leave the salon until my hair was perfect.

I didn't know too much about Charlie other than the basics. Like me, she kept pretty much to herself unless it had something to do with work. I got the impression that life hadn't been easy for her and knew should she choose to open up, she would. Today she had her fiery red hair pinned back with a set of fashion chopsticks stuck expertly into her loose bun. Tendrils of hair framed her round face, and a warm smile graced her features. Every time I came in, I made a mental note to somehow get to know her better, but life often got in the way.

"Absolutely!" I grinned as I tucked my feet on the chair's rung. "I can't tell you how many times I've seen that photo. The purples, blues, and greens are gorgeous!"

She whipped the black plastic cape around me and began running her fingers through my hair. "Did you want a trim after to keep it healthy?" She held up a section, showing me the length she intended to cut. "Probably about half an inch would do it."

Closing my eyes, I relaxed into the swivel seat. "I'm in your capable hands, Charlie. I trust you."

A while later, I sat with my head under a dryer, the foil hiding the different dyes within its folds, making me look like I was trying to ward off a legion of space aliens. I'd started off reading another magazine, but it didn't take long before my mind wandered to more enjoyable thoughts.

Like Micah.

His kisses.

The way his eyes widened ever so slightly—giving away how he truly felt whenever he saw me.

How amazing he was with Holly, even when he was being super protective.

He had so many incredibly sexy traits that dazzled me. He made the dashing heroes in my books pale by comparison. I was less interested in reading the pile of romance novels by my bedside and more into experiencing my very own real-life fairy tale.

Part of me warned that I was bordering on delusional—that there was no such thing as the perfect guy. Sooner or later, things would sour, and Micah would walk away. If it was too good to be true, it usually meant that some kind of flaw would surface and tarnish the sparkle.

I didn't want the tarnish.

As silly as it sounded, living where I did, surrounded by supernaturals, I wanted the magic.

"Sedona, dear, perhaps you could settle an argument."

Peering over the top of the magazine I was pretending to read, I found myself the center of attention. Irene Beckett and two other town members, Laverne and Sybil Carson, huddled closer, their hair set in curlers. The way Irene wet her lips with anticipation and her eyes twinkled told me all I needed to know.

Micah. They had caught our kiss goodbye and had been gracious enough to lull me into a false sense of security before pouncing. It almost felt like I was their trapped prey, caught in their web until they gained the answers they were seeking and set me free.

I visibly gulped and faked a smile. Hoping against hope, I feigned ignorance. I wouldn't be making this easy for them.

"Hi, ladies. The salon seems the place to be this morning." I was tempted to lift the magazine back off my lap. I glanced at the clock. I still had another fifteen minutes under the heated dryer.

Sybil leaned in and stared at my foiled head. "Did I see right? You're having your hair colored blue?"

The three human women must've been in their seventies, and I couldn't tell whether they approved or not.

It didn't matter. "Yep, plus purple and green. I call it the mermaid look."

Sybil scrunched up her nose. "It should be interesting," she muttered, her gaze never leaving my covered hair.

That was pretty tame for Mrs. Carson, because she usually had no qualms letting you know exactly how she felt. The three of them shared that same trait. When they all zeroed in their focus on you— heaven help you and God bless. There was a rumor circulating town that they could be so sharp-tongued, their words could flay flesh off bone. An exaggeration, maybe, but the imagery made me shudder.

Her almost kind response further warned me they had another agenda. They had questions, and I was the one who could satisfy their thirst for gossip.

"Miss Mathews," Irene chirped, a sugary smile twisting her lips into an insincere grimace. "Did I see right earlier? Are you and Micah Westbrook an item?"

Before I could answer, Laverne interjected. "I should hope so.

Sedona isn't the kind of girl for such grand displays of affection in public. Micah is definitely her beau." She nodded as if it was a commonly known fact and therefore didn't require me to respond.

"You shouldn't be that open with members of the opposite sex, Sedona, dear," Sybil countered, her eyes tinged with concern and her voice low. "You wouldn't want others to think you're something you're not."

I stifled a chuckle. "Thank you for worrying about me, Mrs. Carson, but I'm okay. Yes, Micah and I have started to date."

The three of them collectively took in a deep breath. It made me want to take a bazillion steps back. They reminded me of a nest of cobras, drawing back before they struck.

"About Micah . . ." It was Irene who finally revealed the true reason they surrounded me.

"Mm-hmm," I murmured, praying they'd think better of prying. No such luck.

Irene continued. "Has he told you much about himself? Like who he is or where he came from?"

"Or why he doesn't allow his sweet niece to go to the public school? Why would he prefer to homeschool when we have a fine educational institution at his disposal? Havenwood Falls High is one of the best in the country," Laverne bragged, her chest puffing out with pride.

"I don't really think I should be talking about this without him here." If there was one thing I'd learned, it was the need to be diplomatic. "I'm sure if you asked him, he'd be happy to answer your questions."

It was a bald-faced lie but I didn't care. There was a small voice inside that wanted to add that I couldn't share what I didn't know. My knowledge about Micah was limited as it was. The few tidbits I'd managed to glean were pitiful.

Sybil bounced a little with excitement, and her voice grew louder. "I heard he's part of the witness protection program, and that's why he's here. That he witnessed something so horrifying, he needed to go into hiding."

Her gaze darted back and forth conspiratorially.

"Sedona, are you all right?" Laverne's tone lost its previous nosiness, and motherly concern replaced it. She reached out and touched my hand. "Did we say something wrong?"

Irene zeroed in on me, and I could feel her gaze hungrily search my face for hidden clues. Heaven help everyone if this woman had been gifted with being an empath. She'd gorge herself on all the secrets she'd uncover, because there was no way she would maintain respectful boundaries.

Their stares felt heavy. I shook my head. "I'm fine, and to answer your questions, again, maybe you can ask Micah. He's the best one to share his story."

Something in my voice must've convinced them they were barking up the wrong tree and to back off. They whispered amongst themselves quietly before offering me those sugary smiles again.

"We're glad to see you happy. We just wanted to make sure he was worthy of you."

"Yes, yes," Sybil added, casting a sidelong glance of agreement at Laverne. "Only the best for our beautiful Sedona."

My face heated at the compliment. The way they seemed to bounce back and forth between pushing for gossip and buttering me up with praise gave me a headache.

"Sedona," Charlie interrupted, her eyes evaluating the scene as she gestured for me to come back to the chair I'd been in before. A silent sorry exchanged between us. "I think we're ready to rinse out the dye."

Excusing myself from the meddlesome trio, I finished up my appointment, happy with the results.

All that was left was to find Micah. All this talk about him had me craving him.

Who was I kidding?

I was ready to sink into his arms and take up where we left off outside Shear Magic. If there was one thing I was beginning to know about that man, it was that one kiss would never, *ever* be enough.

CHAPTER 10

"*M*mmm, that smells delicious!"

Micah came up behind me and placed his hands on either side of me, resting on the kitchen countertop. His breath was soft against my ear, and it was suddenly difficult to concentrate on chopping up the vegetables we'd be having with the steaks he'd be grilling.

Focusing on the knife in my hand, I tried not to moan out loud when his breath was replaced with his mouth. A bolt of desire shot through my body, and a wave of shivers made me squirm a little against him.

If he had even a fraction of an idea about how he affected me, he would probably tease me without mercy. Not that I wouldn't enjoy every blissful second, but with a sharp object in my hand, I couldn't guarantee it wouldn't end up bloody somehow.

"That marinade smells divine," I agreed, taking a small bite out of the green bell pepper sliver before offering him the rest. "My mouth keeps watering every time I take a breath."

"And here I was thinking I was the reason." I didn't need to turn around to know that Micah wore a devilish grin that would've melted me on the spot. For someone who had been reluctant to let me in, Micah wasn't wasting time in showing me exactly how he felt.

Whenever we were together, whether in public or private, he was always reaching for me. And I ate it up like I was starved for affection—a woman thirsty after a lifetime of drought.

"I have one word for you, mister," I retorted, scraping the cutting board clear of bell peppers. All that was left was to slice some tomatoes and dice the cheese, and my salad would be complete.

"And that would be?" He spoke softly because he was too busy nuzzling my neck, leaving trails of blistering heat.

"Holly."

Micah let out a long, exaggerated sigh. "I guess that's my cue to see if the grill is ready."

Surrounded by the cold and snow outside, a small covered patio out back protected the state-of-the-art grill—and its griller—from the weather. He'd only just come inside from turning the gas on before he'd snuggled up behind me.

"Well, you were complaining earlier how hungry you were." I turned around to face him as Micah gave me the room to move. The second I locked eyes with him, he pressed against me again.

There was a hardness now that made me gulp—whether nervously or lustfully, I wasn't quite sure.

His voice was rough and husky. "My appetite has changed. I'm more interested in . . ." And instead of telling me what he wanted, Micah showed me.

There was no tentativeness or shyness about the kiss he leveled me with. It held all the power and determination of a man who had no problem claiming what he wanted. Not that I was in any position to refuse him, as my body softened into him and my arms worked their way up around his neck.

With his fingers in my hair, tugging the back of my head firmly, he totally owned the kiss—setting the pace as his tongue brushed against my mouth. I acted instinctively and parted my lips, moaning the instant his tongue touched mine.

Everything about Micah overwhelmed me in the best possible way. He made it hard to breathe—to think—to remember that only moments ago I was warning him we had a teenage girl in the house with us. He was both gentle and brazen, giving me just a tiny taste of submission before he took control and dominated the kiss.

I let him.

I encouraged him.

I drowned in him.

It was painfully blissful in the agony he stirred within me, because all I wanted to do was grab him by the hand and take him to his bedroom. We hadn't really talked about it, but as his tongue danced with mine, I was willing to show him that behind every girl was a woman just begging to let loose and indulge in her wildest fantasies.

I wanted to be wild.

I wanted to rock his world.

He set me on a rollercoaster of indescribable emotions that frankly scared the crap out of me, because they felt so new and raw.

The kiss was over way too soon.

Leaning back in to steal one last taste, I stared up at Micah with what felt like stars in my eyes. "Where did that come from?" I sounded all sexy and raspy.

"Just a promise of what's to come." The look he gave me set off a flurry of butterflies inside my stomach. It was one that whispered he was talking about more than just kissing.

We were combustible.

All I could do was grin like a dork, making sure to slap his butt on his way out to the grill.

"My gosh, I thought you two would never stop." Holly peered around the corner from her room. She clutched her stomach like she was in pain and gagged repeatedly. "I thought my eyes might bleed."

I burst out laughing. "Just you wait."

I didn't say anything else. I already knew she had a crush on Austin. If given a chance, I was sure she'd kiss him, too.

"Yeah, but still." Holly walked over to the island counter where I was standing and peered at the salad in the bowl. Before I could stop her or caution her to wait for dinner, she plucked out a cucumber chunk and shoved it into her mouth. "Not where we eat."

With each passing day Micah and I spent together, I also got a chance to get to know his sweet young niece. She had very little memory of her parents, and her uncle had basically raised her. There was no mistaking how much she loved him, and it was endearing to hear her share small story after small story of things he'd done for her growing up.

The tales weren't anything too revealing—other than how totally committed and doting he was. He denied her very little, and in return, Holly showed him a level of respect well beyond her years. She trusted him completely, even when she didn't understand his constant need to move. Holly would follow him to the ends of the earth and jump into space if he asked.

Such devotion was impressive.

"Did you get your homework done?" I asked, changing the subject. That was the other thing I admired about Micah . . . he'd nurtured in Holly an incredible love of reading. Earlier, I'd gotten another chance to look at the shelves of books Holly called her own personal vault of knowledge, and her eclectic tastes were evident in the variety of books I saw.

If she had even the slightest interest in it, chances were she also had a book or two about it.

"Yep. I finished that book about Henry the Eighth you got me!" she answered with excitement. "I'm kinda sad that it's over."

She definitely was a kindred spirit. I had those same feelings—what I called a book hangover. The greater the adventure or tale, the deeper the sadness.

"Quick, tell me what you loved most about it . . . a fact." The tomatoes were finally sliced into fourths and spread out over the top of the lettuce.

She shrugged. "Hmmm, I thought it was interesting that for a man who thought he was popular with the women, he wrote really bad love letters. I guess it was a good thing he was king, otherwise he would've never had a family." Another thing about Holly was, despite her not liking to see her uncle make out, she was a horrible romantic. "But he was also very musical, so maybe that's how he charmed them."

My knife cut through the small block of cheddar. After cubing two strips, I offered them to her before dumping the rest in the salad. "I don't think it really matters what he did. Like you said, he was king. He could do pretty much whatever he wanted."

Before I could say it, Holly spoke. "Well, wasn't that what he was infamous for?"

With my part of the meal completed, I quickly washed my hands at the sink and peered out the window to see how Micah was doing. Judging from his smile, it was time to take out the steaks to him.

"You want to take this outside to your uncle?" I asked, holding the rectangular glassware containing the meat. "I'll finish setting the table if you want to come help after?"

Nodding, Holly took it from me. "I like it when you come over, Sedona. Micah talks to me about what I read, but it's not the same." Her smile was sweet and innocent.

"Well, you know where to find me."

Our conversation came to a halt as Micah came bursting into the kitchen. He was no longer relaxed. Something had lit a fire under him, and his eyes reflected the frenzy.

"Holly. Hide. Now," he barked out his order. "You go with her, Sedona."

Holly didn't argue. She dropped the glassware on the floor, and it shattered on contact, as she rushed out of the room. Sauce slowly started dripping from the fresh meat, a small pool spreading outward.

"What's going on?" I began to ask, but Micah was already halfway out the door.

Calling out over his shoulder, he repeated his demand that I follow Holly. "Don't argue with me. Just do it."

The patio was lit by two overhead light fixtures. As I took a few steps down the stairs and into the backyard, the light began to fade, the sun finally setting. Micah was already moving into the gradual darkness, and ignoring him completely, I chased after him.

"What's going on?" I repeated, running until I finally caught up with him. He was stalking around the perimeter of the house's property, brushing against the solid fence that encased it.

His gaze was constantly scanning his surroundings. If it was at all possible, he seemed larger, more terrifying, more like a battle-hardened warrior than the carefree man who stole kisses earlier.

This time a chill went through me, because this was the same Micah I caught a glimpse of that day he came barging into the store looking for Holly. He carried himself like a man who would kill first and ask questions later—if he even bothered to ask at all. He looked like someone most would cross the street to avoid.

It was alarming how powerful the transformation was.

"Micah!" I called out, expecting him to stop. He didn't.

"Why won't you listen?" There it was—that ever so slight sound of exasperation. It made me wonder how many times he'd had similar conversations with Holly before she responded the way she just had.

His question made me pause, and I also began looking about. The night was quiet with a chill in the air that I was only just now feeling. From the way Micah was vigilantly studying the woods, his pace never slowing as he circled around the house and back to the patio, I knew that this wasn't merely some crazy paranoia on his part.

"Is someone here?" I let out a sigh of relief when I was finally able to join Micah. "Micah?"

"I have a quartz grid around the house. They're specifically spelled to ward against malicious intent and to protect all who reside on the property. Whenever there is a threat lurking by the boundary, the crystals are programmed to alert me immediately." Micah finally looked at me long enough so I could feel his seriousness.

"And they went off?" I asked, already guessing the answer. That would explain his inspection of the property. Something had obviously triggered it. "And?"

I felt like an ass always asking questions, but he didn't always give complete answers.

He nodded. "I won't jeopardize her safety. The second I'm alerted, I act." Her being Holly.

"Are we under attack?" I asked, suddenly feeling sick. "Oh no, I left her alone. I didn't listen to you." I closed my eyes, wishing I could take back my stubborn ignorance. I started back to the house, but Micah reached out and stopped me.

"My wards are strong enough that no one with malicious intent can breach them. Whatever it was that triggered the crystals is outside."

That made this all the more creepy—my beloved woods were now filled with sinister shadows.

"So we're safe?" I repeated as a throbbing headache started blossoming.

That's when it hit me.

"Micah? How many times has this happened? How many times have you given Holly that order?" All I could think about now were the steaks abandoned on the kitchen floor amidst shattered glass. She hadn't even taken the time to carefully place the dish back on the counter before rushing off. Holly had simply dropped everything and obeyed.

"Too many to count."

His confession hurt my heart. It hurt my soul. It made me weep for the kind of vigilance it took to always be that ready to respond—to act automatically without thought. It made me want to pull Holly into my arms and hold her until the world was a safer place. It felt unfair that this was their lifestyle . . . like they were merely pretending to live between each attack.

"Who are you afraid of?" I asked, searching his eyes for a hint. Gently, I cupped the side of his face, hoping that the intimacy of my touch would encourage him to share. "Is someone hunting you?" All I could think of were the mobster movies I watched on television, where someone would witness a murder and have to go into hiding.

His expression turned to one of pain. "Don't ask me that, Sedona. You know I can't tell you. Not because I don't want to, but because the less you know, the safer you are."

"But you're not safe and neither is Holly." I stated it as a fact. After what I'd just witnessed, it was impossible to casually brush it aside.

Speaking of Holly.

I started heading back into the house, and Micah joined me. "Is this all she knows? Please tell me this hasn't been her entire life."

Visions of them bolting into the night with only the clothes on their backs filled my mind. I imagined them moving to new town after new town, always having to look over their shoulders, never trusting a soul.

He tugged me to a stop, my hand in his. "And this is another reason why I didn't want to bring you into our lives. To be with me, to be around Holly, you're also putting yourself in danger. I can't ask you to be so careless with your life."

I could feel him pulling away. I'd finally seen behind the iron curtain where he kept his secrets hidden, and it had scared him. He wasn't even trying to disguise the fear in his eyes as he looked at me.

There was no way I was going to let him retreat.

As we entered the kitchen again, I stopped dead in my tracks and turned around. I was about to do something I vowed I would never do.

I slipped my hand into my pocket and pulled out my phone. "If you can't confide in me, then there's someone I think you should talk to." When he went to interject, I shook my head, determined to get this next part out before I second-guessed myself. "If you truly are in that kind of danger, you're going to need help."

"So who do you suggest?"

Dialing the last number I thought I would, I took a deep breath before answering.

"You need to talk to my aunt."

CHAPTER 11

J couldn't keep from pacing outside the closed door. Every instinct in my body yelled for me to run fast and far, because while I'd been the one to initiate this discussion, I had no idea what was happening inside between my aunt and Micah. From the moment they met, I'd been excluded from the conversation.

I could never tell which way my aunt would spin something, and a niggling feeling whispered that our prior discussion about me using my gifts to uncover his secrets may arise.

The thought of jeopardizing what was growing between us turned my stomach sour. Maybe I should've been honest from the beginning and told him.

I'd tried to talk with him before—to explain that despite what my aunt might say, I hadn't wanted to spy on him. It had been the very last thing I wanted, and I had adamantly refused her.

Yes, the Court used empaths when they needed to discern the intentions of others, but it had never sat well with me. Only under extreme persuasion and duress would I cave to their badgering. Thankfully, they had other empaths they could employ. It was my aunt who relished the opportunity of reminding me where my duty lay.

I had no problem helping and doing my part. It was the uninvited prying into the emotional psyches of people that left a nasty taste in my mouth.

The door handle quickly turned, and the door swung open.

The look on Micah's face was calm and professional. He shook the hand of my aunt, murmuring something to her before stepping out into the hallway.

Perhaps it wasn't so bad, I thought, inwardly sighing with relief.

Perhaps she'd stuck strictly to what I'd shared with her—that Micah may need additional help from the coven in protecting his beloved niece.

That was when he finally turned to me and lowered his guard. Thunder and anger blasted at me so hard that I staggered backward from the force.

His glare was like a lance piercing my soul.

"Sedona," Aunt Millicent said, staring at me over the glasses perched on her nose. "I appreciate you informing me about Mr. Westbrook's needs, and I believe we've reached an appropriate compromise. He has officially registered himself and his niece as permanent residents of Havenwood Falls and kindly shared his intentions of moving here. The coven won't be requiring your services after all."

I couldn't speak even if I wanted to, as the realization hit me like a ton of bricks—there was no way Micah wouldn't understand her meaning. Now I knew the reason why he dropped his guard and let me in. Now I knew why a storm brewed deep inside him.

My mouth flapped open, and I struggled to find the words.

"Thank you, Aunt," I mumbled, regretting that I'd been foolish enough to trust her. They said that family was everything and that there was nothing you couldn't turn to them for. My intentions had been sincere—I'd earnestly believed meeting with her would result in some kind of comfort for Micah. I didn't want him feeling so alone. While I hadn't expected him to share his secrets with everyone, he could believe the coven would step in and join his efforts to protect Holly.

I looked at him, hoping that by some miracle he would stay long enough to listen to me explain. He had to know that I would never spy on him, that the times we'd spent together were sincerely because I wanted to be friends—not because I was my aunt's secret weapon.

His brows furrowed in disappointment and hurt. There was no need for me to press against his walls and judge his emotional status. The truth was plastered across his face with a flashing neon sign over his head.

Any trust we'd established together had been obliterated, and tears began to well in my eyes as I watched the shutters fall inside him. What had started between us was now over—a fleeting moment of happiness. Whatever hopes and dreams I held that maybe, just maybe, he could be the one evaporated in a puff of smoke.

"Were you wanting to talk to me, Sedona?" Aunt Millicent interrupted, her voice filled with arrogant impatience. In that moment, I wished I could blast her far away. I'd confided in her how much Micah was beginning to mean to me, and she'd ignored my feelings and acted in true Millicent fashion—nothing mattered but the coven and its agenda.

I stood staring at Micah, imploring him with my silence to please give me the chance to explain. Words still failed me. All my life, words and sentences had filled every waking moment, but now, I was confounded over what to say.

For a moment, I thought he was also quietly willing me to say something—anything so the ugly truth didn't hang between us. But as each second ticked by, his jawline twitched from the clenching of his teeth.

I knew the precise second when he gave up.

It was also the exact time I found my voice, but it was too late.

"Micah, wait!" I called out as I watched him turn and head toward the exit. I couldn't let him leave like this.

He paused in his tracks, his back still to me. "There's nothing more to say, Miss Mathews."

His use of my last name felt like a dagger in the heart.

Reaching out, I gently grabbed his arm, hoping he would face me. "It's not what you think! I honestly thought this would help. I didn't want you carrying your burden alone!"

Micah whipped around, his features twisted with anger. "So it's not that you were asked by your aunt to use your gifts on me, to find out why I was here in Havenwood Falls?" When I went to answer, he shrugged off my hand and gestured for me to stop. "All those times I felt you pressing against my wards, trying to read me—it wasn't because you were curious, but because you were working for the coven? All the times you asked me to trust you, to let you in, was any of it true, Sedona? Or was it all a charade . . . a game?"

It was my turn to feel hurt. "Seriously, do you think so little of me that I would do that?"

"Honestly? I don't know what to think right now. All I know is I can't stand here a second longer. I told you I didn't have time for friendship and romance . . . for whatever has been building between us. I was truthful when I said that I wasn't expecting you. I have one mission, Sedona, one task before me, and I allowed myself to become distracted by you."

I could feel what was approaching—the sledgehammer of pain that was swinging fast toward me. Out of desperation, I stepped toward Micah, only to have him retreat farther away.

"Please don't say it," I implored. I didn't care how needy that made me sound. Tears threatened to spill over my cheeks, and I shook my head in denial.

"You've left me no choice. Respect my wishes, Sedona. We can't be friends, and I ask that you don't encourage Holly to come to the bookstore anymore."

I drew in a jagged breath. All while my aunt watched on, like those who slow down as they pass a car accident. The casualty this time was my heart.

"Please." One word. It was all I could utter as my mind raced to find the perfect thing to convince him this was a horrible misunderstanding. The problem, however, was I knew this could've been avoided had I been open with him. Countless conversations flittered through my mind, showing me missed opportunities where I could've broached the topic.

Micah had entered the meeting I'd arranged blind. I'd assumed my aunt would stick strictly to what we'd discussed, and now she'd reduced me to an ass who looked like she'd been hiding something from the man she was dating.

In his eyes, I had betrayed him.

"Sedona," my aunt said. "Let the man leave."

Fury boiled up inside me, and I whipped around to level her with a hateful glare. "Don't you think you've done enough? You were meant to help him, not make things worse. I told you I didn't want to be used as some kind of tool in your arsenal. I refused you when you asked. At no time did I ever agree to spy and pry at your request. Why would you give that impression?" I took another deep breath, my hands shaking at my side.

"I'm not responsible for how others interpret things. Besides—" With a jaunty smirk, she pointed behind me. "He doesn't seem too interested. I would think any man who respected you and held any kind of affection would stick around long enough to hear what you had to say in your defense."

The emotions I had struggled to rein in broke free, and the tears finally fell. "I didn't do anything wrong! You were the one being deceptive! He was someone important to me, and you trampled over everything. Your position with the coven doesn't justify you acting like a . . ." I bit my tongue at the last moment before I hurled at her words that would've disappointed my mother.

"Watch your tone, young lady," Aunt Millicent chastened. "Remember who you're speaking to."

Once upon a time, I admired the woman before me. Part of me had hoped to make her proud, but life had shown me a different path, and I wouldn't be carrying on her legacy any time soon.

"That's the problem. You're the one who's forgotten who she's speaking to." Not waiting for her reply, I shook my head sadly and walked away.

She didn't call out for me to stop.

CHAPTER 12

I tossed the book back onto the counter in disgust.

"I don't know why I bother," I complained, a slight whine in my tone. It was no use. The stories I once loved to escape into had banned me from entering, and I was left trapped in my own reality.

It didn't matter which book I tried, my heart just wasn't in it since last week, when Micah had walked away. He wouldn't answer my calls, and true to his word, Holly had stopped coming to the store. Even Austin was missing her.

"Just give him time, love," Maxwell gently counseled. His usual snark was gone, and in its place was a grandfatherly concern. "If you two are meant to be, just give him time."

"What does that even mean?"

"It means, you working yourself up into a tizzy isn't going to solve the problem. Take a deep breath and show a little faith." For a ghost who often liked to tease, Maxwell's advice was actually sound.

Pity I wasn't done wallowing in my sorrows.

"I guess this is it. I'm officially dubbing myself the Cat Lady of Havenwood Falls. I can be eccentric and kooky and die a spinster." The defeatist tone in my voice was pathetic. Glancing to the side at

Maxwell, I murmured more. "I just really liked him." I let out another frustrated huff.

"Well, I can always go talk to him. Perhaps rough him up and make him see the error of his ways." My friend cracked his knuckles menacingly. I knew that he was trying to cheer me up, but a part of me knew, if given a chance, Maxwell would've been kicking down Micah's door, demanding answers.

I started giggling. "How would he take you seriously if you took a swing and your fist went right through him? I'm grateful for the sentiment, but I think it's best I just do what he says and leave him alone."

I'd gone through our brief argument over and over in my head—viewing it from different perspectives. There was no ignoring the fact he felt betrayed. He'd warned me from the beginning that he didn't have the luxury of letting people close to him and Holly.

"Perhaps, given time . . ." I muttered out loud, staring out across the town square. I could scarcely believe that life was moving on as if nothing was amiss, and meanwhile, my world had been tossed upside down.

Who'd have thought I'd have fallen so quickly for him?

The door jangled as Austin stepped through. He cautiously approached the front counter where I'd been sitting.

"How is it going today?" He eyed me curiously, as if he was an empath too, and was assessing the situation.

He was another person who was worried.

"I'm not falling to pieces, if that's what you're wondering," I retorted with a slight snort. "Relationships end all the time, Austin. Life goes on. It's no big deal." That last part was a lie. It was a big deal, but I wasn't going to give in to the constant temptation of climbing back into bed and forgetting the world for a while. "Besides, we have work to do."

That elicited a loud groan from Austin.

"Then what about my heart?" He staggered forward with his hand over his chest like he was wounded. "I miss Holly and her million questions about everything."

"Again, you're a senior and she's only fourteen years old," I reminded him, sounding like a broken record. Not that it mattered either. Holly was homeschooled, and for all I knew, Micah was planning on leaving Havenwood Falls completely. He had suggested that the last time I saw him, but an insistent feeling inside me whispered to be prepared.

"I know," he blustered, rolling his eyes. "I'm no cradle robber. All I'm saying is she was a great study partner. It's a shame she couldn't keep coming in. I went out to her house the other day, but Micah said she was resting."

At the sound of his name, my insides started whirling about like butterflies. "You did?"

A jumble of questions flickered through my mind. I just couldn't give them voice as the words stumbled before reaching my lips.

Behind Austin, Maxwell's ghostly form reappeared, and he threw me a saddened look. He heard the hope I still felt.

Austin's school messenger bag dropped behind the counter with a heavy thud. "I think it's safe to say you're not the only one moping about."

I slapped his shoulder. "Who's moping?"

Maxwell mouthed the word at the same time Austin answered, "You."

"Well then," I replied, standing up from the counter stool and straightening myself out. "Consider this an intervention." I snatched up one of the flyers Eloise had asked to put in the store. "No more hiding away. I'm going to the psychic fair coming up, and who knows, maybe I'll get my fortune read—figure out why I'm so disastrous in love."

My declaration made the sadness in Maxwell's eyes deepen before he faded away.

"That's the spirit," Austin cheered, a smile returning to his face. "Who knows, maybe Holly will be there, and we can at least convince Micah to let her come back to the bookstore. We were developing a pretty close friendship."

Shrugging my shoulders, I warned him not to get his hopes up. If there was one thing I knew, it was that Micah was unflinching when it came to Holly. He never did share why he was so overly protective, but to me, it didn't really matter.

He wasn't the only stubborn one.

While my mouth said that it was time to move on and there were plenty of guys out there, my heart screamed something different.

He couldn't simply walk in and out of my life like that without some kind of explanation.

It was time to corner him and demand one.

CHAPTER 13

A slight breeze caused the candle's flame to dance, tendrils of potent incense smoke twirling upward.

Callie gripped my hand tighter, staring down at my palm with all the concentration she could muster. The tip of her tongue peeked out between her lips, and it was hard to take her seriously.

"So what do you see, oh powerful swami?" I asked, barely containing my amusement. The annual spring equinox festival was in full swing, and the cold weather didn't deter people from attending in the slightest. It was as if the promise of spring hung heavy around us—blinding us from the presence of residual snow with whisperings of sunshine and warmth.

Havenwood Falls loved to celebrate, and Eloise always organized an incredible Into the Mystic New Age & Psychic Fair. It was one of those opportunities to bring the supernatural community members together with the human ones, and for one day, rejoice in the differences and share gifts otherwise hidden. They said that Halloween was when the veil between the dead and the living was the thinnest, but for me, it was this time of year that held its own brand of mystique.

Usually we had to be careful not to give away our secrets and reveal our true identities. Tonight, however, it was all in jest and for entertainment. It was amazing how humans could suspend disbelief for a few hours in the name of community and charity.

Callie cleared her throat and leaned over closer, her finger tracing over a line on my palm. "You have quite an adventure coming your way." Pausing for a dramatic sigh that was meant to convince me of her authenticity, her voice lowered to a soft rasp. "You will fall madly in love with . . . a carnival ride operator, who will sweep you off your feet. He will win your heart at the top of the Ferris wheel."

I burst into laughter and withdrew my hand. "Impossible. I'm scared of heights."

Rolling my eyes, I crossed my legs and sat back in the chair. If there was anyone in town that I felt I could be close friends with, it was Callie. She ran the local consignment store, a place that I regularly got lost in as I sorted through the many treasures she had. I always teased her that I was tapping into my inner dragon because all I wanted to do was buy everything that caught my eye. Unfortunately, my bank account didn't agree.

Spoilsport.

"You can't argue with me," Callie countered, waving her hand before her like she was beckoning the spirits of her ancestors. "Perhaps I should gaze deep into the crystal ball and see what truths lurk there."

Her long brown hair fell like a curtain over her eyes, and she tucked it behind her ears. Her style was a little more eclectic than mine, but tonight Callie's outfit screamed gypsy fortune teller. Despite the weather, she wore a full-length skirt with assorted beads sewn into patterns in the fabric. Her jade-colored peasant shirt matched her skirt and brought out the green in her eyes. She was such a striking woman, but that wasn't what I liked about her. She had the same quirky personality and sense of humor as I did. She never failed to leave me laughing or smiling.

"Ahhhh, I see it now," she whispered in hushed tones. She waved me to join her peering into the ball. "There is someone. Oh, he's tall, dark, and handsome." Callie fanned herself, all part of the show. "Girl, you're going to fall so hard for this one."

Playing along, I grinned. "Does this stranger come with a name?" In the back of my mind, Micah's name floated to the surface. It brought a hint of sadness that I pushed back down. "How will I recognize him?"

Her gaze flickered over my shoulder to where the festivities were still happening. Each vendor was given a large space to set up in, and she'd chosen to have a canopy-like tent that would keep in the warmth from the portable heater by her feet. What humans didn't know was that the coven had also placed a spell over the fair so that the elements wouldn't ruin the event. So while we all donned our favorite coats and boots and walked around with rosy cheeks, no one completely froze.

It was another perk of living in a supernatural town like Havenwood Falls.

"Something tells me he has a sweet tooth for snow cones." Callie's smirk told me that she was being a little too specific for a reading on my future.

"What?" I asked, already turning about in my seat. My eyes instantly found the meaning behind her comment. Micah was currently talking with Zoey, a resident frost dragon, at her snow cone booth. Most didn't see it, but Zoey made her treats by blowing her cool breath, and she had a way of making anything taste delicious. Holly was standing to the side of him, happily pointing to the different flavor bottles. My lips formed a silent *O*.

I'd been looking for him all night, anxiously hoping he'd come, yet here he was, and I had a sudden case of nerves.

"I can't, Callie," I confessed, slumping back in my seat as I faced her. "I screwed up and broke his trust. There's really no point falling for someone who doesn't even want to talk to you anymore." A slight quiver filled my voice, and I took a quick breath, praying I wouldn't cry. It was crazy to cry over a guy—no matter how incredible he looked.

Or kissed, my own thoughts betrayed me.

"I don't know what happened, but I know there was a spark of something between you. Why don't you go over and at least try?"

"Did you know a summer on Uranus lasts twenty-one years? Or that it rains diamonds on Jupiter and Saturn?" My cheeks flushed when I realized that instead of sharing how I felt, I'd resorted to my fact-sharing like it was an armor I wore. I rubbed my brow and let out my own sigh. "Sorry, force of habit, I guess."

Sympathy filled Callie's features, and she placed her hand gently over mine. "It doesn't take any kind of magical gift to see that he means a lot to you, Sedona. You can't hide away with your books forever. If he's someone you want, sometimes you have to fight for him . . . fight hard."

"And if he doesn't want to be won?" I asked, chewing on my bottom lip and staring at Micah again. The lights that were hung around the different booths gave the top of his head an angelic glow. My heart ached to go talk to him, to say hello, to say anything. I just didn't know how to speak—how to say the right words.

"Why don't you start with hello, and take it from there." She squeezed my hand affectionately. "Besides, a gypsy demon doesn't lie about such matters. It's not over between you two. Trust me."

I still wasn't convinced as I stooped to the side for my purse. As I opened it up, Callie shook her head and pointed outside. "Consider it a freebie."

Her smile helped banish some of the butterflies causing a ruckus inside my chest.

"I couldn't," I uttered.

"How about you name your firstborn after me, and we'll call it even?" Her teasing remark made me burst out laughing, and Micah looked over to where we were, his gaze searching. When it met with mine, I gulped loudly.

"I can't do this," I murmured, willing my feet to work. "I'm not some heroine in a romance book."

"You're right, you're not. You're Sedona Mathews, badass owner of Shelf Indulgence, and damn it, I'm never wrong about these things, so off you go."

Micah was still standing, staring at me, while Holly began eating the huge red snow cone he'd purchased for her. I'd expected him to disappear into the crowds, but he hadn't. It was as if his feet wouldn't work either, so I threw caution to the wind.

"Wish me luck," I exhaled. "I might be back later to see if your guides know a way to mend a broken heart." My smile was weak, and I knew it.

A *pfft* sound erupted from Callie's mouth, and I took it as a warning to quickly hustle before she took matters into her own hands. Leaving the safety of the softly perfumed tent, I stiffened momentarily as a chill went through me. I approached Zoey's snow cone stand and returned her smile when she asked if I was interested in getting one.

"They're so delicious," Holly gushed, taking another mouthful that painted her lips and tongue a bright red. "I got one called Dragon's Blood."

I could hear her talking, but my gaze hadn't left Micah's. Testing the waters, I stepped closer. "Hey."

For a second I thought he was going to ignore me, but to my great relief, he nodded.

"I wasn't planning on coming tonight, but this one was going a little stir crazy cooped up in the house." He gestured to Holly, who was still trying to tackle the large icy dessert. "I also figured certain eyes would be watching for me to attend like a good community member."

There was a not-so-subtle dig at the coven, my aunt in particular. She was big on participation and looked down on those who chose to live a more reclusive life.

"I think you're fine," I murmured, peering up into his eyes. God, I missed him. "So, how are things?" The moment it came out, I could feel the awkwardness between us blossom. "I haven't seen you in town lately."

The lines about his eyes crinkled as he gently smiled. "I've been busy. I run most of my errands either really early in the morning or late at night." He glanced about, his eyes scanning the nearby groups of people. "And you?"

How could I possibly sum up everything I was feeling into a few succinct words?

I shrugged, deciding to respond as nonchalantly as possible. "I've been okay. Busy, the same as you. The bookstore keeps me occupied." As if to test the Fates, I quickly turned to Holly. "You're missed at the store. Austin mourns his study buddy."

"I'm sure he does," Micah fired back between clenched teeth, the muscle in his jaw twitching. Obviously, some things didn't change.

Holly had a different response. Her eyes grew wide with interest, and she perked right up. It had nothing to do with the sugar coursing through her body, and everything to do with mentioning my teenage employee.

"Do you know if he's here?" Her head whipped back and forth. She craned her neck to see if she could spot him. "No offense, Uncle, but you suck when it comes to helping me."

Micah didn't look upset in the slightest. He was probably gloating over how he'd saved her from the evil clutches of male hormones and lust.

"Holly," he warned, his tone suddenly stern. He shook his head at her, and it did the trick. She closed up and returned to focusing on her treat.

I hated the awkward silence that fell around us like the choking grip of the Grim Reaper. My own emotions bombarded me—anxiety, loneliness, desire, need, hope, and frustration. All I wanted to do was to reach out and touch him, but Micah felt too far away.

Take a risk, a brave part of my psyche urged. *Speak up.*

"Micah," I blurted out roughly. My hand whipped out to take his. I was so terrified of missing the moment—any moment—with him that it felt impossible to hold it all in without screaming. Steadying myself, I briefly closed my eyes. When I opened them back up, Micah was all I could see.

"Please." I squeezed his fingers with mine and searched his face for any hint to what he was feeling. His mouth softened a fraction before he tugged me toward him. I stumbled against him.

"I can hear you better when you're closer." He was staring at me with the intensity of a million suns. Instead of scorching my skin, it warmed me from deep within. "You were saying?"

Staring up into his beautiful blue eyes, I finally found the right words.

CHAPTER 14

*T*here are many types of kisses in the world.

While I was in no way an expert, I knew they held the power to sweep you off your feet, lifting you high into the air, before gently cascading you back like a feather on a breeze. True, it was an extremely romantic ideal that each press of the lips could elicit such pleasure, but for as long as I could remember, I'd hoped against hope that such kisses existed.

I'd read my fair share of books. I lived vicariously through both classic and modern literature—swooning over knights and their princesses. I knew that kisses could reveal an extraordinary range of intimacy, but I also knew that *the* kiss with *the* right person held enough force to decimate them all.

All the legends.

All the myths.

Each and every kiss that had gone before it.

They paled in comparison to the feeling bubbling inside me as Micah cupped my face so carefully, his thumbs brushing back and forth across my skin, his fingers in the hair at the back of my head.

He owned that kiss.

He sealed that kiss.

It held a promise that it wouldn't be the last and that while we had more to discuss, we would face whatever came together.

Micah feathered his mouth over mine again before he pulled away. Slowly, the sounds around us filtered back, and the chill from the air reddened my cheeks.

I could taste him in my mouth—his emotions, so raw and delicious against my tongue. It was a perk of being an empath. I didn't just feel what others felt—I could also taste it.

Forgiveness. Openness. A willingness to try again.

The kiss held more than I'd hoped for.

"Let's get Holly and head home," Micah said, his lips against my temple, his breath grazing across my skin.

"You don't want to get your palm read by Callie? Perhaps she'll give you the winning lottery numbers or something?" I couldn't help the lighthearted teasing or the huge grin on my face. It didn't matter that the town was still covered with snow and that winter was having a hard time relinquishing its control to spring. I was warm all over.

He rolled his eyes as he turned about, looking for Holly, his arm slipping around my shoulder. "I'm feeling pretty lucky." His voice grew faraway, and Micah dropped his arm as fast as he had embraced me. "Why would I . . ." His voice trailed off.

His worry provoked my own. I started looking about, not knowing what was happening. "What is it?"

"Where's Holly?"

Two words, and the happiness that had just been brimming over inside me vanished.

"She was just here. Maybe—" I whipped about and raised onto my tiptoes. "Maybe we embarrassed her with the public display of affection and she's over by one of the stalls, giving us some privacy?"

"She knows not to wander without saying something." Micah didn't bother to hide the concern in his voice. "She wouldn't leave without telling me."

I trailed beside him, trying to convince him that he was worried for nothing. "She's a teenage girl, Micah. She's going to defy your rules and do what she wants. Just take a deep breath. I promise you she's okay. You're going to scare her if you don't calm down."

The look he threw at me spoke volumes. In the time it took for me to give my little spiel, his anxiety had ratcheted up a few notches from worry to full-on warrior mode.

"Micah?" I grabbed his hand to pull him up short. "What aren't you telling me?" When he brushed my question aside and craned his neck to peer over me, I was tempted to punch him in the gut or stomp on his foot. "Hello?"

He must've snapped out of whatever thought had locked him in because he shook his head, and finally answered me.

"You're right," he replied feebly. "She's probably gotten distracted." His nods looked more like he was trying to convince himself than me.

"You know—" I had his complete attention now. "Maybe she headed over to the store to see if Austin was there? He was meant to come tonight after locking up at the end of the day. I haven't seen him yet, so maybe they're together?"

His nodding slowed as sense penetrated his dark thoughts. "How about you head over there now, and I'll check a few places we stopped by tonight? There was a crystal necklace she fancied. Maybe she went there?"

It was good to hear him breathe. The warrior guy he'd briefly morphed into was a little scary. It made me wonder again what kind of supe he was.

I pulled out my phone and glimpsed at the screen. "We'll meet there in fifteen minutes. If either of us runs into any problems, call. Okay?"

I turned up the volume on my phone before pocketing it again. I also had it on the vibration setting, just in case.

His kiss lacked the intensity from earlier as he absentmindedly pecked my cheek.

He was worrying for nothing. Holly was a teenage girl prone to distraction and due a few moments of defiance. He'd find her and scowl, and all would be okay.

This was the beginning of our happily ever after . . . or at least the possibility of one.

Life was perfect-ish.

Damn pesky feeling.

~

"HOLLY?" I called out, dumping my unused keys to the store on the counter. The door being open with lights still blazing was a good sign. She'd probably come searching for Austin, seizing a quick moment to touch base with her friend.

Reaching for my phone so I could call Micah, I chuckled softly to myself. He was such a worrywart. Maybe this would finally convince him to relax the death grip he had over her.

"Austin?" I hollered, wondering if they were in the back storeroom or something. Each step I took, however, felt like I was wading through quicksand with concrete slippers. I shook my head—once, twice, three times sharply. Something was wrong . . . very, very wrong.

Emotions hit me like a ton of bricks and stripped away every defense I'd ever erected. The sensations obliterated all reason until all that was left was fear.

Blinding.

Bile-inducing.

Nauseating.

Fear so powerful that it took me a few seconds to ground myself the best I could as I ran toward the pulsating source. Holly.

"Holly!" I screamed as I entered the storeroom to find her whimpering in the corner, her legs and arms bound, a strip of duct tape stuck over her mouth. Angry tears streamed down her reddened face, and she struggled to break free from her restraints.

A million thoughts flickered through my mind, one being that Micah had been right all along. He had warned me of danger, told me there was a reason he was so guarded. I stumbled to grab hold of my phone, my fingers shaking, barely keeping the device from falling to the ground.

Muffled cries filled my ears.

"Give me a second, Holly," I muttered, abandoning the phone so I could work on the tape cutting into her skin. "Who did this to you?" I stammered, rambling with a slew of questions part of me knew she couldn't possibly answer yet.

Adrenaline coursed through my body as I shook my head once

more. Emotions were jumbling over and over in my head, distorting my vision momentarily. The tape failed to give way no matter how gently I tried tugging at it. The last thing I wanted was to rip away her soft skin, but the greater her panic swelled, the more deafening it sounded in my ears.

"I need you to calm down, honey. You're safe now. I promise. Micah's going to be here. I'm trying to get this off you, but I need you to stop fighting me, okay?"

With trembling hands, I cradled Holly's tear-streaked face and looked deeply into her eyes. I pushed out every soothing thought and feeling I could muster, pushing down and past my own terror.

When that didn't work, I reached back around to the chain clasp behind my neck and released the black tourmaline pendant I was wearing. I didn't even think. I simply reattached it back around hers.

Grounding her would ground me.

Placing my palm over it, pressing it against her sweat-drenched skin, I closed my eyes and said a quick spell to help unravel the tape so it wouldn't rip too much of her flesh with it. My heartbeat slowed with hers, and with it, the room became easier to breathe in.

The tape at the corner of her mouth finally gave way, and with a quickly fired apology, I yanked it off. "Better?"

Holly nodded. "I didn't know," she sobbed, her words broken up.

"Where's Austin, Holly? Is he hurt? Did he go get someone?" One more tug, and I had her hands free. Her skin was a mottled red—blotchy, hot, and angry. "I need to call the police . . . Micah . . . I need to make sure whoever did this doesn't come back."

I was rambling, my body still shaking as I pressed the back of my hand against my forehead. I was way out of my league. I'd never been in a situation like this before. Hell, I'd never even had to deal with shoplifters. I'd been blessedly kept from harm's reach my entire life, and nothing had prepared me for the intensity of the adrenaline and shock.

Dragging in a deep breath, I focused on the air filling my lungs. I focused on the feel of the clothes on my body. I focused on the sensation of my heart thudding in my chest. It was a technique I employed whenever I was overstimulated and was a surefire way of finding the balance I needed to act.

I may have been only a fact-wielding bookworm and not some lethal warrior badass, but I wasn't some fainting damsel in distress either. Micah needed me to keep my head about me until he got here.

I stood, moving toward the door. Holly was busy working on the tape around her ankles.

"Hopefully whoever did this was scared off." I was being optimistic, a trait that hadn't failed me in the past.

Austin blasted into the room, knocking me over. "Sedona! You're here! Quick, you need to get down and hide . . . they're back!" A frenetic energy bounced off him, plowing into me.

Wait, wait . . . wait, my inner voice screamed. Something wasn't right.

"You?" I gasped, leaping to my feet in confusion. Instinctively, I stepped in front of Holly, protecting her. "Austin?" I croaked in disbelief.

My gaze dropped to his hands—in the left, Austin held a gun, and in the right, a roll of duct tape.

He raised the weapon to my head, a cynical smirk on his face. Damn, he didn't even look like the high school student I'd taken under my wing and given a job to for the past year. He didn't feel the same either. Austin felt bitter, the taste burning the top of my tongue with its acidity.

"I can't stand another second living here, Sedona. If you knew who we were surrounded by . . . the monsters . . ." Austin's eyes bulged a little in his head as he glanced about nervously, the gun in his hand dipping. "You would've done the same thing if you were looking at failure. I was promised scholarships. I played by all the rules, and then I get the brush-off. Ask me what happened, Sedona." When I didn't answer fast enough, Austin shook the gun at me angrily before swinging it to aim at Holly. "*Ask. Me.*"

I gestured for Austin to calm down with my hands, hoping to convince him to lower the gun or at least aim it back at me. "What happened, Austin? Tell me? Maybe I can help?"

He shook his head, and beads of sweat flicked from his damp hair. "How do I know you're not one of *them*?"

The way he emphasized *them* made me wonder. Austin was human.

"Did something happen at school?" I took a tentative step away from Holly, forcing him to keep his attention on me. "Did you have a fight? Fail a class?"

I knew he'd been anxious over an exam he had, but I was so used to his normal adolescent neuroses that I tended to tune the overflowing emotions out.

"I was promised a theater scholarship to any university of my choice . . . wherever I wanted to attend around the country. I was told it was all but official, so I didn't bother submitting for any other funding options. They said I didn't have to worry about the financials, and to just focus on my academics and my extracurricular drama workshops. I did everything I was told, but I guess people lie."

I took a bolder step. Austin's face was like thunder, his brow twisted into furrows. My heart hurt for him, because he had talked about nothing else since his counselor had advised him at the beginning of the school year. I guess something had changed.

"Surely there was a mistake. Put the gun down." I took a step toward him, my arm still outstretched. I had never worked so hard at layering my voice with calm, soothing tones. "How about we go in to the high school tomorrow and ask for a meeting?" I was closer now. "This isn't how you solve the problem, however."

"Let me go, Austin, please. Maybe my uncle could help too." Holly's sniffles snapped the distracting spell I'd been weaving.

"Actually, you are my ticket out of here. Imagine my surprise when a stranger pulled me aside, said he worked for someone he called the Collector, and offered me easy money. All I had to do was answer questions about people around town. The money was crazy good, so of course I jumped all over it. And then he started asking about your uncle and said if I ever saw you, to call him, and he'd make it worth my while."

His laugh bordered on maniacal, his smirk turning into a snarl.

"I don't care that they gave my scholarship to that freak anymore. I don't need it. With the money I'll make delivering you to this Collector guy, I can study anywhere I want in the world."

I was a riot of contradicting emotions. My heart hurt that the young man I'd grown to love was nowhere to be seen in the angry and bitter diatribe Austin was delivering. I wanted to erase away the hurt and promise him I'd find a way to get him to college without reducing him to the gun-wielding attacker he was now.

But that was nothing compared to the word echoing in my head. *Freak.*

Somehow, Austin had discovered that it wasn't just humans who lived in Havenwood Falls, and based on his brief description, one obviously stole what he thought was rightfully his.

"You've underestimated my uncle if you think you're going to leave this store!" Holly yelled, her courage kicking in.

"No, I believe that's what I should be saying to you," Austin spat. Desperation drenched his words. "Now get up. We need to go."

Holly's gasp sounded seconds before mine escaped through my lips.

Cocking back his fist, Micah slammed a punch so hard that it lifted Austin off his feet and threw him into the shelves before he crumpled to the ground. The gun skittered across the floor until it came to a stop.

"No. I believe my niece was right the first time."

CHAPTER 15

I was at a loss for words.

The Devil himself couldn't have painted a more formidable and awe-inspiring scene than Micah standing there in all his menacing glory. Electricity rippled off him in tsunami-sized waves as he surveyed the scene before him.

He was breathtaking—magnificent. In all my short life, I didn't think I'd ever seen a man look so incredibly sexy, yet in the next breath look as if he could rip your face off with his teeth. When he said that he took care of his niece and wouldn't allow anyone to place so much as a finger on her, he meant it.

Austin groaned weakly on the ground. Micah had completely incapacitated him. Based on the death glares he was still leveling at someone I'd thought was a friend, he'd let Austin off easy.

"Is everyone okay?" Micah growled, his breathing ragged and chest rising rapidly. He rushed toward Holly, who met him halfway. Her arms were around his waist in the blink of an eye, her face buried into his shirt as she sobbed buckets of tears.

"I'm so sorry, Micah," she repeated, over and over again like a broken record. Her shoulders shuddered as she struggled to control her crying, her small frame dwarfed by his larger one.

"Shh, sweetheart. It's okay. I'm here. This wasn't your fault. He caught me by surprise as well." Micah rubbed Holly's back in a fatherly manner as he cradled her in his arms. "There's nothing you could've done." He glanced over to me, his eyes doing a quick once-over to check I was okay. He relaxed a little once I nodded. It could've been worse than the bruised skin where Holly was bound and a bad case of the shakes.

"How did they find us? We were careful. I promise you, I didn't tell Austin anything!" Holly's sobs had turned into broken words echoed with hiccups.

I came closer and wrapped my arms around them both—enveloping Holly between us. "Who are they?" I whispered, looking cautiously at Austin. "What's going on, Micah? Why did my employee suddenly become a psychotic, gun-wielding kidnapper?"

I didn't know what hurt most—being kept in the dark by Micah or that I had been so blindsided by Austin. I'd become so accustomed to withdrawing inwardly and not using my gifts that I'd totally missed any telltale sign that he had been plotting anything.

"It's a long story," Micah began, placing one more kiss on top of Holly's head. "One I think is overdue. Let me get Holly home, and we can talk." He kicked at Austin's still body. "I'll call Sheriff Kasun while we're on the way."

"Hopefully the police department doesn't have their hands full tonight with the fair going on," I added. I dragged trembling fingers through my hair. My brain was having a difficult time processing the last fifteen minutes.

How did I go from getting my fortune read to this?

Micah took hold of my hand and squeezed it, gently pulling me with him as he guided Holly out into the main floor of the store. I tried not to look up when we passed by shelves. I felt violated—the safe haven I'd created for myself from my inheritance felt confining and defiled. I knew it was just a building and that the real blessing was no one was hurt and Austin's plans had been diverted, but it didn't stop the pain from pressing down on me.

"We'll smudge the store thoroughly," Maxwell offered feebly, his ghostly form barely present. "Don't let this break you, Sedona. You didn't know."

"I should've known!" I exclaimed, forgetting I was the only one who could see my phantom friend. My anger blistered my insides—the rush of changing emotions drowning me. "I'm a god damn empath, and I had no idea!"

"No one's mad at you, sweetheart," Micah comforted, and for the first time since this nightmare started, he wrapped his arms around me.

That's when Holly shocked me.

"I think she's talking to the ghost, Uncle." And she pointed straight at Maxwell. I couldn't tell who was more stunned—me or him.

"You see me?" he said, flustered.

"You see him?" I echoed, my eyes growing wider by the second. "Are you all keeping secrets from me now?"

She'd caught Micah off guard, too. His attention flipped back to her. "See who?"

Holly's smile was so genuine and pure, it made my heart ache. "Well, yeah. When no one introduced him to us, I figured that he was a secret. If there's one thing I know how to do, it's how to keep one."

Maxwell's pale jaw hung open. If it wasn't for what had just happened, I would've relished watching him be so flabbergasted.

"I had no idea." Stroking his mustache, he gestured to Micah. "Can he see me?"

Holly shook her head. "I don't think so. Unless he's being a complete jerk and ignoring you."

All eyes turned to Micah, who looked adorably clueless. "Someone needs to fill me in now. You have a ghost?"

Stifling a yawn, I was partway through saying yes when another one hit. "I guess we have more to talk about than we thought." I turned around and gave my bookstore one more look. "But how about we leave that subject for another day? I'm still trying to wrap my head around this."

It was on the tip of my tongue to complain about the monster headache pounding away like hail on a tin roof when a blinding pain unlike anything I'd ever experienced pierced my body, dropping me instantly to the ground.

"Sedona!" It was Holly I heard screaming, but all I could see was Austin dragging himself out of the storeroom, his now smoking gun beside him.

He shot me. The sentence sounded weird inside my head. *He shot me, and I'm bleeding.*

Fire blazed through me, burning over every nerve until they lay blistered in its wake. I couldn't keep myself standing. No matter how many times I told my brain to move—to do anything—it responded with more agony until all that was left was to close my eyes.

The ground felt hard beneath my body. I'd fallen, but someone was lifting me up.

"Sedona," the voice cried out. It sounded so far away, though. All I knew was that in the maelstrom of intensity, that voice was the only thing tethering me to life.

I'm dying. The thought floated in and then floated out.

"I'm dying," I croaked. That's when the shock set in, and I started to laugh.

～

"YOU NEED TO HEAL HER, Micah. There's no time."

Holly. That voice belonged to Holly.

Awareness slowly creeped back in, and the blissful ignorance faded away until all that was left was the harshness of reality.

I was lying in my bookstore.

Austin had tried to kidnap Holly.

Micah had stopped him.

Austin had shot me.

I was now bleeding out in Micah's arms.

"She's right," I answered weakly. "By the time you reach the doctor, it'll be too late."

My blood stained the front of my shirt, and for some sick reason, all I could think was how annoyed I was that my new shirt had been ruined. I'd barely bought it from Callie's Consignments the day before, and it was now destroyed.

Micah placed his hand over the bullet's exit wound. "The coward shot you in the back," he barked, applying pressure.

I winced at the contact, but didn't attempt to move his hand. I couldn't if I tried.

"Heal her!" Holly screamed again. "I don't care if you've kept who you are hidden to protect me. Heal her now, Micah!"

My brain was muddy, but I still tried to understand what she meant. My head lolled to the side as the edges around my vision grew darker.

Micah lowered his lips to my ear, and I savored the warmth of his breath. *Cold.* I was so cold.

"I didn't want you to find out this way, sweetheart. I thought my secrets were more important, and with it being too late to even get Elias here, there's no other choice. Close your eyes." When I didn't, he gently brushed his fingers over my lids and shut them for me. I stiffened at his touch. "Don't be scared. I've got you."

"Elias?" My mouth formed the word but nothing came out.

"I guess you could say he's my brother."

I didn't hear the rest. I couldn't, as the most peaceful, glowing, soothing light filled me. It was everywhere—with no ending or beginning. It penetrated every shadowed corner of my soul, purging away the pain with a different kind of fire.

A healing fire.

A *holy* fire.

"Micah," I cried out, my body arching as I felt that warmth spread relentlessly throughout me. Cells sung with restoration. Wounds healed. Pierced organs rebuilt themselves. It was miraculous, and it all emanated out of Micah and into me.

I didn't want to move or speak. I didn't want to do anything that might break that incredible connection forging out of him and into me. The walls that he had kept so painstakingly erect were nowhere to be found as he let me in and healed me completely.

When it was over, and my weary fingers rested on the ground, my body drenched in sweat, I slowly opened my eyes and gasped.

Micah filled the room.

No, his *wings* filled the room—each illuminating white feather ruffled from being unfurled. I'd had my suspicions about what kind of supernatural creature he was, but never had I guessed he was divine.

"You're beautiful," I murmured as tears filled my eyes. "My gosh, Micah. You are beautiful."

He silenced me with his lips as he lifted me back into his arms. I could barely hear a commotion happening outside as Elias's handsome face came into view.

"I felt you," he said to Micah. "I got here as quickly as I could, so if you want to keep your identity secret still, I suggest you hide yourself before the police arrive, wondering who fired a shot."

Indecision warred in Micah's face. "Can I truly hide my nature now? They're going to want answers." He continued to ignore me, but I caught his gaze darting over to Holly, who now stood with her arms wrapped around her body.

"Blame me. Tell Kasun what happened, but when it comes to healing Sedona, say the Fates were smiling, and I was the first to arrive here."

Micah shook his head firmly. "No. I can't ask that of you."

"True, but I'm offering, and this way you get to disclose to whomever you choose in your own time. Quick." Elias cast a confident look outside, and I envied that he could take this all in stride. I was a mess. "You won't have privacy for much longer. The shifters would've heard the gunfire."

The decision was made with a brisk nod. "Thank you."

Elias reached out and stroked the side of my face. "I'm sorry you were hurt, Sedona. Hang in there. We'll get you home quickly."

Leaving to go meet with the police when they arrived, Elias slapped Micah's back. "Take care of your women."

I tried not to let that rankle as I cozied up to Micah more.

"You're an angel. My angel."

"What I am is a fool."

I didn't get a chance to argue with him. With the angelic powers he held, Micah lulled me into a restful sleep.

CHAPTER 16

"*P*enny for your thoughts."

It was the next day, and despite my feelings from last night, I'd opened up Shelf Indulgence this morning as though nothing had happened. True, I was still ignoring that back storeroom, but —baby steps.

Just like Rome wasn't built in a day, erasing what Austin had tried to do would take some time.

I said I was working, but honestly, that was me sitting at the front counter, staring out into the town square. I could see Maxwell hovering in my peripheral vision, but I didn't have anything to say.

Apparently, he was tired of my silence.

"It was my fault." It was the thought among many that had stuck to the forefront of my mind all day. When Maxwell didn't answer or argue back, I slowly looked at him. "I should've known."

"You're being too hard on yourself. You're young, and your gifts are young."

I had no idea how long he'd been rehearsing that, but I wasn't buying any of it. To me, they were merely words—excuses—we said when we hoped to placate someone. The blame had to fall somewhere, and as the empath, I couldn't deny I felt responsible.

"Austin was my employee. I introduced him to Holly. Do you

know how often we talked about her together . . . speculating about why Micah was so secretive? All this time, under my nose, and I had no clue."

"Do you actively read people?" He gave me a stern look. I was surprised he didn't pair it with pointing one of his pale slender fingers at me. "Are you all-wise, all-knowing?"

"Maxwell!" I exclaimed, slamming my hand down hard on the counter. "I. Should've. Known." There was no way I was going to budge. I'd had all night to stew in my insecurities and musings.

"Fine." He threw his hands up in frustration. "Then you need to share the blame and guilt around. Don't be greedy, Sedona. We all deserve a huge serving of self-loathing this morning."

I snorted in disbelief. "How do you figure that?"

I clicked on the computer's keyboard, bringing the screen to life. Letters and numbers filled the brightness, but it all looked like a jumbled mess to me.

Maybe I should've stayed home like Micah had suggested.

"This entire town knew or at least has seen Austin, and no one noticed he was unhappy. How many times does your aunt come in here to harass you? A high-ranking coven member, and she didn't sense anything either. You didn't see her nefarious deeds alarm go off, did you?" He was being silly, but I saw his point.

Relenting a fraction, I took in a deep breath. "I promised them both things would be okay."

That was what stung the most. I had convinced Micah I was someone safe to befriend and then look what happened—our world had exploded in gun smoke and violence.

That's when the real reason buried under all my guilt surfaced.

"He's going to leave, Maxwell. I saw it as plain as day when he was healing me. When he arrived in Havenwood Falls, he vowed that at the first sign of trouble, he would leave immediately with Holly. He would never risk her safety again, once he knew a place was too dangerous. And before you say it, do you honestly think I'm the best person to tell him to stay?"

"Yes, Sedona! Can't you see he feels something for you?" His eyes lit up with passionate fervor. "And before you argue with me, a man can tell these things about another man. You stole his heart."

"But that was before, and this is now," I fired back. "Too much has happened."

"You didn't see his face when you were shot, or the blatant fear that threatened to break him when you said you were dying. I'm telling you, Sedona, quit being stubborn and go talk to him."

Micah and I had agreed to meet later, after I convinced him I'd be okay. Holly was his priority, and from what he'd shared, she was still pretty shaken up.

"Face it, Maxwell. My spinster status is still secure. He won't be staying."

Tuning him out, I stared back out the window.

And I need to somehow let him go.

I MUST'VE DOZED OFF, because the next thing I was aware of was Maxwell yelling loudly to rouse me.

"Sedona, get up now!"

Chills skated over my sleep-dazed senses as I cracked open an eye.

"Sorry, I guess we should just lock up for the day and go home. I'm not much use here anyway." I'd tried all day to keep busy with orders and light dusting, but my heart just wasn't in it. Untouched books sat beside me at the front counter. Even the delicious treats from the bakery that I sold to customers with their purchases remained uneaten.

"He was leaving Havenwood Falls, but I convinced him to wait long enough to say goodbye." Maxwell was as solid as I'd ever seen him, his hands fidgeting with agitation. "You don't have much time, though. Hurry."

A million thoughts raced through my mind. "What? Micah was here?" Stretching out the tight kink in my neck, I looked about. "Why didn't he wake me?"

"Sedona," Maxwell exclaimed again, sounding like he wanted to shake me. "There's no time to explain."

And with that, my ghost friend disappeared—only to reappear outside the bookstore in the middle of the town square. A loud squawk went up us he startled a few people taking a brisk walk through the center.

Once he knew I'd seen him, Maxwell popped back in, amused by the astonished expression I wore.

"You left!" I gaped. "How the heck did you do that?"

He reached for my hand. It breezed through my own. Some habits, no matter how long ago used, were still hard to break.

"We don't have time, Sedona. Please. For once, do what you're told and go to Micah's home. He told me he could hang around for an hour—no more. Go, or you'll miss out on your chance to tell him how you feel."

The world felt like it was crashing down around me—sounds blurring until all I could hear was the truth. Micah wasn't even going to tell me what had happened. He wasn't even giving me the courtesy of saying goodbye before he and Holly disappeared.

When he'd taken me home the night before, it was with the understanding that once we were all better rested, we would talk about everything. Any question I had, and I had many, would be rewarded with answers.

Yet here was the painful truth—I hadn't even warranted that level of respect.

"It's better this way," I replied, rapidly shutting down each and every feeling I had. I didn't want to feel anymore. I was done being empathic, and I was over opening my heart, only to feel it break. When Maxwell tried to argue, I dug in deeper. "His life is not his own. If it was, I truly believe he would've come himself."

I picked up a chocolate mint brownie I'd placed on a plate earlier, but didn't take a bite. I crumbled the treat between my fingertips instead, making a mess.

All I could see, however, were all those precious seconds and moments of possibilities—all the what-ifs that could've been mine and Micah's.

"Are you seriously going to spout that bullshit to me?" The corner of Maxwell's mustache twitched as he began chastising me.

"Do you really think anything I could say to him will make a difference? It's not like he's been forthright with anything other than his reluctance in being more social."

"I watched you all these years, Sedona. Witnessed your loneliness and struggles with being empathic. Micah wasn't the only one keeping others at arm's length. What does it say that a beautiful young woman's two closest friends are a stubborn old ghost and a three-legged cat? Somewhere along the way, you got hurt . . . whether from other people's thoughtlessness or unresolved grief over your parents' deaths. You keep to yourself and surround yourself with other people's stories." In a grand gesture, Maxwell waved his hands about to the various shelves that lined the store. "Here is one irrefutable fact for you, Sedona . . . there is no greater story than the one you write yourself. Your tales and your adventures."

He was giving quite the impassioned speech, and I half wondered how long he'd been storing it away for the perfect opportunity. Holding my head in my hands, elbows crooked on the counter, I searched my heart until all I could do was whisper.

"What if I tell him to stay and he leaves anyway?" I'd finally given voice to the real fear hiding behind my bullheadedness. "What if he was never mine to ask?"

"Isn't that what life and love is all about? I'm not saying you have to be madly in love with him, but aren't you even the slightest bit curious? Go. You'll regret it if you don't." Maxwell's features softened, and his gaze filled with tenderness. "Besides, I barely tolerate the cat you have now. I can't imagine the chaos here if you added more felines to the mix."

I started laughing. "I love you, Maxwell. Thank you." Pushing the chair back and grabbing my coat, I wrapped a thick woolen scarf around my neck and tugged a beanie on my head. "What's life without a little risk?"

It may have been the lighting, but I thought a hint of tears glistened in his eyes. "It's what makes all the darkness and uncertainty worth it, sweet girl. Now go and don't return without him."

I didn't even bother replying, locking the store up behind me, before rushing toward Micah's home. The paths were a little icy and slick, but that didn't stop me.

I had no idea what I was going to say when we were face-to-face. Perhaps words weren't needed.

Maybe it was time to lay it all bare with nowhere to hide.

CHAPTER 17

*H*e was standing in the backyard, overlooking the fence that provided a barrier to the beautiful rich forest of Colorado. All around him, melted snowdrops fell from nearby pines, the air crisp and cool.

I was sure he could hear me approaching as the snow crunched beneath my feet. It wasn't until I was right behind him that he spoke to acknowledge me.

Micah looked exhausted, and his Adam's apple bobbed slightly as he swallowed. "He said you'd come."

Every instinct I had told me to touch him—to somehow convince him that whatever dark thoughts he was having, it would be okay because we could face it together. The words felt like lies, however, because we both knew that it hadn't mattered in the end. Someone had found them, and used Austin to try to hurt Holly.

"I'm still not sure how Maxwell left the store. As long as I've known him, he's been like a permanent fixture. I just assumed he was destined to haunt the place forever." My hand reached out, only to fall short. Micah didn't move closer, either.

"I'm not going to lie. He scared the crap out of me when he suddenly appeared out of nowhere, but I guess he had a lot on his mind that needed to be spoken."

He still hadn't looked at me.

"You'll get used to him. Maxwell can be rather long-winded when he chooses to." I trailed over to a small path of thawed ground, smiling at the brave little flower trying its hardest to thrive in the frost. "It's amazing how resilient we can be when we have to." It was a random kind of thought that simply fell out. I crouched over and gingerly stroked the pretty purple petals.

"But it would be better to never be placed in that situation to begin with," Micah countered. Even though I'd been musing about nature and the coming of each new season, he was referring to something much closer to home.

"Do you honestly believe that? That life should be as easy as possible with little opposition?"

When he turned to answer, the familiar Micah I'd first met stood looking down at me. Gone was the man I'd seen heal me—love in his eyes, wings unfurled at his back. There had been nothing separating us last night, and now he'd returned to being tight-lipped and shut off.

He shrugged. "I don't know what I believe anymore." Removing his hands from his heavy black coat, Micah helped me stand. "I wasn't lying when I said I wasn't expecting you. I just also know that they will never stop coming for her."

By her, he meant Holly.

"You can't keep running, though, Micah. I'm not saying you have to settle down and live the rest of your life out in Havenwood Falls, but sooner or later, you're going to run out of places to hide. Wouldn't it be better to make a stand where you will at least be surrounded by the support of friends?"

"Are you volunteering for that position, Sedona? Are you ready to die for me and Holly?" Pain filled his face, the first true emotion he'd let show. I wanted to comfort him, cradle his cheek with my hand while we tried to work things out. There were so many things I wanted to say and do, but I didn't.

Damn if my fear wasn't still there.

"I'd be a liar if I said last night wasn't an eye opener. I'm not arguing that with you at all. You told me things could get dangerous, and they did. I just don't think you necessarily have to do it alone. Aren't you tired of always being strong?"

This time I did lightly rest my hand on his arm, and he didn't shrug it off.

"I am old, Sedona. I have existed from almost the beginning of time, and I've experienced so much ugliness in this world. It doesn't matter the time or people—humanity can be cruel with its thirst for power and greed. I never questioned my duty as an angel—a sentinel of mankind. I protect at all costs." He tilted his head to the side, catching my gaze. "I also destroy at all costs. My life was never truly my own, because I was only ever viewed as a weapon."

"But?" He hadn't said it, but I knew one was coming. There was always a 'but' that marked those moments when everything changed, paths diverted, and lives altered.

"And then there was Holly."

Micah shoved his hands back in his pockets, and with his gaze now held by some invisible thing in the distance, he lowered his voice to a hushed tone.

"She's special. She has . . . gifts . . . abilities that could have a profound impact on the world as we know it. And just like me . . . in the wrong hands . . . she could be a weapon of mass destruction."

My mind raced as it flickered through all the different powers and types of supernatural creatures that existed. None of them really screamed the sweet, naïve, fourteen-year-old girl I'd come to know.

"Holly?" I questioned, confused. I cast a backward glance to the house. "She seems so . . ."

Micah barked out a brusque laugh. "Normal?" I nodded quickly. I wanted to pry and ask what she was, but Micah beat me to it. "She's a fledgling oracle who's still trying to understand and learn to use her gifts. In time, she will have the ability to predict situations of great importance and shape them either to the benefit of all or to destruction, if the wrong people control her. With her approaching powers, she could level civilizations, undoing them with a few syllables. She's a weapon that should only ever be wielded when all other hope is lost."

"So you were assigned to protect her?" That made the most sense to me, because it was exactly what I'd been watching him do from the moment I'd met him. It was actually one of those endearing qualities I'd admired of his.

His next words chilled me to my core. "No, I was ordered to destroy her. She is such a wild card that the powers that be deemed it safer to have her killed than risk those with evil intentions using her."

It was my turn to laugh, mine coming out more strangled than his. "And it's not evil to kill a child?"

My voice rang out, and it startled some nesting birds in the trees. Their wings flapping through the air afforded us a temporary moment to pause and breathe. I was only beginning to catch a tiny glimpse into the secrets Micah held, and I already felt like I was drowning.

"It wasn't my position to question my superiors. I was ordered to take her from her home and dispose of her like she—" His voice cracked under heavy emotion. It revealed that despite what he'd said, Micah had grown to love his young charge, and the thought of harming even a hair on her head was utterly abhorrent. "Like she was chattel."

"But something changed," I encouraged, hoping to keep him talking. I tightened the coat around me with the hope of staving off the cold air. There was no way I was moving until I'd heard everything he was willing to share.

Micah snapped out of whatever he was seeing in his mind's eye and approached me once more. Tucking a stray hair back beneath the hem of the beanie, he studied my features until his gaze finally rested on mine. "I looked in her eyes, and I knew that not only would I give my life for her, but that I would spend the rest of my days roaming the earth in order to keep her hidden."

"Micah?" I whispered, feeling completely mesmerized by his confession.

"Sedona," he answered. "It's the same way I feel as I look at you now."

A loud breath escaped from my mouth as his new admission registered. "But you'll still leave."

A stray tear dropped down over his cheek—one single lonely tear that held all the emotions he kept bottled up.

"Because my duty to her trumps what I feel for you. If I stay, there is the very real risk I will lose you both." Before I could say anything, he shook his head, and dug a small velvet pouch from his pocket. "So before we have to leave, there's something I want you to have . . . need you to have. It's the only way I can walk away knowing you'll be okay."

With nimble fingers, he undid the loose knot, and slowly withdrew a beautiful silver chain, but it wasn't the idea of jewelry that made me gasp out loud or my hand instantly cover my mouth.

Hanging from the chain was a silver-filigreed vial that contained an ethereal, glowing substance that seemed to pulse with energy and life.

"Promise me you'll wear this always, Sedona. It's not a lot, but it's enough of my grace to heal you should anyone come looking for us once we're gone. I couldn't bear leaving you defenseless."

My fingers touched the vial, and the liquid responded to my touch. The emotions emanating from it were identical to the glorious feeling of peace and love from last night.

"Your grace." I was completely in awe. "I can't accept this."

I held it back out to him—half hoping he wouldn't take it, because if this was all I could have of him, I would cherish it until my last breath.

"I wish I were a different man. I wish we had met under different circumstances, but we are who we are." He took a step back. He was already distancing himself from me.

Something Maxwell had said inserted itself into my thoughts.

He'd asked me whether Micah was worth fighting for, whether telling him how I felt was worth the risk of possible rejection.

That answer was now a resounding yes!

"We are who we are," I finally said, dropping all of my own insecurities and boundaries. This could possibly be the most vulnerable we might ever be, and it was time to lay it all bare. "I can't predict the future like Holly, and I'm sure as heck no divine creature. My name is Sedona Mathews, and I'm an empath who still has so much to learn. I'm going to make mistakes. I don't have any special survival skills to offer. All I have is me and my capacity to love with everything I have."

And that's when I realized it was bigger than that—larger than just him and me.

"And this is Havenwood Falls. We may have our secrets and flaws, but we are also fiercely protective of our own. Hurt one of us, and you hurt us all. Stay with me. Stay here with us all. Let the town help you protect Holly. No one wants to hurt a child. You might be surprised to find yourself surrounded by others who are equally ready to face the future and the unseen."

Another thought surfaced. "And Micah? Holly isn't the only one here in town with these kinds of powers, so knowing that, don't you think we're better equipped to help?"

"There's more to who Holly is . . . more to who her father is that makes her a target to anyone privy to that knowledge."

I opened my mouth to question him about it, but Micah immediately gestured that he wasn't ready to divulge that particular secret. "It's a secret that I will guard to the death, and even then, there is no force under Heaven that would make me utter those truths."

I knew better than to press the issue. I was simply grateful he'd opened up enough to let me catch a glimpse of what he was dealing with. It was an incredible burden, and one I would figure out how I could best help him carry.

"I'm not suggesting you talk with my aunt again." That little admission caused a smile to curl the edges of his mouth, a soft chuckle rumbling within him. "But there are other coven members who you can talk to. Members of the Court. Someone . . . anyone. All you need to do is ask. We can face this together. You will have the support you need."

"I can't ask that of you or of strangers." He kept shaking his head, but I didn't let that deter me from speaking my truth.

"You don't have to ask, Micah. Don't you see that? I've grown to love Holly, and given a chance, the town will too. You just need to let us in." My hands now lay on his chest, my fingers over his heart. "You just have to give us a chance."

We stood there quietly as the sky began to darken. Neither of us spoke, and it was difficult not holding my breath because my insides were churning with nerves.

Micah's slow grin was like an elixir on my soul. "Did you know that someone sold the air guitar they played at a Bon Jovi concert for five dollars and fifty cents on eBay?"

"Is that so?" I smiled, cocking my eyebrows.

Shivers shot through me as Micah trailed his finger over my cheek. "I figured if I'm going to stick around, I'd better come up with my own source of knowledge. Can't let you have all the fun." His soft chuckle warmed my insides.

"I can't promise what tomorrow holds," I said, and I tightened my grip on the front of his coat. "But we'll face it together."

"Is that so?" Micah brushed his lips over mine, and I felt my body relax.

"That's a fact." Then without waiting, I pulled him in and claimed his mouth, kissing him with everything I had.

Life might not get any easier, and dark days may be headed directly toward us, but in that moment the only truth that mattered was this . . .

Strange things happen in Havenwood Falls, but this is our life.

Oh, and angels are amazing kissers.

Watch for *Addicted to You*, the continuing story of Sedona, Micah, and Holly, coming early 2019.

WE HOPE you enjoyed this story in the Havenwood Falls series featuring a variety of supernatural creatures. The series is a collaborative effort by multiple authors.

Books in the main Havenwood Falls series:

Forget You Not by Kristie Cook
Old Wounds by Susan Burdorf
Fate, Love & Loyalty by E.J. Fechenda
Covetousness by Randi Cooley Wilson
The Winged & the Wicked by T.V. Hahn & Kristie Cook
Alpha's Queen by Lila Felix

Ink & Fire by R.K. Ryals
Lose You Not by Kristie Cook
Tragic Ink by Heather Hildenbrand
Nowhere to Hide by Belinda Boring
Flames Among the Frost by Amy Hale
Rock Me Gently by Susan Burdorf
From the Embers by Amy Miles (June 2018)
Defying Gravity by Kallie Ross (July 2018)

More books releasing on a monthly basis

Also try the YA line, Havenwood Falls High.

Subscribe to our reader group and receive free stories and more!

IMMERSE yourself in the world of Havenwood Falls and stay up to date on news and announcements at www.HavenwoodFalls.com. Join our reader group, Havenwood Falls Book Club, on Facebook at https://www.facebook.com/groups/HavenwoodFallsBookClub/

ABOUT THE AUTHOR

International and #1 Multi-Genre Bestselling Author Belinda Boring is known to many readers as the Queen of Swoon and also the Queen of Cliffhangers. Her Mystic Wolves series has topped many charts along with receiving several awards and nominations such as Paranormal Book of the Year, Best Debut Book, and being in the Top 3 Best Rated on Amazon. With additional titles like Bittersweet Melody, Bittersweet Symphony, Enchanted Hearts, Loving Liberty, and Broken Promises, it's easy to see why readers are captivated by this swoon-worthy author!

Facebook: https://www.facebook.com/pages/Belinda-Boring-Author/200626723318915

Twitter: https://twitter.com/BelindaBoring

Instagram: https://www.instagram.com/BelindaBoring

Website: http://www.belindaboringauthor.com

Pinterest: http://pinterest.com/belindaboring/

Amazon Author Page: http://www.amazon.com/Belinda-Boring/e/B005C1IRFC/ref=sr_tc_2_0?qid=1384912397&sr=8-2-ent

Newsletter link: https://docs.google.com/forms/d/e/1FAIpQLSfGcIfO_GUFrNkUP_B-ZM4xvNb662E75dKmvn6WVvKeXEVyfg/viewform

ACKNOWLEDGMENTS

I can't begin to tell you just how excited I am to be part of the incredible Havenwood Falls world! A huge thank you to Kristie Cook and all my fellow authors for letting me be part of the team. You guys are so inspiring, and I'm 100% serious when I say we need to move to this town ASAP. #itsreal2us

As with every project, there's a supportive crew of people who surround me:

To my author coach Jessica Gibson—not only are you one of my bestest friends, but you also understand what's needed when I squirrel hardcore and go off on a tangent. Thanks for keeping me on task and sane through all the crazy. #stuckwithme4life

To my beta readers: Stephanie Krause, Lisa Markson, Julie Engle, Jane Elizabeth Stahl, and Cindy Mayberry—I appreciate you all so much! Thank you for being so excited about Micah and Sedona. Your feedback and love have been such a blessing! #swoonaddicts

To three amazing readers: Brenda Anderson, Amber Jones, and Jade Hakin—I hope you enjoy seeing the facts you entered the giveaway with! Thanks for all your support to not just me, but all the authors within this amazing series. Muah! #seeyouatthenextparty

To Laura Benedict, Susan McCray, and Michelle Boyes—you guys definitely put up with my crazy! Thank you for the many hours you listen to me bounce ideas off you and talk on and on and on about Micah and Sedona. Words can't describe how much I love you! #ioweyoubigtime

Last, but never, ever least, my own personal muse and soul mate, Mark—we did it! We survived the year of HELL and this story is the celebration of it. You are why I write romance and why I love all things swoony. You are in every hero I write and YOU, my darling BFF, will always be my happily ever after. #abazillionkisses4you

Thank you to everyone who purchases this book and gives Micah and Sedona a chance. Thank you for loving Havenwood Falls as much as I do. Whenever you're in town, make sure you stop by Shelf Indulgence and say hello . . . you are always welcome!

Much love,
Belinda #dare2fly

AN EXCERPT

~ A Havenwood Falls New Adult Novella ~

Havenwood Falls

Flames Among the Frost

Amy Hale

Flames Among the Frost (A Havenwood Falls Novella) by Amy Hale

Jetta Mills has felt stifled most of her life. She's a rebellious creative who's had to bend to her father's will, as well as the rules of her hometown Havenwood Falls. Needing a break from it all, she skips town for an adventure far from the smothering influences she's used to. Unfortunately, trouble always has a way of finding Jetta, and she quickly learns that the best place for a frost dragon shifter such as herself is back within the warded borders of home.

When Conrad Monroe is hired to find a thief and bring her back to face justice, the trail leads him to the Colorado mountains and the path of Jetta Mills. She's gorgeous, talented, and a whole lot of trouble. He doesn't know what he's getting into with Jetta and the town she calls home. Jetta has no idea that Conrad has quite a few secrets of his own.

Jetta's seeking real freedom while Conrad's planning to lock her away. But sparks fly between the two as the line between deceit and truth quickly becomes blurred. When the smoke clears, the truth may be the only real path to redemption.

FLAMES AMONG THE FROST

AN EXCERPT

I'd be lying if I said I'd never imagined myself in jail. I'd always been a hot mess with a talent for getting in way over my head. I'd never considered myself a bad person, but I was certainly no angel either. I always ran with the wrong crowd, said the wrong things, dressed the wrong way, and generally pissed off my father by merely existing. Lawrence Mills had been making my life miserable for years, although if you'd asked him, I'm sure he'd have told you the same about me. Despite my love for the rest of my family, I had to escape him. Which, in a roundabout way, was why my ass was going numb as I sat on a cold concrete bench in a six-by-eight cell.

"Damn," I muttered as I adjusted my position. "Hey assholes," I yelled, "are cushions against your religion or something? I can't feel my legs anymore."

I didn't expect an answer. It'd been six hours since I'd been arrested, and outside of my being booked, no one had spoken a word to me. My roommate, Frankie Hopkins, told me she'd be here to bail me out, but I'd yet to see her.

I stood and stretched, hoping to bring some of the feeling back into my limbs. The bland, gray cell was chilly, but actually the perfect temperature for someone like me—a frost dragon shifter. We generally preferred the cold to the heat. I guess when your roots traced back to Iceland, loving the frigid temperatures made sense. It still pissed me off, though. The jackwads didn't even offer me a damn blanket. I think they hoped I would freeze. If so, the joke was on them.

The large metal door at the end of the hall opened, and I listened as footsteps approached. A uniformed officer and Frankie appeared on the other side of the bars. Her tall slender frame, shoulder-length red curls, and blue eyes were a welcome sight after hours of staring at the same cinderblock walls.

"About time," I growled, as the officer unlocked the door. His name tag read Barnes.

"You're free to go, Ms. Mills." Officer Barnes's expression appeared as if those words were painful to push past his lips.

I looked at Frankie, and she smiled. I shoved past them both and stalked down the hall to collect my personal items. The lady behind the window slid a paper bag toward me, and I inspected the contents. I grabbed the pen attached to the clipboard and signed to verify everything was there. Frankie held my jacket open, and I pushed my arms through before stuffing the bag into my pocket.

"May I go now?" I asked with more than a little disgust in my voice.

She nodded. Without another word, I walked to the main doors, Frankie on my heels. I pushed one door open, turned to face the officers standing in the lobby, and flipped them off. "Thanks for nothing."

Frankie rolled her eyes as she shut the door behind us. "Is it really the best strategy to piss off the cops who just arrested you?"

"Are you kidding me?" I glared at her. "Was I supposed to thank them for falsely arresting me, handling me like a piece of meat, and then ignoring me for hours?"

"Of course not," replied Frankie, "but being a bitch isn't going to help anything."

"But . . . I'm so good at it. It'd be a shame to waste my talents."

Frankie put one perfectly manicured hand on her hip. "And it wasn't exactly a false arrest. You did break into that safe, right?"

I didn't know how to explain what had happened. Partially admitting to the altered version of events would make more sense to her than the truth ever would.

"The item I was after belongs to me. I didn't want any of his other shit." I grimaced as I searched for her car in the now dark parking lot. "Thanks for bailing me out."

"Oh . . ." Frankie's voice was hesitant. "I didn't actually bail you out."

My eyebrows rose. "So, how'd you spring me?"

"It was Brandt. I talked him into dropping the charges." She looked nervous.

I felt my temperature rise. I shook my head as I found the nearest wall and leaned against it. As my eyes closed, I saw large claws, scales, and reptilian irises flash in my mind.

"Damn it, no!" I shouted in frustration.

Frankie placed a hand on my arm. "I'm sorry, Jetta, but I couldn't come up with the cash. I didn't know what else to do! I promise it'll work out. Brandt said he'd forgive everything that has happened. That's better than a bail bond, court, and a record, right?"

Frankie didn't understand that, while I was really pissed at her for working out a deal with Brandt on my behalf, the "no" was not about her negotiations. I was commanding my inner dragon to stay back. Being a shifter could be amazing at times, but this was not the time or place to let the beast come out to play. Anytime I felt threatened or upset, she tried to push through and take over. I couldn't allow that. Not again. I wasn't back home in Havenwood Falls anymore, where stuff like that was somewhat normal. This was Atlanta, and supernatural creatures of any kind were still considered part of myth and legend. My kind wasn't welcome in the human world.

I opened my eyes and released a heavy sigh. "So, what did you promise him?"

I quickly walked to her car, not waiting to see if she was following.

Frankie's heels clicked as she ran to catch up. "Not much. Just that you'd give him a chance."

"Oh hell, Frankie," I shouted.

"C'mon, just one dinner. Let him attempt to wine and dine you one more time. Enjoy an expensive meal, then brush him off and move on." She spoke as if her plan was simple, but she didn't know Brandt like I did. She didn't know I'd already been down that road.

"No one walks away from Brandt Sawyer if he feels he's owed something. It's why I'm in this mess to begin with." I frowned. "And now you're in the middle of it, too." I pushed my hands through my hair, still caught off guard by the length since having extensions put in. "Damn it!" I banged my fist on top of her car.

She unlocked the car, and we both climbed inside. "Stop being so dramatic. You act like you're dealing with a mobster or something."

I looked at her and wondered how she could live in such a big city all her life and still be so sheltered. "He pretty much is. He'll use our friendship against me."

"Oh shush." She started the car. "He's an arrogant, rich club owner, and your boss, but I highly doubt he's fitting anyone with cement shoes in his spare time." She rolled her eyes as she pulled out of the parking lot. "I know I haven't known you for long, but your paranoia has gotten really bad lately."

I shook my head. "It's not paranoia. The man is insane. He—" I cut myself off before I let my secrets slip. Frankie didn't need to know all the dirty details about my evening with Brandt. Or the reason it all went to hell. "Let's go home. I'm tired."

She nodded and steered us toward our apartment. We drove the rest of the way in silence, but once inside, I made a beeline for my whiskey stash. I opened the bottle, poured a healthy amount in a tumbler, and downed it in one swallow.

"It's gonna be one of those nights, huh," Frankie stated in a flat voice. She wasn't a fan of my drinking, but I'd made it clear from the beginning that I had vices and those vices would move in with me. Another perk of being a dragon—or con depending how you looked at it—it took a lot of alcohol to get us shit-faced. Thankfully I had a well-stocked bar.

"Yep," I muttered. "It's absolutely gonna be one of those nights." I poured another glass and threw it back, letting the comforting burn slide down my throat. "Do we have mac and cheese? I'm starving. Getting arrested makes a girl hungry."

Frankie jerked her thumb in the direction of the kitchen. "Cabinet."

I nodded and strolled the few short steps it took to travel from our living area to the kitchen, the whiskey bottle my constant companion.

～

The alarm clock screamed in my ears. I rolled over and glared at the blue glowing digits. Seven a.m. wasn't terribly early, but it felt that way when you'd consumed all the alcohol in the house. I slammed my fist down on top, knocking the clock to the floor.

"Shiiiiiiit," I moaned loudly as I rolled over. My mouth felt like I'd swallowed a distillery. All I wanted to do was go back to sleep, but I really needed to run errands before rehearsals that afternoon. *Rehearsals! Work!* I bolted upright in bed as my mind reeled with the events of the previous night. Brandt. Our fight. The safe. Jail.

I couldn't stay here, not now. I slid from the bed and pulled my suitcase out from underneath. Tossing it on the bed, I unzipped it and made a beeline for the dresser. Without care or organization, I dumped the contents of my drawers into the suitcase, followed by my clothes in the closet. I had to sit on the lid to zip it shut, but after no small amount of effort, I managed to force it closed.

"I need to get dressed," I muttered as I realized I'd just packed everything. Out of the corner of my eye, I saw the clothes I'd worn the previous evening. Frowning, I looked them over. They were wrinkled, but even worse was the blood on the right sleeve and back of my shirt. I wasn't sure if all that blood was mine. Some of it may have belonged to Brandt. Both of us were injured the night before. Anger seethed beneath the surface. I had to take care of this problem before it became impossible to correct.

I pulled my bloody blouse on over the T-shirt I'd slept in and slid my legs into my jeans. I crammed my feet into my boots, not caring that I was without socks. I took a few minutes to pack the rest of my personal items scattered around the apartment, and then I hauled it all out into the living area near the door.

My eyes scanned the small two-bedroom apartment I'd been calling home for over a month. The dingy yellow paint, the kitchenette, the tattered secondhand furniture. I'd miss it all.

"What the hell are you doing?" Frankie whined as she stepped out of her room. She was rubbing her eyes and yawning, her red curls a wild mess around her head.

"I'm going home." I grabbed my jacket from the back of the sofa and put it on.

"What?" The shock of my announcement woke her up fully.

"I tried this. It didn't work. It's time to go back to Havenwood Falls."

She stepped forward and put a hand on my arm. "Are you sure? You hated it there."

I nodded. "Now, I hate it here more."

Frankie frowned, and I realized what I'd said sounded harsh. I pulled her in for a hug. "It's not you, sweetie. I love you. It's this city. I'm better off in a small community. And I can't be in the same area as Brandt. It's not safe."

Puzzled, Frankie sighed. "Okay then. I think you're overreacting, but do what you gotta do."

I slipped her a wad of cash. "This should cover my part of the rent for the next six months. That'll give you time to find a suitable roommate, and you won't have to accept the first weirdo that answers your ad."

She grinned. "You mean like I did with you?"

"Exactly." I smiled. "Don't let another freak cross that threshold. You were lucky with me. The next one might not be so great. Be picky."

She pulled me in for another hug. "I'm gonna miss you, roomie. You're weird, but I like that."

"I'll miss you too," I said softly. "I need to load this stuff in the Jeep, and then I'm out of here. Do not engage with Brandt or any of his goons, okay? Once I'm gone, he'll likely leave you alone."

She nodded. "Will do."

It took three trips to haul all my belongings to the Jeep. Once my stuff was packed away, I said a final goodbye to Frankie and pointed my vehicle in the direction of Sawyer's Bar. I'd been away from home for roughly 41 days. I'd tried to assimilate, but the time had come to accept defeat. I had one final stop to make before I put Atlanta in my rearview mirror.

Purchase *Flames Among the Frost* at your favorite book retailer.